I0762518

THE LEGENDARY ADVENTURES OF DOC COPPER

& THE MAD DASH OF FIRE FACE

THE LEGENDARY ADVENTURES OF DOC COPPER

& THE MAD DASH OF FIRE FACE

DARek ISAACS

New York, New York

Good Books books may be purchased in bulk at special discounts for sales promotion, corporate gifts, fund-raising, or educational purposes. Special editions can also be created to specifications. For details, contact the Special Sales Department, Good Books, 307 Fifth Avenue, 4th Floor, New York, NY 10016 or info@skyhorsepublishing.com.

Good Books is an imprint of Skyhorse Publishing, Inc.®, a Delaware corporation.

Visit our website at www.goodbooks.com.

10 9 8 7 6 5 4 3 2 1

Library of Congress Cataloging-in-Publication Data is available on file.

Cover design by Johanna Sáenz

Print ISBN: 978-1-964219-16-5
Ebook ISBN: 978-1-964219-37-0

Printed in the United States of America

THE LEGENDARY ADVENTURES OF

DOC COPPER

& THE MAD DASH OF FIRE FACE

A fierce wind swept across the Baja, whipping up sand as thousands of cheering spectators squinted against the pebble-laden gust, eagerly awaiting the start of the legendary race.

But Doc Copper was impervious to the desert elements. The thirteen-year-old embraced the wind, stinging sand, and the promise of unforgiving desert heat that waited for him. He longed for the agony of thirst, the threat of the unknown, and the danger of unmitigated speed. When he was in its throes, it meant he was doing the very thing he was born to do: racing.

But this time, it was more than just a race.

He stared ahead at the vast, barren Baja desert that stretched as far as the eye could see. Somewhere out there was the battle of his life and a chance for racing glory. His big, dark brown eyes popped with intensity and teetered on the tip of insanity as his body flowed with high octane adrenaline. He felt the engine pulse beneath him as the pistons fired in perfect sync. The heat from the engine began to steam up his leg, but it was the right kind of pain.

Doc pressed his chest against the bars. He pulled the clutch, shifted the high-strung racing machine into first gear, and pushed the engine within a millimeter of the redline. The engine roared, almost lurching forward, primed for the popping of the clutch.

He tilted his head, and yelled out, "This is going to be legendary!"

Mac Irons, his navigator, responded with his customary, blunt, and choppy way, "Yep."

Mac's intense anticipation pushed beads of sweat down his brow and cheeks, and they began to soak into the padding of his helmet.

Doc glanced to his right and left, seeing nothing but enemies flanking them. "The entire planet's coming after us," he said.

Mac grunted back, "Yep."

"Let 'em come," Doc replied.

"Now you're speaking my language," Mac replied.

Ethan Oxidant, the British racer to Doc and Mac's left, yelled over the roar of the engines, and as loud as it was, nothing could drown out Ethan's narcissistic scorn. "Hey, Doc, nice ride. I'm a little surprised it still runs."

Doc knew exactly what Ethan meant, and his scoffing did nothing but add more fury to the raging fire. "Hold that thought," Doc yelled back, and then pointed to the desert. "We'll pick this up out there."

Mac spoke into his helmet's headset, "That punk would make a nun pull a switch blade."

The Australian team held down the spot to Doc's right, and the Aussie driver lifted his helmet just enough to spit on Doc's front tire. "Let me guess," the Aussie said, "you want to make this race great again?"

Mac threatened with his fist. "How 'bout I make your face great again?"

Doc and Mac never wanted to war so bad, and Mac yelled into the madness, "Doc, if you don't crush these guys, I'm going to let Fire Face kick you in the face."

Doc rifled back, "If I don't crush these guys, I'll let him kick me in the face."

A young girl walked out into the sandy, cacti-riddled starting line. She began waving a flag in front of the greatest junior off-road racers the world had ever assembled.

"Mac," Doc said, "have you ever heard of American Exceptionalism?"

"Yep," Mac cracked his neck.

Doc grinned, "Here comes exhibit A."

"Roger that," Mac quipped back.

Another strong gust kicked up the desert silt. Doc pushed in his goggles, making sure the seal was tight.

The girl was waving that flag high above her head, and then Doc saw the slightest pause in her motion. "HANG ON!" he screamed.

The flag dropped.

Chaos.

* * *

One Year Earlier

Fireworks popped, cracked, and left a smoky haze in the rafters of the indoor arena at the national sixteen and under ATV championships.

"Yeah!" Doc Copper cheered as he let loose of the handlebars of his beloved Honda racing ATV, which he had named *The Drakon*. He thrust his arms up high as he soared fifteen feet in the air while crossing the finish line.

Doc skidded upon landing, and then busted out his customary donut celebration, kicking dirt into the first rows of the cheering fans.

As he spun his ATV to a stop and stood up on his pegs, he saluted Old Glory, which hung proudly in the rafters. That made the crowd love the boy even more.

He patted his four-wheeler like it was a faithful friend and then found his mom and dad in the crowd and gave them a big thumbs up.

His dad, Dean Copper, the famed steeplechase racehorse trainer, reached fatherhood utopia as he saw his boy achieving both of their dreams. But his mother, Rachel, succumbed to utter mortification. Not because their only son had just become the youngest national champion ever in the sixteen and under division at merely twelve years old, but because he was a fearless daredevil, with all the giftedness of a natural born racer to go with it.

Dean didn't need a cypher to understand the puzzle on Rachel's face, and he tried to remind her that this was the path she had chosen for Doc. "Hey, remember what you wanted?"

"Remember? Remember what?" she asked.

Dean had to yell above the crowd noise. "You said you didn't want him racing horses."

Indignant, Rachel stared her husband in the eyes. "How is this any better?"

Dean pointed to the jumbotron. "Look."

The big screen zoomed in on Doc and *The Drakon*. The announcer roared, "Doc Copper! Your new national champion!"

The crowd erupted with cheers that overpowered the thumping victory music that shook the arena. Confetti showered down, and strobe lights flickered to the point of disorientation.

Doc gazed upward through the clouds of confetti to see himself on the big screen. He smiled as the camera circled around. He made sure to show off the back of his classic, brown leather motorcycle jacket. It had a standing collar with dual, off-white stripes adorning the sleeves. Stitched into the back of the shoulders was the custom embroidered logo that read, "Copper Racing."

That day, Doc Copper was submerged in the euphoric ecstasy of the overindulgent star-hungry craze in America. And then he saw the smiling girl with the three-foot-tall trophy walking his way, and he didn't know if he'd ever be the same again.

His hometown news website from Bell Buckle, Tennessee, gave Doc the front page the next day. It read:

DOC COPPER!

SON OF LOCAL HORSE TRAINER STUNS.

BECOMES YOUNGEST ATV NATIONAL CHAMPION EVER.

* * *

Present Day

"Dad! Dad!" The now thirteen-year-old's voice resonated throughout the Copper farmhouse. There was an amped up energy coming from the well-mannered, southern boy, and Dean knew something was up.

Dean turned slowly, careful not to spill his nearly overflowing coffee. He heard the feet coming hard and fast to the kitchen, but he kept his eyes down on his coffee. He attempted to walk toward the commotion. Big mistake.

BAM!

The two collided as Doc turned the corner, and coffee went everywhere.

"Doc," Dean protested, "are you kidding me?"

Doc's southern voice exuded charm, even in a situation like this. "Dad, not a big deal."

Dean raised his eyebrows, "Well, it ain't nothin'."

Rachel was in the next room and heard the ruckus. She popped her head in. "What just happened?"

"Nothing," Doc said.

Rachel's eyes found the puddle of coffee on the floor. "Really?" she said, "Because somebody not called 'Mom' will be cleaning that nothing up."

Doc stood unfazed as he waved a letter in front of their eyes.

"What's that?" Dean asked.

Doc flipped it around and cleared his voice to add unnecessary theatrics. "*Dear Doc Copper,*" he read. "*The United States Junior Racing Association is pleased to inform you that your point total on the USJRA ATV dirt track circuit has placed you as the top junior racer in Tennessee.*

You are hereby invited to Wyoming next month for the honor and challenge of racing in the USJRA Champion Off Road Racing Cup. The winner will be named the Junior Eighteen and Under National Champion."

The cheers that exuded from Doc and Dean rattled the fine china in the cabinets. Racing was synonymous with the Copper men, and the thrill of high stakes racing turned both into primal barbarians.

"That's what I'm talking about, boy," Dean shouted as he put Doc in a fatherly headlock.

"Wait," Doc said, "there's more."

"More?" Rachel asked surprised. "What's more than that?"

"Hit me with it," Dean pushed.

Doc continued to read the letter,

> *As you may know, every four years the greatest event of junior off-road racing occurs, the legendary Quad Continental. This world-renowned desert race is a one-thousand-mile crucible that pushes the limits of racer and machine. This year, the off-road national champions from eighty countries will descend on the unforgiving desert of Baja California in Mexico to compete for the honor of being the Quad Continental World Champion. Therefore, the Wyoming race will not only name the US National Champion but will also determine who represents The United States of America in the Quad Continental. Young man, start your engine! The USJRA.*

The jumps, claps, hugs, stomps, hoots, and hollers of the Copper men consumed the kitchen and nearly broke the leg of a chair in the celebration.

Rachel, however, merely offered a strained smile. She knew her son was going to race as if tomorrow would never come. She coughed a bit, just to get their attention. "It seems like a lot of older kids will be in this."

Doc and Dean acknowledged the sound of her voice but didn't pay much attention to it beyond that. She raised her voice a little more. "Maybe we could think about it? Sounds pretty dangerous."

Her last statement didn't even register to the Copper men whose ears had checked out to all things contemplative.

Dean smacked his lips and nodded. "We got a trip to plan!"

"We do, and I need my crew," Doc added.

"Yeah, you do," Dean agreed. "This is a once in a lifetime opportunity. We gotta make it count."

Rachel sighed.

Those next few weeks seemed to move slower than frozen molasses for Doc, but it did give him time to fine-tune *The Drakon* for the *next* biggest race of his life. Dean also got the big diesel truck freshly serviced, and they took the gooseneck livestock trailer in for an acid wash. Doc gathered everything he could think of to pack it top to bottom, and when the trailer got back, he was ready to turn it into his mobile racing garage.

* * *

THE DAY HAD COME FOR THEM TO TRAVEL TO WYOMING, AND NOTHING could have been more exciting for the Coppers. However, as Dean shifted the rig into gear, Rachel gave him a glance that told him she had something to say.

"Well, alright," Dean said. "What is it?"

"I don't like this," she replied.

"Don't like what?"

"Don't give me that. You know exactly what."

"Um . . ." Dean really didn't know, so he guessed. "Doc's a racer. This is what he does. He knows there are risks, but he accepts that. I thought you were cool with all of this."

Rachel showed a bit of frustration. "While that is something, that's not what we're talking about, and you know it."

Dean shook his head. "*I* know it? I literally don't. I didn't even know we were talking. I just saw a look."

"Well, I don't like it," Rachel replied, "so never again, Dean. Read my lips. Never again."

Dean's jaw dropped. "For all things good and holy, just tell me what you're talking about."

"The boys, Dean." She was frustrated that she even had to say it. She pointed back to the horse trailer where Doc and his two friends were riding. "It's not an RV. We're responsible for their safety."

"Oh." Dean blew that off. "My brothers and I did that all the time growing up. We never got hurt."

"Well, things are different today, and you know it."

"It is different," Dean agreed, "but what if it shouldn't be? Is it really all that bad that we expect our kids to toughen up a bit? So what if one of them takes a bump and falls over. We want them to be men, don't we?"

That perturbed Rachel. "Don't you go there with me. You know I agree with that. What if we get pulled over with the kids back there in the horse trailer?"

"We're fine. I've never been pulled over by the police while pulling the trailer. The cops know that we country folk are pro-blue, and they respect us, because we respect them. It's all good."

Rachel sighed. "I hope you're right."

Dean was a bit surprised that Rachel acquiesced so quickly. "Really? Did I just win an argument with the lawyer? Wow, this is a big day for me," he said with a laugh.

Rachel laughed a bit, too. "Yes, and it will be your last win. So, soak it up."

"Will do." Dean smiled. "But one more thing. Are you hinting that you would rather have the boys up here with us all the way to Wyoming? You want J-Dog up here the entire trip?"

Rachel grinned. "Sustained. Even on his best day, J-Dog is an acquired taste."

"That's what I thought." Dean laughed. "I win again."

The boy nicknamed J-Dog Dynamite had been Doc's best friend since they were four. Doc often wondered if J-Dog's mother had just plum given up on trying to influence his dressing habits, because he essentially wore the same thing each day: an old straw cowboy hat, pilot sunglasses, camouflage cargo pants, tan lace-up desert combat boots, and of course, his sleeveless, white, cotton t-shirt which always had a hand-painted message on it. Today, his shirt had a picture of an American flag, bearing the caption he scripted above it: "Try burning this one, jerk face."

Rachel knew that wherever J-Dog was, trouble always followed.

Recently, J-Dog had focused his entire ornery, early adolescence into his streaming channel, called Wild Dog TV, causing widespread anxiety for all the adults in the know.

Nothing was off limits for him. The more inflammatory his takes, the more online reaction he got, and it forever bugged Rachel that a thirteen-year-old boy with a seemingly supernatural gift to stir a pot got so many views.

But he wasn't alone in his viral escapades. His cameraman was Alfie Ping, a foreign exchange student from Malaysia that lived with J-Dog. One could spot Alfie from a mile away by the bright red nylon jacket he always wore. He and J-Dog acted like brothers, and they fought like cats and dogs. They were two of Doc's best friends, and they went to every race they could, streaming their lives along the way.

Dean glanced over at Rachel as he gave the diesel engine a bit more fuel. "Honestly, honey, we're lucky to have them. I know J-Dog is ornery as all get out, but both he and Alfie are good kids. They are a heck of lot better than the norm in today's world."

"I know, I know," Rachel agreed. "It's just never easy when they're all together. I need a rule where Doc can only have one friend over at a time. Otherwise, it's like a carnival after midnight."

Dean chuckled at that as he merged the rig onto the next highway. "They're just boys being boys. They're fine, and they're back there in the gooseneck making memories that will last a lifetime."

"As long as they're safe," Rachel warned.

"What could happen back there?" Dean argued. "They are literally locked in a cage. What trouble could they possibly get into?"

Rachel snapped back, "What trouble? This is J-Dog we're talking about. He invents trouble."

"In a cage? Really?" Dean protested.

"Especially in a cage."

"Come on, Rachel. How bad could it be?"

Rachel batted her eyes. "Why don't we just check what they're doing?"

"Check?" Dean asked incredulously. "We just got started, and you want me to pull over and check?"

"You don't need to pull over, Dean. You know J-Dog and Alfie are probably streaming that stupid internet show. What do they call it—Barking Dog or something?"

Dean corrected, "Wild Dog. Wild Dog TV."

Rachel's head snapped around. "How did you know that so quickly?" Her eyes widened in shock. "You watch it! You subscribed, didn't you?"

Dean couldn't contain his laughter now. He loved how indignant Rachel would get with the boys' antics. "I might have clicked some things. It's actually kind of funny. The kid has talent."

"Talent? That's what you call it?" Rachel turned in her seat to face him. "He absolutely offends everyone. That's his talent."

Dean calmed his laughing, but still smiled. "He's declared war on safe spaces. I'm not sure he knows that, but that's what he's done."

Rachel squinted her eyes. "You're a closet Wild Dog fan. I should've known."

Dean laughed. "Maybe I am. They're funny. They're good kids, Rachel. And honestly, I think it's kind of what this world needs."

"Oh, really? What the world needs?" Rachel challenged. "Why don't we just log in and see what the world, as you claim, needs right now?"

"Oh boy." Dean wished he could have that last comment back.

She got her smartphone out and opened the app. She clicked on Wild Dog TV with J-Dog Dynamite, and she winced when she saw it. "Oh goodie, they're streaming right now," she sarcastically squealed. "Let's see what the full faith and approval of Dean Copper looks like in real time."

Dean emptied his lungs and fluttered his lips. "This could hurt."

"Oh look, Alfie is in the picture, too." Rachel stared at Dean. "That means they got Doc to film it. They roped our boy into their tomfoolery."

"And shenanigans." Dean decided to push some buttons. "It's both tomfoolery and shenanigans."

Rachel held up her finger and stopped the conversation abruptly. She studied the screen on her phone. "What is that? Where did they get that?"

"What?" Dean asked, and she showed him the phone as he was trying to drive.

"Where did they get that from?" Rachel asked. "That's gotta be six-feet tall."

"It looks like a Mickey Mouse blow-up doll," Dean answered. "They must have packed it."

Then out of nowhere, J-Dog slugged the giant inflated Mickey Mouse right in the face.

"Woah!" Rachel said, "he just punched Mickey."

And sure enough, J-Dog not only punched Mickey but also unleashed a wildly violent mauling of the blow-up mouse doll, kicking, choking, punching, and throwing the mouse all over the trailer until it popped on a bolt.

"You see that?" J-Dog yelled at the mouse as it deflated into a limp, crumpled up plastic bag. "How does that feel? You can't have your cheese and eat it too, you little rodent."

J-Dog walked over to the camera and pushed his face right into the lens. "You kill Han Solo, I kill you."

Dean was beside himself laughing, and Rachel closed the app. "I can't watch that anymore. I just can't. I'm listening to the radio." She turned the nob on, and Dean's favorite country music station started blaring, but Rachel didn't like that either. "I suppose country music is better than watching J-Dog's show." She laughed a bit. "Look at what I've been reduced to, Dean. In the first fifteen minutes of this cross-country road trip, I'm already listening to country music."

Dean loved his wife, her wit, and her way. He never thought he would've convinced a big city girl like her to move to the country with him. But he was so glad that he had.

Dean tried to explain, "You just gotta get used to road trips. There is a way to do it. We have twelve hundred miles to go before we get to Wyoming. So, sit back, roll the windows down, and listen to some country music. That's how we pass the time."

"Fine, I'll listen," she said. But it didn't take thirty seconds for her to protest the song. "What did he just say?" Rachel asked.

Dean leaned forward and tapped his forehead on the wheel. "They'll be more songs, honey. They're not all like this."

She listened intently to the lyrics, and she blurted out loud, "He did say that!"

Dean laughed.

Rachel lifted both hands, open palmed, toward the radio dial. "He just sang that he was a man somewhere in between Jesus and John Wayne."

Dean acknowledged the lyric, "Hmm, hmm."

"Who writes that?" Rachel asked. "Who sits down on a stump with a guitar and thinks that's the gripping lyric?" She looked at Dean and paused, waiting for a response.

"What?" he chuckled, "I didn't write it. It's not me."

"I'm going back to the Yelping Dog. I want to see how bad they mutilated that mouse," Rachel said.

"I guarantee they won't be on the mouse anymore," Dean replied. "J-Dog jumps topics fast."

Dean was right, the boys were onto something else altogether.

This time, there was no violence or heavy action; rather J-Dog was sitting calmly in the gooseneck part of the trailer. He was rubbing his chin as if to portray a deep, powerful thought was percolating.

"So," J-Dog exhaled long and then spoke in a slow, punctuated, and well-elocuted manner, "My parents, bless their hearts, wanted to increase my sensitivities they said. They wanted to expose me to more cultures, experiences, and points of view." He sniffed and glanced upward as he took off his cowboy hat, dusted it off, and repositioned it on his head. He adjusted his pilot glasses. "They thought there was room for me to grow in these areas. So, to do this . . ." He paused and kind of fluttered his hands before quipping, "They imported a China man."

Alfie shouted from behind the camera. "I'm Malaysian of Chinese descent. Get it right!"

J-Dog rolled his eyes and waved it off. "Tomāto, tomâto."

Alfie continue to yell, "You think it's a picnic for me? There was no mention of bunk beds on the form."

"Simmer down, Jackie Chan," J-Dog said. "Today's the day your ship comes in. We have a question from one of our viewers that, shockingly enough, is for you. Now, I don't know why they don't want to hear from me when I'm available. But this individual, for some unknown reason, wants to hear from you."

"Because he values sophistication," Alfie retorted. "That's why."

"Well, sophisticate this, rice cakes," J-Dog replied. "Our viewer asks what holidays did you celebrate over in Malaysia?"

"Oh," Alfie replied, "that's good. The big three, really: Easter, Christmas, and Jamaican breakfast."

J-Dog followed up, "Any more? No Independence Day? No chase the cobras out of the baby's bedroom day?"

Alfie put his hand to his head as he thought as hard as he could. "I know we celebrated more when I was very young, but I can't remember my first memories."

Up in the truck, Rachel turned her phone off, and then slowly put it away into the center console. She looked at her husband who was trying not to bust a gut as he was driving down the interstate.

"You know, Dean, the internet lives forever," she lectured.

* * *

THE REST OF THE SIXTEEN-HOUR ROAD TRIP TO WYOMING WENT AS well as twelve hundred miles in a truck and trailer can go. The only surprise to Dean and Rachel was that the boys never wanted to come up to the cabin. They found the windy, loud, bumping, rattling environment of the stock trailer to suit them just fine.

They had a cooler back there, tons of food, each other, and imaginations to boot. That's all they needed.

And, eventually, the Copper rig finally reached the Wyoming Fairgrounds with the sun just starting to come up.

Doc's excitement began to build. "Here we go, boys," Doc said, gripping the slats in the trailer and pressing his head through the opening.

Most of the other racers were there already. There was one slip for every state champion. Fifty racers in all, and the campground was already bustling with activity.

"You know," J-Dog said as he perused the scene, "if I weren't such an internet sensation with followers hanging on my every word, I think I would like to race, too. There's a vibe here that's easy to get into."

Alfie was inspecting his GoPro camera and drone kit, and he quipped at J-Dog, "You would lose."

J-Dog shook his head. "I'd be great, but I just can't—" he exhaled and tipped his cowboy hat back "—I'm just too important to too many people."

"Yep," Doc remarked, "I can only imagine its tough having your own life when you're trying to build a cult."

That got a smile out of J-Dog. "It is. I gotta care for the flock."

"Don't forget all the orange drink in the plastic jugs you gotta buy," Doc added. "That's cult leader 101."

J-Dog nodded. "Heavy is the head that wears the crown."

"I'm ready," Alfie changed the subject as he stood up from his stooped position from tinkering with his high-powered drone. "You've got your eyes in the sky, Doc."

"Perfect," Doc replied as the conversation switched to racing, and he pulled out his smart tablet to study the radar app. "We've got a high chance of getting rain tomorrow morning." He looked over at Alfie. "Will your drone fly in heavy rain?"

"Should," Alfie answered.

Dean found the slip for the Tennessee State Champion, and he had no shortage of fatherhood pride pulling the Copper rig into that spot. After he killed the engine and popped open the door, he reached over to nudge his sleeping wife. "Hey, honey, we're here."

She stirred a bit and opened her eyes. "Oh, alright." She sat up straight and found her bearings. She looked around at the fairgrounds and saw all the other teams, their rigs, and the early morning activity. "Wow, this is something."

Dean felt the refreshing pre-rain Wyoming breeze as he stretched his legs outside. "Hey, Rachel, I'm going to roll down your window. It feels great outside."

"Okay," she said as she wiped down her eyes and flipped down the visor to look at herself in that tiny mirror. "Yikes," she said as she stretched out the circles under her eyes and took in her somewhat matted hair.

By that time, the boys were already out of the trailer, and J-Dog walked by Rachel's open window and looked inside. "Good morning, Mrs. Copper," he said.

Rachel didn't want a conversation with J-Dog to be one of the first things she did that morning.

But J-Dog smiled and was rather sweet. "You look really good this morning, Mrs. Copper."

Rachel was taken back a bit but appreciated the manners. "Well, thank you. All things considered, right?"

"Yeah," he replied, "you only look like you've been living in a truck for maybe sixteen hours. Definitely not eighteen."

And there he was. Rachel forced a closed lip smile and heard Dean call for Doc on the other side. She took the opportunity to say, "Looks like they're talking back there. You should probably go see what's going on."

"Yep, they're going to need my two cents. Well, with inflation, that's like thirty-seven dollars," J-Dog replied as he reversed course back to the trailer.

By the time J-Dog reached them, the three others were already in the middle of a conversation.

"Take the day to rest, boys," Dean said. "The race is tomorrow morning, eight o'clock."

Doc replied, "I want to be at the starting line no later than seven-thirty."

"I agree," Dean answered, "and we'll have to leave here by seven, probably, to get there. It's a long race, and the starting line is a fair bit away."

"This isn't where the race begins?" J-Dog asked.

"This is the finish line," Doc replied as he pointed toward the fairground bleachers and racetrack. "I'll be coming in from the west, and I'll be winning the race right there."

"I like how you think, Doc," J-Dog said, "so where will the trailer be?"

Dean explained, "We'll drop Doc off at the starting line, and the three of us will drive the truck and trailer back here."

Doc piped up, "Alfie, will you be able to control your drone from that distance?"

Alfie nodded to affirm.

J-Dog then deduced, "The trailer is my command center, and I'll stream the entire race from the GoPro on Alfie's drone. Then, I'll split screen the drone's race footage with my award-winning commentary."

"You can do that?" Dean asked.

The three boys laughed at the naivete.

"Sweet soul," answered J-Dog. "You and the Mrs. can just sit back in the bleachers and watch the show."

Alfie added, "We'll bring the action to you."

"Well, that's cool," Dean replied, "I like it."

"Okay, then. We've got you guys sorted," Doc said. "Now, look what I've got." He smiled as he showed the screen of his iPad. "I've downloaded the entire topography of the area and then superimposed the racecourse on top of that data. I've already started to calculate my desired RPMs on each climb and descent for ideal engine output. I'll have heavy fuel burn when I need it, but I'll strategically conserve where I don't. The good news is I think I can manage with half a tank of gas for the last leg of the race."

"Why is that good?" J-Dog asked.

"It's good because everyone else will top off their tanks at the pit stops, which makes them heavier. I'll stop the fill halfway at the last one. I'll be a touch lighter, ergo faster."

"Whose running the pit stops?" Alfie asked.

"Volunteers," Doc replied. "There are four pits, and volunteers fuel up all the racers."

"How much faster will you be?" J-Dog asked.

"Not much, but in a race like this, you don't need much. I'll be dragging at the back of the lead pack, which will also give me power in reserve, and then I'll sling shot around them on that last bend coming into the stadium. I'll have extra engine, and I'll be lighter. I've won this thing already."

"Easy, Doc, you're racing forty-nine other champions," Dean chimed in. "Don't count your chickens before they hatch. I've learned that the hard way with Fire Face."

"Not the same thing, Dad," Doc countered. "I've got the data." He tapped his old leather cylindrical tube.

"Dude," J-Dog said, always admiring Doc's wit, "doesn't it feel good to be a genius? I think it does. I think it feels good to be a genius."

Alfie shook his head. "Doc's the only genius here, J-Dog. You're on the wrong end of the scale."

"Hey," J-Dog argued, "I'm a genius, too."

"No, you're not," Alfie pressed. "Doc has a one hundred and sixty-five IQ, and he dropped out of Mensa because it was boring. What do you got?"

J-Dog dusted off the front of his shirt. "I know I'm a genius *because* I'm a genius. In fact, that's my next shirt I'm making. So, my brilliance will be forever codified."

Doc laughed.

Alfie scolded, "That's circular reasoning, you moron!"

"Not it's not. It's logic," J-Dog countered, "because if someone really is a genius, then they would know that they're a genius, because a genius would know those type of things. If you don't know if you are a genius or not, then you're not a genius, because a genius would know those type of things." J-Dog smacked his lips and snapped his fingers. "There you go. See? I'm a genius because I know I am."

Doc shook his head. "But the problem with your reasoning, J-Dog, is that morons get the wrong answers all the time. That's what makes them morons."

J-Dog snapped his head toward Doc. "What's your point?"

"The point is, a moron would conclude that they are a genius, because morons reach errant conclusions. Likewise, if a person who thinks they may be a moron, realizes that they are not a genius, then it's likely that they are not a moron, because they reached the correct conclusion that they are not a genius."

Alfie raised his hand as confusion arrested his face. "Does it matter who asks the question?"

Dean jumped in, "So, if I follow, and I think I do, if a person truly believes that they are a genius, then they are either a real genius or a complete moron."

Doc nodded. "Precisely."

A few seconds of silence went by, and J-Dog said, "Well, that settles that. I think we all know which side of the fence I fall on."

A couple more seconds passed, and Alfie replied, "Yes, I think we do."

* * *

THE NEXT MORNING, DEAN, RACHEL, ALFIE, AND J-DOG DROPPED Doc and *The Drakon* off at the starting line of a race that had his future riding on it. Not only was he going to race for another national championship, but he was racing to represent the United States in the greatest off-road race of all time, the legendary Quad Continental.

At just thirteen, all the other racers had at least two years on him, but those were the odds he liked. He wanted to be overlooked and doubted. Being the afterthought only drove him to go harder and faster.

"You ready?" J-Dog asked.

"I was made for this," Doc replied as he zipped up his leather coat, pulled on his helmet, and strapped on his gloves. "Are you guys ready?"

"Locked and loaded, brother," J-Dog replied. "Our connection is hot. We'll start the livestream as soon as we get back to the trailer."

"And you, Alfie?" Doc asked. "I'm starting to feel drops all ready. It's going to be a wet race. Your drone is good?"

"One hundred percent," Alfie replied. "No question. I'll be your eyes in the sky."

"Perfect, and remember Dead Man's Curve."

"I've got your back," Alfie replied with confidence.

Doc gave a thumbs up as he climbed on *The Drakon* and fired up the Honda engine. It roared like the racing machine it was. He looked around at all the other racers going through the same motions at the starting line, and he knew this was going to be a dogfight out there.

J-Dog and Alfie put on their headsets and switched them on.

"Can you hear me, Doc?" J-Dog asked.

Doc replied into his headphones, "Loud and clear."

"And me?" Alfie checked his comms.

"Yep," Doc replied.

"Good," Alfie said.

Dean and Rachel glanced at each other, amazed at the skills and equipment that these boys had. But Rachel saw the weather turning and gave in to her motherly instincts. She walked up to Doc one more time as he revved his engine. She raised her voice over the popping of the pistons, yelling loud enough that some of the other racers even heard. "Doc, listen, it's going to storm. It's going to be muddy, wet, and dangerous. Please just be safe. It's okay if you don't win. There will be other races."

The racer from Kansas shouted over, "Yeah, it's okay if you don't win. Mom knows best!"

Doc didn't reply to the Kansas racer. But he looked at his mom and shook his head. "No, Mom, that's never okay."

It was in that moment that Doc's mind switched from just a southern boy from Bell Buckle, Tennessee, to a whole different persona. To say that Doc had a game face would be an understatement. He became the game. Every other aspect of his life was fully forgotten. Only one thing mattered in that moment in time: the race.

Rachel got the point and walked back to the rig where Dean was waiting. Alfie and J-Dog were already loaded up in the trailer. She glanced upward, just in time to see Alfie's drone jettison out of the back of the trailer and zip off high into the western sky.

"Time to roll," Dean said as he shifted the truck in gear.

She opened the door and climbed in. "Will they have a screen to see the race at the fairgrounds?"

"This isn't NASCAR, honey, but the boys in the back have you covered."

"The drone?" she asked.

"Wild Dog TV, live and in living color."

"You've got to be kidding me." Rachel shook her head.

"You know," Dean said as he chuckled, "if you create your own account, you can get bonus coverage today."

"No." Rachel pointed at Dean. "I will not dignify this."

"Are you sure? You get discounts on t-shirts."

"He sells t-shirts? You're lying."

"I think he sells them, but I'm not sure he delivers, yet. It's complicated."

"Again, I'll be representing him soon."

"He's fine. He's what they call an influencer. They live by different rules."

Rachel curled up her lips. "J-Dog needs direction. He doesn't need to be influencing anybody. Honestly, I don't want to talk about it."

Dean slowed his roll. "I'm just having fun, Rachel," he said. But over the next few minutes, he studied his wife a little bit more as he drove back to the fairgrounds. He could see something deeper was happening within her. "Honey, you okay?"

"I don't know, Dean." She looked out the window and saw the dark clouds coming. "Are you sure Doc can handle this? You know he's not going to hold back, even if the weather gets crazy."

"He's a racer, Rachel, and a good one. It's in his blood. If we try to stop him from racing, it won't work. He won't stop . . . we'll just lose our son. We either do this with him, or he does it without us."

Rachel shook her head but didn't respond. She knew Dean was right, but she didn't have to like it. Then a few heavy drops fell on the windshield of the truck. "This storm is going to wreak havoc on him out there," she said.

"Yep, but the good news is all the racers are in the same boat," Dean replied.

"By the looks of it," Rachel said, "they may need a boat."

"Right," Dean chuckled. "Hey, reach behind you under the seat. I've got some ponchos back there. The fairground bleachers don't have any cover."

* * *

Squeezing through hundreds of parents and other fans, Dean and Rachel found their way to the bleachers just before the race began. They had left behind J-Dog and Alfie at the trailer to stream.

Dean pulled out his phone. "Are you going to say it?"

"Say what?" Rachel shot back, a bit defensive.

"That you are thankful for J-Dog's show," Dean said playfully. "That is, if you want to watch the race."

"Just give me that," Rachel said as she grabbed his phone and put one of his ear buds in. Dean used the other.

By the time they logged in, J-Dog was in full swing with his performance. "If you are just tuning in," he said, "welcome to Wild Dog TV. I am your fearless leader, the man with the gift of gab, a smile that lights up the Milky Way and melts the hearts of cheerleaders everywhere. I am J-Dog Dynamite. If you want today's special t-shirt—" he pointed down to the wording on his sleeveless white tee, *I know I'm a genius because I'm a genius,* "—just send me money and lots of it, and don't forget to send a donation so I can continue to feed our favorite foreign import, the Malaysian Spitfire himself, Alfie. Trust me, he's not cheap. He'll only eat chicken necks."

Alfie quipped on the other side of the camera, "You've never gotten me chicken necks."

Rachel put her hand to her forehead as she watched the boys. "Are you kidding me?"

"I know," Dean said through boyish laughs.

"Does Alfie just take it?" she asked.

"Oh, no." Dean shook his head. "Alfie snaps. Just give it time."

"This is hard to watch," she said, but then she went back to it, like a moth to a flame.

J-Dog continued, "If you are new to our channel, you must know that we do not discriminate. We are equal opportunity offenders. We welcome both the bulimics and the obese, the freaks and the geeks, the fools and the wise, the beautiful and the ugly. Hey, Alfie stick your mug out here, I need proof of concept."

"Why do they need to see me?" Alfie shouted from behind the camera. "I have glorious features."

"Yeah, you're quite symmetrical, just show us your face," J-Dog pressed, "and maybe flex, too."

"No!" Alfie shouted.

"Come on, Alfie, we're doing this for posterity. There needs to be a record that I don't discriminate against the aesthetically disadvantaged."

Alfie pushed back, "I'm about to aesthetically disadvantage your face. Don't make me reach for the bamboo again."

"You know the cowboy in me welcomes that, but dude, remember your drone? The race is about to start."

"What?" Alfie yelled. "You're right. I see Doc!"

"Listen everyone," J-Dog said, "the boy, the myth, the legend, Doc Copper—all the way from Bell Buckle, Tennessee—is about to open up a can right now on this entire racing field. We're going eyes in the sky, split screen. Let's roll!"

* * *

UMBRELLAS SPROUTED UP ACROSS THE COUNTY FAIR BLEACHERS. Dean and Rachel huddled up against each other as the rain started to come down hard.

"I'm glad I sprang for the waterproof phone," Dean said.

"It's going to be tested," Rachel replied.

"That picture is so clear," Dean said, shocked at the graphics and professional output of the stream. "They actually did the split screen. I can't believe that aerial view. Alfie's drone is awesome."

"I see Doc!" Rachel had completely forgotten she was watching J-Dog's platform, and she leaned over and whispered in Dean's ear, "Let's keep this low key. I don't want all these people trying to watch our phone."

"Sure," Dean understood.

The fairground's stadium announcer's mic crackled and popped as the old audio system tried to come to life. "Ladies and Gentlemen," he echoed, "we are going to have a wet, muddy race. Though we may not like it, I can tell you from experience that these racers are going to eat it up. This is what they live for. The racers will be just fine, but the storm coming in is going to hamper our ability to know what is happening out there. Obviously, an all-terrain, long-distance race like this makes it impossible to really watch it. But I will give you updates as I get them. We do have a jumbotron. We will try to post info up on that as it comes in. There are support vehicles at pits, so we'll know something. On that note, I think the race is seconds away from starting."

The whole stadium sat wet and silent, resigned to the idea that they wouldn't know any pertinent details until the very second the racers entered the fairgrounds for the final stretch. Consequently, murmurs, whispers, and casual conversations spattered up around the bleachers, just to help people bide the time.

But then that calm was broken when Rachel stood up in the crowd and screamed, "Go, Doc! Go, go, go!"

Dean pulled on Rachel's poncho. "Real subtle."

She sheepishly looked down, "Oh, I couldn't help it. They started."

"Yeah, I gathered, and um, so did everyone else."

All eyes turned on her, and then someone right behind her leaned forward and piped up, "Excuse me, are you actually watching the race?"

"Yes," Rachel replied, and realized she couldn't uncrack that egg. "We're watching on our phone."

"Where?" another asked with excitement.

"It's, um—" she coughed a bit, nearly mumbling the answer "—it's called Wild Dog TV."

"Oh, cool," the man said. "My kid watches that."

"Great," Rachel deadpanned. "Have they tried the Bob Ross channel instead?"

In a matter of seconds, fingers across the stadium began tapping apps, clicking agreements, and accepting cookies to log onto the webcast through all the avenues J-Dog had created.

The domino spread of smartphones lit up the bleachers like a candlelight vigil as the storm made it as dark as early evening. Once the crowd was logged in, they began cheering and shouting with the action.

The entire stadium became the single largest gathering of Wild Dog viewers in the world.

Then, much to the dismay of Rachel and the wild amusement of Dean, the inevitable happened. The old, fuzzy, nineties-era jumbotron on the north end of the stadium popped on, and sure enough, the race was piped in. The unique perspective of the Wild Dog was unleashed.

* * *

THROUGH THE JUMBOTRON, THE CROWD COULD SEE THE ATVs push hard through the sheets of driving rain. Most of the racers had opted for high tech water shedding fabrics that day for their jackets and pants, but Doc wouldn't trade his brown leather racing jacket for the world, and today, he was going to feel it. The jacket was quickly getting water-logged, but he'd live with that. That jacket was part of his persona, part of his transition from young teenager to racing prodigy, and when he zipped it up, it was go time.

Each state champion charged over the unforgiving landscape, the crowd cheering wildly from the action delivered by Alfie's drone. Doc weaved in and out through the racers, trying to get into that perfect drag position at the tail of the leading pack.

"Come on now, come on," Doc grunted to himself as rain cascaded over his helmet. "That's it," he said to his 450cc Honda racing ATV as he found the spot he was looking for. "Let's stay here for a while," he said, the engine humming with perfect pitch.

But then slinging rooster tails of muddy water and debris from the racers in front of him shot up like geysers, splashing an opaque wash of mud and water everywhere. "That's the thing with being in the back of the pack," Doc muttered as he took his racing glove, which had a mini-wiper built into its thumb, and squeegeed his racing goggles to a translucent haze. "That will have to do."

Doc saw Alfie's drone high in the sky. Alfie focused the GoPro camera in tight on Doc's back, showing all the viewers the embroidered Copper Racing across his shoulders.

J-Dog opened the communications with Doc. "Hey, Doc Copper, this is your friendly world famous icon. You are live on Wild Dog TV. Why don't you give all the fine people a wave."

"Kind of in the middle of something, J-Dog," Doc said in his smooth southern tones, but he did manage to give a thumbs up.

Doc felt his tires lose traction, sliding on a hard patch of slick watery clay. "Woah."

"You okay?" J-Dog asked.

"Yep, all good," Doc replied. "But play time is over. Things are getting bad out here. I gotta ride."

"Alright, brother, go win this thing," J-Dog said.

"Plan to."

* * *

FROM ALFIE'S DRONE'S SKY-HIGH VIEW, THE RACERS MIMICKED A flock of birds. The cluster curved back and forth, seeming to move as one collective soul in and out of turns. But the weather began to break up that body.

Then Alfie's drone got caught in a violent swirl up in the atmosphere and he lost control of it. He furiously pulled, pushed, and fought the controller to try to gain some semblance of flight. The view from the camera shook with violence, making the picture nearly indistinguishable.

"Watch out, Doc, this is close," Alfie yelled, "it may come down."

Doc looked up, but a sudden barrage of lightning strikes dazzled his eyes and washed out his view of the struggling drone.

BOOM! Lightning crashed into the ground.

The sound was deafening. It might as well have been a nuclear blast to Doc's senses. Blinding light gushed around him enough to make him think that his days were over.

"Holy Moses!" Doc shouted as fuzz busted through the headset.

"Woah," J-Dog yelled, "what just happened?"

Doc's stressed voice answered back, "Lightning!" He worked to regain his bearings. "That was close," Doc said, "I saw it hit the ground."

"That's intense and oddly impressive," J-Dog replied. "I mean, under the circumstances, there is a litany of things that could have followed "holy," and you kept it kosher with "Moses." Well done, Doc, you're going to win a Dove award for that."

Doc replied to the pressing situation, not the commentary, "It's bad out here, guys."

BOOM! Another lightning strike obliterated Alfie's drone, sending shrapnel to the ground.

More than that, the strike set off a mini-electromagnet pulse that fried the comms in Doc's headset.

"Hello, hello?" J-Dog tried to connect with Doc, but there was no response.

Dean, Rachel, and the whole stadium gasped as their feed to the race suddenly ended.

Rachel grabbed Dean's arm. "What happened?"

"Nothing," Dean replied. "We just lost the race feed. That's it. I'm sure Doc's fine."

"Then I'm turning the rabid dog off," Rachel said. "I'm not going to watch it if I can't see the race."

Dean chuckled. "Let's not turn it off yet. They may get it back."

* * *

ALFIE CRIED, "MY LITTLE ANGEL!"

"Oh man!" J-Dog dropped his head. "We had a live feed, and now it's gone. The comms with Doc got knocked out, too." J-Dog looked at Alfie. "We'll lose some views over this. No other way to say it."

Alfie's face reddened with distress, and his eyes teared up. "That's what you're thinking of now? All your views? Are you so calloused? What about Doc? What about my drone?"

"You're right, you're right, Alfie. I'm sorry. I should have focused on your pain," J-Dog said as he went and got his iPad and zoomed in on Alfie. "Keep crying for the feed; it will show everyone our humanity."

"That's it," Alfie snapped. "Turn it off."

"You're going to have to make me, panda man," J-Dog said.

Alfie pointed at J-Dog. "Your parents will soon be childless, and I will replace you in their will."

"Oh, my goodness," J-Dog replied, "you've got your rice sheaves all up in a bunch."

Alfie pursed his lips. "I've got my bamboo stick, and I'm not afraid to use it."

"Use it on yourself," J-Dog lectured. "It was your little drone that crashed, and evidently, it was the drone that attracted the lightning which fried Doc's comms. You need to get your little Philippine mind in order."

Then things went insane.

"*Malaysian* mind! I'm from Malaysia!"

J-Dog scoffed. "Wouldn't it be smarter if all you guys just formed one country? Doesn't that make sense? Your Olympic medal count would go way up. You could stop clinging to one bronze every twelve years."

"That's it!" Alfie had had enough. He jumped in the air and contorted into an ancient martial art fighting stance. He pursed his lips, and with his distinct accent, he let out a long "Oooohh!" He motioned toward J-Dog. "Come, and I will teach you respect."

"Oh, yeah?" J-Dog replied. "You're going full Samurai?"

J-Dog straightened his cowboy hat, raised his right fist, then his left, and conjured up his best Clint Eastwood impression. "Go ahead. I'll fry your wanton."

Rachel covered her face as she gawked at the chaos. "Dean, do something. We are responsible for them. This is happening in your trailer."

"Okay, okay." He took his phone, opened an app, and started tapping.

"What are you doing?" Rachel looked over. "Aren't you going down there?"

Dean raised his hand. "I got it."

Rachel looked at his phone, "Uber Eats?"

"I'm going to send them some burgers. That'll make 'em lose interest."

Rachel shook her head. "All these years and I still don't understand how your mind works."

"I just know boys," Dean laughed. "And honestly, this is normal for J-Dog and Alfie. This is what they do," he said in a matter-of-fact way.

Rachel just lifted her eyebrows.

"How do you think they got so many subscribers?" Dean explained.

Rachel shook her head, incredulous.

"J-Dog and Alfie act like brothers. The difference is, in this day and age, they broadcast it. My brothers and I fought all the time growing up. But we just did it in the barn. These guys do it online."

"Well, they shouldn't," Rachel said, and Dean wasn't going to argue that point.

Then, across the big jumbotron, the crowd saw a bamboo stick fly across the trailer and knock the iPad off the perch, sending it tumbling to the trailer floor. The stadium roared and Rachel was mortified as sounds of crashing and banging resonated throughout the fairground speakers.

Rachel rolled her head toward him. "At least you sent them burgers."

Then the stadium heard J-Dog yelp, "Ow!" And then he tried to tap out, saying, "That's my ear, Alfie! That's my ear!"

"Why do you care?" Alfie snapped back. "You never use them!"

But then the audio and video feed into the stadium abruptly cut out, and the jumbotron went black. The race announcer came across the intercom and cut into the action.

"I'm sorry, ladies and gentlemen, we just got a call from our legal department, and we are being told we must end the feed to Wild Dog TV for too many reasons to list."

"That took them long enough," Rachel said. "And, if they don't have the race footage, I'm not going to watch their antics on my phone either."

"Fair enough," Dean said as he closed the app down.

* * *

THE TORRENTIAL RAIN MADE THE SILTY CLAY INTO A BED OF GREASE, and it demanded every bit of concentration from Doc. He gave a cursory glance to the sky, and he didn't see any chance the storm was going to relent. "Time to lock in, Doc," he said to himself.

He opened his throttle to ninety percent. He didn't want to go full bore yet, but he wanted more. "Just a little faster," he said.

It was still hard to see through his goggles. The rooster tails were spraying mud all over the place, but then Doc saw something happen to the racers in front of him. He couldn't make it out, but it seemed like an unnatural shift in the pack. "What are you doing, boys?" he asked.

Then it happened. The dirt was too slick. The visibility too hampered. Someone lost their line, and then a domino effect of swerves and fishtails broke the unity of the lead group.

COLLISION!

One racer failed to shift in time, and a front tire clipped the rear end of another. The impact at that speed sent the back ATV into an irrecoverable spinout. With that velocity, the four wheels lost all contact with the ground and twisted into a barrel roll. The rider was able to stay on the four-wheeler through one complete belly turn, but not the next four. A huge wall of water, mud, and broken plastic parts exploded into the air, and the rider was jettisoned, like a stone out of an ancient slingshot, out of the race.

"Whoa!" Doc yelled, and quickly turned his handlebars, but the muddy desert floor didn't give *The Drakon* the traction Doc wanted, and he barely changed his path at all.

Doc crouched down to miss a flying chunk of fender that zipped over his helmet, and another wave of mud splashed his face, coating his goggles.

He frantically wiped his goggles, but he couldn't clean off the muddy, brown swirls. Then, he felt something more coming. It was just a gut feeling, but it made him tap the brakes, just a little. It was like it occurred in slow motion in Doc's mind. He saw another four-wheeler lose control in front of him, sliding sideways. The two right tires started to lift on the ATV. Doc knew a crash was coming and so did its rider. Milliseconds before that four-wheeler went into a crocodile death spin, the rider bailed out. He dove as far as he could away from his machine, hoping the racers coming up on his six were skilled enough to miss him. Without the weight of its rider, the four-wheeler popped into the air, flipping over and over again with destructive power.

The boy who dove off hit the ground and slid like he was on a slip-and-slide. That probably saved his life, for he was a long ways away from the path of the other racers when he finally came to a slushy stop.

Doc looked back at the crash as he zipped by, and amazingly, the rider looked alright. His ATV, however, was a mangled mess.

The crash sent a ripple effect through the group. The seasoned riders began to think in unison, and all abided by a slower pace until the terrain would allow a bit more aggression. It was an act of self-preservation that seemed nothing but prudent.

Doc leaned his body left and provided just a bit of turning pressure to his handlebars, testing how well he could turn in the muddy mess. He found some traction, and he drifted to the back left of the lead pack. The move lost him the ability to drag, but that made his view life-savingly better. Trading a little bit of wind advantage to evade the dirty sprays from the muddy rooster tails was a tradeoff he was willing to make.

It was then, in the clearing, that Doc felt the moment arrive. Every race had one. There was a clear danger that the weather and terrain brought to this race, but Doc had learned that in the middle of calamity there was also opportunity. It was the moment where the race would be won or lost. He felt it, and knowing this moment was what made him different.

His instincts triggered a do or die mentality. He knew it was now or never. And here, in the midst of this thunderous western storm in Wyoming, any sense of self-preservation gave way to a predatorial aggression. He was consumed by the adrenaline that surges when going in for a kill.

He craved the racing's edge of calamity, the rush of chaotic nirvana. He cast aside any fear of injury or harm. This game rage dismantled any inhibitions, doubts, or hesitations. His breathing quickened. His pupils dilated. His heart doubled in beats per minute. Energy surged through his arms and legs.

He was a racing addict, no two ways about it, and he lived for this moment and the mayhem that came with it.

* * *

Dean and Rachel huddled under the poncho in the pouring rain. The main thrust of the storm that had engulfed Doc and the other racers had not yet reached them.

"How can they not tell us what's happening in the race?" Rachel asked. "You would have thought that they would have prepared for this."

Dean replied, "Not a lot of money in youth ATV racing, but I don't think it's going to be much longer before we see them. Trust me, they're coming hard and fast."

"I wish we knew if he was ok, at least," she said. "I just think we should have waited two more years before putting him in this kind of race. He's so young."

"He's built for this," Dean said simply.

Rachel wasn't satisfied with that answer, but then the announcer's voice came across the fairground intercom, "Ladies and gentlemen, it has been a wild and wet race, but I think I see them coming if my binoculars don't lie. Still a long way out, but I think the lead pack is reaching Dead Man's Curve!"

* * *

"Dude," J-Dog complained, rubbing his head and ear as he ate the burger Dean had delivered from Uber eats, "eight pounds of pressure can pull an ear off."

"Stop your bellyaching. Why do you need them? They are completely unused," Alfie said as he stuffed his face with French fries.

"Because I'm saving them for marriage."

Alfie gave him a suspicious glance.

"Yeah, I'm that kind of guy," said J-Dog. "I have high moral fiber."

Alfie chugged down a root beer. "You're saving your ears for marriage? That makes no sense."

"Yes, it does, Alfie. My wife will be very honored that she's the first person I've ever listened to." J-Dog tapped his head as if he revealed deep wisdom.

"Where do you get this stuff?"

"I've got deep wells of knowledge inside of me." He paused. "But we got more immediate issues."

"And what are those?" Alfie asked.

"I'm not pointing fingers, but your drone was supposed to give Doc some eyes in the sky. Remember?"

"Lightning strike is an act of God. That's not my doing."

"Maybe so," J-Dog said, "but, do you remember what is coming up near the end of the race?"

"Oh, no. Dead Man's Curve."

"That's right, Alfie, Dead Man's Curve." J-Dog spoke condescendingly. "Doc said Dead Man's Curve was the critical part of the race. Everyone has to slow down. Remember?"

"It's an S-Shape canyon. Makes you crash." Alfie put both hands on his head. "He's trusting us with his life."

"Yes, Alfie, and the plan was to use your drone to see Dead Man's Curve from the air. We would then tell Doc it was coming. Now Doc is going to die because of you." J-Dog shook his head. "Not placing blame. Not pointing fingers, but you'll have to tell his mom how you, and you alone, are responsible for the death of her only child. If this goes bad, I gotta send you back to China."

"Malaysia," Alfie corrected. "But I think we can help him."

"How?"

"It's mathematics. Doc showed me how to do it," Alfie said.

"What?" J-Dog asked. "Why didn't he explain it to me?"

"Probably because you're saving your ears for marriage."

"Alright, Professor, what is it?"

"This is a classic story problem. If Doc is X distance away from Y, traveling at N miles per hour, then how long will it take for Doc to reach Y?" Alfie clapped his hands. "See? I got it!"

"Okay, great, then what's the answer?" J-Dog said.

"What do you mean?" Alfie asked.

"What's the answer of how long before Doc reaches Y?" J-Dog asked.

"I gave you the answer," Alfie argued.

"No, you didn't," J-Dog replied. "You gave me the story problem."

"Is that not the answer?" Alfie asked.

"No! That's the problem! Now you have to solve it," J-Dog gasped.

"How do you do that?" Alfie asked.

"Are you that dense?" J-Dog waved his hands around. "You, um, got to use e=mc2 and, you know . . ." His voice trailed off. "Multiply that by Pi."

Alfie crunched up his eyebrows, "Alright, so Pi is 3.1416, right?"

"3.1264 is like an abbreviation," J-Dog said, scrambling the numbers. "You have to use all of it if we want the right answer."

Alfie shrugged. "I have an idea; let's just look at where he was when we lost communications."

The two boys hunkered down together and looked at the map of the race. Alfie whispered to J-Dog without moving his lips, "We're being streamed right now, everyone is watching this."

J-Dog whispered back also without moving his lips, but pointed at the map as if he knew something, "I know; we look like idiots."

Alfie replied while tapping on his temple and giving a thumbs up, "We gotta come up with something, and fast."

"Okay, I got this, go along with it," J-Dog whispered, and then he stood up. "I've got it!" he announced boldly. "If my calculations are correct, using Pythagorean's theorem, Doc Copper is there!" He pointed to a completely fabricated spot on the map. "Do you concur, Alfie?"

Alfie stood up. "I concur."

"Alright!" J-Dog clapped his hands together. "Time to save Doc Copper's life."

"Ah," Alfie exhaled, and he smacked himself on the forehead.

J-Dog looked at him, "What?"

Alfie walked over to J-Dog and whispered, "I feel so stupid."

J-Dog wrinkled his brow. "Good, that's growth."

Alfie spoke, trying to keep the stream from hearing, "I think I figured it out for real this time."

J-Dog whispered back, "Really?"

"Yeah," Alfie replied, and then showed him the map while holding a piece of scrap paper and a pencil. "The map has a legend on it. I think he was about twenty miles away from Dead Man's Curve when my drone went down, give or take."

"Alright," J-Dog said.

"Doc said he was going to try to average sixty-five miles an hour, but in that rain, he is probably only going fifty or fifty-five, give or take."

"That makes sense," J-Dog answered.

Alfie scribbled things on the paper. "If I'm right, then I think he was about twenty-one minutes away from Dead Man's Curve, again give or take."

"That was about—" J-Dog looked at his watch "—ten minutes ago."

"Give or take?" Alfie asked.

"Yes, of course, give or take, Alfie." J-Dog confirmed and looked at Alfie a bit inquisitively. "Did you just learn that phrase?"

"Yes, and I've been waiting to use it," Alfie replied.

"Congratulations on the execution," J-Dog said. "Are there any other phrases you've been waiting to say?"

"Yes," Alfie replied. "My hips don't lie."

"Good luck fitting that one in." J-Dog rolled his eyes. "But we have to warn Doc, and his comms are fried."

About sixty seconds of precious time ticked by as the boys thought it through, and then Alfie's eyes brightened. "I know what to do."

"Tell me," J-Dog said.

"You have to do so something first," Alfie said.

"Name it."

Alfie pointed at J-Dog. "Give me your shirt. Your genius shirt."

"What? You want my shirt?" J-Dog asked.

"I want the genius shirt, because I came up with the solution, and you didn't. You're the opposite of a genius."

"You're crazy. You're not getting this shirt."

"Then you'll have to tell Mrs. Copper that you killed her only son."

"Are you out of your mind?" J-Dog gasped.

"I know how to save Doc. Give me the shirt," Alfie insisted.

"Fine," J-Dog acquiesced as he took off his white shirt that said, *I know I'm a genius, because I'm a genius,* and slung it at Alfie, hitting him in the face.

"Wow!" Alfie looked at J-Dog's shirtless physique. "You have no muscles, and you are very pale."

"Shut it!" J-Dog now yelled. "Now, tell me. What do we do to save Doc?"

Alfie started putting on the shirt as he explained his plan to J-Dog. "Mr. Copper keeps emergency flares in the horse box in case he has a flat tire or something. So, we light the flare."

"I get it," J-Dog said. "Doc will expect us to signal him when he's getting close to Dead Man's Curve. Now, what's the rest of the plan?"

"The rest?" Alfie said.

"Yeah," J-Dog pressed. "We've got the flare, but what's your plan to get the flare to where he can see it."

"I was going to light it. It's bright."

J-Dog stood completely still. "Stand outside and light it?"

Alfie nodded. "Yeah."

"Give me my shirt back." J-Dog held out his hand and snapped his fingers. "Give it. You're an idiot."

"No, you gave it to me."

"It has to be worn by a genius, and clearly, you are not a genius. Give me my shirt back."

"No."

"I gave it to you because you said you fixed our problem, but the only thing you came up with is lighting a candle outside. Now, give me the stupid shirt!"

"No." Alfie was resolute.

"Then, I'm going to take it off of you."

"You can try."

The two boys collapsed on each other in a wrestling embrace and fell to the trailer floor, rolling around and banging into the gates and walls of the trailer. J-Dog grabbed the shirt and managed to lift it up over Alfie's head, blinding him with it. J-Dog almost succeeded in removing the shirt when Alfie yelled. "Stop, okay, okay!"

The two boys stopped and stood up. Alfie took off the shirt and held it in his hands. "I have an idea. I will rip the shirt in two, and you can have half, and I can have half."

J-Dog took a step back and shook his head. "No, don't rip the shirt. Just give it to me. It's mine."

"No, I will rip it. We each get half the shirt."

Alfie grabbed the shirt and began to pull. The boys could hear the threads began to pop.

"Wait!" J-Dog dropped down to his knees. "Wait! Don't hurt the shirt. You keep the shirt. I would rather you have the shirt than to see it ripped in two."

Alfie paused a bit, looking surprised at the genuine plea from J-Dog. "This shirt really means that much to you?" Alfie responded softly and caringly. "You would rather me have it and wear it than to see it torn apart?"

"Yes." J-Dog nodded. "Yes."

"I see," Alfie said, and then violently ripped the shirt in two, holding the two halves up in the air.

"No!" J-Dog cried out.

"You," Alfie shouted, "were callous and only thought of yourself when my drone was destroyed by lightning. Now *you* know the pain of loss."

"What have you done?" J-Dog's mourning quickly turned to anger. "That's the only shirt I brought."

"What?" Alfie asked. "We're on a five-day trip."

"Exactly, and that's my shirt."

"You only brought one shirt?"

"Duh, yeah," J-Dog replied. "How many shirts did you bring?"

"For a five-day trip, I brought five shirts."

"Seriously, Alfie, you pack like a girl."

Alfie quipped, "You pack like you're homeless."

"Doesn't matter; you ripped my shirt. So now I must light you up with the paintball guns!" J-Dog stopped for a second. "Oh, I've got an idea."

"What? To shoot me?" Alfie asked.

"Oh, this is big. Really big."

"What is it?"

"Doc and I snuck our potato canon on," J-Dog said. "It's in the gooseneck."

"You shoot potatoes?"

"We shoot them; we don't shoot at them," J-Dog explained.

"I don't get it," Alfie said.

J-Dog straightened his hat. "Of course you don't. It's American ingenuity, son. Time for a demonstration."

* * *

After retrieving the potato cannon from the gooseneck, J-Dog and Alfie climbed up onto the roof of the trailer. J-Dog held up the bazooka-sized potato canon, and with no shortage of pride and bravado, explained this piece of artillery to Alfie. "A few years back, I came to Doc with an idea. Nay, a vision. And I offered to invite him into the design process."

Alfie blurted, "You needed him to make it for you."

"Let's not sweat the details," J-Dog replied. "Through our collaboration, my vision became a reality. I introduce to you the Red Spud."

He lifted the PVC-pipe canon into the air.

"Now," he continued, "this is America's answer for when we get invaded by the Chinese army." He paused, slightly. "I've never said this before . . . no offense."

"None taken. I'm Malaysian," Alfie concurred.

"Sure you are. When the Red Army invades our shores, we will blast them in the face with our Idaho sourced, superior complex carbohydrates."

Alfie summarized that plan, "Yeah, yeah, I get it. So, they compare their rice with the Idaho potato, and they see they are hopelessly outmatched, and then they'll turn around and go home."

"Wow!" J-Dog was impressed. "I never thought you would put all that together."

"I've lived with you for years. You're no Rubik's cube."

"No, I'm a thousand-piece jigsaw puzzle of a clear, blue sky. But let's move on to the main event. This is how this works. We're going to have to jam a potato down this PVC pipe," J-Dog said while pointing to the business end of the potato canon, "and we'll have to bury your flare into the potato."

He flipped the cannon around. "We unscrew this cap on this side, and normally, we would spray hairspray into the combustion chamber, and replace the cap."

J-Dog then showed Alfie a hole in the side of the PVC tube. "As you can see, Doc already prepped the chamber with a fuse. So, we will light the fuse, aim it, and boom. We launch the potato and the flare three hundred yards into the air. Doc should see it and realize we are signaling the coming of Dead Man's Curve, thereby saving the life of Doc Copper. Honestly, we are bonified heroes."

Alfie enthusiastically nodded. "Yeah, that's a great plan. We can do this. But there is one question."

"Shoot."

"You said you would normally spray hairspray into the combustion chamber. Are we not doing that?"

"Well, evidently, Doc went into his secret little lab and kind of made a homegrown chemical to use instead of hairspray. He said he wanted to, and I quote, 'better account for the natural existing thermal inertia . . .' yada, yada, yada. Its nerd speak. In layman's terms, he wanted a bigger bang."

J-Dog pulled out of his back pocket a twelve-ounce white tube that had a screw top. "I got it here."

"What's written on it?" Alfie asked.

"It's hard to read Doc's handwriting, but I think it says 'super-activating heat accelerant. For Doc's use only.' Then there's a little asterisk, and it says 'welding shield.'"

"Oh, no," Alfie said, "you need protection to use that stuff."

"Dude, look at me. I'm tough as nails, and I've got my authentic Top Gun Edition pilot glasses that I bought in the value bin right after I rode the Top Gun rollercoaster. These things are used to shoot down enemy MiGs. I'm good."

"If you say so," Alfie said, and then tapped the iPad. "But we gotta get this show on the road. Doc will be at Dead Man's Curve, kind of now, I think."

"Then, step back, and let the master do his work," J-Dog said.

J-Dog set the modified PVC pipe on one end and reached into the bag of potatoes that Alfie had carried up on the roof. He pulled out the biggest one. He began jamming the potato into the open end of the PVC pipe.

He then flipped the pipe over and unscrewed the thick, threaded, PVC butt cap on the other end, and then tried to pour the 'super-activating heat accelerant' into the combustion chamber, but it didn't immediately come out.

"Huh?" J-Dog said as he looked down the hole to see why it wasn't coming. "It's a gel. That's why it's in a tube. I got to squeeze it out." He jerked his head back and blinked. "Whew, this stuff really stings the eyes." He squeezed the entire bottle into the combustion chamber. "I think Doc said it didn't need much, but extraordinary circumstances need extraordinary measures, so I'm using it all. I'm nothing if not thorough."

J-Dog then screwed the butt cap of the potato canon back on tight.

"Now what?" Alfie asked.

"Now we light the fuse. But since we are in a rush, you are going to light the flare, and use the flare to light the fuse, and then stuff the flare into the potato that's already in the canon. I advise you to find your inner Bruce Lee and move fast."

Alfie studied the potato gun and the desired combustible outcomes, and then shook his head. "I think I'll let you do that."

"You are such a scaredy cat," J-Dog said. "But fine, I will be the heroic figure here. I'll be the fifth face on Mount Rushmore. But I only have two hands."

Alfie muttered, "You may only have one after this."

"What?" J-Dog asked.

"Nothing," Alfie replied.

"Let's do this. Take the plastic tip off the flare," J-Dog said. "And Alfie," J-Dog continued, "do you see the tip of the flare?"

"Yes."

"Okay, it works like a match. On the plastic cap, you will find striking paper."

"I see," Alfie replied.

"Give me the flare," J-Dog instructed, and Alfie handed it to him. J-Dog took the flare and began to bore a hole in the top of the potato. "If I dig a hole now, it will make it easier to stick this into the potato when we are on the clock, so to speak."

"I don't get to say this very often," Alfie remarked, "but good thinking, J-Dog."

After J-Dog dug a hole in the top of the potato, he rebalanced the potato gun on his shoulder. He then held the flare out toward Alfie. "When I say 'when,' strike the top of the flare, just like a match."

Alfie reached out and struck the flare, sending sparks in the air, and it ignited the fire-cracking torch.

"What are you doing?" J-Dog yelled.

"You said when you said 'when,' to light the flare. So, I lit the flare."

"I said *when* I said 'when.'"

"Right, you said 'when.' So, I lit the flare."

"No, I was only explaining that 'when' was the word to listen for."

Alfie waved his hands. "Right, I listened, and you said it twice, so I lit the flare."

"No, I had to say it again. It was the next time I said 'when!'"

"Three 'whens?'" Alfie asked.

J-Dog was flabbergasted. "Don't you understand context?"

"English is my third language! This one's on you."

"Fine," J-Dog said, "but no more screw-ups. Alright? Now, I can't light the fuse to the canon with the flare until we are ready to fire. So, tell me when Doc is close enough to Dead Man's Curve, and that's when we'll light it."

"Okay," Alfie said. "But how long does it take for that fuse on the cannon to burn?"

J-Dog looked at it up and down. "Ten seconds, maybe. Probably ten seconds. Don't you think?"

"You don't know?" Alfie asked.

"I've never done it, but it would be crazy if someone made a fuse that didn't burn for at least ten seconds, right? What would be the point of a fuse if it was shorter?"

"I suppose," Alfie surmised, "but we'll find out." Alfie then looked down at the iPad. "I'd light the fuse."

"What, now?" J-Dog yelled. "He's already at Dead Man's curve?"

"Give or take."

"You are so *not* skilled labor," J-Dog criticized. He lit the fuse on the potato canon and sparks quickly scorched the rope racing toward the combustion chamber.

"Oh!" J-Dog yelled at the speed of the spark.

"That's a five second fuse!" Alfie pointed and yelled.

"You think, Sherlock?" J-Dog screamed as he frantically stuffed the flare into the potato. "Going to be close!" he yelled as he lifted the potato canon and placed it against his right shoulder and aimed it at the sky.

"You're aiming the wrong way!" Alfie yelled.

BOOOOOM!

The explosion was nearly deafening as copious amounts of super accelerant nukified inside the PVC and blew the potato and flare over a thousand feet high, sending a streaking orange, potato-burning comet through the western sky.

The blast was further intensified by the accelerant's vapor reigniting with the flare's flame, causing an engulfing fireball blowback into J-Dog's face.

The percussion blast of the canon, absorbed by J-Dog's right shoulder, sent him careening off the top of the trailer with legs spread high and wide. His body thudded on the prairie grass below, deflating his lungs like a popped balloon.

"Ugh," J-Dog moaned, trying to suck in air, but it was going to be a few seconds until his lungs recalibrated.

"J-Dog! J-Dog!" Alfie yelled, clambering down the ladder. "Are you alive? Are you alive?"

He rushed to his friend's side and knelt. By that time, J-Dog resumed breathing, but he was still stunned by the impact and stared agape into the sky.

Alfie put both hands on J-Dog's chest and started to compress. "One, one thousand."

"Ow!" J-Dog protested, trying to stop him.

"You have to let me help," Alfie said and pushed again. "Two one thousand."

"OW!" J-Dog yelled and smacked Alfie in the head. "I'm not dead. Stop it."

"I'm saving you!"

"No, you're not. Get off me!" J-Dog shoved him, and tried to sit up, but then he laid back down, groaning. "Nope, too soon."

Alfie stopped his CPR attempt and looked at J-Dog's now smoke-blackened face, and he sat back. "Oh, I thought you were dead."

"Couldn't breathe, yes. Dead, no."

"That's good. Did you notice it was a five second fuse?"

"Now that you say something . . ."

Alfie stared at J-Dog's burnt face, so much so that it became awkward.

"What are you looking at?" J-Dog asked.

"Where are your eyebrows?"

"What?" J-Dog reached up and patted his face. "Alfie, give me your iPad."

Alfie handed him the iPad, which was still streaming, of course, and J-Dog quickly flipped the camera to see the damage.

"AGGGHHHH! MY FACE!"

"Um," Alfie tried to intervene, "it's not *that* bad."

"I don't have eyebrows. I don't have eyelashes, and I even lost my nose hairs! I look like a cartoon villain."

"Well, look at the bright side," Alfie said.

"What bright side?" J-Dog demanded as he studied his blackened nose in the camera.

"You were always ugly, so what's a little more ugly?"

J-Dog was beside himself. "What?"

Alfie explained, "See, if you were beautiful and then this happened, then you would experience great loss. But there's not much difference between ugly and then more ugly. So, I'd say you dodged a bullet."

"Oh no," J-Dog said, "I'm concussed. I normally would outwit you, but the explosion has compromised my brain."

Alfie hemmed and hawed. "Well, again, I'm not so sure," he said as he walked over and picked up the broken, charred, and mangled sunglasses with shattered lenses. "Here are your glasses." He brought them to J-Dog as he looked them over. "Wow, now that is irony."

"What?" J-Dog asked.

"Look," Alfie handed the sunglasses to J-Dog and pointed at them. "*These* are from China."

* * *

DOC STRAINED HIS EYES TO SEE THROUGH HIS MUDDIED GOGGLES, and he saw the pack start an incline. He stood on the pegs to get a better view, but his vision was still hampered by the weather and the ascending terrain. He was blind to what was past that hill. He thought it might be Dead Man's Curve. "That's got to be it," he said to himself.

Doc knew that Dead Man's Curve was strategically put in the race to slow the field and condense the pack heading into the final stretch. The small hill that rose and fell into the dangerous S-shaped canyon was a perfect tool to do just that, and he knew that how he navigated the corner would be the difference between winning and losing.

He talked to *The Drakon*, "I feel it; it's coming."

The front pack had opened a lead on the rest of the field, and Doc bided his time at the back of it. The pack of racers started a climb, and in a staccato-like rhythm, all started to brake and ease off the throttles. "They think it's Dead Man's, too."

Then, he saw it, the orange potato flare comet firing across the sky. He laughed, "That's good enough for me."

Of course, there was no way to know, for sure, what such a flare could mean. There had been no discussion of launching a burning signal in the sky. But Doc knew J-Dog and Alfie, and that was enough to believe the unbelievable.

* * *

"DEAN," RACHEL ASKED AS SHE POINTED TO THE SKY. "WHAT'S THAT?"

Dean looked at the streaking orange flame sparking high in the western sky. "I don't know," he said slowly as he studied the comet-like arc. "Is that coming toward us?"

"Dean—" Rachel's concern emanated the need for immediate action "—it's coming toward us, but I'm a little concerned about where it came from."

"I see it," Dean said. "I should probably go check the trailer now."

"Yeah," she said and then put her hands over her head. "OH!" she gasped as did the rest of the stadium crowd.

The flaming potato flare torpedoed into the oven pit of the hot dog vendor down at the food court. The grease and paper hot dog wraps ignited, setting the whole unit ablaze.

More than one onlooker captured the inferno on video, along with the jumping man in a giant hot dog costume who just watched his cart go up in flames. He was an eternal meme within seconds.

Dean gritted his teeth, not wanting to look at his wife and knowing he was going to get the blame for this if both their intuitions were right.

Rachel shook her head. "I bet you ten to one that we just bought a food cart."

Dean didn't quite run to the trailer, but he jogged.

* * *

When Dean got to the trailer, he found a shirtless and charred-face J-Dog sitting on a chair on the roof with Alfie sitting next to him.

"Hey!" Dean called.

J-Dog walked to the edge. His cowboy hat found its way back to his head. It was charred black as well, but J-Dog liked it. He thought it made him look tough.

"Howdy, Mr. Copper. What's up?"

"What's up?" Dean asked. "Why is your face black? Where's your shirt?"

"Well, sir, there was an incident," J-Dog replied.

Dean kept going, "Did the incident have to do with the flare we saw in the sky?"

J-Dog and Alfie fist bumped each other with pride.

"Awesome," J-Dog said, "you saw it."

"The whole stadium saw it!" Dean dropped his head. "And so did an unsuspecting hot dog vendor." He turned and muttered, "That's going to cost me."

"That means Doc saw it, too," J-Dog reasoned.

"You did that for Doc? Why?" Dean asked.

"Dead Man's Curve," Alfie replied. "We lost contact with him, so . . ."

"Oh," Dean said, putting it all together in his head. "Smart . . . sort of."

* * *

Doc quickly veered to his left to move out from behind the lead pack. He needed a clear runway if he was going to hit that high point just right. Then a guttural command came from the southern boy as he commanded his ATV, "Give me all you got!"

Doc shifted down and hammered the throttle. *The Drakon* roared. The lower gear brought instant torque and acceleration. He rocked back into a crouched stance and banked further left, giving him a free lane up the hill. This was Dead Man's Curve, and he wasn't slowing down at all.

Game rage continued to possess Doc, and like a loaded slingshot, he hurled by the slowing group as he barreled toward the embankment, heading into the dangerous drop and curve. When he reached the tip of the ascent, he didn't slow at all, but gave it one last twist of fuel.

Euphoria found Doc in a way only racers can understand. The thudding and churning of the terrain gave way to the graceful glide of flight as he soared off the steep twelve-foot embankment.

His eyes drifted down and he saw the two hairpin turns of Dead Man's Curve zip by beneath him as he cleared both with room to spare.

THUMP! He came back down to earth.

The shocks bottomed out and Doc's butt slammed into his seat, only to be bounced back up into the air from the collision again and again and again until a permanent connection to the ground was made.

Through it all, Doc held his line, and more importantly, he torched the field with the all-or-nothing move as every other racer chose to snake their way through the decline and hairpin turns.

Doc Copper now had an insurmountable lead over the pack. The stadium crowd rose with cheers as they saw one ATV out in front that nearly raced alone.

As he got closer, Rachel stood up, and her scream notified everyone that it was the boy from Bell Buckle, Tennessee, that now owned the pack.

Doc blasted through the entrance to the county fairground stadium all alone. He was welcomed by a standing, cheering ovation as he had *The Drakon* at full throttle. He still maintained a tight racing crouch, and he gunned it around the oval track.

Rachel screamed with ecstasy from the stands, not because he won, but because he lived.

Doc stood up on his pegs, flipped up his collar again, and thrusted his arms high into the air as he crossed the finish line.

The stadium announcer thundered in the speakers, "Your national champion, Doc Copper. Next stop, the Quad Continental!"

Doc throttled down and spun donuts for the crowd before scooting to a stop. He jumped up on his seat and saluted the flag, and the crowd roared.

* * *

AFTER THE WIN IN WYOMING, THE LIFE OF DOC COPPER WOULD never be the same. The constant barrage of the press wanting interviews, pictures, and specials on the young racer came nearly every day. However, it suited Doc just fine spending most of his on-air time with his buddies on Wild Dog TV.

Dean came to grips with the fact that Doc had become the most fearless racer he had ever seen. He just prayed his natural giftedness would keep him safe, at least as safe as any racer could possibly be.

Rachel went from anxious, unsettled, and worried to stone-cold mortified at the idea of Doc racing in the Quad Continental. She now had firsthand knowledge as to what lengths her son would go to win a race.

She used to have dreams that he and his gifted mind would follow in the footsteps of many in her family as a lawyer or a surgeon. Now, those dreams traded places with nightmares that some horrific crash would take all that potential away.

Following the win, Doc had built a relationship with the United States Junior Racing Association. They were the national governing body of off-road junior racing, and he was their champion. They pinned their hopes on him to bring home the trophy of the legendary Quad Continental, something that had evaded the United States for many decades.

The upper brass of USJRA all had their own ideas on how Doc should ride. They discussed strategies, goals, and expectations for him. Doc was quick to point out that, had he strictly applied the concepts they were advocating to the Wyoming race, he would have finished seventh. They didn't really believe the boy and his calculations, and the frustrations with his "youthful stubbornness" began to mount.

Most importantly though, Doc and the USJRA discussed the specs and delivery of the super desert UTV racer being especially built for the Quad Continental. Doc became instrumental in the final mechanical touches to the machine and insisted on some specs that the power brokers disagreed with. But as the champion, he had won the right to make those calls.

When he took delivery of the official Team USA UTV, J-Dog made sure to stream the ceremonial unwrapping of the machine for the world to see. It was a high gloss red, white, and blue thing of beauty, with the American flag painted in wavy, patriotic glory on the hood.

The side-by-side boasted an engine that was eleven hundred cubic centimeters strong. It made his four-wheeler look dainty in comparison. The desert machine was designed to hit an easy one hundred thirty-five miles an hour while in the silty sand of the Baja. Everything was state of the art, from the built in GPS display, satellite link-up communication capability, and power outlets designed to heat special clothing to counter the desert chill that would come with racing at midnight. Every bit of technological advantage and mechanical brute force was packed into this machine.

The USJRA pressed as hard as an organization could to handpick Doc's pit crew for the race. They wanted seasoned vets, under their own watch, over every bit of operational choice, training, and race day execution.

What the USRJA didn't expect, though, was when Doc discovered in the fine print that, as champion, his team was his call, and he ended up declining all their offers.

Doc knew he didn't need their technical expertise or mechanical acumen, for he was already smarter than they were. Rather, he needed a crew he could trust with his life, the kind of crew that would use a potato gun to send a warning flare when all else fails.

So, he told the USJRA thank you, but no thanks. "I'll take it from here."

* * *

On a sunny Sunday afternoon at the rolling hilled Copper farm, Doc was out in front of his dad's beautiful horse barn. He was tinkering with the fluid levels in the Baja racer and revved the engine loud enough that everyone within a country mile could hear it. Those riding in the big, black Chevrolet Tahoe rolling down the long gravel driveway could hear it, too.

"I'm telling you, J-Dog," Doc said as he stepped back from the front hood of the side-by-side, wiping grease off his hands with an old blue, terrycloth towel, "I need someone who can actually ride this race with me. This is a pilot and navigator race."

"Do you absolutely have to have one?" J-Dog asked.

"No, it's not mandatory to have a navigator, but it would be insane not to have one. That's why it's a UTV frame, and not a four-wheeler."

"I just never knew you to need someone else," J-Dog said.

"This race is different, and that is why, even with Jonah in the crew, we're still shy one man. I need a full-time navigator for the Quad Continental. I don't have to remind you, but someone who can race with me for well over one thousand miles under those desert conditions is hard to come by. I need to find an alpha male, tough as nails, with the fight of a honey badger in him. That's a tall order."

J-Dog tipped back an ice-cold glass bottle of root beer and took a swig. "Ye of little faith," he nonchalantly crooned. "I've been playing coy." J-Dog winked. "I took care of you, Doc."

Doc rolled his eyes.

"You did?" Alfie looked up from his cross-legged, seated position in the grass. "I'll believe that when I see it."

By the time the Tahoe pulled around the gravel circle in front of the horse barn, Doc, Alfie, and J-Dog had strolled out to greet it.

The back door to the big SUV swung open, and Jonah Bell jumped out. Jonah was big. The thick-boned, heavy set thirteen-year-old was already north of two hundred and thirty pounds and about six feet tall. He was wearing his vintage Ohio State Ted Ginn, Jr., jersey, and his favorite Air Jordan throwback sneakers to go along with it.

Jonah's voice and persona had all the deepness, soul, and charisma of a black southern Gospel preacher, and he gave his customary greeting with his one-of-a-kind oratory inflection.

"Ding, ding! Bell is in the ring," he said and did a chest bump with Alfie, which dropped Alfie to the ground.

"Oy!" Alfie blurted as he accepted Jonah's outstretched hand to help him back up.

"Sorry, little man," Jonah laughed. "We need to get some weight on you. Your rice and carrot diet ain't cuttin' it. You need some southern cookin'."

J-Dog walked around Jonah slowly and in a way that everyone knew some kind of remark was coming. "So, Ted Ginn, huh? Interesting choice."

Doc dropped his head to the ground and chuckled a bit. "Here we go."

"So what, J-Dog?" Jonah replied. "What's your point?"

J-Dog took off his cowboy hat and scratched his head. "I thought you would be more of a trenches type of guy. I thought you looked up to someone a little more rotund. I mean, Ted Ginn? That's a skinny, little fast guy."

Jonah got a little testy. "Ginn is cat fast. Long strides, high knees, accelerates like a cheetah. Just. Like. Me."

"I'm sorry," J-Dog quipped. "Maybe you mean a Cheeto?"

"Oh!" Jonah raised his voice, "I see, you startin' up. Alright, I can go there. Because you know my daddy can whip any man in the county, and I can whip my daddy. I'm looking at you, and you're my light work."

Alfie shook his head. "You always say that, Jonah, but I don't understand it. Are you not both in the county?"

"Jonah's not a man, Alfie," J-Dog said. "That's the only way that makes sense."

Doc started chuckling. "We got to this spot faster than usual."

One of the back windows of the Tahoe lowered, and a girl's head popped out.

"All I heard was a cheetah!" The girl giggled like the newly minted teenager that she was. "And if you're a cheetah, then you're the slowest cheetah I've even seen, because you can't outrun me."

"Please, no girl's outrunning me," Jonah said as he looked at the boys while twirling his finger around his temple. "She's been sippin' out of granddaddy's fruit jar if she thinks she's outrunning me. I'm a specimen built for speed."

Doc smiled. "What's up, Flip? Didn't know you were coming, but you're always welcome."

"Yep, low maintenance chick," J-Dog quipped. "You can point her in a direction, and she'll just go entertain herself. Gotta admire that."

Flip was as cute and giggly as a girl could be. She couldn't be caught without flashing a bright smile and bouncing those medium brown pig tails. But that only told half the story.

She was a true freak of nature. Otherworldly athletic and never saw a game she didn't need to win. She earned her stripes with the boys, once and for all, when they were all about ten years old. She had twisted J-Dog's arm until he agreed aloud that camouflage should only be available in pink. That's the type of street cred that tends to last amongst the boys.

She didn't dress like a normal girl, either. Rather, she dressed like a girl who never left the ballpark. She could always be found wearing an athletic shirt with its sleeves cut off, a pair of jersey-knit shorts with white tube socks pulled up to her knees, and of course, well-worn athletic sneakers, often cleats, depending on the day.

Today though, she took it to the next level, and Doc was amused. "Flip, you're wearing eye black."

"Athletes' eye shadow," she laughed. "I played a double header last night and didn't want to shower because I was coming to a barn today." Then she blurted, "I stole beven sases!" She paused, shook her head, and giggled. "Seven bases. Agh, why do I always do that?"

That is why they called her Flip. From the time any of them knew her, she would flip letters around in words, and it always made for colorful conversation.

Doc smiled. "The sun is out today, so I gather the eye black is appropriate." He then elbowed Jonah and whispered, "As soon as your mom gets out of here, we can get rolling."

Jonah hemmed and hawed a bit. "Yeah, 'bout that . . ." Jonah looked back at the van. "There's this thing."

"What thing?" Doc asked.

A passenger side door opened.

Doc's eyes squinted, and he lowered his voice, "Did you bring someone else?"

"So, Doc," Jonah cautioned, "J-Dog told me that you're still missing a navigator."

"Yeah," Doc pressed, "but I don't know what that has to do with . . ." He pointed to the person who stepped out of the front door. All eyes went to the sunshine blond girl who climbed out of the front seat of the SUV.

Her bouncing blond hair was pulled back perfectly with a big pink bow which matched the pink bows on her bright white sandals. She wore leggings decorated with butterflies and a white fluttery blouse with a picture of a prancing unicorn fully adorned with glitter. She had manicured nails with little sparkling stones glued to them, and the shade of her nail polish must have come out of the same bucket as her lip gloss.

Alfie's eyes popped. "She's so shiny."

"Hello," the new girl said.

Doc didn't care. "That's not my navigator," he quipped.

"No, she's not," Jonah agreed, "but that's one of the things I was talking about."

"I'm not a thing," the shiny girl said in protest, but no one paid any attention to her.

Doc began to boil a bit. "Jonah, this is a strategy session on winning the legendary Quad Continental. This isn't a party. This is business."

Jonah replied in a high-pitched retort, "I know, but, man, my hands are tied. You feel me? She's the daughter of my momma's friend who just moved to town. I got pinned into it. Momma said so."

"Are you kidding me?" Doc raised his hands.

Jonah stared at Doc, and with a low deep voice, rumbled, "Momma said so."

"Well . . ." Doc fought with the idea for a moment. "She's not my momma. She's your responsibility."

Jonah's eyebrows almost hit his hairline. "Have you met my momma? She ain't no one's responsibility. If you want to go tell her, I know she'll roll that window down. I'm warning you, though, she still ain't allowed to fly on Delta."

"Alright, alright, fine. I know you wouldn't do this if you didn't have to. I just didn't think anyone else would be here."

Then a back passenger door opened. "Good," a boy's abrupt and choppy voice was heard on the other side of the Tahoe, "then you'll love seeing me."

Doc looked at Jonah with cold eyes. "Et tu, Brute?"

"Agh," J-Dog grunted, "Doc went all linguistic. He might take this worse than we thought."

A cloud of dust stirred up as the Black Tahoe drove away. When the dust finally settled, there stood none other than Mac Irons. The broad-shouldered, inner-city kid from the streets of Memphis, who was as tough as the asphalt he grew up on.

* * *

DOC'S TEMPER SPIKED, AND HE TOOK TWO QUICK STEPS TOWARD Mac, but he was quickly interrupted by the new, preppy blond girl. She tossed her shoulders back and stood with impeccable posture. "Good morning to you," the bubbly girl interjected. "Perhaps I could introduce myself?"

Her out of place demeanor jarred the scene and brought some levity to a situation that was about to get out of hand.

"Fine. Introduce yourself." Doc's last strand of patience was being pulled. "By all means."

The girl took a deep breath and made an announcement as if she was standing on a Broadway stage in front of a sold-out crowd, "I am Penelope Parsippany, a poet of epiphany."

Jonah's head dropped. "Why does she *always* do that?"

Alfie looked around bewildered. "Who's she talking to?"

J-Dog smirked. "Hey, sweet cheeks, you're on a farm, and we're not your glee club."

Jonah offered some explanation, "She's like a poet or something. I don't know."

Penelope smiled and responded with perfect elocution, "Yes, Jonah, you are correct. I am a word maker. I provide perfect prose to bless the heart and tickle the toes."

Alfie raised his hand. "I don't want my toes tickled."

Flip jumped in, "Can you kick a kickball or not? That's all I need to know."

"Ooh, I'm not much for athletic confrontation," Penelope responded, "but I can make words drip like honey and make the mundane sunny." She then clicked her heels together, for whatever reason.

Flip was baffled. "I don't know what to do with that."

J-Dog took off his cowboy hat. "She's Mrs. Willy Wonka meets Dr. Seuss. I'm getting a cavity just listening to her. Hey, Doc, don't you have a horse-drawn carriage she can ride away in?"

Doc was frustrated with the whole situation. This was supposed to be the key planning day for the Quad Continental, but now he had a circus on his hands.

Mac Irons reveled in the chaos, and he flashed a patronizing grin toward Doc. "Got your tutu in a twist?"

Doc clenched his fists as he stared down the Memphis kid.

Mac was wearing what he always did: a plain, white, V-necked t-shirt and faded blue jeans with slight tears and stains throughout. He had short, spiky, sandy brown hair, buzzed nearly to the scalp on the sides. He wore old broken-in basketball shoes and a rawhide leather necklace that was threaded through with a half-a-dozen iron ball bearings.

Doc and Mac, at first glance, were completely different. Doc's charming southern accent with eloquent speech scratched up against the quickened, choppy bluntness of Mac. Doc had thick, wavy, dark brown hair and boyish good looks, and Mac came with a squared off fighter's jaw that testified to giving out more than he ever got.

Both were leaders of the pack. Both hated the other for it.

"Irons," Doc deadpanned.

"Copper," Mac countered with equal disdain.

Doc jabbed at him. "You're finally using multiple syllables, Mac. Good to see the improvement."

"You're not braiding your hair yet, pretty boy. I'll take that as a good sign," Mac shot back.

Doc shook his head. "Mac, any other day, and I would rip that chain right off your neck."

Mac had a shark-like stare. "You make sure you find me when that day comes."

Doc bent down and picked up a handful of gravel from the drive. He ground it up for a few seconds and then flung it down the driveway.

"Dang it, boys!" he yelled at Jonah and J-Dog. "This is my team. Heck, this is my barn and my farm." He pointed at Jonah and J-Dog. "You better believe that whoever is riding with me as my navigator is my call."

"Now, Doc," Jonah interrupted, "listen, we all want to win this thing, and both J-Dog and I knew you'd hate this. But—"

"Well, if you knew I would hate this, then your deduction skills to bring him really lack any semblance of intelligence. I expected more out of both of you."

"Hey," Jonah said, "listen. You said this race was over a thousand miles through a desert and you needed someone tough enough to do it with you. That's Mac Irons."

Doc shook his head. "No, he's not tough enough."

"Now, Doc," J-Dog interrupted, "everyone knows Mac doesn't feel any pain. That's pretty tough."

Doc was incredulous and flung his arms in the air. "He doesn't feel pain because he has a medical condition called congenital analgesia! He's not tough; he's brain dead!"

Penelope gasped and placed her hand over her chest. "Oh, my heart!" She looked at Mac with sincere empathy. "We should hold a telethon."

J-Dog laughed. "Yeah, we'll make little ribbons out of barbed wire and stick it to his chest."

"Can we focus, boys?" Doc scolded. "The answer is no. Besides—" Doc looked at Mac "—why would you want to help me win a world championship? Last I checked, I wasn't high on your friends and family list."

"Ain't doing it for you, Copper. I'm in it for the money."

Doc looked at Jonah. "Really? You told him about the college scholarships?"

"Well, duh!" Jonah responded as if the answer was self-evident. "Why else would he race with you? He thinks you're just a pretty boy with fancy toys. He can't stand ya!"

"Yep," Mac agreed.

J-Dog chimed in, "Doc, it's called swinging a carrot."

"But it's my carrot," Doc quickly countered and turned to Mac. "Mac, I'm sure you can Uber your way back to wherever you came from. It's my call, and you're out."

"Now, Doc," J-Dog stepped in, "calm down. Both Jonah and I agreed on this, and you know that me and Sumo don't agree on much."

"Hey," Jonah said, "watch your tongue, little man. Remember last time."

"Whatever." J-Dog ignored him. "The point is, you need a navigator, and it can't be me cause I'm web-streaming the whole race. It can't be Alfie since he's my camera man, and besides, if he was your navigator you'd probably end up in an Asian rice field. We can scratch Jonah off the list, obviously, and Flip's a girl. So, you know."

PANG!

Out of nowhere Flip rifled a red dodge ball that pinged off the side of J-Dog's head, knocking his cowboy hat and new pilot sunglasses off his face. The ricochet sent the ball twenty yards away.

"OW!" J-Dog stumbled back and cradled his face. "What's wrong with you?"

Flip giggled. "That's right, I'm a girl. Ba-bam!"

Alfie pointed at J-Dog's face. "You have VOIT stamped backwards on your cheek."

Flip turned to Penelope. "That's called dodgeball, and he didn't dodge. I win."

Jonah bent over with a big ol' belly laugh, then sighed. "I know that hurt."

Alfie nodded. "Yeah it did. Flip's like an Altoid. Small, white, and curiously strong."

Penelope was getting concerned and tried to turn the conversation. "Why can't Jonah be your navigator?"

Jonah smiled. "There is wisdom in that question, Penelope. Of course I could do it. But I'm running the pit crew. Oil changes, tire rotations, and things like that take mad skills. That's my role."

J-Dog brushed off his cowboy hat and stuck it back on his head. His stinging face led to even a more contentious and sarcastic mood. He rubbed his cheek. "I'm sorry, Jonah, did you say you could be the navigator?"

"Yeah, of course," Jonah replied.

"Are you out of your mind?" J-Dog asked. "Out in Wyoming, Doc left a gallon of gas out of his four-wheeler just to save weight."

Jonah lowered his voice as his displeasure grew. "I don't see where you're going."

"Jonah," J-Dog shouted, "you would sink him like quicksand."

"Oh, I get it." Jonah nodded. "Muscle weighs a lot. Yeah, I'm a chunk of granite." He shoved his shoulders back.

J-Dog grinned. "I'm sorry, Jonah, my ears are still ringing a bit. I thought you said you were a chunk of granite?"

Jonah curled his lips a bit. "That's right."

J-Dog feigned deep puzzlement. "Are you going to let your belly in on that secret?"

The slights coming from J-Dog were now starting to pile up. "You're itching for a beat down, little man," Jonah warned.

Penelope smacked her lips and used her punctuated pronunciation while she waved her index finger. "No, no, no, we don't go there. You just point those words out the door to the don't-come-back store."

Flip looked around at everyone. "Does everyone else hear her? Or am I dreaming?"

That slowed down Jonah for a moment. "It's all good. J-Dog's comments don't mean nothing to me."

"No, Jonah. Don't do that to yourself," Penelope instructed. "Don't deflect your feelings. You owe it to your heart. It's okay if it hurts."

Jonah stressed, “Really, Penelope. Let it go. I’m straight.”

J-Dog couldn’t help himself. “No, Jonah, little Barbie 2.0 is right. You owe it to your heart.”

“Boy,” Jonah threatened.

Penelope continued, oblivious to the pot she was boiling as she kept trying her own brand of intervention. “Jonah, all you need to do is be the best you that you can be, because you are such a better you than anyone else could ever be.”

J-Dog slow-clapped. “Oh, bravo, thank you, Miss Renaissance. I feel so enlightened. Jonah, I didn’t know you hired your own self-help therapist. Let me guess, she told you to weigh yourself in smiles!” He laughed and laughed.

Doc tried to caution, “J-Dog, you’re really pushing. This isn’t going to end well for you.”

Alfie shook his head. “Do we have a first aid kit?”

“Affirmative,” Doc replied. “It’s for horses, but yeah.”

J-Dog laughed. “Hey, Jonah, I have a bag of skittles. Come and get your happy.”

“DING, DING!” an infuriated Jonah yelled and bull-charged J-Dog.

Penelope gasped, “What’s happening?”

“Welcome to the Bell Buckle Gang,” Alfie shouted as he stepped out of the way of the big ball of aggression.

J-Dog kept laughing while quickly backing up. “Oh look, a hungry, hungry hippo. Can I pet him?”

THUMP! Jonah engulfed J-Dog and steamrolled him into the grass.

“UGH!” J-Dog grunted as the wind got knocked out of him. The commotion was loud enough that even some of the horses in a nearby field jumped and snorted.

"Whatchya say, son?" Jonah taunted as he laid on J-Dog, completely smothering him so that J-Dog nearly disappeared under the big mass. "I can't hear you," Jonah mocked. "Where's your witty comeback, now?"

A gasping voice was heard from underneath, "You think I'm witty?"

Jonah raised himself up and then power flopped his belly right down on J-Dog's head.

"You like that? Huh?" Jonah said.

J-Dog's reply was too smothered to make out.

The kids surrounded the pile, but no one intervened.

"Shouldn't we do something?" Penelope asked.

"Nah, it will be over soon," Alfie said calmly.

"I got a dollar on twenty seconds," Doc offered.

"Ten seconds," Alfie countered.

"You're on." Doc looked at his watch.

Jonah dominated the skinny, overmatched boy, and kept driving him deeper and deeper into the ground. Jonah lifted himself up so J-Dog's face could be seen, "What? Are you trying to talk, son?"

J-Dog took the opportunity and yelled at Doc, "Horse tranquilizers! Horse . . ."

"Oh, so we're not done yet?" Jonah said. "I gotcha."

Jonah lifted up his shirt and stuck his armpit in J-Dog's face. J-Dog began squirming now as wildly as he could, but Jonah pushed his armpit deeper and deeper into the boy's mouth and nose.

J-Dog freed his mouth for a moment. "Dude! They're so hairy! And wet!"

"That's right, Dog!" Jonah yelled back. "I got man pits!"

J-Dog fought to turn his head, and got out a scream, "My mouth was open!"

Then there was a sudden calm. Jonah could feel J-Dog go limp underneath him.

The struggle was over. J-Dog tapped out. "Okay, okay, okay."

Flip giggled. "It looks like camouflage is still pink."

Doc looked down at his watch. "Twenty seconds."

"J-Dog," Alfie yelled, "you can't even lose right!" He handed Doc his dollar.

The boys got up off the ground. J-Dog was filthy, and Jonah was satisfied.

"What does that come to now, Doc?" J-Dog asked.

Doc immediately answered back, "Jonah, one hundred and fourteen to J-Dog's . . . zero."

"What?" J-Dog asked. "I thought it was only one hundred and thirteen."

"Well, it *was* that," Doc pressed.

"Oh," J-Dog acquiesced. He brushed off his hat and put it back on his head.

Penelope was aghast. "They do this quite often?"

Flip whispered to her, "Don't worry, they're only boys." She giggled. "I'd take 'em down Reco-Groman style!" She flexed.

"Greco-Roman," Penelope corrected.

"I've heard it both ways," Flip replied.

The tussling between the two boys deflated the tension a bit, but the bigger issue wasn't going away.

Doc looked at Mac Irons, "Do you even know what you are trying to sign up for, kid?"

* * *

DOC LED THE GANG AROUND THE SIDE OF THE BARN WHERE THEY saw the incredible UTV desert racing machine.

Jonah lifted his hands to his head in admiration. "Ooh, check it out!"

The side-by-side racer was stunning. The airbrushed flag on the hood, the metallic stripes, swooshes, and stars that swept over the rest of the red, white, and blue painted panels gleamed like crystal.

Doc grinned, climbed in on the driver side, and pressed the push button ignition. It came to life with a wild roar, and Penelope quickly covered both her ears. The guttural growl brought a grease monkey like Doc into a mechanical nirvana.

Doc stared at Mac who walked slowly around the racer. Mac reached out and slid his hand across the smooth waxed surface as he circled the machine. He curled his lips a bit and tilted his head. "Not bad."

Doc killed the engine and responded, "Not bad?"

"This is what money buys. That's all it is," Mac replied.

That chapped Doc. "Right, *money* did this," he said as he grabbed the USJRA racing publication magazine that was lying on the navigator's seat next to him. The front cover was Doc standing next to the UTV, holding the big trophy from the Wyoming race.

Doc got out of the vehicle and slapped Mac on the chest with it. "Read it," Doc demanded.

Mac grabbed the magazine and scanned the front.

NATIONAL CHAMPION DOC COPPER

RACING PRODIGY DOC COPPER BECOMES YOUNGEST NATIONAL CHAMPION EVER. SETS TRACK RECORD IN THE PROCESS AND NOW TURNS HIS EYES TOWARD THE QUAD CONTINENTAL.

"Money didn't buy that," Doc stated. "I beat a field of champions to win that. Set a record doing it."

"Nope, it was money," Mac countered.

"I won the race," Doc argued.

"How much money did it take to get you there? The hotels, gas, the four-wheeler, the truck and trailer that I see over there. I see tens of thousands of dollars. I mean, I've got a newspaper route. I have to buy my own shoes. You don't have a job. You get to play with these toys that mommy and daddy buy. You won because of money, pretty boy."

"Oh, I get it," Doc countered, "you're jealous. You think you've been dealt a bad hand, and I'm just unfairly privileged." Doc chuckled a bit. "You've actually bought into the exact thing that the worst part of humanity wants you to buy into: that you're a victim, and it's okay to hate those dirty privileged people. Let's eat the rich!" Doc laughed at Mac. "Yeah, you're nothing special, Irons. You're garden-variety fast food, and you'll be the useful idiot they all want you to be. Go ahead, stew in your jealousy."

Mac clenched his jaw. "I'm not jealous of you, Copper, and I didn't buy into anything. You, on the other hand, have had *everything* bought for you."

Doc snapped his fingers in Mac's face. "Hey, hear me clearly, Irons. I'm going to do you a favor. I'm about to talk to you in a way no one has." Doc looked him square in the eyes. "I will not apologize for my mom and dad. I'm not going to feel guilty for living and loving the life they worked so hard to give me. When I do my best with what they give, I'm living their desires for me. So go pout with left-stream America. They'll love your victimhood and drink your tears. But, here, at the Copper farm, we put people like you in the rearview mirror and don't look back. You are free to wallow in your self-pity while I move on. I won't even remember your name, and that's saying something, because I remember everything."

Mac wanted to punch him so bad. He hated that Doc made him think. "You've just had better opportunities than I've had, Copper. It doesn't make you better than me."

Doc shook his head. "I don't think I'm better than you, as you say it, for all of this—" He waved his arms around. "I know I'm better than you because I don't walk around bitter like you."

Mac almost swung, but Doc kept talking.

"What now, Irons?" Doc asked. "J-Dog and Jonah, against all my wishes, picked you to come to my farm today. And low and behold, the very opportunity you despise me for having is set before you. Funny how this works, huh? You have an opportunity to prove your worth. In theory, you could convince me, via merit, that you can ride with me and win the international race of a lifetime. So, are you now going to complain that you got this opportunity when every other Memphis kid you know—" Doc flashed air quotes "—was *robbed* of this opportunity? Aren't you the dirty privileged one now? Should you live your life feeling guilty that this chance was given to you and not to everyone else? What say you, Mac Irons?"

Mac seethed a bit under his breath, but he really didn't know what to say.

"Yeah, Mac," J-Dog quipped in a nonchalant way, "Doc's really good at arguing."

Mac looked at the kids standing around him, and they were all waiting for his response. "Fine, Copper. Tell me what we're doing here."

"See, you're learning already, maybe there is hope for you, after all," Doc jabbed, but Mac didn't say a word.

Doc laid it all out, "This is a one-thousand-mile race that takes place in Mexico, in the Baja California desert. It is grueling and dangerous, but it pays by changing the lives of those who race it, and immortalizes those who win it." Doc turned to the desert machine. "This eleven-hundred cubic centimeter engine produces one hundred fifty-five horsepower. It goes from zero to sixty in three point seven seconds with a top end speed north of one hundred thirty miles per hour. Now, the terrain and the other racers make it unlikely that we reach those speeds very often. However, we will get there at times as we fly over every kind of razor-sharp rock and jump ravines, while plucking out the four-inch cacti spikes from our suits and any skin we have showing."

"No biggie," Jonah interjected, worried that Mac may be having second thoughts now that he heard how dangerous it was going to be. "You don't feel pain. It's all good."

Doc gave Jonah a wry glance. "It will be one hundred and ten degrees in the daytime and under fifty degrees at night. Your hands and feet will go numb from the hours of non-stop racing. You'll be hungry and thirsty in one of the most remote places on earth, but I won't stop. I'll keep going harder and faster because we'll be trying to avoid the crash-up derby that this race is famous for. To top it all off, we are racing against the very best racers in the world."

Mac's eyes scanned the faces of the other kids. "Is that all?"

"Well, if you haven't deduced," Doc explained, "all of this happens while I'm at the helm. Your life will hinge on how I race. You may not feel pain, Irons, but I'm pretty sure you can still die, unless you have a brain condition for that one, too."

"He ain't exaggerating," J-Dog said. "Only ten percent of the teams, on average, even finish the race. In fact, eight people, since 1942, have died."

"Not to pile on more," Jonah said, "but the two of you would be the youngest to ever attempt the race."

"My kind of odds," Mac remarked.

"They're not your odds yet," Doc corrected. "I haven't seen anything to make me think you should be the guy sitting next to me."

"What about you?" Mac shot back.

"What do you mean?" Doc asked.

"How do I know you're skilled enough to do this?" Mac argued. "If I'm going to risk my life you better be good enough to win."

"I'm good enough," Doc said. "Trust me."

"I'm not going to trust you. I need more."

Doc shook his head and laughed. "Mac, I don't need to prove anything to you. I'm in the race whether you are or not." Doc then sarcastically promised, "In the unlikely event that you prove to me that you can help me win the race, then I'll do anything you need me to do to prove my worth." Doc tilted his head, and grinned. "You first."

"Game on," Mac said with a dagger in his eyes.

* * *

THE KIDS WALKED AROUND TO THE EASTERN SIDE OF THE BARN TO a grassy square. The field was an amalgamation of seemingly unrelated objects, but it had been clearly constructed for a purpose.

There were about two dozen square alfalfa bails spread out across it. Most were grouped in either pairs or trios with their own unique angulation. Some of them were stacked, others lying flat. Some were standing on end, propped up against each other. There were old tractor tires spread around and stacked in various formations, nearly as plentiful as the bails. Someone had dug two L-shaped ditches deep enough to hunker down into. There was a circular pen of sorts, made of makeshift wooden plats that were roped together via bailing twine and a huge pile of what appeared to be broken branches, but it was large enough for a few people to crouch down behind. There were old racing barrels on the field along with a V-formation of about twenty or so burlap sacks, each filled with crimped oats.

"What am I looking at?" Mac asked.

"This is just how we have some fun," Doc said as Jonah, J-Dog, and Alfie laughed.

"Oh, yeah," J-Dog smiled, "this is going to be awesome."

Doc walked over to an old tack box that sat up against the side of the barn. He opened it and began to pull out rifles.

"Are those guns?" Mac asked with a little alarm.

Doc nodded. "Of the paintball variety."

Doc handed out an array of paintball rifles to J-Dog, Alfie, and Jonah. He offered one to Penelope, but she declined. He tried to hand it to Flip, but she pulled out a slingshot. "I got this."

"Fair enough." Doc grinned and pulled out a face mask, complete with an eye shield and a throat guard. He tossed it to Mac who caught it.

"It's simple enough, Irons," Doc said. "You start at that side of the field." Doc pointed to the east, and then he pointed to the opposite, western side of the field. "And over there is a pole with a horseshoe on it." Doc shrugged. "You just have to get that horseshoe."

"And you guys get to shoot me with your paintball guns until I get it. That's the gig," Mac deduced.

"That's the gig," Doc replied.

"Do I get a gun?" Mac asked.

"Not the first time. Consider this an initiation phase," Doc replied.

Mac shook his head. "Did everyone get such special treatment?"

"Yep," Doc said.

Jonah, Alfie, and J-Dog all nodded.

Alfie even added, "I still get nightmares."

"Now," Doc said, "you don't have to do this. No one is making you. And once we start, if you want to tap out at any time, simply wave and scream like a three-year-old little girl, and we'll get the picture. There will be no hard feelings. No judgments that you sissified your way out. Hear me, there is no shame in you crying and begging for it to end. At any time, you can grab your skirt and go home."

Penelope gasped. "We are not giving Mac a safe space at all."

"No, Honeybuns," J-Dog said, "but we *are* creating an internet space." J-Dog looked at Doc. "Give me and Alfie about five minutes. We need to stream this."

Doc grinned ear to ear. "I think that is an excellent idea."

"Wait, wait," Penelope pleaded. "I think we need to step back and breathe. I want to make sure that Mac feels he has a place to express himself."

Mac kept his eyes squarely on Doc. "You don't want me to express myself."

It only took a few minutes for J-Dog and Alfie to make sure that every square inch of that battlefield was surveilled by smartphones, tablets, and GoPro cameras.

"Doc," J-Dog yelled, "Wild Dog is ready to go live."

"Good," Doc said and turned to Mac. "One more thing."

"What?" Mac asked.

"I'm going to need you to sign a waiver."

"A waiver?"

"It's a basic boilerplate really. It's just a little something I drafted for the next time social services show up. My mom was complaining. So, ergo, the waiver."

Doc pulled out his phone for the digital document, and Mac signed the phone.

"Perfect," Doc said, "now we're free to light you up like the Fourth of July."

* * *

MAC STRAPPED ON HIS HELMET, ADJUSTED HIS FACE SHIELD, AND crouched down in a sprinter's stance. His eyes scanned the approximate football-sized field and found Doc, J-Dog, Alfie, Jonah, and Flip positioned at key bunkers along the way. Penelope stood off to the side with her palms covering her cheeks.

Mac mapped out his starting path from ditch, to bail, to barrel, to bunker, and took a deep breath.

J-Dog had primed the internet pump and sent out his push notifications that the event was going live, and hundreds of thousands had already logged on to the stream.

"Irons," Doc yelled out from a perch built on old wooden plats, "all you got to do is get that horseshoe."

"Yep," Mac replied.

"Then, on my count of three," Doc said, "one."

POP.

Mac took a paintball right in the face, snapping his head back and splattering paint all over his face shield.

"Sorry, sorry," Alfie yelled. "I got excited."

J-Dog remarked, "Don't put a gun in his hands if you're trying to avoid a war."

"I can't see," Mac said as he tried to wipe the paint off his visor.

"Two, three!" Doc yelled.

On that mark, a barrage of paintballs peppered Mac, pinging all over his body.

"Agh!" Mac yelled as he took heavy fire. He bolted to his right, keeping his head down, as paintballs zipped everywhere around him, and into him. He made it about twenty yards and slid headfirst into a ditch that had been walled up by old tractor tires. He yelled out, "So, it's going to be like this, huh?"

"Ready to give in?" Doc quipped.

There was no line of sight on Mac, so they held fire. Mac took a breath, got on all fours, and slowly crawled to an edge and peeked around the corner.

ZIP. A paintball flew right by his face.

Jonah hollered, "Oh man! I almost gotcha. Did you see it?"

"I saw it," Mac said as he retracted to the safety of the bunker. "Alright, next move," he said to himself aloud.

Doc picked up a walkie-talkie and depressed the button. "Alfie, deploy the high-altitude attack."

"Roger that," Alfie said. He picked up his remote for his new and heavily modified high-speed drone.

The drone was high enough that it almost looked like a bird. Alfie used the camera to zero on Mac in the tire bunker.

"Target acquired," Alfie said. "Dropping bunker buster now."

Mac never saw it coming. He was still on all fours when the paint grenade landed directly on his back. The height of the drop produced an audible thud when it pegged him, and it exploded in a yellow wash of paint.

"Direct hit!" Alfie yelled.

"Oh man," J-Dog shouted out, "how could you let him hit you like that, Mac? I'm never going to hear the end of it."

"I'm an ace!" Alfie yelled out.

Mac reached behind him to the small of his back where the grenade had hit, and although it didn't hurt, he knew he was going to have a bruise with deeper purples than a plum. He growled, dug one foot in the dirt, and bent low into a sprinter's stance. He waited a bit and then ripped out.

"There he goes!" Doc yelled, as Mac made a beeline for the horseshoe. No longer was he trying to find cover in bunkers or slowly pick his way through the field. It was a straight-line sprint to that shoe.

"Open fire!" Doc yelled, and every single rifle filled the air with paint balls. Though many missed, a lot also found their mark, and little bursts of paint popped all over his body. Penelope seemed to yelp with each impact and acted like it hurt her more than it hurt Mac. It probably did.

Doc grabbed the walkie-talkie. "Jonah, he's coming at you."

"I got him," Jonah said. He set down his rifle and picked up a cord. He waited for Mac to reach a spot, and then he yanked it as hard as he could.

The trip wire came up perfectly, and Mac hit it in full stride. The unsuspecting boy tumbled at sprinter speed, face planting into the tall fescue grass.

Doc picked up a secondary rifle and aimed carefully at Mac lying face down and prostrate on the ground.

PING. Doc nailed him. Right in the glutes.

Mac was sufficiently lit up by paint balls and paint grenades, but what had just hit him was different. He reached back and felt where it had hit. It wasn't the same thing. There was a hole in his pants. He pushed in, and when he pulled his hand back around, he saw blood. Sure as shooting.

"That's it." He stood up, took off his helmet, and slammed it into the ground. Then he started walking, and only walking. He stomped his way out in the open toward that horseshoe. A few more paint balls hit him as he walked, but he didn't care.

J-Dog leaned forward from his position. "Would you look at that." He stopped shooting, and so did the other boys.

Then a single paintball hit Mac. It left a big blue splotch on the back of his head, and Flip let out a giggle. "I got him!" She waved her slingshot.

Mac got to the pole, and except for where the face shield had protected him, there was not a square inch of him not splattered with paint. The boys had lit him up, and he knew it. He bent down, picked up the horseshoe, and then flung it into the field.

Doc, Jonah, J-Dog, and Alfie walked toward him, grins across their faces. They had just had the time of their lives, and they assumed Mac had as well.

That wasn't the case.

Mac seethed when Doc reached him. "You shot me with something else. What was it?"

Doc laughed. "It was nothing big. Just a little BB gun. It didn't hurt, did it?"

"It made a hole in my jeans," Mac said as the boys went around and looked.

"You shot him in the butt with a BB gun?" Jonah asked.

"You said he didn't feel pain! What's the big deal?" Doc replied.

J-Dog bobbed his head a bit. "I'm kind of uncomfortable, being on video, looking at Mac's butt," J-Dog said, as he adjusted the GoPro camera that was strapped to the outside of his hat like a miner's light. "But I got a question. If there's a hole in his jeans, then where's the BB?"

"I'm sure it's somewhere out in the field," Doc said. "It pinged him good, and it bounced off."

"It didn't bounce off, Copper," Mac said.

"Say what?" Jonah asked. "What do you mean it didn't bounce off?"

"It's still in there," Mac said.

"The BB is in your butt?" Alfie gasped.

"No way," Doc protested. "Maybe you're not as immune to pain as you claim, and it just hurts."

Mac put his finger on his back right cheek and pushed. "It's in there. I feel it."

J-Dog put his hands up. "First off, I want to thank all of you for this incredible content. I can guarantee this will be the most viral Wild Dog ever." J-Dog smiled, raised his eyebrows and his two index fingers, and started nodding like he had the biggest idea ever. "What would make it even better is if we go full on Civil War battlefield and dig the BB out. Alfie, quick, go get a wooden spoon for Mac to bite. Doc, please tell me that there is whiskey somewhere. We've got to sterilize my pocketknife."

Mac shook his head. "If anyone tries to dig a BB out of my butt, they'll be digging you out of the ground. And at this point, I'm mad enough that I'm okay leaving the video evidence."

"Well, actually, you don't even need to get it out," Doc said. "It's not a lead BB. It's copper. It won't hurt you." Doc laughed at the irony that the BB was copper. "Just consider it something to remember me by."

Mac stared at the boys, wanting to hit all of 'em.

"But I'll tell you what," Doc said, "if you think you want to ride with me in the desert, I'll let you have a crack at it, as long as you can actually do the job of being a navigator. You've earned yourself a chance. I'll give you that."

"Oh, no," Mac shook his head quickly. "No, no, no. This isn't done. I owe you."

"You owe me," Doc deadpanned.

"That's right, remember our little deal? Plus, you're the ones who need a navigator. You need someone tough enough to ride with you, and I don't see people lining up for it, Copper. So now, *you* need *me*. You have to prove to me that you're tough enough to win that race. Because I'm not doing it for fun, and I'm sure as heck not doing it for your racing glory. I'm in it for the money. I need the scholarship, so it's time for you to prove yourself to me."

J-Dog, Alfie, Jonah, Penelope, and Flip all turned and looked in unison at Doc for his response.

"Alright, Irons," Doc spit on the ground, "what do you have in mind?"

Mac shrugged. "Simple. Just ride that horse."

* * *

Doc stood as if time stood still. He replied slowly, "What horse?"

"You know. *That* horse," Mac answered. "The whole way here, Jonah wouldn't stop yapping about this one big horse. Supposedly, he's too dangerous to ride. Supposedly, the fastest horse ever. What'd you say his name was, Jonah?"

Jonah took in a deep breath and sighed. He looked over at Doc and shook his head to say that he was so sorry. He then quietly replied to Mac, "Fire Face."

"Yeah," Mac said loudly and pointed at Doc with enthusiasm with one hand as he wiped paint off the side of his neck with the other, revealing a welt that was already swelling. "I want you to ride Fire Face." Mac looked around, knowing that he just pulled a trump card. He scoffed, "Come on, guys, this will be fun. You know what you just did to me. This will be like that. Good times. Unless, of course, you're just a garden variety, fast food, all talk, kind of kid."

Mac had just laid down the gauntlet in every conceivable way. Doc also knew this was the one thing he just couldn't do. Doc's dad would kill him if he messed with the big stallion.

"You can't be afraid, are you?" Mac continued and laughed. "Are you actually a horse trainer's son who's afraid of a horse? I mean, that would be poetic, Copper. Imagine, you wanting me to ride with you in the most dangerous race of all time across a desert in a foreign country, and you can't even ride your own horse on your own farm. Now, *that's* rich."

Doc didn't respond.

"Wow," Mac mocked him, "the kid who's so good at arguing can't even muster a sound."

Doc still didn't speak. Mac didn't know what he was asking, but it didn't matter.

Mac had figured out where it hurt, and he pushed, "Or maybe, your dad's not a good enough horse trainer. Maybe no one can ride the horse, because at the end of the day, your dad's just not any good."

Doc straightened up with that. "Irons, you need to measure very carefully what comes out of your mouth next, boy."

"Hold on," J-Dog intervened, "let's just take a breather." J-Dog knew, maybe more than any of the other kids, what was at stake. He knew, even with all his outlandish instigations, that there needed to be someone to pull back the reins just a bit.

"Mac," J-Dog said, "I get what you're doing. You want a little pay-back. And you know something? After what we just did, I get it. But you don't know what you're asking. Listen, I'm not even sure Fire Face is a horse. He's more like a monster. Honestly, he's probably the reason we don't have any unicorns. He hunted them all down and murdered them."

"Whatever," Mac said. "All I hear is excuses for a pretty boy finally being called to the mat, and he doesn't have the guts to do it after all." Mac laughed. "You're all talk."

Doc had lost control of the situation, and he knew it. If he backed out now, he'd forever be the horse trainer's son who was afraid of horses.

His face lost all expression, and he barely moved his lips when he said, "You want it, you've got it."

Then, for all the wrongs reasons, he walked toward that arena.

* * *

DOC SLID THE LATCH ON THE METAL GATE AND IT SWUNG OPEN. HE flipped a switch on a breaker box, and the old halogen lights flickered to life in the arena. Instantly, the kids saw the stallion.

The horse was in the center of a large pen made of ten-foot long by eight-foot-tall metal gates all linked together. Fire Face had been stomping in the pen, even before they arrived, creating a dust cloud that hazed the arena.

The big stallion gave a snort and sped up his stomping and stirring, clearly showing an agitation that they were coming into his domain.

He began to prance in tight circles as they walked closer to him. His circles gravitated toward the edge of the pen, and there was an almost hypnotic rhythm that came from the strong prancing of the hooves. He began rubbing against the cage as he circled, causing the metal to rattle louder and louder as they approached.

The kids got within twenty-five feet when the stallion abruptly stopped and reared up with a shrill cry, before coming down with thunderous force. He froze like a statue just long enough for the dust to settle.

"Fire Face," Doc said as the kids stared in awe.

A person didn't need to be a horse enthusiast to be mesmerized by the appearance of the stallion. He looked like the reassembling of all the DNA of the perfect horse brought into existence by God Himself in the Garden of Eden. He was not merely a horse; he was The Horse. The seminal blueprint for all horses to follow.

Fire Face gave quick understanding to his namesake. His coloring was that of smoldering deep red splattered on artic white. Nature had painted him so that he looked like he was on fire. Red inferno-like color and patterns kindled out of his nostrils and encircled his eyes, fanning out over his face, neck, chest, and abdomen with the final spark ending in the rump. His thick, flowing, bright white mane looked like rising, pure white smoke when he pranced as it whipped with power above the thunder of his strides.

He held his head in that stunning downwardly cocked position. His huge muscles tremored throughout his body. His neck was thick, bulging, and it made his head look refined and even a little small in comparison.

His neck connected into a broad, powerful chest which was constantly bustling and rippling due to the incessant tapping, pawing, prancing, and rearing of the front legs. His shoulders challenged the prevailing thought of how wide the shoulders could be on a thoroughbred. They seemed more like what you'd see on a Clydesdale than on a streamlined runner.

His belly was as tight as a barrel. Not an ounce of fat. His hindquarters looked like they had been carved out of a solid block of marble by Michelangelo himself. His thick white tail would drag on the ground if it wasn't for the fact that he unceasingly snapped it around like a bullwhip. The kids looked on with almost a reverence, and if not that, then a deep, frightened respect.

The mighty horse reared up with explosive quickness and slammed his front hooves into the metal cage, warning them to stay back. Fear dropped like an anvil upon Doc's chest. He realized, in that very moment, that the choices made in the briefest of time, the ones that you can't take back, can impact the rest of your life.

* * *

DOC POINTED TO THE NORTH END OF THE ARENA, "ALFIE, MAKE sure that gate is latched. This rodeo stays in the barn." Then he pointed to the south side. "Jonah, go check that one."

"Flip and Penelope, you can't be here." He pointed to a connecting gate that went into another barn that housed the stalls for the normal horses. "I don't want you anywhere near this."

Alfie couldn't believe what he was hearing. "Doc, you're not actually going to do this, are you?"

Jonah added, "We can think of something else. You don't need to ride this horse."

Doc glanced at Mac, but Mac didn't say a word. He just spat on the ground.

"You think you're street tough?" Doc said to Mac. "Well, this is country strong."

Mac rolled his eyes. "Well spoken. Still waiting."

Penelope didn't understand any of this as she walked with Flip to the gate. "Why is this happening?"

"They're boys," Flip replied, "and they went and got something in their head."

Penelope was dismayed. "The boys I knew back in Rhode Island just played video games, watched TikTok, and ate junk food."

"Oh," Flip replied, "well, these here are real boys. And my mom said if they live long enough, these are the type of boys who become real men."

"That's a big if," Penelope replied.

* * *

Fire Face sensed the anxiety of the kids, and it fed his energy. It sent pulses through his body that only quickened his steps and flamed his aggression.

"You want a saddle or something?" Jonah asked nervously.

"We'd never get a saddle on him," Doc replied.

"You gotta be kidding me!" J-Dog took out his phone. "Are you allowed to call nine-one-one and say there is *about* to be an accident?"

Doc explained with a stern voice, "This is how we're doing this. I'm going to climb onto one of these gates. When he passes by, I'm jumping on him."

"What?" Jonah asked in exasperation, his voice rising several octaves. "That's your plan? That's the best your one-hundred-and-sixty-five IQ can come up with? Jumping on him?"

"Honestly, Jonah, what do you expect?" J-Dog asked. "I don't think Fire Face will stop for a sugar cube."

Doc ignored the objection and conversations. "The moment I'm on him, J-Dog, you're going to swing open that gate—" he pointed at very specific location "—as wide and as fast as possible."

"Okay, hold on." J-Dog raised his index finger, switched on his iPhone camera to selfie, and hit the record button. "If you're watching this video, it means I'm already dead. A bright star extinguished. An icon lost too soon to the annals of time."

"Shut up already," Alfie protested. "Why is everything about you?"

"Why is everything *not* about me?" J-Dog replied. "That's the question we all need to be asking ourselves."

Doc continued, unmoved by J-Dog's antics, "Once I ride Fire Face out, Jonah, Alfie, and J-Dog, you get into the pen as quickly as possible, and close it behind you. Now, this should go without saying, but I'm saying it. You better be out of the way. Because he will absolutely and without reservation or remorse run you down."

"What about me?" Mac asked.

"You signed a waiver," Doc replied. "You can get as close as you want."

Doc took a long look at Fire Face, and fear encased him. But this was a rite of passage, albeit one of his own making, that he couldn't avoid.

He slowly walked around to the back of the pen, staring at this rogue beast, who was prancing faster and faster around that circular metal structure. Doc climbed up on the gate and crouched like a spring with his right foot on top and his left foot on the second rung as he used his hands for balance.

"J-Dog, as soon as I'm on him, you open the gate, and get out of the way."

"I got it," he responded.

As Doc sat on the top rung, his mind was flooded with thoughts and emotions, and the one that kept running through his head most was what happened to the last jockey who had tried to ride Fire Face. The horse had left the poor man with a broken back. And everyone considered him lucky.

J-Dog saw a transformation come over his oldest friend as he crouched on the gate. Doc's face changed; his whole body changed. Copper's eyes became hard as steel, and J-Dog saw his knuckles turn white as he gripped the top bar tight, ready to hoist himself on the horse.

"He's doing this," J-Dog whispered, and he readied the gate.

Alfie heard him and asked, "I'm surprised you're not streaming it."

"We don't need the video evidence."

Doc was counting Fire Face's steps around the pen and calculating when he would go. When the stallion passed the fifth time beneath him, Doc decided that on the next one he would jump.

Doc saw every single step around that pen, and as Fire Face made the last turn, with only steps now between both of their fates, the horse looked up at Doc, and their eyes met.

Fire Face snorted, flung his head up, and seemed to dare Doc to try it.

Doc jumped.

* * *

THE JAR OF LANDING ON A WIDE, HARD BACK, SHUDDERED UP HIS spine. Doc felt Fire Face's skin twitch underneath him. His knees banged against the giant shoulders which were turning like a steel-forged crank. Doc buried both of his hands in the thick white mane and wrapped his fists deep into the long strands. He squeezed his legs as tight as he could. It felt like squeezing a rock. Fire Face's ears flattened back, and he leapt straight up into the air with an extraordinary explosion.

J-Dog unlatched the gate and began to open it, but Fire Face saw his confines breached, and when he landed from his initial jump, he cut directly toward the gate that was only barely cracked open.

The stallion barreled into it with his chest and the gate crashed open with perilous force, smashing into J-Dog. It sounded with a loud bong as the metal frame connected with every part of J-Dog's body, and it sent the boy flying backward with the force of the bolting horse. His body twisted in the air and his arms flailed wide as he tried to brace for his own collision with the ground, but nothing could brace him for crunching face first and mouth agape into a freshly discharged pile of horse dung, making his face look like it was splatted with a very wrong type of pie.

Fire Face was out of his cage, and as the stallion tasted sweet freedom, he turned toward the southern gate of the arena and erupted in a torrential sprint. The velocity of Fire Face's acceleration flung Doc backward, his head whipping back and his arms snapping to pain-inducing extension.

Fire Face's head and neck flattened out as he extended his huge legs out in front of him, trying to cover as much ground as possible with each stride. Jonah cupped his face and screamed as he and the other boys shut themselves into the horse's pen.

The magnitude of the moment hit Mac Irons as he watched Doc cling to the raging stallion. "He actually did it."

It only took a couple of seconds, and the kids knew they made a big mistake. But their mistake was not that Doc needed to ride Fire Face, as disturbing as that was, rather it was not realizing that the arena had no hope to hold that horse.

Fire Face bolted toward the gate, and there was not an odds maker alive who would wager on that stallion stopping.

Doc regained his balance and posture just enough to look up. Through the bouncing thickness of the white mane, he could make out the gate in front of him, and the wide-open field on the other side. Doc pulled his body up right behind Fire Face's shoulders. He choked up on his grip in an attempt to anchor down to the neck. He squeezed as hard as possible with everything he had from his legs to his hands. He leaned forward and buried his face into the plume of the mane until his chin was inches from the thick, muscular neck.

Then he felt the propulsion of Fire Face's hindquarters. The five-foot-high gate that stood between Fire Face and his freedom might as well have been a foot. In a celestial moment, the thundering of the hooves beneath Doc stopped. The pounding of the powerful strides was suspended, and the sound of the rhythmic machine beneath him disappeared to allow the hard breathing of the horse to be heard. Doc held on as tight as he could as this gorgeous creature soared to freedom, clearing the gate and then landing outside in the fresh fescue, which felt like nothing but fulfilled dreams to that stallion.

But J-Dog found his own level of despair as he sprinted out of the arena, wiping his face clean of the manure, and screaming and spitting out the pasty chunks he hadn't already swallowed.

* * *

Tall grass whipped around the hooves of Fire Face as he galloped toward the wooded truck path that led to the back forty. The thundering rhythm of Fire Face's strides reverberated in Doc's chest.

He could feel each stride getting a little longer and faster, and over an eighth of mile into this run, the stallion was still speeding up.

Doc waited for the wild bucking, rearing, and fighting that happened to every jockey who ever had a go on Fire Face. Today, though, it never came. This was unbridled, unrestrained, straight-line speed by way of thundering hooves. It was a horse doing what it was bred to do.

Doc's intense, primordial fear began to subside, and it gave way to a reckless, heightened sense of euphoria. This wasn't the same adrenaline junky thrill he got from revving the engine to the redline. This speed was different. It was breathtaking. It was blistering, but it wasn't chaotic or stressed.

It was measured, purposeful, balanced, and precise. Fire Face ran like an organic machine designed with far more complexity than the mere works of man.

The flawless motion of the stallion gave Doc a sure seat under him. He found the perfect sweet spot crouched tight behind the shoulders, his chest laid forward, and his face centered just inches above the surging stallion's neck.

It was a surreal moment with the thick mane flowing all around him. All time, space, caution, and thought seemed silenced and put away while Doc just rode. He stared between the ears of the horse as they flew across the field in unison, as one unit, bonded for one purpose—speed.

But speed like this requires space, and space ultimately ends with distance, and that which had been far off was now upon them. They were quickly reaching the thickness of the woods, and Doc thought it fortunate that Fire Face seemed to be aiming toward the curvy truck path instead of plowing through the trees.

Doc rewrapped his hands in the mane and anchored himself down.

He found himself speaking without the benefit of thought, "Go, Fire Face, go."

The right ear of the stallion twitched backward for a moment to identify the sound. He sensed the instinctual approval of the boy clinging to his back. Doc had bought in. He was there to ride. He wasn't looking to get off, he wasn't looking for the horse to stop, and he wasn't trying to control that which could not be controlled. Animalistic instinct told the stallion that Doc was not the adversary. Doc was the willing passenger who had given way to the spirit and will of the horse.

Doc felt the slightest dip in the back quarters. It was like a clutch was pulled, and then it popped. Fire Face shifted gears and accelerated with unexpected torque.

"Yeah!" Doc yelled as new levels of acceleration were reached. He knew at that moment that no man had ever ridden a horse faster.

Doc kept the vice grip he had with his legs but began lifting his torso just a hair to take in the moment as he finally trusted the surety of the horse. In the moment, he found a victory unlike any trophy he had ever held, and he did what he always did, he thrust his arms into the air as the stallion glided across the ground. Doc stared at the sky and then brought his gaze back to the earth, focusing on the woods ahead of him. Fortunately, Fire Face went directly to the thin, treelined truck path, just as Doc had hoped.

But this brief moment of rapturous euphoria was traded for the cruelest of sucker punches. Doc's spirits sank as he saw what was in front of him. His dad had closed the gate to the truck path. With a fleeting hope and monotone malaise, Doc hoped, "Maybe he'll stop."

Doc never reestablished a firm grip on the horse in time, and Fire Face launched from a full stride to soar over the metal gate. Doc felt his backside separate from the horse, as he was jettisoned into air.

He felt two rotations of his body before he crashed through a collection of big oak branches that cracked, popped, and snapped around him. Mercifully, he missed the trunk of the big oak. Doc thudded to the ground with breath arresting force, bruising his tailbone on a root that refused to be buried.

Fire Face never broke stride, and he was gone.

* * *

MEANWHILE, J-DOG PLOWED THROUGH RACHEL COPPER'S FLOWER bed, spewing flower petals into the air. He didn't even slow down as he reached the front door. He pushed the lever down, acting on faith that the door wouldn't be locked.

It was locked.

J-Dog smashed against the thick wooden door and collapsed in a hyperventilating mess on thc front porch. The impact resonated through the house, and Rachel hurried to the front door to find out what had just happened.

She opened the door to see a filthy J-Dog laying in a heap before her. "Oh my goodness, J-Dog," she said, "what happened?" She put her hand to her nose, trying to figure out where that smell was coming from.

J-Dog reached up with a tired hand and pleaded between deep gasps for breath as the taste and texture of the greenish, brown manure overwhelmed his mouth and colored his teeth and lips. "Mouthwash! Give me mouthwash!"

That was not what Rachel expected to hear. "Mouthwash? Alright, come in," Rachel said in a caring, motherly fashion, not sure what she was looking at. She helped him to his feet, and the two of them walked back through the house to the bathroom. J-Dog left dirty footprints the entire way.

Rachel opened the medicine cabinet. "I've got mint flavored and the original Listerine, which is pretty strong. You probably want the mint."

J-Dog stood there incredulous that Rachel was so nonchalant with the situation. "I need the hard stuff," he said as he impatiently grabbed the yellow Listerine and hit it like a fifth of whisky. J-Dog was pleased that it tasted like it could sanitize a chemical spill. His face distorted as it sloshed around his mouth. He could feel the remnants of the semi-digested hay stuck between his teeth. He violently spat into the sink, splashing it up on the mirror, which perturbed Rachel to no end.

"I'll show you the Windex, too," she followed up with.

J-Dog hit the Listerine again. He swished and swished. The mouthwash was starting to sting. He must have had an open cut somewhere in his mouth from the fall, but he didn't care. He swished as violently as anyone could swish, and he spat again and then gripped the sink with both hands in utter despondency.

"J-Dog? Are you alright?" Rachel asked, trying to decipher the bizarre scene unfolding before her.

He stared vacantly into the mirror as his tongue explored every crevice of his mouth, and then every kind of emotional pain flushed his face again. "Come on," he screamed in frustration, "Floss! I need floss!"

He took another hit of Listerine as Rachel moved a bit quicker now and opened the drawer where she kept the floss.

She held it out to J-Dog. He snatched it out of her hand and began wrapping it around his fists like he was an assassin with a garrote. He spat into the sink and attacked his mouth.

"Gentle, be gentle," Rachel coached, "you're supposed to hug the teeth, not saw the gums."

J-Dog would have none of that. He shook his head and grunted. He then hit a hard spot on his back right molar.

"That's corn! Are you freakin' kidding me?" he screamed in despair. He squinted his eyes and yanked. A chunk of corn, coated with intestinal residue, came shooting out from his mouth and dinged the mirror.

Rachel was aghast. Being the wife of a horse trainer, she finally knew exactly what had happened.

"Oh, crap," she blurted.

"Well aware!" J-Dog replied.

Rachel grabbed J-Dog, tipped his head back, and poured more Listerine in his mouth, joining in the urgency of the moment.

"Swish, J-Dog, swish!" she yelled. "Now spit!" She shoved his head over the sink.

J-Dog listened to the adult supervision for the first time in his life, and so he spat.

Rachel yanked his head back and peered into his wide-open mouth. "What did you do?" she asked as she made J-Dog floss and swish again. She pulled out a toothbrush and handed it to him. "Scrub."

He obliged, grabbed a tube of charcoal-infused toothpaste and squirted it directly into his mouth. He scrubbed and scrubbed, blackening his mouth and lips and finally spitting it out. He washed his mouth out with the tap water and took another hit of the Listerine. He handed the now gnarled toothbrush to Rachel. She reluctantly grabbed it by the tips of her fingers and dropped it into the trash can.

J-Dog swished and spat and did it two more times.

Then, finally, the ordeal was over. His mouth was scrubbed raw and sterilized, so much so that he didn't think he would taste food for weeks. Then, out of exhaustion, he slumped down on the floor and put his arm over the commode while rubbing his face with his other hand.

He slowly reached into his cargo pocket of his camouflaged army pants and pulled out his camping canteen, which was actually an old whisky flask that he repurposed for a better calling in life. He poured out the water that was in it and replaced it with Listerine. As soon as he topped the flask off, he took a swig out of it, swished it around, and spat into the commode.

Rachel looked at the boy slumped over the toilet, clutching the flask like an old friend. His cowboy hat was cockeyed and his pilot glasses had slid halfway down his nose.

"Mrs. Copper?" J-Dog asked, and breathed out as if resigned to some horrible fate.

"Yes?" Rachel replied.

"One day," he muttered with a sigh, "I'm going to get me a wife."

Again, that was something Rachel was not expecting from J-Dog, and she responded with brutal honesty, "That's optimistic."

J-Dog shook his head. "But she'll never kiss me if she knows about the events of today." He bowed his head. "I've got skeletons."

Rachel cracked a smile. "I see what you mean. Are you saying what I think you're saying? You want me to keep all of this our dirty little secret?"

He nodded. "We need a pact, Mrs. Copper."

"I understand," Rachel replied, and she decided to have a little bit of fun. "Then there's a term that you should learn that lawyers use quite often."

"What's that?"

"Leverage," Rachel smiled.

"Leverage? What about attorney-client privilege? Can we work under those terms?"

"My retainer is five thousand dollars. Is that something you're prepared to pay?"

"I'll stick with leverage."

"That's what I thought." Rachel then crossed her arms. "How in the world did all of this happen?"

J-Dog was emotionally exhausted, and he had no evasion left in him. "Doc tried to ride Fire Face."

"What!" Rachel yelled.

"Right." J-Dog bobbed his head. "Then the whole world collapsed, because that thing is not mortal."

Rachel pulled out her phone and immediately called Dean, who was currently cutting alfalfa in a neighbor's field. He stopped everything and came running.

* * *

THE SOUND OF DOC CRASHING THROUGH THE BRANCHES MADE IT all the way to the barn. The kids climbed the gate of the arena and peered into the woods, hoping for some sign of life.

"Oh man, I didn't like the sound of that." Jonah's fears were real.

Alfie put his hand on Jonah's shoulder. "I don't think we thought this through."

"Hold your horses," Mac quipped with a smirk.

"Really, Mac?" Jonah chastised.

Mac shrugged.

The two girls ran over to them.

"We have to find him," Penelope insisted.

"Yep, let's go," Jonah agreed.

"Wait, we got other problems," Mac said as Dean's big truck pulled into the barn, kicking up gravel and dust along the way.

The truck skidded to a stop. An angry horse trainer superimposed over a worried dad jumped out of the truck and slammed the door. Dean walked with a quick, aggressive stride toward them. "Where are they? What happened?" he demanded. He then looked at Mac who was peppered in paint. "And I'm sure that has something to do with this."

The boys didn't say anything. Dean looked right at Jonah. "Speak."

Jonah took a very deep breath, and then he spoke as quickly as he could as if he was pulling off a band aid.

"Doc and Mac got in an argument where they challenged each other's manhood, and so we shot Mac with every paintball we had, and then he made Doc jump on Fire Face to prove himself. Then we all ran for our lives from a raging beast that should not be allowed to be around people, and we believe, at this point, that Doc is in the woods, either hanging by his hair in a tree or in a pile at the bottom. Fire Face is gone, probably never to be seen or heard from again." He exhaled.

Alfie and Mac looked at each other and then back to Dean. They confirmed in unison, "That's it."

Dean went from anger, to shock, to disbelief, to genuine concern for his son in a matter of seconds, and his face showed every emotion as it came and passed.

But then Penelope pointed toward the pasture and exclaimed, "The boy lives!"

Sure enough, Doc was limping back from the woods. The group stared at the sight for a few powerful seconds, and then Dean got his emotions under control, quickly texted Rachel that Doc was okay, and walked out to meet him halfway.

None of the other kids followed.

When Dean reached Doc, he looked him up and down and turned him around. After the examination, the kids saw Dean relax into an emotional relief which told them that, for the most part, Doc was okay. But then like a sudden thunderstorm, Dean switched gears and chewed Doc out.

By the time Dean and Doc got back to the barn, Dean was barking orders to Doc that everyone could hear. "Go get the mare that's in heat, put her in the gooseneck livestock trailer, not the horse trailer, and I'll pull around the truck so you can hook it up."

"Yes, sir," Doc replied.

"What are we doing?" Jonah asked as Doc marched toward a pen in the barn and didn't make any eye contact with the gang.

He didn't want to talk about what just happened, but only about what was next. "We got to catch Fire Face," Doc replied.

"How are we going to do that?" Alfie asked.

"We're taking that mare with us, and if we are lucky enough to find him, we're hoping we can bring him back."

"Is the mare going to call him?" Alfie asked.

Doc ignored the question and looked around. "Where's J-Dog?"

All the kids stopped for a second and realized he wasn't there.

"I don't know," Alfie said, "but it has been a bit quieter."

By that time, J-Dog had left the house and begun a walk of shame back to the barn.

Flip saw him coming. "There he is."

"He doesn't look right, does he?" Jonah said. "He's walking weird."

"Does he ever look right?" Alfie asked.

* * *

THE GANG SAT IN THE BED OF THE TRUCK, WHICH WAS NOW HAULing the gooseneck aluminum trailer with a young mare inside. Dean slowed down and stopped when he reached the closed gate heading to the back forty. Doc hopped out of the bed and walked to the gate that he so wished hadn't been closed.

He opened the gate wide so the truck and trailer could get through. Doc walked back to the truck and said to his dad, "This is where I lost him, so to speak."

As Doc passed the driver's side door, Dean reached out the window and put his hand on Doc's chest to stop him. "You stayed on him this whole way?"

"Yes, sir," Doc replied, still smarting from his stupid decisions. "I got on him in the pen in the arena. We opened it, he ran out and then jumped the gate out of the barn, ran across the field, and I fell off when he jumped this gate."

Dean sat back in his captain's chair in complete bewilderment, and he traded his dad hat for his horse trainer hat. "Are you sure?"

Doc quickly replied, "Pretty sure. Kind of hard to forget. But if you need more evidence, that oak tree has some of my skin on it."

"I'm sorry," Dean said, "I believe you, but it's just no one has ever stayed on him that long. How'd you do it?"

"Well, first, I held on like my life depended on it."

Dean chuckled. "That makes sense."

"Second, he actually never went crazy. He just ran and jumped, and it was wicked fast, Dad. Faster than any horse I've ever been on."

"But you were bareback."

"Obviously, and this may sound crazy, but he was easy to ride once he hit full stride."

"Really?"

"Yes. His back is incredibly muscular and thick, and gives a good seat. Then he's just so smooth. It's like running is the most natural thing for him to do. He flows."

What Doc was telling Dean was something that Dean had never heard, seen, or known. Fire Face had always reacted with violence against all who had tried to ride him in the past. He reared, bucked, and sometimes slammed the rider into the side of the arena. Fire Face treated every professional jockey who had ever sat on him as the abject enemy. No rider, ever, was allowed to be on his back for any amount of time. Period. Fire Face was, in every way possible, the unbreakable horse.

"Okay." Dean scratched his head. "Why do you think he let you stay on?"

"I don't know, Dad," Doc said. "I just jumped on, grabbed his mane, and held on for dear life. Then he ran, and when there was a gate in front of him, he jumped it. It's that simple."

"Bareback and unbridled." Dean said under his breath.

"Yes, sir."

Dean was dumbstruck that his boy not only jumped on that horse but that he also legitimately road him for about quarter of a mile.

Dean didn't speak to that, but the look on his face said it all. There was quiet pride that Dean couldn't express, for it was truly a foolish thing for his boy to do. But he knew then and there that his son was tough as nails.

Doc grinned. He knew his dad was proud of him.

"Hop in the back," Dean said. "Let's go get this horse."

"What about them?" Doc motioned to his friends.

"Oh, they're coming," Dean replied. "They got to help fix what they broke."

* * *

THE DUALLY AND GOOSENECK PULLED THROUGH THE TRUCK PATH and made it to big open pasture.

"Does your dad really think he can catch Fire Face?" J-Dog inquired. "Because I don't see how this is going to work."

Jonah began to get a little fidgety in the bed of the truck. "Are we safe back here with him out there?"

"What do you want," Mac asked, "a shark cage?"

"Yes, as a matter of fact, that would be great," Jonah fired back.

"We're fine," Doc said. "Fire Face isn't going to care about us."

"Why not?" Jonah asked.

"Because the mare we brought is in heat."

"In heat?" Jonah asked, not sure what that phrase meant.

Alfie crumpled his nose. "Why is she so hot?"

Penelope folded her arms in defiance. "I'm not going to be the one to explain it to them."

"No, not hot," Doc said. "She's *in* heat, and Fire Face is a stallion. That's the plan."

"That's the plan?" Jonah asked. "I still don't know what the plan is."

Dean stopped the truck in the middle of the field, killed the engine and got out. He carried out a few flakes of hay and a bucket of grain from the trailer and placed them about twenty feet from the truck. He then led the mare off the trailer and to the feed. He tied two extra-long lead straps end to end, snapped it to her halter, walked over, and leaned next to the bed of the truck.

"He's going to eat? Is that the plan?" Jonah interrogated. "Because that's a really stupid plan. Take it from a big eater. He ain't coming to us for no meal."

"No, Jonah," Penelope said and spoke very slowly, even condescendingly, frustrated that she had to even broach the subject. "It's dinner for two, soft music, starlight."

"Oh, I get it," J-Dog said. "When you say she's in heat, you're using the ancient tongue; you're speaking Amish. What you're really saying is that you're setting up an equine sting, and you're luring him in with pretty miss horsey."

"Oh," Jonah exhaled, "a classic honey trap. Alright, alright."

Alfie was perplexed. "Who brought the honey?"

Mac blurted, "The mare's the honey."

Alfie's eyes widened with illumination. "Ah, little, tiny horse babies."

Dean jumped in, "You see, boys, Doc is really lucky. Because, as chance would have it, this mare is just now coming into heat, and she will attract the stallion. If she wasn't ready, we'd never get this horse back."

J-Dog pulled out his Listerine-filled flask. He took a hit of it, swished it around, and then spat it out. "Doc, I love your farm. Always next level stuff." He then climbed up on the trailer roof. "I'm now notifying you that this lure and trap operation is being streamed." He took another shot of the Listerine, swished, and spat.

Jonah pointed at the flask. "What's in there?"

"Don't worry about it," J-Dog shot back as he put the flask back into his camouflaged, cargo pocket.

The kids watched him fire up his stream. "Welcome to Wild Dog TV. Wild stallion edition."

* * *

For about ten minutes, the kids sat silently while the mare ate the grain. There was no sign of Fire Face.

"Hey guys," J-Dog said from atop his perch, "I'm losing viewers."

"Nothing we can do, J-Dog," Doc said, the reality setting in that his stunt could end up costing his family big.

But then, the honey trap set the hook. The mare neighed and snorted. It was unprovoked, unplanned, but quite welcome.

Dean tilted his head in eagerness. "I'm hoping she knows something we don't."

"Hear that?" Doc said. "Shh, listen."

Everyone primed their ears.

"Yeah," Jonah said, "I heard something."

"That's your stomach," Mac replied.

"Oh, sorry," Jonah replied.

"No, there's something out there," Doc said.

Then everyone could hear it. Faint galloping reached their ears.

"There he is," Dean said.

Then a loud shrill call broke the silence. The stallion appeared in the distance. He reared up high and kicked into the air with his big front legs.

J-Dog feigned a fake Australian accent as he spoke, "If you're just tuning in, we are on location, trying to capture a wild stallion who wants to eat us alive. Be very quiet. Our native guide is about to speak."

Dean kept his eyes on Fire Face. "Listen up. No matter what happens, you do not get out of the bed of the truck. Understand? You, J-Dog, stay up there."

"I ain't moving," Jonah agreed.

"Doc," Dean said, "as soon as I get Fire Face on the trailer, you've got to close that gate as fast as possible."

J-Dog turned the camera on himself. "A daring trap is set."

"Dad," Doc asked, "what about you?"

"I'll be coming out of the front side door of the trailer, with the mare, hopefully," Dean explained.

By that time, Fire Face had set his sights on the mare and was galloping toward them with instinctual vigor.

There wasn't much time. Dean choked up on the lead strap and began pulling the mare gently toward the back of the trailer.

J-Dog zoomed in on the stallion charging at them. "And behold, peace will be taken from the earth."

As the stallion closed quickly on the truck and trailer, he slid hard, bending low and deep on his hind legs, tearing grass as he came to a stop about thirty yards out. His ears flickered, taking in the whole scene from the kids to the mare and then from Dean to the trailer. He snorted, and with clear agitation, he snapped his head back up and stomped forcefully into the ground. He began moving again, prancing sideways, toward the mare, snapping his head and tail along the way.

"Stay in the truck," Dean warned.

Fire Face sped up his approach as Dean led the mare to the back of the trailer. The big stallion got within ten feet of the mare, who was now antsy and clearly intimidated by the aggressive suitor.

Dean quickly stepped into the back of the trailer. He tightened the lead strap, and the mare got her two front feet up and in.

J-Dog was still on top of the trailer, livestreaming the scene. Then he moved to the back edge of the trailer to get a better shot of the action. Unfortunately for him, he was so focused on the tiny camera view that his situational awareness painfully failed.

Fire Face moved quickly, not wanting to lose sight of the mare, and the big stallion closed the gap between himself and her instantly. He lunged at her, and his chest hit the top of the trailer. His head and neck rose above the roof as he attempted an all or nothing mount.

J-Dog was standing at the end of the trailer, filming down when Fire Face launched. The horse's head raised up equal and on plane with J-Dog's, and the fiery fury of his face reached inches from J-Dog's nose.

J-Dog let out a screechy scream that pierced a country mile. The boy stumbled backward with unrestrained trepidation and fell off the trailer. Again.

THUMP. He landed flush on his back. Knocking all the wind out of him.

Fire Face's collision against the trailer jarred even the kids in the back of the truck.

Jonah yelled out, "My momma's going to be mad at me for dying!"

Once Fire Face's front two hooves landed back on the ground, he gathered himself quickly and bolted into the trailer after the mare. The trailer rocked and banged, and sheets of aluminum were permanently dented as heads and hoofs slammed all around into each other and into Dean.

The action was intense, and it seemed to go on a lot longer than it did, but it only took a couple of seconds before Dean dove out of the front side door of the trailer and landed on his shoulder. He quickly rolled to the side to avoid getting trampled by the mare that was leaping out of the trailer right behind him.

Dean jumped up and slammed that door shut and then yelled, "NOW! DOC!"

Doc sprinted to the back of the trailer and swung the back gate closed as hard and fast as he possibly could. He locked it a half second before Fire Face slammed his face into the back of it, trying to escape.

Fire Face locked eyes with Doc, recognizing the boy, and he snorted.

Back on his feet, Dean lunged to the side door and slammed it shut before Fire Face could make his way up to that diminutive opening.

Dean glanced around at the trailer and the stallion that was inside. He was safe and secure.

"Doc," he yelled, "you okay?"

"Yes, sir," Doc responded and popped his head around the back of the trailer.

"Good," Dean said, and then he dropped to one knee and clutched his arm.

"You alright, Dad?" Doc asked.

"I got slammed into a wall in there." Dean stood back up. "I think I broke something," he grunted. "I'll deal with it later."

* * *

Late evening had arrived, and Rachel paced the kitchen, nervously drinking coffee, which only added to her jitters as she waited for her husband and son to return.

"Why is he not texting me back?" she asked, and then she made up her mind. "I'm going out there." But something through the front window caught her attention and she saw the truck and trailer driving through the field heading to the barn. "Oh, thank You, Lord!" She studied the situation from afar. "They're not driving like it's an emergency."

After about five minutes in the arena, the truck, sans the trailer, began driving down the gravel driveway and made it to the house. She opened the garage and went outside to meet them.

The truck pulled to a stop, and Dean and the kids all climbed out. The sight was disconcerting to say the least. Dean and Doc looked like they had been through an alley fight. J-Dog looked concussed, and upon arrival, he took a hit of his flask, swished, and spat.

Mac looked guilty. Jonah was scared. Penelope looked befuddled, and Flip seemed disinterested, throwing a football high in the air to herself. Alfie smiled and waved, happy as he could be, still hoping to have some of the honey that the boys had been talking about.

As Rachel took in the discombobulated pile of people in front of her, she didn't really know where to start. "Tell me what you need," she said.

Jonah exclaimed, "We need to go to church! That was a warning from God that we're on the wrong track. We need to get right."

"Sure," Dean smiled, "but if you could drive me to the hospital first, that would be helpful." He held his arm tight to his side.

Rachel walked to him and gently reached out to touch his arm.

"No," Dean said, "don't touch."

"Okay, sorry," Rachel said. "I'm just trying to help."

"I know, I know," Dean replied as he walked inside to get the insurance cards. "Hey, Rachel, could you remind me to fix the breaker box in the arena tomorrow? It got smashed by a gate or something. I've got live wires exposed, but I'm not fixing it tonight."

* * *

That day and evening was one for the ages at the Copper Farm, and although it was comprised of events that were haphazard, ill-advised, and ridiculously dangerous that brought measures of destruction, it did in fact start to weave a team together.

Doc and Mac began to build a kind of respect for each other. Jonah felt the need to be a type of shepherd for the team. Penelope's eyes were opened well beyond the public schools of the East Coast, and she started a journey of curiosity into this other side of American life. Alfie really loved farm life and began to dream of being an American farmer, and J-Dog developed an interesting OCD tick with that flask, and no one knew why. Flip, though, remained mostly uninterested in the events as she was always looking to begin a game of dodgeball whether anyone else was or not.

The bonding of the kids led to the newly gelling gang accepting Jonah's invitation to attend his southern Gospel, mega-church the next morning. They all were genuinely excited and ready to "have church" as Jonah explained it, but the church may not have been ready to have the Bell Buckle Gang.

* * *

As the kids walked down to the front row of the church, they were met with a seismic flood of sound. It reverberated throughout the giant auditorium as a powerful, black female worship leader's voice boomed, "Come on, put your hands together!"

The congregation responded in kind and the collection of voices made it sound like singing thunder inside the walls.

Penelope gasped as she took in the worship leader. "She really has a presence."

Then five women walked down from the choir to the front of the stage, each holding an individual microphone. Jonah elbowed Doc, "Check it out."

"What?" Doc said as the women prepared themselves to sing.

"That's my family up there," Jonah explained. "You about to hear something."

It was Jonah's great grandmother, grandmother, two aunts, and a cousin. All of them were as big or bigger than Jonah.

J-Dog leaned over to Mac as they looked at the five women and whispered, "I don't think we could stop the run."

"Roger that," Mac confirmed.

Jonah heard the comment. "What'd you say?"

"Nothing pertinent," J-Dog replied.

"Okay," Jonah nodded, but then pointed a finger of caution at them. He then leaned over and nudged Doc. "We'll get the pastor to pray for our race. No way we're losing now."

J-Dog overheard it. "Will he smite the others?"

"No," Jonah said, "it doesn't work that way."

"I'm not sure," Doc said, "remember the plagues? That was major smiting."

"Yes, the plagues!" J-Dog loved the idea. "Let's frog 'em."

"No," Jonah said, "we ain't frogging nobody."

"Come on, at least the French. Let's frog the French," J-Dog pushed.

Rachel leaned over. "Shh, we're in church. Behave yourselves." She then turned to Alveda Bell, Jonah's mom. "Sorry about that. They get rowdy when they're all together."

"Oh," Alveda laughed, "don't I know it." Alveda switched gears. "How is Dean doing?"

"He'll mend, but he did break his arm. He's on pain meds at home recuperating. I'm just trying to keep him away from any farm work."

"If you need anything, you call me," Alveda urged.

"Thank you so much," Rachel said. "You know, it was really sweet for Jonah to invite all the kids to church."

"Yes, I'm so glad we could round them all up. I wish more kids would make it to church."

"I know," Rachel said, "it's bad out there, but all we can do is take care of the ones the Lord gives us."

"Hmm, mmm," Alveda agreed.

By this time, the pastor was front and center of the stage as Jonah's family finished their singing, and the pastor shouted out, "Will someone give me an amen?"

Alfie quickly blurted, "You can have mine."

The pastor looked down at the group of kids taking up the front row. "Hey, there you are. Good seeing you, Brother Alfie."

Alfie smiled big as the rest of the kids were kind of surprised.

Doc leaned over to Jonah. "How does your pastor know Alfie?"

J-Dog interrupted, "I let him come one Sunday."

Alfie objected, “I don’t need your permission.”

Jonah replied with big wide eyes, insinuating that something had gone down. “Oh, he came alright,”

“What happened?” Doc asked with a chuckle.

Jonah explained, “He went up there with an altar call, and everyone started praying, and he started speaking in tongues. He brought the house down.”

“Tongues?” Doc asked.

“It was lit,” Jonah said. “He was riffing man, like an auctioneer, but . . .”

“But, what?” Doc asked.

Jonah began to whisper, “It wasn’t really tongues. It was Mandarin Chinese. But I didn’t have the heart to say anything. Everyone was so happy.”

By then, the pastor zeroed in on the kids in the front row.

“Jonah,” the pastor spoke into the microphone so all the church could hear, “these must be your friends who are going to the big race you were telling me about.”

Instant shivers ran through Rachel’s body. “Oh no.”

Alveda leaned over and smiled. “No need to be nervous. Our pastor can handle the kids just fine.”

Cameras zoomed in on them, and the big screens highlighted the gang in the front row. Doc flipped up his collar, the other kids tried to look cool, and J-Dog took a hit of his Listerine from his flask, and then realized he couldn’t spit. So, he spat it back into the flask.

“Jonah,” the pastor said, “get your friends up here. Come on, we gonna commission you, send you off with a blessing.”

J-Dog grabbed Doc’s arm. “We gotta bring up the frogs.”

* * *

ON THE WAY TO THE STAGE, J-DOG PULLED OUT HIS IPHONE AND began streaming, and between his stream and the mega-church's own online presence, millions were watching the Sunday service unfold.

"Let me get this right," the pastor said, "you're Doc Copper. You must be a pretty good racer?"

Doc smiled.

The pastor kept going, "Because out of all the racers out there, Jonah picked you to be the driver on his national championship team."

The kids slowly turned their heads toward Jonah. Jonah nervously grinned.

"Yes," Doc replied, "I was as surprised as anyone when I got that news."

"I bet you were," the pastor continued. "We know that you are off to the deserts of Baja, California." He turned to the congregation. "That's actually in Mexico, not California. I think we should pray for your safety and even the blessing of your victory, if it is the Lord's will." The kids smiled, and the pastor said, "Everyone bow your heads."

But J-Dog elbowed Doc, and whispered, "Plagues."

Doc shook his head and whispered back, "No."

"Come on," J-Dog said, "we're missing our window here."

"Let it go," Doc replied.

J-Dog would have nothing of that, and he quickly blurted before the pastor could begin, "Can you ask God to make the others lose?"

The pastor stopped, and the whole congregation raised their heads from the bowed position.

"Excuse me?" The pastor smiled and glanced at the congregation, which offered a few laughs back.

"Well, it just seems," J-Dog explained, "that other teams may be praying that they win. We need God to pick a side."

Rachel's face jutted forward, and she turned to Alveda. "Your pastor is about to lose control."

Alveda smiled and patted her on the leg. "They're fine. This is good fun. He can handle this."

But Rachel knew, all too well, that the unimaginable can become quite real with this group.

"I wasn't going to say anything," Doc jumped in, "but it would be nice to secure God's sole backing for this race right now. He picked a side between Israel and Egypt. So, we have precedence."

The pastor smiled. "I understand your point, but since we have all sinned, and fallen short of the glory of God, I don't know if God picks sides quite like that when it comes to races."

J-Dog raised his hand. "So, you're saying we can't plague anyone?"

That took the pastor and the whole congregation off guard, but he laughed it off. "Um, no. We're not going to plague anyone."

Mac grunted, "That's a buzz kill."

"Not even a few frogs?" J-Dog asked.

But Doc never gave the pastor time to respond. "But wait, we have all sinned. If God knows we've all sinned, then He knows how much we've all sinned."

The first few beads of sweat appeared on the pastor's brow as he was quite cognizant of his livestream. "Right," the pastor said, "He knows all of our sins. Every single last one."

"Precisely! Then we've got this," Doc replied. "We petition Him for His sole support on those grounds."

"Oh no." Rachel dropped her head. "Derailed," she said to Alveda as the mega church went uncharacteristically silent.

"What do you mean?" the pastor asked.

Doc explained his point, "If everyone is undeserving, then our case to the Man upstairs is that we are the most deserving because we are the least undeserving."

"Huh?" the pastor asked.

"It's easy," Doc said. "All of our competitors at the Quad Continental are going to be years older than us. It would follow, then, that they have four or five more years of total depravity on their ledgers that we simply don't have because of our relative youthfulness."

"I see," the pastor slow rolled his reply.

Rachel lamented from the pews, "But they are catching up so fast."

"Right," J-Dog agreed, following the argument. "See, we just have thirteen-year-old sin, but they have, like, eighteen-year-old sin. That's way worse. They have whole different categories of sin."

"Oh yeah," Jonah added, "we're like angels compared to them."

J-Dog agreed, "Glowing with halos."

Doc said, "So, I do think this is an open and shut case. So, pastor, if *I* may pray for us."

The pastor kind of jiggled his head, but he didn't really know what else to do, and Doc started praying his case. "Good and gracious God, who is infinitely fair and logical in judgments, who rightly weighs the scales of good and bad and will not turn a deaf ear to the innocence of youth and the desires of said youth's heart—" Doc glanced at J-Dog.

"Solid preamble," J-Dog said.

Doc continued, "Lord, may I first say, please keep us humble in our pursuit of global laurels, awards, and glory as we race to win the Quad Continental." He took a pause to gather himself and then to launch his case. "Now, behold, I have undertaken to speak to the Lord, and You, O wise Lord, know that we are competing against dirty, sinning, worldly young adults. Therefore, if it pleases Your perfect will and if You find little, youthful me to be just eighty percent purer than the lying—"

Jonah interrupted, "Don't push it. I'd go seventy."

Doc thought about it and agreed. "Okay. If You find me a mere seventy percent purer than the lying, sinning, heathens, will you not grant me victory in the great race?"

"Seventy?" Mac chirped. "You shot me with a BB gun."

"Oh shoot. Alright," Doc acquiesced. "Lord Creator, who has a sense of humor, behold, I have undertaken to speak to the Lord, if You would find me fifty percent purer than the wretched idolators who will be in the race, would You not grant all of us victory?"

"Doc," Jonah interrupted, "remember when you snapped a mouse trap to my lip?"

"Jonah, it was an accident," Doc argued, "and how could I know you would go for the cheese?"

"But you laughed," Jonah pressed.

"Fine, I'm sorry," Doc said. "Dear Father in heaven, I have again undertaken to speak to the Lord, and if you find me to be a thirty-five percent cleaner form of flesh and blood than the corrupt and stench-ridden racers of a draftable age, shall You not grant us all victory in the great race?"

Alfie piped up, "Do you remember when you winked at the substitute teacher in sixth grade?"

Doc grimaced. "Do you think that's a strike against me?"

Penelope gasped. "Yes, that's a strike against you. That's her workplace environment."

"It depends," Mac asked, "what was in your heart?"

Doc thought about it. "Shoot, alright."

Jonah jumped in, "Knock off five for that."

"Alright, but this is it, the margins are getting too thin," and Doc knew if he was really going to make the case, he had to go all in and state some unbending truth to garner some goodwill. "Behold, I have undertaken to speak to the Lord, who is the Creator and Judge, who made the colors of the rainbow to mean what they really mean . . ."

J-Dog leaned over and whispered to Jonah, "This is going take a while. I think we're looking at full Copper dissertation here."

"No doubt," Jonah replied, also speaking out of the side of his mouth so his momma wouldn't see him.

J-Dog glanced upwards. "These are really high ceilings."

Jonah looked up. "Yeah, they really are."

J-Dog then offered a curious statement, "Heat and gas rise pretty quickly. That's solid science."

"Yeah," Jonah said as he furled his eyebrows, "I suppose."

"I mean how long are we just expected to stand here?" J-Dog asked.

"Pssshhh," Jonah breathed, "there's no telling."

"That's what I'm saying," J-Dog replied, "and I've got science on my side."

It was only a few seconds later when Jonah sniffed and his face distorted. "Oh."

All expression was arrested on J-Dog's face as he stood motionless.

Jonah's face crumpled. "Do you smell that?"

J-Dog didn't respond.

Jonah's face turned to anger. "Was that you?"

Not anything from J-Dog.

"It *was* you!" Jonah whisper-screamed. "We're in church."

"You said I could do it," J-Dog muttered.

"What?" Jonah jerked his head toward J-Dog. "I did not."

J-Dog spoke without moving his lips, "You said that we'd be here a while and confirmed that heat and gas rise."

"Are you out of your mind?" Jonah said.

"Don't worry," J-Dog said, "high ceilings. It goes straight up. No one else will smell it."

"Dude, my eyes are watering," Jonah said. "Everybody is going to smell that."

"Relax, just let it go." J-Dog started to laugh. "I just did."

Jonah shook his head with real angst and worry. "I had a bad experience in church with this."

"With this?"

"Yeah, with this," Jonah recalled in a whisper. "We used to go to an old single room kind of church. They had these long, antique, dried-out wooden pews. They echoed real good."

Jonah stopped and began to feel uncomfortable recounting the story.

J-Dog encouraged him, "Go on, think of me like a priest."

Jonah continued, "The pastor said something, and so I raised my hand and yelled Hallelujah. And . . ." He stopped, not wanting to finish.

"Free your burdens, my son," J-Dog replied.

"That wasn't all that was freed."

J-Dog tried to keep from laughing. "Did anyone hear it?"

"Are you kidding me? With those old wooden pews? It was like they mic'd my butt."

J-Dog was trying to keep it together but wasn't doing well. "What happened next?"

Jonah's eyes widened and he shook his head. "My momma happened. She was right next to me, and she slapped the back of my head. It knocked me forward and I hit my head on the pew in front of me. That made another one come out!"

"But that one's not your fault," J-Dog replied.

"That's what I said, but Momma didn't see it that way."

"Did you say sorry?"

"Yeah, but my momma ain't Jesus."

J-Dog pulled his face together. "Well, I'm sure the fine church folk forgot about it as soon as it happened."

"I wish. The next week we showed up, and there were pads on the pews."

"Pads on the pews?"

"Pads on the pews," Jonah pressed and shook his head as he wrestled with the painful memory. "Then, at the potluck after church that

Sunday, everyone was calling them gas pads. It was the pastor's wife who said it first."

"Ouch."

"My momma was ready to throw. She said to me, 'hold my King James.'"

"So, you're saying there was some fallout," J-Dog surmised.

"Why do you think we come here?"

The boys paused for a second, and Doc was still praying a thesis.

"Man," Jonah said, "you still stink. Like something died inside of you."

"I know. The gas isn't rising like I anticipated." J-Dog looked around as if he was studying the air. "Must be heavier than the air, big molecules. I blame the avocado and organic toast."

"What?" Jonah was shocked. "Never eat healthy before being in a group of people. It's straight, hard cheese and Pepto. You go for complete system shutdown."

Penelope, who was the next closest to the two boys crinkled up her face, put her finger to her nose, and glanced toward Jonah.

Jonah saw her, and he cranked his head toward J-Dog. "She's looking at me."

"Dude, it stayed right here. It's heavy. It can't migrate."

Jonah was afraid to look over, but he had to. He looked, and sure enough, she was staring right at him, and it was written all over her prim, proper, powder-puffed face.

"Oh, my word," she whispered, scrunching up her nose further, "Jonah, did you pass gas? Are you feeling alright?"

She wasn't as quiet as he and J-Dog had been. He tried to wave her off. "No, it wasn't me." He tilted his head toward J-Dog.

Penelope glared at J-Dog with contempt and judgment. "I should have known. J-Dog, haven't you ever heard of holding it in?"

J-Dog slowly shook his head with condescending confidence. "If you do that it will come back later with seven more of its friends more evil than he."

"So, you simply pay the toll every time it comes due?" Jonah asked.

"That's proper management, yes."

"Oh," Penelope muttered, properly peeved, "you, J-Dog, are so uncouth." Her voice began to rise even more. "You have very poor manners." She turned her head. "You are very bad."

"Hey, Penelope," J-Dog whispered, "if you've been listening in church today, you'll know that I'm only thirteen years old, and so I've barely sinned at all."

J-Dog's shamelessness was too much for Penelope to handle, and she raised her voice just enough for the whole church to notice, "You, J-Dog, are the chief of sinners."

"Oh my!" J-Dog feigned a gasped look. "Penelope, did you just say the word 'chief?' I always make it a point to say 'indigenous leaders.'"

Penelope put her hand on her chest. "Oh, my heart!" Her face fell long and sad. "I did say 'chief.'"

That outburst got Doc's attention, and he decided to wrap up his prayer. "So, that's my case. I hope You find it sound. Amen."

By that time, the cameras in the church had zoomed in on the trio of J-Dog, Jonah, and Penelope. Anxiety riddled Jonah's face when he saw himself up on the big screen. He quickly looked at his mom and mouthed, "It wasn't me, Momma. It wasn't me." He pointed at J-Dog.

To everyone else who had just tuned into that side of the stage, all they knew was what they saw on the screens. J-Dog looked as ornery as a bag full of rattlesnakes, Jonah Bell had nervous perspiration, and a petite little blond Penelope's face hung with a deepening grief.

Alfie slid over to J-Dog after hearing the exchange. "J-Dog, you are a big sinner. I know. We have bunk beds." He grabbed J-Dog's flask, pulled it out of his cargo pocket, and shook it in his face. "And I won't look away anymore as you try to drown your sorrows in this."

The pastor saw a glimmer of hope to recapture control of the service, and he jumped at the chance. "Yes, son," his preacher voice thundered, "there are no answers at the bottom of the bottle. Many in our church have fallen down that black hole. But they climbed back, and you can make it back, too."

That, of course, was when the pastor saw the front of J-Dog's sleeveless, white T-shirt with a homemade custom message on the front. "Now hold on. Ooh, boy." The pastor popped up a bit. "You just hold on. You're not a boy without a true north, are you?"

"Oh no, sir," J-Dog replied and made sure he stood up straight.

"In fact, you may be a young man with conviction in you, hmm? Am I sensing that?"

"Yes, sir. My parents tell me all the time that I will be convicted."

"Hmm, mmm," the pastor hummed. "You're a young man who believes. A young man with passion in his soul." The pastor tapped on his own chest. "I feel that inside of me."

J-Dog concurred, "I feel something inside of me, too."

Jonah whispered to him, "You better hold that one in."

The pastor continued, "Though you may slip up and reach for a bottle with no answers, you still believe that there is grace and mercy for someone like you."

"Especially me." J-Dog replied.

"Maybe, just maybe this is your moment," the pastor said, "your moment to get something off your chest, because I see something written on your chest, son, and I think it means a whole lot to you. And quite frankly, it's something that means a whole lot to me as well. Tell me what your shirt says, son. Tell us all."

J-Dog played it up as he looked down at the word that he had written in big bold letters across his custom shirt. "Pastor, it says, '*Forgiveness.*'"

The pastor's voice deepened. "Oh, boy. You're talking about the word that changed the course of human history."

J-Dog nodded. "Yes sir, I am."

Then the pastor saw Flip looking at the back of J-Dog's shirt, and she was clearly reading something.

"Son," the pastor said, "is there something on the back of that shirt?"

"Oh, yes sir," J-Dog replied.

Rachel covered her eyes from the pews. "Alveda, I can't watch. Please get someone to stop this."

"Why?" Alveda asked. "Do you know what's on the back?"

Rachel just dropped her head, "No, but I don't have to."

"Cameras," the pastor said, "zoom in on this young man's shirt. I want everyone to see it."

J-Dog smiled ear to ear as he turned and revealed what he had written on the back of his shirt.

> *"The more I learn about Hillary,*
> *the easier it is to forgive Bill."*

Half the congregation burst out into laughter. The other half didn't know how they should respond because they knew who they voted for.

The pastor stood there dumbstruck, trying to figure out how to save this capsized service.

"Alright," Flip said to Mac, "time for the mercy rule."

Mac nodded. "Yep, poor guy took one on the chin."

Flip pulled out a baseball from her backpack. "I'm calling it."

Before anyone knew what she was about to do, she rifled that baseball toward an emergency-exit-only door, perfectly striking the push bar, and setting off the alarm. Flip raised her hands in victory and shouted, "She scoots she shores!"

Mac put his hand on the shoulder of the pastor as he watched the sanctuary empty and head to the doors. "You were taking a ten count."

Jonah jabbered, "Saved by the bell." He laughed and looked at J-Dog. "See what I did? See what I did?"

"Nice," J-Dog replied and pointed to his iPhone. "We Wild Dog'd the whole thing. Already viral."

Jonah squealed, "Check it out."

"You know," J-Dog replied, "if someone would have told me that I would be an internet sensation just two years ago, I would have told them . . . that's a virtual certainty."

Rachel picked up her purse to follow the gang outside. "That's a wrap."

* * *

A few days had gone by since the Sunday morning church service and the Fire Face escapade. Rachel and Dean were glad things had started to normalize, but Dean was still hurting, and it would be weeks until his body healed up.

He wasn't able to keep up with his farm duties, and normally he would simply have Doc step up, but with the Quad Continental approaching, he gave Doc an out. Rachel picked up the feeding of the animals and the light work, but some of the heavy repairs went undone.

The doctor argued emphatically with Dean not to drive a truck and trailer from Tennessee all the way to Baja California, but Dean would have none of that. There was no way a broken arm would stop him from making the trip. Eventually, the doctor gave in. He knew Dean wasn't missing his son's shot at a world racing title.

The kids were doing great, and Doc and Mac really began to gel. It would seem that Copper and Iron were simply different kinds of metal, but both were metal, nevertheless.

With the Quad Continental so close, Doc was in full swing in developing a race day strategy. A few years back, Dean took Doc to a Formula One race, and Doc studied the Ferrari team—every acceleration, every turn, and every brake—gleaning all he could from them. Doc learned that preparation provided knowledge and knowledge produced results.

And so, he became obsessive in his pre-race patterns. He charted ideal RPMs for each turn, ideal speed for each straightaway. Before every race, he already knew exactly when to brake and how hard. He was meticulous. He used an old-school compass, straight edge, pencil, and scratch paper, along with spreadsheet calculations. He had weight targets for himself and the machine, which was a habit he picked up from his dad's jockeys, and he practiced the perfect lean into each corner to counter the force of each turn at the precise speed.

Doc's racing efficiencies were so perfected that his calculations always provided an estimated time that would beat the existing track record. His trophies had taught him that if he stuck to his plan, that there would be no way he could lose, barring catastrophe.

This race prep created reams and reams of scrolled up thirty-six by forty-eight-inch blueprint paper, all hand drawn, with old school hand calculations. The average race would have about five pages of Doc's customized race map and calculations. The race he'd won in Wyoming was longer, and it had a dozen pages.

But the Quad Continental had totaled fifty-seven pages of calculations and planning. Doc had worked on it every day for eight weeks. After each sheet was drafted, he committed every detail to memory. Each night, he would review his work product and quiz himself through mind-mapping techniques.

He kept these master plans in a family heirloom passed down from his mom's side. It was an old beat-up cylindrical leather tube with a leather carrying strap. Back in the day, his great-grandfather would keep blueprints of early missile and bomb designs he drafted for the American counteroffensive in World War Two in it. He had never met his great-grandfather, but he was told that the two of them were a lot alike, and so he treasured that leather cylinder and treated it like the nuclear football. During race weeks, it was often slung around his neck. And as Doc's winning streak became well-known, the other racers began to wonder what in the world was in that leather tube.

* * *

THE BOYS WERE ROUNDED UP IN THE BARN'S HAYLOFT FOR A DEEP dive into the Quad Continental racing strategy. Doc had moved square bails around for bench seats and stacked other bails to make a war room table for his racing blueprints.

It took four hours for Doc to explain his schematic. By the end, there were empty longneck bottles of IBC root beer and cream soda strewn everywhere, and empty bags of pretzels, chips, and beef jerky.

"That, boys, is how we do it." Doc flipped the last page of his racing schematic over.

"Oh, is that all?" J-Dog looked around, took a hit from his flask, swished, and then spat off the side of the two-story hayloft. "I mean, couldn't you have just said that we're starting here and then we got to finish here as fast as we can? I mean I would've understood that just fine."

"My legs are numb," Jonah said as he stood up.

"The hay poked holes in my skin," Alfie said. "You should have told me not to wear shorts."

"Sorry about that," Doc conceded. "Good news is, we're done here. We're heading to the arena. It's time for you guys to get more acquainted with the vehicle."

* * *

FIRE FACE REARED UP AND NEIGHED FROM HIS OCTAGONAL CAGE AS the boys entered the arena.

Jonah grimaced. "Let's leave him alone this time."

"Can't argue with that," Doc said. "Now, over here," he added, walking to the UTV that the United States Junior Racing Association had delivered to the farm, "is one of the most advanced desert racing side-by-side vehicles in the world. I say that with a caveat."

"What's that?" Alfie asked.

Doc replied, "Every single team starts out within a spec range on their base vehicle. Then everyone super modifies it. So, even though this is one of the most advanced machines in the world, it will be par for the course in this race."

"No," Alfie interrupted, "I mean what's a caveat?"

That question went unanswered as Doc climbed into the driver's side, took the leather schematic tube, and placed it on the center console. "Here are my special modifications. I've installed the latest onboard monitoring system: an eleven-inch touch screen mounted on a single swing arm. This screen, Mac, will be your world. You'll access the GPS system, data from the speedometer, odometer, tachometer, engine temp, ambient temp, compass, and video chat capability with the pit crew, which J-Dog, you then can stream out to Wild Dog TV."

He raised his flask. "Bringing hope to the world."

Jonah grinned. "This has all the bells and whistles."

"There's more," Doc replied. "Tire pressure monitors, standard radio, satellite phone. Three USB and USB-C ports, and a DC outlet for good measure. Bluetooth connectivity for the communication system in the helmets, and . . ." Doc pointed at some cardboard boxes. "Mac, go ahead and open those up."

Mac took the big boxes off the passenger seat and ripped them open. Inside were brand-new fitted desert-ready racing suits. The red, white, and blue suits were made of stretchy, highly abrasion-resistant Cordura fabric with mesh panels for direct venting on the chest, sleeves, and thighs, with two long exhaust vents on the back.

"These boys," Doc explained, "are top-of-the-line desert rally race suits with molecular armor in the elbows, shoulders, back, and chest along with the hips, thighs, and knees."

"What's molecular armor? Tell me this time," Alfie asked.

"Good question," Doc replied. "It means the molecules stay soft and pliable, but then they instantly harden on impact, displacing the energy so it doesn't go directly to our bodies."

"Space stuff," Jonah said.

Doc continued, "Then we have our racing gloves with carbon fiber reinforced knuckles. Leather race boots and vented racing helmets with the comms built in. We'll all be talking to each other."

"What's that?" Mac asked as he pointed to a wire coming out of the suit.

"That is a special touch I added," Doc said. "The wire gets plugged into an outlet in the vehicle and then powers and heats up our suits at night. And trust me, when it's forty degrees at midnight and we're flying one hundred miles an hour over desert terrain, you'll be thanking me our suits are heated."

"Check it out," Jonah squealed, "there's no way we can lose."

"While I appreciate the enthusiasm," Doc said, "if we didn't have all of this, we couldn't even finish the race. This is over twenty-four hours of racing through the harshest conditions on earth, against the best racers in the world who will have their vehicles just as modified as ours. What will make us win is how well we execute the plans in that leather tube. Those plans are the key."

He patted the leather cylinder and he got out of the vehicle. "We protect that tube with our lives. Now, let's eat."

"I thought you would never say those blessed words," Jonah said. "I brought my legendary *something meaty meat pies*!"

"Dude," J-Dog pleaded, "why do you keep bringing those? Nobody is going to eat anything named 'something meaty.'"

"You just don't have a refined pallet like I do," Jonah fired back.

"Don't worry, my dad got the grill out," Doc said. "We'll be eating like kings."

That night, they slept outside in sleeping bags underneath the starry Tennessee sky. They listened to the coyotes and the crickets. They marveled at the horses running in the night and talked about the imminent epic adventure of a lifetime. There was the natural ribbing that occurred between the boys, but they also knew, and even confessed, that they were amongst the best friends of their lives. Life was good.

* * *

No one really knows when it started. Whether it was early in the evening with just a spark or somewhere deeper in the night. What people did know, though, was that in the deep darkness of a country night, the sky was illuminated by an ominous glow coming from the Copper Horse Farm.

Dean was awoken from a heavy sleep by a nudge from within. His eyes blinked and he sat up, his broken bones panged at the movement. That pain wasn't a concern though—rather, a natural intuition, or a spiritual nudge, or both stirred him to an acute awareness. Something was wrong.

"What is that?" he asked himself, but his words woke Rachel.

She rolled over, and in a groggy, half-asleep fashion she asked, "What is it?"

"Do you hear anything?" Dean's tone was serious, heavy and strong. It was enough to fully awaken Rachel.

A bit alarmed, she sat up. "No. Is everything okay?"

"Shhh," Dean shushed her.

"Is it the boys?" she asked.

"I don't think so." He walked over to the back window and moved the curtains. The boys were asleep outside under the big oak. "They're fine, but—" He stopped. "That's weird."

"What's weird?" Rachel asked.

"Well, I think we left an outside light on." He looked through the window. "Something's on."

He dropped that curtain and went to another window of their bedroom. He moved the curtain out of the way, and what he saw was incomprehensible. He turned to Rachel in a panic. "Call 911! The barn is on fire!"

Rachel gasped and reached for her phone on her nightstand but knocked it off in the chaos. She flung the covers off and lunged to the phone.

Dean's adrenaline coursed through his body. He grabbed his boots and ran through the house at a dead sprint, opened the outside door, and flung it shut. Rattling the night and awaking the boys.

"Dad?" Doc sat up as he saw activity outside of the garage and heard the garage door open. Doc got out of his sleeping bag and walked around the corner to get a full view of all the commotion. That is when he saw it. The barn was engulfed in flames.

The blaze was out of control. The fire was feasting on the hayloft, wooden horse stalls, and dried mulch. It was the worst-case scenario.

"Fire! Hurry!" Doc heard Rachel yell through the walls of the house to the 911 operator.

Rachel looked through the back window just in time to see Doc run to the side of the house. She knew he was going to try to help. Terrified, she lifted up the window and screamed, "No, Doc! No!" But it was too late.

Doc wasn't stopping, but he shouted back, "Horses are in the barn!" He knew his dad was going to try to save them.

Dread seized Rachel's heart. There would be anywhere from seven to ten horses in those stalls, and she knew Dean would try to save every single one of them, even if it meant him not getting out. That's just who he was. She also knew that Doc wouldn't leave that barn without Dean. Rachel's life flashed before her.

The commotion woke up the other boys, and Jonah, Mac, J-Dog, and Alfie got up from their sleeping bags and quickly acclimated to the seriousness of the night, slowly realizing the emergency situation.

Doc sprinted inside the garage, grabbed his boots, and pulled them on just in time to see his dad get on his motorcycle and peel out toward the barn.

Doc jumped on his racing four-wheeler and powered the ignition before he even landed on the seat. The engine replied with racing fury. He popped the clutch, twisted the throttle wide open, and fired out of the shed. He hit the gravel, fishtailing as the tires found their grip.

Out of the corner of his eye, he saw Mac running barefoot and full speed. He was running at the perfect angle. Doc stood up on the pegs to clear the seat, which was made for one.

Mac pointed to the right intersection, and yelled, "Go, go!"

Doc angled toward Mac and sped up to intercept. He shifted gears to time Mac's jump perfectly, and Doc was at no small speed when Mac leapt toward *The Drakon*. Doc swerved the back end toward his airborne navigator who landed on the seat. Mac drove his bare feet down onto the metal pegs, piercing his soles, causing blood to drip. He didn't feel a thing.

"Go!" Mac yelled, but Doc had already hammered down.

On the quarter mile drive, Doc started to count horses as they bolted from the barn.

"One, two!" he yelled. His dad was already in the barn and unlatching pens. "Another, three. Okay, there is four."

Mac pointed. "I count three that came out the other end."

"Okay!" Doc yelled. "That's seven."

Doc blasted to the front of the barn and skidded to a stop next to Dean's motorcycle, which was tipped over but still running.

The fire in the barn cracked and popped, the flames extending much higher than the barn itself, and the heat started to sting their eyes.

Another horse came running out of the front door of the barn.

"That's eight!" Doc yelled. He wanted all the horses out, but mostly he wanted his dad, and he knew his dad wouldn't come out until the last horse was saved. "I think Fire Face is still in the arena."

Then a quarter of the roof from the southern end of the arena collapsed.

"Dad!" Doc yelled with primal fear, and the two boys ran around to that side. The smoke and fire felt like a furnace. They could see inside, and it glowed like a woodburning stove. Nothing could survive in there for very long.

Then, bursting out of the fire and jumping over debris came Fire Face. Dean had reached his pen and set him free.

Something caught Doc's eye. It was the electrical breaker box that Fire Face had smashed with the gate while coming out of his pen when Doc had ridden him. The box was charred, like it had been electrocuted. His mind quickly put together what happened. It was that breaker box that started the fire.

Doc put his hands to his head and looked at Mac. "This is all our fault. The breaker box!" Doc pointed to it, and he didn't need to explain to Mac what had happened. Mac got it.

"Dad!" Doc yelled. "Dad, get out!"

Nothing. Dean wasn't coming.

"I can't see him, Doc," Mac yelled.

Just then, Rachel skidded to a stop in the pickup truck out in front of the burning barn. J-Dog, Alfie, and Jonah were in the bed of the truck, and they jumped out just in time to see Doc and Mac storm into the burning inferno.

"No!" Rachel screamed in terror. Panic overwhelmed her, and she too bolted toward the edge of the arena. The three boys were right behind her.

They all reached the edge of the arena when a loud crash of beams fell, caving in another portion of the arena. That opened a hole in the roof, and a new fresh flow of oxygen fed the hungry fire. Flames shot up out of the top of the barn even higher.

* * *

"Dad! Dad!" Doc yelled as he and Mac jumped over beams and then crouched low to run under the smoke. Orange flames encircled the boys, causing a fiery wall to meet them at every turn. They looked up and noted that the beams which were still erect were glowing from within. "We don't have long!" Doc said.

"Doc!" a voice from inside the fire yelled. "Doc!" It was Dean. The boys heard him, and Dean yelled with all he had, "Get out of here! Now! Get out!" Dean pleaded with as much force as he could, "Now, please! Run!" Hoping against all hope that Doc would obey him.

But his voice gave the boys a homing beacon.

"There!" Mac saw him first.

"Dad!" Doc yelled and coughed as his eyes and face began to cook with heat.

Dean was on his back, trapped beneath a giant beam that had collapsed on his chest. His broken arm rendered him incapable of bench pressing that chunk of wood off himself.

The boys ran to him, jumping debris and dodging flames to get there. Doc knelt next to him. "Dad, we're getting you out."

"Doc, listen," Dean said with a calmness that ran antithetical to the situation, "even if you get this beam off me, the barn is about to collapse. We're out of time, son. You are *my* son, my job is to protect *you.* Let me do my job, and you get yourself and Mac out of here."

"No!" Doc's tears came down his face.

Doc and Mac grabbed the beam and pushed with all their might, but the beam was simply too big and something was on top of it, anchoring it down. It simply didn't budge.

The boys didn't give up, though.

"Doc!" Dean kept trying to reach his boy. "You've got to trust me now, son. You need to go."

Doc stopped trying to move the beam for a moment, and he kneeled next to his dad. "Dad," he said as tears came down his face, "you need to trust me to get you out of this. I can do it. Don't ask me to stop again."

Doc turned to Mac. "I need the toughest Mac Irons you got."

"I'm here."

"Let's go."

Doc and Mac left Dean and ran deeper into the fiery barn.

* * *

RACHEL STARED AT THE FIRE WHICH WAS TAKING EVERYTHING SHE treasured in life away from her.

"Listen to me," she turned to Jonah, J-Dog, and Alfie, "you are staying here. You will not follow me."

Then, with the strength of a wife and the resolve of a mom, Rachel chased her dreams, her love, and the purpose of her life into the death trap in front of her.

The smoke hit her like a punch. It was a direct assault on her face and lungs. It was a murderous environment. Nothing could survive; it was just a matter of how long it would take to kill her.

She hunched over and pushed harder, knowing that the clock ticked against her.

"Dean! Doc!" she yelled as love pushed her deeper into the unbearable heat toward her husband and son.

"Please, God," she pleaded with the faith she had known since her youth, "please, I need You; they need You!"

"Rachel! Rachel!" Dean's voice reached her ear. "Over here!"

"Dean!" she screamed as she chased his voice.

She got to him. He was still pinned under the unforgiving beam. She slid down to her knees, cupped his head with her hands, leaned over him, and pressed her forehead onto his.

"What do I do, Dean? Where's Doc?" she pleaded, and she looked around her as more avenues of escape were being eaten up by the flames.

"Listen, Rachel," Dean said, "Doc was here with Mac. I told them to leave me behind."

Rachel protested. "We can't lose you. He needs you. I need you!"

"Doc didn't listen. He's still in here somewhere."

"Dean, just tell me what to do," Rachel begged.

* * *

Doc and Mac coughed from the smoke, and Doc could feel his skin being singed. Mac knew he was getting burned, but his condition kept the pain more bearable, although the damage to his body was even more severe.

"There!" Doc pointed at the big John Deere as the boys reached the other end of the arena.

"We got to do this fast," Mac said.

The fire had not yet collapsed that side, but it was coming. The hay wagon was burning right under a major support beam, and it was only a matter of minutes before it brought the rest of the arena down.

"I know," Doc said, "we've got to attach that hay fork to the front of the tractor."

The fork had to be moved about five feet. Doc ran up to the side and grabbed the metal cross bar to shove it toward the arms, but it was cauldron hot.

"Agh!" Doc screamed, searing his palms on the metal. His reflexes forced him back as he naturally looked at his hands.

But then Mac yelled with such graveling resolve that he damaged his vocal cords. "AGH! AGH! AGH! AGH!" he grunted. He summoned a deep lion-like growl and grabbed the bar with both hands. He dragged the whole fork to the arms of the tractor with adrenaline-enhanced strength.

Mac's hands were frying as he pulled the big piece of metal, and he knew it. But he wasn't stopping.

Doc grabbed two tractor pins and slid them through the holes once the implement aligned.

"You did it!" Doc yelled.

Mac let go and looked at his palms. They were branded, blood red, outlined in burnt, crispy blackened skin.

Doc and Mac climbed into the cabin of the tractor and the diesel fired up on the first turn, but then—

CRACK!

The sound came from the roof.

"What does that mean?" Mac asked.

"Go faster," Doc replied.

* * *

"Find Doc," said Dean.

Rachel stood up, then leaned over one more time and kissed Dean.

Dean looked at his wife. "Rachel, I wouldn't trade any of this for a life that didn't include you."

Rachel's face streamed with tears. She didn't have words, but then . . .

"Mr. and Mrs. Copper!" came a shout.

Rachel looked back stunned. "What are you doing here?" she yelled as she saw Jonah, Alfie, and J-Dog coming through the fire. "Why don't any of you kids listen?" Rachel yelled.

Jonah wiped the sweat from his brow. "We're going through this fiery furnace together."

"Jonah," Dean yelled, "get your butt out of this barn now, and take them with you!"

"No, sir," J-Dog replied.

Those three boys got under the beam and Rachel followed suit.

"Now!" Jonah yelled.

They all put everything that had into it, but they couldn't do it either. It was anchored.

"Come on!" Jonah yelled. "Again!"

They tried, but still nothing. Rachel's heart sank as she saw the man she loved crushed and about to burn up right in front of her.

"Look!" Alfie warned.

The roof began to buckle.

"Listen, boys," Dean said, "this roof is going to be gone in seconds. You all have to get out, now!"

Dean looked at big ol' Jonah squarely in the eyes. "Jonah, I'm asking you, not as adult to a child, but I'm asking you now, man to man." For the first time, tears came down Dean's face. "Please, get my wife out of here. Please."

Jonah stood up straight. "Yes, sir. It will be done," he replied with a sad, but strong, resolute voice.

Dean didn't say anything but nodded with thanksgiving in his heart and on his face.

Jonah turned and picked up Rachel Copper like she was ten pounds. He slung her over his shoulder against her protest. "I'm sorry, Mrs. Copper, I gave my word," he said as tears came running down his cheeks. He knew they were leaving Dean behind to die.

Rachel screamed for her husband, and she beat Jonah's back with her fists in panic and fear, but he didn't stop. Jonah plowed through the smoke, holding his breath, and barreling through any kind of debris that was in his way.

Alfie and J-Dog followed close behind, but they were scanning the barn for Doc and Mac. The fire was everywhere, and it was either now or never for all of them.

"Wait!" Rachel screamed in a way that Jonah knew something just changed. She pointed from her position slung over Jonah's big back. "Doc!"

Doc and Mac busted through the smoke and flames driving the big John Deere.

"Yeah!" J-Dog and Alfie yelled as Jonah turned.

"That's my boy!" Dean yelled from beneath the beam. "He got the fork!"

Doc dropped the hay fork to the ground and never slowed as the two metal spears slid on either side of his Dad's body. Dean didn't even have a moment to consider how he would be impaled if Doc's aim was just a little off.

As soon as the fork was under that beam, Doc yanked that hydraulic lever back with conviction. The John Deere overpowered the beam and half of another truss that had kept it down, and lifted the mass right off Dean's body.

Jonah saw that Dean was freed, and everybody was there to help, so he put his head back down and charged ahead. He was still going to get Mrs. Copper to safety.

Dean's chest popped as he felt the immense pressure on his abdomen lifted.

Then Mac ran to Dean to help him up.

"I've been told this hurts," Mac said as he took Dean's broken arm, slung it over his own shoulder, and then lifted.

The pain of being violently jerked to his feet had never felt so good to Dean.

Doc kicked open the door of the tractor cabin and Alfie and J-Dog helped Mac lift Dean into the cabin with Doc.

Once in the cabin, Doc spun the tractor around, freeing the fork from the debris, and aimed the tank-like tractor toward the open end of the barn.

Mac ripped off his shirt and then ripped it in two. He threw half to Alfie and half to J-Dog. "Wrap your hands, climb on, hold on!"

Alfie and J-Dog wrapped their hands with Mac's shirt, and they both climbed on to the hay fork with Mac and held on to the metal spears of the fork, which were burning hot. Doc lifted the fork, rising the boys high up in the air with it. He shoved the gear shift forward and rammed through the fallen beams and through every other object in their way.

Jonah had reached the end of the barn, and he and Rachel tumbled out of it onto the cool, dew-covered grass. As soon as they landed, they turned back toward the red glowing inferno, hoping for the best but fearing the worst.

Alfie looked up. "We have to hurry!" He pointed as the rest of the roof began to give way.

Doc gave the tractor all the fuel it had, and it lurched forward as the boys clung on for life on the front fork. Pieces of roofing bounced off the cabin, and the boys were holding their breath and dodging debris falling from above.

"Almost there!" J-Dog yelled, but a wall of fire stood in the way.

"Deep breath! Eyes closed!" Mac yelled and turned back to Doc. "Go!"

Doc heard him. He aimed that tractor, found his line, and punched it through like he was racing, just before the barn's total collapse.

All Doc saw was a wall of flames and smoke. He knew his friends on the outside hit first, but then that awful red gave way to the crystal-clear breeze of the Tennessee night and its waves of cooling grace.

Doc didn't stop that big John Deere until they were fifty yards out of the burning inferno. But once he did, J-Dog, Alfie, and Mac jumped off that front fork and immediately collapsed to the ground in utter and total exhaustion.

They sucked the chilly night air into their hot lungs. They laid in the sensation of the cold, dew-covered grass that soothed their singed skin. They blinked their way to fresh, clear tears that were cooled by the clean night breeze. They experienced the triumph of salvation from the grip of fiery doom.

Rachel ran to the tractor at a dead sprint. She climbed up into the cabin and hugged and kissed Dean and Doc with the purest of ecstasies and with praise and jubilation on her lips. Her family was miraculously graced with life when death seemed certain to take it that night. It was a moment that would define their lives forever.

The boys hugged each other with deep emotional embraces. Their bonds were cast with an eternal alloy. Forged through the fire, refined through the fiery fight, the boys were becoming men, and they were now more than friends; they were family.

* * *

THOUGH THE MOON HADN'T FINISHED ITS ROUNDS AND HADN'T given way to the sunrise, the glow of the Copper Horse Barn gave off its sad illumination, providing some light as the embers glowed with persistence.

The oddity of experiencing great loss, while also feeling the rapture of salvation, was not lost on the Coppers. It was one of those great mysteries of life on Earth. To have both emotions simultaneously present seemed paradoxical, and yet, here they were. In the midst of both, the love of family proved to be greater, and its strength nullified the loss of wealth.

Soon, both Bell Buckle ambulances had arrived. The paramedics did admirable work, but it was clear they could only help Dean so much. They were preparing to transport him to the hospital, and even he was alright with that decision.

Every fire truck in the county had answered the call as well, and the fire fighters created a moat around the glowing embers, just to make sure nothing could spread to the hay fields.

The local sheriff was there. His deputies, along with fire fighters, were checking the area for arson. Barn fires were not always innocent accidents. But they didn't see any signs of malicious play. It became pretty apparent that the broken electrical box was the culprit. Dean's broken bones had provided just enough discomfort for him to put off fixing it, which he deeply regretted now.

For young Doc Copper, the full-frontal assault of the irrefutable fact that foolish antics had caused all this calamity brought a lasting concussion to his conscience. Of course, the pain was soothed by the lives preserved, but he had already begun to count the losses, and they were high.

The barn was gone, and so was all the equipment inside. They had insurance, but there would be an entire season of lost time just to get the farm back up and running.

Then there was Fire Face. The gifted stallion who never had a racing prime. Without that arena where he could be cordoned off away from the other horses, there was no facility left that could keep him at the farm. He was too dangerous, too strong, just too wild. This fire had just ended Dean's ability to even try to salvage the greatest horse he had ever seen.

The fire also saw the Quad Continental go up in smoke, along with everything that came with it. The extraordinary UTV for the Quad Continental was destroyed. There wasn't enough time or money to build another one, as they were supposed to leave for the race in a few days. The pages and pages of plans and his family's leather cylinder that kept those plans were destroyed. Losing his great-grandfather's leather cylinder hit Doc as hard as almost anything.

On top of that, without the Quad Continental, Doc had to wrestle with the fact that the adventure of a lifetime for the Bell Buckle Gang was gone.

* * *

DEAN LAY ON THE GURNEY WITH RACHEL AND DOC BY HIS SIDE. The paramedics had an oxygen mask on him. His arm was in a sling, and they had immobilized the rest of his body, unsure of the extent of the damage done to him.

Dean shook his head and tried to take off the oxygen mask with his one good arm. The medics tried to stop him, but he wanted to talk to his family, and so they obliged.

"Alright, Dean," a paramedic said, "your lungs are seriously jacked up. You'll need respirator help for a few weeks, and you have a long recovery ahead of you. So, say what you need to say, and then let's get you to the hospital."

You could see that those words hit Dean hard. He was the owner, trainer, and the farm hand, all tied into one.

Rachel squeezed his hand. "It's okay, Dean. You're alive. That's all that matters."

He took off his oxygen mask, and immediately he felt a burn and struggle with his breathing. "How is everyone else?" he gasped out. He placed the mask back on in a hurry.

Rachel replied, "You got it the worst. But Mac burned his hands bad, and his feet are in rough shape because he was barefoot the whole time. He says he's not in pain, though. The other boys got out without too much damage. They have some burns, but they are of the cream and ointment type. It's a miracle it's nothing worse."

Mac sat on the backstep of the ambulance. Both his hands had deep burns, and the medics had wrapped them with reams of gauze until they were mummified. His feet were wrapped in gauze as well, and he pulled his socks up over them.

Mac pled his case with the medics as he held up his mitten-like hands, "I can't walk around like this. I look like an idiot."

"Just keep 'em on," the medic urged.

J-Dog took a hit, swished, and spat from this Listerine flask. "Dude, how are you going to go to the bathroom?"

Mac's eyes sharpened like a hawk. "Are you streaming me right now?"

"Would it be a problem if I said yes?" J-Dog replied.

* * *

Rachel kissed Dean as they loaded him into the ambulance. "As soon as we get all the kids to their homes, I'll be in."

"Take your time, love. I'm fine," Dean comforted her, but they both knew he wasn't fine.

Doc was next to the gurney, and Dean reached out and grabbed his hand. "Doc, son, a father could not be prouder of a son than I am of you. Now, you don't worry about me. It takes more than this to keep your old man down. I love you, son."

"I love you too, Dad, and don't worry about the farm. I'll do all the chores, and I'll find a way to build the barn back that I burned down."

"Doc, stop. Accidents happen. No one blames you."

"But, Dad—" Doc tried to interrupt.

"Nope, not going to hear it. You're my hero tonight. There is no blame for a night like this. We're all safe. We won."

"I love you, Dad."

"Love you too, son. Now, call your friends over here."

The boys came to the edge of the ambulance. Dean took turns looking each one of them in the eye. "Words don't do justice for what you mean to all of us. I owe you my life, and in my book, you're all family now." He took time to focus in on Jonah. "Jonah, if you ever need anything, you call me. I'll drop whatever I'm doing, and I'll come running. What you did tonight for my wife, I'll never forget. I'll always be in your debt."

Jonah couldn't respond with words, but his smile told all. That kind of statement coming from Dean Copper carried as much weight as any statement could.

"Alright, guys," the medic said, "we got to get him off to the hospital." With that, the medic shut the door.

Doc didn't want to leave his dad, but he also knew he needed to be by his mom's side, and so he stayed.

* * *

A SOMBER CLOUD HUNG OVER DOC COPPER THE NEXT DAY. Doc sifted through the ashes where the barn used to be, just to do something. But the destruction was total. There wasn't anything that could be salvaged.

Rachel drove up from the house and around the driving circle out front of where the barn used to stand. She rolled down her window and called, "Hey Doc, it's time to go see your dad."

Doc stood up and brushed the ashes off his clothes. "Everything is lost, Mom. We lost everything."

"No," she corrected him, "not even close to everything. We have family. We have friends. And guess what; we have God. God didn't leave us alone in that fire. He was standing there with us—He is the only reason we all got out."

"He may have spared our lives, but He sure did take everything else." Doc didn't even try to hide his grief.

Rachel didn't want to overly correct Doc right then. They had all been through the trauma, and she wanted to let love rule the moment. She smiled at the tired, broken-hearted boy. "Doc, I disagree," she said tenderly. "Sometimes, we don't know how much we have until it is almost gone. And because I have you and I have your dad, I have more joy right now than I ever have had in my life. Maybe, just maybe, losing all of this, and losing it in the way we lost it, was God's way of refocusing our lives, our pursuits, our vision on the things that matter most."

Doc wiped down his face, leaving some black ash streaks on his brow. "I understand, but it still hurts."

"I know, honey. I know."

* * *

THE DAMAGE DONE TO DEAN'S LUNGS WAS MORE SEVERE THAN ANYone wanted to hear. The tiny burning particles that seared their way into his soft interior flesh had crippled Dean's ability to breathe. The scabbed lungs struggled to absorb the oxygen needed from the air, and he was dependent on the constant aid of a mask that kept pumping heavily oxygenated air into his lungs. He removed it only when he needed to speak.

The pain meds gave him enough comfort, and helped him act better than what his serious condition would otherwise suggest, but he was still a grouchy patient, that's for sure.

"Why doesn't this work?" he grumbled as he kept pressing the nurse's button over and over. His annoyance had already flatlined. His throat felt like someone had just sanded it with steel wool, and any agitation on top of that was simply too much for his common courtesy to bear. Finally, the nurse arrived.

"What took you so long?" he complained. "I've been pressing this flashy thing forever."

"If you must know," the nurse answered calmly, "I had some other patients that needed my help as well. You are not an exclusive patient here, Mr. Copper."

Rachel and Doc walked into the room at the tail end of the conversation.

"You're doing great," Rachel said to the nurse apologetically. "He can get grumpy."

"Oh, he's fine," the nurse said, "or he will be as soon as he finds out I control his pain medication."

Doc studied all the apparatuses going in and out of his dad. "Those have got to be uncomfortable," he said.

"Evidently," Dean quipped, "*how* uncomfortable is up to her." He stared at the nurse.

The nurse smiled as she walked out of the room, calling over her shoulder, "Don't forget to press that button if you need anything."

"Can you believe this?" Dean said to Rachel.

Rachel replied softly, "She's a good nurse, and you know it."

Dean turned his head away. "I know. I'm just chapped at being out of the saddle for such a long time."

"How long are they saying?" Rachel asked.

"The doctor doesn't want me to do any hard work for at least three months. He says I need to make sure I don't breathe too hard."

"I can understand that," Rachel replied.

"We have two pressing issues, though," Dean said.

"Those are?" Rachel asked.

"One is Fire Face. You and Doc can't take care of him. He's just too dangerous. I've accepted the purchase offer from Ben Fallow."

"But, Dad," Doc interrupted, "the boys and I got him back in the trailer after the fire, just like you taught me. I can take care of him."

"But how many times is there going to be a mare in heat when he gets out?" Dean asked.

Doc didn't respond. He knew his dad was right.

"Listen," Dean said, "I've texted Fallow. I've already accepted the offer. It's done."

That was hard for Dean to admit, and Rachel knew it. Fire Face could have been Dean's magnus opus, the biggest opportunity of a trainer's life.

Rachel reached out and touched his hand. "That was a good offer, Dean. I don't know of any other horse stud that would buy a racehorse that has never even raced."

"I know. Ben has always been a bit of a gambler. It's just that the whole thing is a reminder of what could have been. Fire Face is the fastest horse I've ever seen."

Dean turned to Doc and marveled at how he had stayed on that horse. "You really stayed on him that whole way?"

"Yes, Dad. I just anchored into his mane and held on with everything I had. I was waiting for the bucking and spinning, but it never came. He just ran and cleared the two gates, and I just didn't hang on well enough for the second, or we'd still be running."

"Dag gone it," Dean lashed out with a concession. "It's the bridle. Has to be the bridle. There's nothing left for it to be. Doc, when you rode him, he was in control?"

"Total," Doc agreed.

"There it is, then." Dean shook his head. "Evidently, he didn't mind you being on him, because you weren't telling him where to go and how to do it."

Doc surmised, "I doubt a jockey would be willing to ride him with those conditions."

"Right," Dean conceded, "he can't be raced. The one thing Fire Face needs is the exact thing we can't give him." Dean sounded different this time when talking about Fire Face. This time it was final. It was a concession. It was an admission that he couldn't break that horse.

Rachel tried to console him. "Dean, I think we understand that you did more with that horse than any trainer could have."

"We'll never know," Dean replied. "It is what it is. It's over now."

"What's issue two, then?" Rachel asked.

Doc answered for him, "The Quad Continental."

Dean nodded. "Right."

"I have nothing to ride," Doc said. "It's completely destroyed," Doc said. "It looks like someone packed it with dynamite and blew it up."

"Oh, sweetie," Rachel's heart went out to her boy. "Is there time to get another one?"

"No, not with the same specs," Doc explained. "One, it would take too long to build out, and we are supposed to leave for Baja soon. And two, it would need to be inspected by the racing commission, and that deadline has passed."

"Then there is the other problem," Dean said. "Even if you had a vehicle, there is no way I can drive you all the way to Cabo San Lucas. I'm sorry, I just can't."

"I know, Dad. I know."

"Let's pause on all of this," Rachel said, "and let me put on my lawyer hat. These are extenuating circumstances. I think there may be some moves we can make."

With that, Rachel found herself in the paradoxical position of fighting to keep Doc in the one race she was so apprehensive of him participating in.

* * *

THAT EVENING, RACHEL CALLED DOC TO THE KITCHEN TABLE where she had papers strewn all over. Doc sat down and saw scribbles in the margins, yellow highlighted sections, post-it notes, bold arrows, and x's all over the official rule book of the Quad Continental. It reminded him of what his blueprints looked like when drafting his race strategies.

"So," Doc said, "this is where I get it from."

"Oh, yes, Doc," Rachel said, smiling. "You have a lot more of me in you than either of us would like to admit. You got your brawn from your dad." She smiled. "But where do you think you got your brains?"

Doc was fine with that. "Considering all we've gone through, I'm ready to say you. So, please impress me."

Rachel got serious. "I did find a way to get you in, and perhaps if we had more time, I could litigate a better option for you. However, because we are out of time, we've got to go with this."

Doc exhaled, cautiously happy and very curious. "Alright, hit me with it."

"I read every page of the official rule book," Rachel said, "and there is a hardship provision in it. It was exactly what I was looking for. It states that in the face of financial hardship or other extreme hardship where a sanctioned vehicle is not feasible or attainable, then that team may, and I quote, 'run a clearly deficient vehicle that is demonstrably less capable than the approved sanctioned vehicles.'"

Doc tossed up his hands. "That's great, Mom. I'm allowed to race the slowest vehicle in the field. Fantastic."

"Yes," Rachel said, "but you can still race."

"You want me to ride my 450cc Honda four-wheeler in the legendary Quad Continental?" Doc asked.

"I wouldn't say that's what I want, but it's the only option you have."

"I'm going to be severely underpowered compared to everyone else."

"I understand that."

Doc protested the idea with all his might. "You are giving me an option that's nearly impossible to win with. That's not an option at all! Let's call Dad. He'll side with me on this."

"What side is that, Doc?" Rachel sat up straight and leaned in as if she was interrogating a witness. "The side that has you at home with no chance to win? Or this other option that gives you a chance? A small chance, yes, but a chance. Because, let me think, is a small chance greater than or less than absolutely no chance at all?"

A few seconds of silence ticked by.

Doc couldn't believe it. He just got out-argued by his mom.

Rachel smiled a bit, knowing the conundrum she'd just put Doc into.

"You got so lucky!" Doc flashed an annoyed grin. "I was emotionally compromised and tossed you up a softball. No way I'd walk into that if we weren't on the heels of all this junk."

Rachel beamed. "I just Babe-Ruthed you over the fence. Called my shot and everything." Rachel sat back and pulled out nail polish from her purse. "Much to learn, have you."

"You're gloating." Doc shook his head. "You are actually rubbing it in."

"What do you know?" Rachel said. "You and your dad aren't the only ones that like to win." She unscrewed the top of the polish and pulled out the brush. "I totally won, and it wasn't even that hard."

"Oh no!" Doc stood up and began walking around the kitchen table. "It's so on! You're not going to win against me again. I'm not taking the loss." He raised his voice as he paced. "It's unbelievably on. I'm going to take your little rules, and I'm loading up *The Drakon*, and I'm going to win this race on your one in a million chance, because I'm Doc Copper, and I'm in it to win it!"

"There's my boy." Rachel smiled again. "I knew I could get you to come around," she said as she brushed her nails. "I got you to be so enthusiastic about *my* idea."

"What?" Doc stopped cold in his tracks. "You did it again. You totally manipulated me!"

"Some would call that 'leadership.'"

"It's manipulation," Doc rebuked.

Rachel conceded the point. "Yes, it is manipulation, but it sounds better to call it leadership."

Doc exhaled and looked at the ceiling fan. "I can't believe that you got me to side with your crazy idea. I'm not sure what to say to that."

Rachel blew on her nails. "Let's keep Dean in the hospital just a little bit longer. I think I can do a lot with you."

"Oh, that's cold, Mom."

"Dad's not here to save you, Doc. You're in my courtroom now."

How that roasted Doc, but she was right. She got him ready to declare war on the Quad Continental armed only with his trusty four-wheeler and his gang of friends.

* * *

RACHEL AND DOC WENT BACK TO THE HOSPITAL TO TELL DEAN their plan in person.

Dean looked at them like they'd both gone crazy. "The Quad Continental on your four-wheeler? That's a tough ask, Doc."

"You don't think I can win?" Doc paused, and then asked the question that had been heavy on his mind: "Should I race knowing that I'm going to lose?"

Dean grimaced a little. Most of it was the pain in his throat though. "Doc, you know me. We race to win. I don't believe in racing to lose. Heck, I earn my living making sure everyone else is the loser, so I'm not going to tell you to concede before you even go."

"I hear a 'but' coming, Dad."

"But you have to be honest with yourself. Learning to win takes understanding your weaknesses. If you do this, you need to know where you are weak and bury those weaknesses so deep in your strategy that they can't come out. Your four-wheeler is a sizable weaknesses going into this race."

"Trust me, I know."

"I know you know." Dean's eyes and face became a bit more serious. "There's more, though. Considering we all almost died recently, there are some things I don't want to keep to myself any longer."

Rachel gave Dean a curious look.

"I've never said this to you before, Doc, because I'm your dad, and I'm not here to puff you up. I want you to work hard. I never want you to think you're entitled or owed anything just because. There is real value in life when you achieve something that you *work* really hard for. And I want that for you. I want you to strain, strive, and sweat for what you get. I don't want everything to come easy. I don't want you to think talent alone will win every time, because it doesn't."

"Dad," Doc interrupted, "are we getting to the stuff you've never said? Because, Lord knows, you've told me all of this before."

Dean laughed a bit, and he waved his hands, asking Doc to not make him laugh because it hurt his throat and lungs too much. He calmed himself down. "Okay, you're right. Here it is. Son, this is what I've always known but have never said." Dean got really serious, and he readied himself to give the most heartfelt speech he had ever given to his son. "Doc, you are the most gifted racer I have ever seen. If you were a jockey, you'd win. If you were in Formula One, you'd win. For crying out loud, if you had a paper route, you would do it faster than anyone ever has. So just go and do this thing. Go to the Baja, take your four-wheeler, and cut loose. Race on instinct. Hit that throttle and just race. Shoot, son, if you do that, I don't care if you're on a tricycle; ain't nobody there going to beat you."

Dean sniffed a bit as his eyes reddened and teared up. He wanted to say more, but he choked up.

Doc reached out and touched his father's hand as Dean fought back the tears. He looked into his father's eyes. "Dad, I thought you were going to tell me something I didn't know." He grinned and winked at his old man.

Dean curled up his face. "Oh, you ornery little runt."

"But, Dad, I'm the most gifted little ornery runt you've ever seen. I'm the best."

"You little—" Dean stopped himself. "Leave it to you to take something like this. . . . Here I am, with tubes going in and out of places they ought not be going in and out of—"

Rachel shook her head and grimaced.

"—And, Doc, you can't even be . . ." Dean stopped. He didn't know how to finish. "You better believe that's the last time I say something like that to you."

"Well," Doc chuckled, "good thing for me I remember everything, and I'll do my level best to make sure you remember it too." Doc smiled ear to ear and glanced at his mom who couldn't believe how he was poking his dad.

"When I get out of here, boy," Dean said, pointing, "I'm going to whip up on you, and I can still do that."

"Now, Dad, careful of all your tubes!" Doc just laughed and laughed.

That even got a chuckle out of Rachel, which drew the ire of Dean.

"What are you laughing at?" Dean asked.

Rachel smiled and kept chuckling.

Dean looked at his wife and decided to drop a bomb on her. "I don't get to say this very often, Rachel, but you didn't think this through, honey."

Rachel stepped back, not sure where this was going. "What do you mean, hon? What didn't I think through?"

"You got your boy all fired up to race in this race."

Rachel responded slowly, not sure where this was going, "Yes, I did."

"Well, as my very compassionate son just acknowledged," Dean explained, "I'm all in tubes. The doctors say my innards are really messed up and they got me pumped full of pain killers. I've been ordered to bed rest."

"Right . . . ?" Rachel began seeing where Dean was heading.

Dean grinned. "You just became the designated driver."

Rachel's face went blank.

"Doh!" Doc blurted.

"Don't worry," Dean said, "the dually has cruise control, and the gooseneck pulls true. I'll even give you a country playlist for your listening pleasures. By the way, you are welcome to have all those kids ride up in the cabin with you the whole way to Mexico. I'm sure J-Dog will be awesome."

Rachel's countenance dropped with the weight of reality. "Oy vey."

* * *

"THANKS SO MUCH," RACHEL REPLIED AS SHE HUNG UP THE PHONE. She then called out the front window to Doc who was still outside after pulling an all-nighter to get everything ready for the big trip. "The Detwilers said they would drop hay and grain in the fields for the horses while we're gone."

Doc replied with a thumbs up and then took a long, deep breath. He had washed and waxed the dually to a crystalline shine, amongst other things. But the work he did on the dually was nothing like the transformation of the thirty-two-foot aluminum livestock trailer. Now *that* was remarkable.

The boys had gotten together and completely remodeled it to resemble more of an RV than a cage for animals. It was now complete with air conditioning, sleeping quarters, a fridge, couch, and a camping gas cooktop. They plumbed it with a water tank and sink.

They even put in a plumbing-free cartridge toilet, which everyone swore they would not be the one to empty. Rachel, Penelope, and Flip steadfastly refused to even acknowledge its existence, let alone use it—especially because it slid out of a drawer beneath the refrigerator. Doc was thrilled with his space-saving design, but only a makeshift curtain could be used to give any cover, which seemed tragically uncivilized for anyone not a boy.

The trailer had a tool-equipped, functioning mobile garage for *The Drakon,* along with a very secure, large free roaming pen for the unexpected passenger, Fire Face, which had everyone quite nervous.

Doc left nothing unimagined, and the boys left nothing untried. With Dean in the hospital, no one was there to stop the quite irreversible modifications that were made.

The Drakon was likewise as modified as Doc could get it in short order. Yet, even with the modification, his top end speed wouldn't be close to his competitors. *The Drakon* would be conspicuously underwhelming, underpowered, and ill-equipped for the most demanding desert race in the world.

* * *

WHEN THE TIME HAD COME TO LEAVE THE FARM IN BELL BUCKLE, Tennessee, Rachel wasn't quite sure how she'd gotten to that moment. "Sure, no pressure, Rachel," she muttered to herself as she saw Alfie chasing J-Dog around the trailer, threatening something in a foreign language. No doubt J-Dog deserved it.

Flip was performing cartwheels and handsprings while Penelope sat in the front seat of the dually writing poems in a pink book and seemed quite giddy while doing it.

Jonah and Mac were on top of the trailer quarreling about a checklist. Doc had a big highway map rolled out on the hood of the truck, meticulously marking their trip with every fuel stop and rest stop along the way. However, he was insistent that no one needed a restroom break, since his cartridge toilet was more than adequate for the whole lot.

Then there was the large, equine elephant in the room. Fire Face was secured in the back quarter of the trailer. Ben Fallow, who had agreed to purchase Fire Face, was in Southern California. It was a kind stroke of luck that this year's edition of the Quad Continental was in Baja California, directly south of Fallow's horse stud. They would be able to drop off Fire Face near their last stop before crossing the border and heading south toward Cabo San Lucas.

It was for this reason that Rachel found herself secretly pleased that Dean wasn't able to come. Not that she wasn't going to miss him, but he would have struggled watching his greatest horse move on to someone else's pasture. Rachel was sad, too—she always enjoyed seeing the big stallion. He was, in fact, the most strikingly beautiful and majestic horse she had ever seen. She remembered thinking that if there was ever a horse that simply couldn't be ridden, then it just had to be him, for his spirit and presence loomed too big to have a rider.

Separating Fire Face and the makeshift living quarters in the trailer was the mobile garage. Everything a grease monkey would need to prep *The Drakon* for the grueling desert race.

Rachel took one more look at the kids she was responsible for, and she said a prayer and blessing over them and for herself. She then reached into the driver side of the dually and pushed the ignition button. The deep grumble of the diesel was the sound Doc had been waiting to hear.

Doc looked around at his gang, his pit crew, and his best friends. "Time to roll!"

* * *

THE DUALLY HUMMED DOWN THE HIGHWAY WITH RACHEL AT THE helm. She handled the wheel better than one would think, considering her limited practice at it. She also deeply enjoyed the girl time with Flip and Penelope in the cabin, and her heart sang amazing grace that the boys were quarantined in the trailer behind her.

However, as well as she handled the rig, she did nearly drive it right off a bridge going through Memphis, Tennessee.

"Oh, my heart!" Penelope gasped and then grabbed the walkie-talkie. She pulled it to her mouth and pressed the button. "Excuse me. Hello? Pardon me, boys, are you there?"

Doc grabbed the walkie-talkie they had back in the trailer, "Doc here, shoot."

"You may want to look out the right side," Penelope said.

The boys rushed to the side of the trailer and looked through the plexiglass window they had installed. And sure enough, a giant banner was hung on the corporate headquarters of a hunting and fishing outfitter.

"Check it out!" Jonah squealed.

The banner read:

Go Doc Copper!
Win the Quad Continental!
America is behind you!

J-Dog and Alfie had been streaming about the Quad Continental with every opportunity they had. Apparently, and to the dismay of Rachel, Wild Dog TV had a reach further than anyone ever could have imagined.

Jonah jumped in the trailer as he reacted to the highway sign: "We pop culture! The world is watching us. Do you know what this means?"

"Outside of people watching us?" Alfie asked.

"It means," Jonah continued, "we get to tell people what to think. We blow a flute and they follow. Our generation is clueless. Schools have already brainwashed everybody. They sold an open mind, but all they gave was an empty head. So, they'll listen to anybody, and now that anybody is us!"

Alfie looked at his own hands with awe. "I have so much power."

J-Dog bobbed his head. "So true. So true. This is what we call, 'a defining moment.'" J-Dog continued with a wry, nearly conniving grin. "To celebrate the occasion of our great world influence and rise to global power, I think we all should come together and tell Jonah just how much we care about him. Because, let's be honest, he is the candy cane that stirs our milkshake."

Mac leaned over and whispered to Doc, "Do you know anything about this?"

Doc replied, "Nope, but are you surprised?"

"Nope."

Jonah stopped abruptly and eyed J-Dog with suspicious eyes. He began cracking his knuckles as a conspicuous warning for all to see.

J-Dog acted apologetic when he said, "I know this looks like a bedsheet." He pulled out a large t-shirt out of his knapsack.

Jonah growled, "You are treadin', son. You are treadin'."

"Relax," J-Dog said, "this is my gift to you." He lifted up the extra, extra, extra-large cotton, white, sleeveless, homemade t-shirt with a J-Dog special written on it. "This comes from the deepest regions of my heart," J-Dog said. "As you can see, the front of the shirt says, *Public Service Announcement*." He then pointed as if he was on a game show showing off a prize. Then he flipped the shirt around. "And on the back, it says, *I defeated Anorexia. Ask me how.*"

In one unified motion, Doc, Mac, and Alfie all slid backwards, clearing the way for a steel cage death match at highway speeds.

Jonah's eyes widened and his pupils dilated. Emotions instantly spiked in the big boy. He stared at J-Dog with a solemn face and stomped quickly up to him. "J-Dog," he said, seizing him by the shoulders and with a powerful grip picked him up in the air.

"I got a dollar for fifteen seconds," Doc said under his breath.

"I'll take the over on that bet," Alfie replied.

But then Jonah gave J-Dog a giant bear hug and squeezed him tight. "This, J-Dog, is the most thoughtful thing anyone has ever done for me," he said as hc pressed his cheek flush against J-Dog's.

"Really?" a shocked J-Dog asked.

Alfie did a doubletake. "I beg your pardon?"

Jonah began tearing up a bit and found a little southern soul. "To think that I am going to be the face of creamy chocolatey hope for all those skinny, sickly, frail little twigs out there! That really blesses me. You, J-Dog, are my blessing today."

J-Dog cleared his throat. "You know me, I'm always trying to be a blessing. Now, can you put me down? Our cheeks are touching."

Jonah dropped J-Dog as he wiped a tear, "Oooh! Check it out!" Jonah squealed. "I got a big idea!" He took off his shirt and put on the one J-Dog gave him. "Let's shoot a commercial. I'll be holding two of my homemade meat pies, but I'll dip them in chocolate. Then I'll look at the camera and flex my jaw line and say, 'I'm anorexia's biggest enemy.'"

J-Dog tipped his head. "That's viral soup that eats like a meal."

"Yeah, that's right," Jonah said. "I'll be such an inspiration that I could have my own talk show."

"Of course," J-Dog agreed, "Wild Dog would eat it up."

"Let's expand the enterprise," Jonah continued with epic jubilation. "I'll have a special segment on cable news. We'll call it, *Food's No Foe! with Jonah, Ring the Dinner, Bell!* Oooh! Check it out! I'll have a cookbook and everything."

Alfie shook his head. "That will never work. I'm sorry, Jonah, but Food's No Foe is a big fat no go."

"What? Why?" Jonah asked.

Alfie leaned forward as if it was self-evident. "Because everybody knows you have to be a blond to have a show on cable news."

* * *

THAT NIGHT, RACHEL PULLED THE RIG INTO A TRUCK STOP NEAR Hot Springs, Arkansas. The dually needed diesel, the girls needed a bathroom break, and they weren't going to be caught dead using the cartridge toilet in the trailer.

As the boys climbed out of the back to stretch their legs, Jonah couldn't hide his disappointment. His face hung low like a basset hound.

Penelope saw the sadness that he didn't even fight to hide. She placed her hand over her heart. "Jonah, you big teddy bear, what's wrong? Why so down?"

J-Dog answered for him. "He's being held down by the man."

Flip caught the sarcasm, and she pointed at J-Dog. "Sit, J-Dog, sit!" She giggled.

Jonah tried to explain as they walked into the convenience store. "Here's the thing, Penelope. I was going to solve the plight of anorexia for all time. But because of quotas, focus groups, and status quo, I'm being denied the opportunity to do so."

"That sounds awful," Penelope replied, "but what is the hang up, precisely?"

"Evidently, I can't be a prime-time cable only TV host unless I'm a blond."

"Really?" Flip asked.

Doc nodded. "It's the balance of probability."

Penelope crinkled her nose. "So, what's the rub?"

Jonah used his hand to circle his face. "I'm black!"

Penelope sweetly smiled. "You are a big chocolate brownie, and that is sweet enough for me."

"Well, for you," J-Dog said, "but we play in the world of high stakes, and there are certain models and ratings. It's a bit much for you to understand, doll."

"Well, Jonah," Penelope replied, "I love your ebony locks, but they don't have to be ebony."

J-Dog grabbed his flask, hit, swished, and spat. "You know something, I stand corrected. Penelope, I think you have a bead on this."

"Yeah," Jonah added, "what's on your mind?"

"Honey," Penelope said, "I can make your hair look like drops of sunshine."

Mac walked up, hearing the back end of the conversation. "Okay, what'd I miss?"

"Really?" Jonah asked.

"Yes," J-Dog emphatically agreed, "Jonah, you have to give the people what they want. Only then will they listen to you."

Doc nodded. "Yep, that's leadership—or manipulation. I've heard it both ways."

Alfie agreed, "It's the itching ears."

Jonah looked at the boys. "Should I?"

All responded in unison, "Yes."

"Well, okay, alright," Jonah smiled. "I am trying to save the children after all."

J-Dog put his hand on Jonah's shoulder. "Yes, it's for the suffering children."

"Come with me, Jonah," Penelope coaxed. "This little mart will have something for us."

Jonah asked her, "How good am I am going to look?"

"Jonah, when I'm done with you, you will be looking at golden goodness on top of that big, rich chocolatey face."

Jonah beamed. "Ooh! Check it out! I'm creamy delicious! Anorexia doesn't stand a chance!"

With that, Penelope and Jonah opened the door and walked to the beauty products, which were right next to the CB antennae and above the cans of RAID.

* * *

The boys saw that Rachel was ordering pizzas at the small restaurant in the truck stop, and they figured they had a few minutes to pull their caper off.

"Are we doing this right now?" Doc asked.

"Absolutely," J-Dog replied as Jonah and Penelope went into the trailer and shut the door behind them.

By the time Rachel walked out with the boxes of pizza, Jonah emerged with a big toweled turban wrapped around his head.

"Dude," J-Dog said, "you look like an African prince."

"It's because I *am* an African prince," Jonah fired back. "I don't have this jaw line for nothing."

"What's next?" Alfie asked.

Penelope smiled. "We let everything set for just a bit, and in a little while, we'll need to rinse his hair out."

"Will Fire Face's bucket do the trick?" Doc asked.

"What?" Jonah asked. "You want me to dunk my head in a horse bucket?"

"I don't see why not?" J-Dog said.

"It's what we have, Jonah," Doc said.

"Alright, then. I'm not high maintenance. I'm chill."

"Okay, good," Penelope said. "I'm going back to the front with the girls, and I'll trust you to finish up then. Don't wait too long, alright?"

"Yeah, I got this, sure." Jonah was all smiles.

The boys loaded back into the trailer, and Rachel fired up the dually and hopped on the highway for another long stretch of driving. Meanwhile, the boys got joking and Jonah forgot to rinse out his hair for a few revolutions around the clock. Then a little longer and a little longer still.

Finally, later that night, Rachel pulled the rig into a campground, and Jonah stepped out of the trailer and walked around back. He dunked his head in that big old water bucket, but he noticed that his scalp began to burn just a little bit, so he went ahead and dunked his head a few more times for good measure, just to play it safe.

He then wrapped the towel back around his head and waited for the sun's morning glow for the big reveal.

* * *

THE NEXT MORNING AT THE CAMPGROUNDS WAS EVERYTHING JONAH could have hoped for. The sun brought a truly special rendition of its morning glory. The sky was awash with many hues of yellows, oranges, and blues. The temperature was cool, and the breeze was slight, and when Penelope and Flip stepped out of their log cabin, they were met with the sounds of rustling leaves and singing birds. It was the perfect end to a restful night and brought a promise of a wonderful day.

Predictably, the boys opted to sleep in the trailer. J-Dog, Alfie, and Jonah were inside the living quarters, and Doc and Mac were on the roof in sleeping bags.

Mac woke up first and he banged on the roof to wake the boys underneath, but all he did was stir up Fire Face who wasn't pleased with the ruckus. "Right, he's here," Mac said to Doc as he sat up and wiped his eyes.

About that time, Jonah had gotten up from his cot and stretched. His turban was still firmly upon his head.

"Well, let's see it," J-Dog said the moment he opened his eyes.

"I want to do it outside," Jonah replied as he opened the side gate and stepped out. "Oh, this is beautiful. Perfect for my big reveal."

"Wait for me," Alfie could be heard saying as he rolled out of bed.

"Where are Penelope and Flip?" Jonah asked.

The two girls heard him as they made their way over. "Here we are!" Penelope smiled and waved.

"Oh, good," Jonah said, and he turned to J-Dog. "Do you want to video this?"

"Are you kidding?" J-Dog quipped. "This is my magnum opus," he said as he aimed his iPhone right at the big boy. "Let's be organic with this. I'm recording already. Just go, dude."

"Alright." Jonah took a deep breath as he reached up and whipped the towel off his head like a magician pulling a tablecloth off a dining room table stocked with dishes.

GASPS.

Jaws dropped and eyes bugged out.

"That looks, uh," Alfie said quite painfully, "good."

Jonah studied the reactions of everyone, and then glanced up to the top of the trailer where Doc and Mac were staring down. "Is it blond?" he asked.

Mac replied bluntly, "It's blond."

Doc tilted his head in curiosity. "I didn't know she was going to straighten it. How'd she even do that?"

"Straighten it?" Jonah asked nervously.

Jonah's previously thick, three-inch, well-kept, and well-trimmed hair seemed to triple in height as the bleach blond strands stuck straight up from his head.

J-Dog raised his flask, not even able to contain his laughter. "Penelope, we salute you. You've created Iowa-sourced corn silk." Hit, swish, and spit.

Alfie shook his head. "That shucks." He looked around. "Do you see what I did?"

Jonah met the ribbing in stride, "You guys are kidding, right? I look good. I always look good." Yet he was met with faces that didn't seem like they thought Penelope's bleaching had quite hit the mark.

Then Rachel's voice came from inside the cabin. "Hey boys," she yelled, "can you tell Jonah his mom wants to FaceTime?"

That got Jonah's attention. "FaceTime? Right now? Momma? Quick, someone give me their phone. I need to see my hair."

J-Dog was more than willing to oblige. "Absolutely, take a gander." He switched it to selfie, but kept the streaming on.

Before Jonah grabbed the phone, Doc tried to offer some counsel. "Jonah, cool heads prevail."

Jonah looked at his hair and his face became still as stone for a few seconds. Then his bottom lip broke and began to quiver. "Momma wants to FaceTime. Oh, man, Momma wants to FaceTime."

"Cool heads, Jonah, cool heads," Doc tried to intervene, but the train was off the tracks.

Jonah had a full-fledged conniption, and the whole campground heard him. "I gotta get my black back! Because Momma . . . Oh man, I gotta get my black back!"

Alfie tried to calm him down, but it was futile as Jonah turned his ire toward Penelope.

"It's that Penelope! She did this!" He threw up his hands. "Penelope Parsippany a poet of epiphany. Are you kidding me? She's more like Penelope Parsippany, a poet of I'm going to jack someone's life up today!"

Penelope gasped and placed her hand over her heart. She turned to Flip. "Well, that's uncalled for."

Doc climbed down the trailer and grabbed the towel. "Relax, big fella, we'll get you through this. Just put your turban back on for now."

"Yeah, yeah. I'll put my turban back on."

Alfie offered his two cents, "Yes, tell your Momma that you're playing make believe and you're the Sultan of Bell."

"What?" Jonah blasted Alfie. "You want me to tell my Momma that I'm wearing a turban on my head as a young black man who is playing make believe as the Sultan of Bell? That makes me sound stupid!"

J-Dog replied, "No, that doesn't make you sound stupid. Letting Penelope bleach your hair with gas station swill, that makes you sound stupid."

"You said to do it!"

"Listen," J-Dog said, putting his arm around him, "we can point fingers or take what life throws our way. You know the saying, when life gives you lemons . . ." He looked at Jonah's hair and didn't finish the idiom.

"You want me to squeeze lemonade out of my head?" Jonah asked.

Mac talked out of the side of his mouth, "Shoe kind of fits."

"I'll be Mr. Brightside," J-Dog said. "You may just get your cable show after all. Your chances of being newsworthy just went up. Now, go talk to your mom. I'm sure she just wants to hear your voice."

Jonah did make it through the FaceTime with his mom, and though she ridiculed him for wearing a towel as a turban, he was able to survive relatively unscathed. He wasn't sure what his next step would be, though. He would take it one crisis at a time.

* * *

RACHEL TOOK THE RIG, HOPPED ON THE SUPER SLAB, AND BROUGHT a heavy foot to the fuel. The next layover, Lord willing, was Big Bend National Park in southern Texas. It was another long-haul day, but the big diesel was made for trips like this.

Once on the highway, the boys got back to hatching plans.

J-Dog coerced, "Listen, Jonah, the best way to get over being sour about the lemon on your head is to do a show."

"But . . ." Jonah pointed at his hair.

Doc jumped in, "Jonah, I really think this may be okay. You look . . . vibrant."

"Vibrant, yes," J-Dog confirmed. "If I were you, I'd be more concerned about the camera adding ten pounds."

Alfie jumped in, "But you have a healthy body image, so you're good."

"Thank you, Alfie, I do have a healthy body image. Because it wouldn't take much for someone to pound J-Dog for running that mouth like that, but actually I'm . . ." He paused searching for the words.

J-Dog filled in the gaps. "You're bigger than that." He laughed at his own pun.

"In a sense, yes. I've had a little time to think, and I remembered what this is about. I'm doing this to help people who have to put in extra holes in their belts because they can't buy them small enough off the rack."

J-Dog took his hat off and placed if over his chest. "They need healing."

"Exactly," Jonah said, "and who better to bring them that than a man with the kind of eating experience I have."

Mac cracked a smile. "Congratulations, you have a purpose-driven life."

With that, the boys fired up the mobile studio in the horse trailer as they barreled down the highway.

* * *

"WELCOME ALL! I'M J-DOG DYNAMITE. FOR ALL OF YOU PLAYING along at home, we will be at Big Bend National Park tonight on our way to the Quad Continental. Today is a very special day for Wild Dog TV. We have a t-shirt to sell."

That got a double take from everyone. No one knew he was going to pitch that, but Jonah gave him an enthusiastic thumbs up.

J-Dog continued, "It comes from our very own, the new and improved, Jonah Bell, now and forever known as the Black Blondini."

Alfie zoomed the camera in on Jonah who ran his hands through his spiked blond hair.

"Oooh, check it out!" Jonah squealed. "I like that. The Black Blondini. I'm the pop culture answer to the crazies."

"Sure," J-Dog quipped, "you're the anti-Kardashian."

Jonah peered intensely into Alfie's iPad and launched into a spiel no one saw coming. "Do you dodge a frisbee because you fear a collision? Does a strong breeze take you to the next block? If this sounds like you, then, I've got a—" he pointed to his white cotton tank top and read it "—a public service announcement."

Mac then tossed Jonah two of his homecooked meat pies. He caught them and spun around to show the back of the shirt, and he recited it, "I defeated anorexia. Ask me how."

He took a big bite out of a meat pie. "You can join our crusade and receive this finely knit t-shirt and show your support for curing anorexia, if the price is right!"

Jonah laughed and turned to his friends. "Did you see what I did? I said if the price is right."

Mac chimed in, "Don't forget to spay or neuter your pets."

"Oh, no," Doc said as if he knew something that the others didn't. "Triggered."

Without any warning, J-Dog took off his hat and flung it into the ground with prejudice. "Really, guys, really!" J-Dog growled.

Doc snapped his fingers. "J-Dog, stay with me. You've come so far. You don't want a relapse."

J-Dog took a hit, swished, and spat. Then again and again.

"What just happened?" Mac asked.

J-Dog cracked, "That has always goaded me. Every dang show!" J-Dog's voice began to rise.

Doc urged, "J-Dog, no good will come from this,"

"I can't let that go, Doc."

Jonah raised his hands. "Okay, what is going on?"

J-Dog took off his sunglasses in deepening distress. "This is the Wild Dog, for crying out loud, I can't let that stand. I mean, how sinister is it, that a man named Barker, *Barker*, mind you, made it his life mission to castrate dogs? What kind of sadistic darkness is that?"

Mac laughed. "This show took a twist."

J-Dog went on an accelerated rant, "It's evil. Barker's a Bond villain. He worked his ways into America's living rooms with spinning wheels, plinko, and chickadees, all just so he could rob dogs everywhere of the chance of having a little, loving, litter. I mean, why? Why?" J-Dog yelled and looked into the camera. "Who doesn't love puppies? Bob Barker, that's who." Hit, swish, and spit.

* * *

Rachel downshifted the diesel as she pulled into Marathon, Texas, just before nine o'clock that evening. "Wow, would you look at this," she mused as she admired the very old Gage Hotel, which was the crown jewel of downtown. It had a tannish brick façade with a weathered patina that spoke to the many decades it had survived. "Did you see that metal sign as we drove in?" Rachel asked the girls. "This town was established in 1882."

Flip cracked her knuckles. "Looks like it, too."

"Oh my," Penelope crooned, "I'm raptured away at its beauty. Look at the open-air patios, and the pueblo-styled architecture. It's just so authentic. I bet many cattle drives came through these very streets."

Flip giggled. "Look before you step."

Rachel parked the rig right on Main Street, and her eyes couldn't help but see the horizon of Big Bend National Park. "I'll tell you what, girls, this little place may just be worth the entire trip. This is spectacular."

"I agree," Penelope said as she took in the rugged, harsh, and unforgiving landscape. "It's breathtaking. I'm so inspired by it. It feeds my soul."

Flip shrugged. "I don't see any ball fields."

The boys were still climbing out of the trailer when Rachel, Flip, and Penelope made it to the front foyer of the Gage Hotel.

Penelope cupped her cheeks and screeched with excitement at the small sandwich board sign that sat outside the front of the door. It read:

PROUD PARTNER OF THE TEXAS COWBOY POETRY
GATHERING.
TONIGHT AT 10:00.

"Poetry by cowboys!" Penelope exclaimed. "Oh, friends, how enchanted be thine heart!"

The boys were trying to get out of the trailer without incident, but Alfie and J-Dog insisted on exiting at the same time, neither giving an inch to the other. Predictably, they got a little stuck in the gate before Jonah shoved them through.

J-Dog heard the excitement from Penelope as he straightened up his cowboy hat. "Poetry, by cowboys? Not a chance."

It was more than a chance, though. It was a certainty, and Penelope made it her mission to ensure everyone was there that night.

* * *

THE OUTDOOR PATIO HAD A HICKORY AROMA EMITTING FROM THE warm, glowing fire pit. The clear Texas sky brought piercing starlight from the heavens, and a big, brusque cowboy filled the air with some fancy fiddling. There must have been a hundred cowboys gathered there that night with enough facial hair to weave an Indian rug.

Penelope herded the gang to the event, and they found a large empty table in the back. The waitress was quick and kind, and she brought them ice-cold longneck root beers, which the boys clinked together before every sip.

J-Dog sat down in his chair, pulled out his flask, and took a hit, swished, and then—to his great satisfaction, there was a spittoon waiting for him at his feet—and spat. "Now that is awesome," he said to the spittoon, "but there is no way these cowboys are reading poetry. Poetry is probably code for fight night."

The fiddle player stopped and tipped his hat to the crowd. "Much obliged." He received a nice applause as he stepped down from the small, wooden platform.

Then a guitar-strapped, leathery-skinned cowboy walked to the stage. He swung his leg over a saddle that was turned into a stool. He touched his bolo tie like it was an old friend. He then peered into the distance with squinty eyes and began plucking that guitar with a haunting tune. After a few measures of mood music, he began to speak, and Penelope was eager to hang on every gruff word.

He had a warm, gravelly voice, a testament to the many harsh Texan summers he'd seen, and a longing for the cooler winters that never came soon enough.

"Howdy, y'all. I'm Benny Brew, and I wrote this poem just for you." He glanced down to his right and spat. "And many thanks for your spittoon."

"It's begun," Penelope whispered with anticipation.

That old cowboy conjured up a deep sound of rebuke, laced with a dose of Texan pride, and spoke with a burning zeal, straight into the western sky.

"You'll fill the ol' Grand Canyon one wheelbarrow at a time,
Buck your way through the galaxy and poke ol' Orion in the eye
Break a thousand mustangs and shoe 'em in a night.
Long before you touch this bolo tie."

Penelope clutched her chest. "I am not alone."

The cowboys erupted with cheers, whistles, hollers, winks, and spits. They were all pleased; it was a proper hit.

Penelope turned to the gang. "I can really feel his love for his tie."

A disgruntled J-Dog replied, "I feel something."

"Do you think," Penelope asked the gang, "they would allow me to recite one of my poems?"

J-Dog had had enough. He lashed out verbally in the back, for the whole gathering to hear, "No, these are cowboys. They're not going to let your pink, glittery fingernails near that stage."

Penelope lowered her head sadly. "I think they might."

"You're out of your cotton candy mind," J-Dog protested. "In fact, I'm so sure of it, I will recite one of your poems if they let you up there, and actually liked anything you did." J-Dog paused for a second and then backtracked a bit. "Just as long as you have something manly enough for a man such as me to read."

Penelope brightened up and asked, "Would you read a poem about dinosaurs? Is that manly enough?"

J-Dog looked around the table at the boys with ridicule and sarcasm pouring off his face, "Yeah, sure, Doll, I'll read a poem about dinosaurs."

"Hmm." She reached for a pen and pad in her pink purse and started whispering to herself as she jotted down a few lines, "I'm Penelope Parsippany, a Poet of Epiphany . . . Done. A poem about a dinosaur."

Penelope just challenged J-Dog in front of everyone, and that chafed him like he was wearing shorts on a bad saddle. So, he pushed all his chips in on this big Texan play. He took off his pilot glasses and taunted Penelope with buckets of bravado and hubris. "If they let you and like you, then I'll not only recite your prissy poem, but I will recite it while twirling your pink umbrella, like Mary the poet Poppins, and you can even stream it on Wild Dog. But it ain't going to happen. Not here in Texas. These cowboys are my kin folk, savvy?" Hit, swish, and spit.

"Ooooh! Check it out!" Jonah squealed. "We got ourselves a poetry shootout in the wild west."

The soft, mild mannered Penelope wasn't cut out for this aggressive play. "Well, I just thought . . ." She trailed off. She was about to fold while holding a straight flush. But this hand wasn't over because a wild card just got flipped.

Flip stood up and pointed at J-Dog. "Oh, it's on! Game time! Batter up! Bottom of the ninth!"

She went and stood behind Penelope and started rubbing her shoulders like a trainer pumping up a boxer before a big fight.

"Don't listen to him, Penelope," Flip railed with a strangely booming voice. "This is what you are going to do. You're going to WORD UP!"

Every cowboy in the place turned around to see what all the fuss was about.

"I like that," a shaky Penelope replied.

"Yeah, you do," Flip continued. "You're not afraid. He's just a little taco dog. He yips and yaps, and you're going to slap one of those cones around his head."

Jonah found his high pitch voice. "Oh, no she didn't! She just went all Bob Barker on you!"

J-Dog tried to interrupt, "Hey, that's below the belt—"

But Flip's pregame speech was already rolling, and the whole patio was listening. "You're about to drop some language!" Flip coached.

Penelope was a little startled. "I don't know. Maybe he's right. Who am I to these cowboys?"

Flip got right in her face. "Don't even let that thought out into the air. You forget you ever heard it. You're going to smash your words into his face until there is nothing left of him, but a tongue-twisted, mouth-wash-spitting, pile of scrabble chips who can't even spell 'I.'"

The boys waited for a J-Dog comeback, but it didn't come.

Jonah double shot a fist pistol right a J-Dog. "Baboom! Ouch."

Mac looked at a speechless J-Dog. "Roasted, dude. Roasted."

Alfie grabbed Jonah's arm. "Did she just throw the kitchen sink at him?"

Jonah furled up every bit of face he had. "Son, she threw the sink, and then she went back and got the tub!"

"J-Dog," Doc said, "I don't do omens and stars aligning and things of that nature. But, dude, it means something, something kind of big, that Flip didn't mess any of those words up. It kind of feels like you're tied to the railroad track and that train's coming."

J-Dog feigned bravery, but something was in the air that even he could sense.

Then an old cowboy stood up. "I think the little lady deserves the stage."

* * *

ALFIE CLICKED ON THE IPAD AND BEGAN STREAMING LIVE AS Penelope walked through the middle of the packed room of cowboys up to the wooden-slatted platform.

"Alright," Alfie whispered into the iPad, "we've got a Texas-sized poetry fight."

Penelope made it to the front, and Benny Brew tipped his hat. "Little miss, you got the stage."

"Thank you," Penelope said with a beaming smile as she stood with impeccable posture and took a deep breath. "Good evening, good cowboys. I am Penelope Parsippany, a Poet of Epiphany." And with that, Penelope began her oration with piercing pronunciation:

> *"If you could see what I see, between distrust and honesty,*
> *and not fail to listen by hearing uncarefully*
> *that walking in sandals of heroes and vandals,*
> *a flame doesn't burn on a barely wet candle."*

One could have heard a piece of straw grace a spur in the silence that overcame the room. A few seconds went by as Penelope stared at the mesmerized crowd. Then the silence was shattered by revolvers doing what revolvers do, and that was followed by cowboy-sized cheers and hoorays.

A standing ovation rocked the Gage Hotel that night as a poetry legend was born in Marathon, Texas, and revealed to the world on Wild Dog TV. Penelope Parsippany indeed became the Poet of Epiphany, and J-Dog now faced a pink-colored reckoning.

A cowboy turned around at J-Dog, who looked like he'd just seen a ghost. "Welp, it looks like you're next." He spit in a spittoon.

* * *

J-Dog fumbled with the paper that had Penelope's dinosaur poem written on it, trying to delay the inevitable, but there was no stopping what was heading his way. He was next, and he slowly walked toward that small wooden stage that might as well have had a guillotine propped up on it.

"Wait," Alfie said. J-Dog stopped with an anticipation of being thrown a lifeline, but alas, that moment didn't come. Alfie had grabbed Penelope's pink umbrella and ran it to him. "Here you go." Alfie even opened it up for him.

J-Dog took the umbrella as he felt the first bead of sweat populate upon his brow. His eyes scanned the room of cowboys fixated on his every move, and he was keenly cognizant of the millions of views coming from his very own show.

As he passed the cowboys, they each took their turn imparting words of wisdom.

"You don't poke a bear, son."

"Let a sleeping dog lie, son."

"Take it like a man, son."

Penelope was waiting for him on the stage with a big smile. She was completely out-of-touch with the humiliation she was leveling on the boy, and she welcomed him to the stage.

"Come, come!" She took his hand and walked him to the mic. "Good cowboys and poetry connoisseurs," she said and then winked at J-Dog, "and I suppose all of your Wild Dog viewers, hmm?"

J-Dog could only respond with a nervous chuckle.

"It is my great pleasure to introduce to you a good friend of mine, Mr. J-Dog Dynamite."

"J-Dog!" The crowd shouted back with laughter and cheers.

Penelope continued, "J-Dog is going to perform for you a cutesy little poem that I find to be just adorable."

J-Dog grimaced at the word choice, and he grumbled, "Let me just get it over with."

With that though, J-Dog earned a rebuke from a cowboy in the front row. "Let her finish, son. Be polite to the lady."

Penelope curtsied to the cowboy and then leaned into the mic. "I think, to respect the art of poetry, this poem which J-Dog is going to recite should be performed by capturing the historical context of the work."

"Historical context?" J-Dog protested. "You wrote it four minutes ago!"

"Nevertheless," Penelope replied, "I wrote it imagining I was being cuddled by a thick wool turtleneck under a waxed cotton jacket topped off with a tartan scarf overlooking a northern sea."

J-Dog wagged his head back and forth. "That's your context?" he asked with incredulous outrage. "Well, Sugar Snap, I'm fresh out of northern seas."

Penelope giggled. "Of course you are, but I think performing it with a Scottish accent would suffice."

"Scottish accent?" J-Dog's face distorted to reveal the depth of his embarrassment.

An old cowboy from the back shouted, "This was the bed you made, son."

Alfie whispered into the iPad with shear jubilation, "May this forever live on the internet."

J-Dog succumbed. There was nothing he could do. He began twirling the pink umbrella, which were the agreed upon terms, as he watched Penelope step down from the stage. He then looked down at the paper, and back up at the cowboys, and then down again. He took a hit, swished, and spat, and then with the best Scottish accent he could conjure and with a trembling voice, he began.

> *"It'd be a might bit smelly to put jelly in my belly, if I had to share my jelly, but never my belly with the belly of a smelly bellusaur."*

Penelope clapped and cheered, "Bravo!"

Then the whole room erupted in laughter as J-Dog's tail was sufficiently between his legs. The amount of joy those cowboys took in his humiliation was nearly as much as the boy could bear. At least it was over, though, and he took refuge in that. He turned to shuffle off the stage.

"Again!" came a shout from a cowboy in the crowd, and everyone else thought that was a good idea as well.

Those cowboys made J-Dog do it again and again and again until they lost count and the laughter began to hurt.

And thanks to Wild Dog TV, the Texas Poetry Gathering at the Gage Hotel in tiny Marathon, Texas, became the worldwide clearing house for backyard, stockyard, and barnyard poets.

* * *

THE NEXT DAY OF TRAVELING ON THE OPEN HIGHWAY HAD COME and gone. The day was long, and the sun was down, but they weren't quite to Tucson, Arizona, yet, which they had circled as a good mile marker for the journey.

"What's this?" Rachel whispered to herself as she felt the frustration of seeing a long line of red break lights ahead of her on the highway. She slowed the rig, and to her chagrin, she had to bring it all the way to a stop.

She rolled down the window and stuck her head out, noticing that many people had shut off their vehicles completely and some had gotten out of their car and were walking around.

"Wonderful," she said.

Both Flip and Penelope were asleep in the cabin, and she was hoping the boys would be as well, but she was less confident in that. She looked as far as she could to try to figure out what the holdup was, and then she noticed something. "We could have done without this."

Penelope woke up. "What's going on?"

"I don't know exactly," Rachel said. "I think it's a vehicle check. Probably looking for drugs or illegal immigrants."

"Will they stop us?" Flip asked as she woke up.

"I would be surprised if they didn't," Rachel acknowledged.

Meanwhile, in the back, none of the boys were asleep.

"Check it out!" Jonah squealed. "We got military up here."

"Oh, this is so cool," Doc said as he pressed his face against the slats.

"I'm getting my drone out, let's see what they are doing," Alfie said as he opened the side gate and launched the drone into the sky.

Rachel saw and heard some activity going on in the trailer, and it made her a bit uneasy. "I'm going to regret this," she said. "Penelope, will you see if they're streaming anything?"

"Sure, Mrs. Copper," she replied. It took her a few seconds, but she did pull it up.

Flip saw the action on the phone. "Do you want to guess?"

"They are," Rachel said.

The girls affirmed.

"That's not going to help," Rachel said.

Back in the trailer, Alfie said, "Look, look. My aerial view is catching all the action."

"Hey," Doc said, "zoom in on that van. Can you get audio?"

"Most drones can't, but my name's not Alfie for nothing. I have a super-modified directional mic that isolates and then disperses interference, and only scoops up the intended audio."

J-Dog replied, "I don't think so. That doesn't make sense."

"Your head doesn't make sense," Alfie shot back.

Doc looked at the drone's footage. "This is getting good," Doc said. "You can tell the agents are suspicious of that van."

Alfie's drone caught all the action, and at that point, the passengers were standing on the side of the road while border agents questioned them.

The agent asked the men, "Who are you guys, and where are you going?"

"See?" Alfie boasted. "I told you we could hear audio. Don't ever question my drone again. It's my friend."

The clear leader of the pack replied, "We're just a band, and we're heading to our next gig."

"A band, huh?" the agent pressed.

"Yes, sir."

"Are you famous? Anything I know?"

"I don't know if we're famous, but we got a few songs out there."

"What's the name of your little band?" the agent asked.

"Loud Lungs."

Doc studied the scene. "There's nothing going on here; they're legit."

The agent asked the band, "One question then. Are there any drugs or murdered victims in your van?"

"No, sir," the lead singer replied.

Alfie elbowed Mac. "We've got to come up with an answer for that and fast."

Mac replied, "'No' should do it."

"We'll try that," Alfie said.

"We're next, guys," Doc said. "They're coming our way."

The aerial view caught the border patrol officers approaching the front of the dually.

"I got an idea. It will be huge for views," J-Dog said as the border patrol officers started to talk to Rachel. "Watch this."

"Bad feeling about this," Mac said under his breath.

"Wait," Doc tried to intervene, but he was too late.

"Help me! Woe is me!" J-Dog began to wail. He mustered such a disturbing sound that Fire Face reared up and slammed his head against the top of the aluminum trailer.

BOOM! The sound carried up and down the highway.

J-Dog continued in low sorrowful moans that reached the ears of every border agent on the detail.

"Taken from my village," he cried, "fed only cardboard, instead of bread. Alas, now I long to eat from the horse's trough. Oh, the humanity!"

What came next happened as fast as a bolt of lightning.

* * *

"MA'AM! SHOW ME YOUR HANDS!" ONE BORDER AGENT YELLED. Rachel thrust both hands out of the window. That same border agent motioned to two others to converge on the trailer as both Penelope and Flip crouched in their seats.

A border agent walked cautiously to the trailer, one hand on his holstered side-arm.

The agent looked inside of the slatted windows and saw a trailer full of kids. "Oh man," the agent said, "we've got a full trafficking operation here."

Rachel heard that comment. "Sir," she tried to reply, "this is one big misunderstanding."

The agent at the trailer instructed the agent outside the driver's side window, "Don't let her out of your sight."

Rachel laid her forehead against the steering wheel. "Sir, if you would allow me to explain."

"Not the time," the agent barked, and Rachel zipped it. He flashed his light right in her face, which revealed Flip and Penelope curled up. "We got two more kids up here with the woman."

The lead agent walked with purpose and pride around the trailer. "Let this be a lesson for you all. The evil doers are getting cagey, sophisticated. Dressing the operations up, making them look like soccer moms."

Rachel kept her head down and tried to offer a calm response, "Sir, that is not what is happening."

The agent at her window snapped back, "Then you tell me, what's happening? Are they your kids? Where are you taking them? Why are they locked up in a livestock trailer?"

Rachel replied, "This will sound a little off, but it's the truth. We are going to Mexico, crossing the border near Tijuana, and one of the children is mine, the rest are not. As to why they are in the trailer, it's because they wanted to be. If you would spend five minutes with them, you'd want them to be back there too."

"You are taking kids who are not yours across an international border?" the agent grilled.

"Yes, but that's not the key takeaway here."

"That's it!" he yelled. "Get out of the truck. Slowly and keep your hands where I can see them."

It was almost midnight, and Rachel got out in the middle of the highway with her arms high in the sky.

Another border agent pressed his face against the slats of the trailer, trying to see inside. "Are you kids alright? Did this woman abduct you?"

"Abduct us?" Doc almost laughed.

The agents opened the side door, and the kids exited in a single file.

"Oh, boy," Alfie said as he looked at the video on his iPad which captured Rachel's COPS moment for all the internet to see.

Rachel was fuming on the inside as she stepped out of the truck, but she knew she had to keep her cool. The agent walked her toward the hood, and when they reached it, the agent took one of her hands and pulled it down behind her back and then the other, handcuffing her. He then laid her head down on the hood. "Stay still," the agent said as all the kids were then lined up on the side of the road in midst of the miles of stopped traffic.

The lead border agent flashed his light up and down the line of kids. "Who cried out for help?"

J-Dog's eyes connected with Rachel's. She mouthed the word, "Leverage," and J-Dog saw the daggers in her eyes.

Fear flushed his face, and he remained completely silent.

J-Dog knew if he didn't fix this right here and now, the mystery behind his flask of Listerine would be revealed to the world. He glanced up and saw Alfie's drone, and the bright red dot from the camera, revealing, in no uncertain terms, that the world was watching. The stakes were high.

Unfortunately, for Rachel, one of the border agents saw the message. "She just said something to someone."

"What'd she say?" the lead agent asked.

"I don't know, but it was a threat."

Rachel shut her eyes. She could hardly believe how this was spinning out of control.

The lead agent walked over to Rachel, who still was bent over with her head on the hood. "What kind of person are you?" he asked with accusatory condemnation.

She breathed out heavy and sighed. "I guess I'm somewhere in between Jesus and John Wayne."

* * *

"WHO CRIED FOR HELP?" THE LEAD BORDER AGENT ASKED AGAIN.

Everyone pointed at J-Dog.

"Who me?" J-Dog replied with the most innocent, boyish charm he could conjure. "I don't remember asking for help. Can you expound, good officer?"

The agent furled his brow. "You said, and I quote, 'Help me!'"

"Huh," J-Dog lifted his hat and scratched his head. "That might have been misinterpreted. Did you hear anything else?"

This vexed the agent, and he pursed his lips. "You said, 'woe is me,' and that you were taken from your village and forced to eat cardboard."

J-Dog nodded and held up his index finger in acknowledgement. "Right. Okay, that does jog the memory. Hmm. Was that wrong?"

The agent now was ticked. He looked back at Rachel, a seemingly normal woman who was handcuffed and faceplanted on her truck. He pointed to her. "That woman, right there," he said forcefully and sternly, "did she abduct you? Are you being trafficked, taken, hi-jacked, kidnapped, held against your will, or harmed in anyway?"

"Oh, sweet goodness, no," J-Dog replied, "she is a pillar of all things good and holy. A shining beacon in times of darkness. In fact, I would hope one day she would count me as one of her own. Her people shall be my people, and her God shall be my God."

"Unbelievable," the agent said, and he turned around in exasperation. "Uncuff her, now."

Alfie said under his breath, "We're streaming this whole thing."

Jonah tilted his head over to Mac. "Best show ever."

"Five stars," Mac replied.

Doc shook his head. "I'm never going to hear the end of this one."

The border agent was properly peeved at this point, and he waved his finger at J-Dog. "Do you see this line of cars on the highway that have come to a complete stop waiting on you to get through this check?" The officer never gave him a chance to reply. "What's your name?"

"J-Dog Dynamite, sir."

"No, your real name."

"Oh, um . . ." J-Dog looked over at the kids. Some of them didn't even know his real name, because he had gone by J-Dog since the time he was two. He leaned close to the officer and whispered something that no one but the officer could hear.

"Okay," the officer replied as he started tapping stuff into his smart pad, and then the officer's eyes open up big and wide. "You've got a juvenile arrest record. Why am I not surprised?"

Alfie and Doc started to laugh. They knew what was on that record.

"That wasn't my fault," J-Dog protested. "Everyone knows that."

"It says you got caught stealing equipment from a health club. How is that not your fault?"

J-Dog defended himself, "They had a big sign outside that said *free weights*!"

* * *

IT WAS NOW HALF PAST MIDNIGHT AND THE HIGHWAYS OPENED UP AS the rig sped toward Tucson. Rachel was exhausted from all the lunacy and was looking for a decent place to spend the night, but there was some unfinished business at hand.

She grabbed the CB, pressed the button, and conjured up the best trucker voice she could. "Breaker, breaker one-nine, breaker, breaker one-nine, I'll give y'all a moment to get your ears on for all those truckers hitting the night shift on the super slab. Come on."

That got the attention of the boys in the trailer who were constantly monitoring the airwaves.

"That's funny," Doc said. "That sounds like my mom."

Alfie had his iPad out and started streaming the CB radio and all the audio that came out of it.

"What are you doing, Alfie?" J-Dog asked. "This isn't Wild Dog material."

Alfie ignored him.

The boys turned up the volume on the CB to hear what was coming next. It didn't disappoint. They heard Rachel's distinctive voice. It was different, though . . . a bit off.

She said, "I am Woman's Wrath, and I'm coming at you with a real time, immediate press release for all those Wild Dog viewers out there and anyone else that simply needs to pass the time."

"What?!" the kids yelled.

"I'm a cinematic genius!" Alfie raised his hand.

Jonah screeched, "Check it out! That's your mom."

"She's having a moment," Mac said.

Doc nodded. "That whole ordeal back there might have made her snap."

"She's off the reservation," Alfie added.

J-Dog wisecracked, "And we're in Arizona. That's saying something."

Alfie shook his head. "Poor woman, who can blame her? I bet she has PTSD. I know living with J-Dog, I do."

Alfie's comment hit J-Dog in the chest like a rusted anchor. Dread befell the boy. His worst nightmare was about to be played out. He grabbed Doc's shirt with both hands and stared at him with wild eyes. "You've got to stop this! She's going to—"

"Going to do what?" Doc asked.

J-Dog glared at Alfie and began running his finger over his throat. "Cut the stream. Cut the stream!"

Alfie didn't, and J-Dog tackled him, trying to grab the iPad. "Kill it, I said!"

"Oy!" Alfie grunted as he went tumbling while still streaming the mayhem and fighting to keep the iPad away from J-Dog.

The tight area of the trailer made it quick work for Doc, Mac, and Jonah to converge on J-Dog. They pulled him off Alfie, and the show went on.

Alfie defiantly stood up and pointed the iPad right at J-Dog, who was on the floor of the trailer under the weight of Jonah, Mac, and Doc. "You need many doctors," Alfie scolded, "and many pills with many side effects!"

The word was out that chaos was reigning yet again on the internet show, and the views began to spike into the millions.

J-Dog gave one last freaky spasm to get out from under his friends, but alas, it was to no avail. He failed to reach his target, and he knew it. His fight was done. A heavy bout of realization fell upon his mind. He went limp as he laid on the trailer floor.

The boys felt his acquiescence to the inevitable, and they got off him.

Still on the floor, J-Dog slowly sat up. Defeated. Resigned to the inevitable. "I'm finished," he said, and he raised his flask in dejection. "It's been a heck of a run, boys." The broken soul looked right into the camera and spoke to all his followers. "Remember me as I was once was. Remember what we once had. Never forget the good times." Hit, swish, and spit.

Jonah was dumbfounded. "Can somebody tell me what kind of nonsense we fell into? I honestly don't know what the heck is going on? Mrs. Copper is turning into a comic book villain, and J-Dog's a big sack of crazy."

J-Dog pointed to the CB as the boys waited.

Up in the truck, Rachel depressed the button and spoke with lethality in her voice. "I saw J-Dog Dynamite eat—" she paused for drama "—horse poop." Then straight from the gut with haunting tones, she added, "And he liked it!"

She then pressed the CB right up against her lips. "This is Woman's Wrath. Over and out."

Mac snapped his fingers. "Mouthwash. Flask. Makes sense."

The boys started to put it together.

"You ran out of the arena," Alfie said, "when Doc rode Fire Face."

"Screaming like a little girl," Jonah added.

"That's when it happened," Mac surmised.

"I'm sorry to say I missed that," Doc grinned. "I was otherwise engaged."

J-Dog hung his head and divulged all the sordid details.

* * *

A FEW HOURS WENT BY AFTER RACHEL OUTED J-DOG, AND AS WITH most things, the gang migrated to other interests, but they erupted as the big rig crossed the state line. "California!"

But J-Dog couldn't join in the jubilation. "Who cares?" he moaned. "I'm finished. I'll forever be the kid who ate poop." He pressed his flask against his cheek. "I have scoured the internet, and that video is already everywhere, and—" J-Dog started to lose his grip again. "The memes, Doc, oh my gosh, the memes!"

Jonah answered bluntly, "There are worse things."

"Worse things? Like what?" J-Dog incredulously asked.

Jonah scratched his head and thought a bit. "At least you're not the Antichrist. You got that going for you."

Doc added, "Jonah's right. Being the Antichrist is way worse. In fact, people will probably forget all about you once he's on the scene."

Jonah winked at Doc and then put his right arm around the sulking J-Dog. "My granddaddy always said there is a silver lining to everything, and even now, I see one for you. People will forget that you're a big horse poop eater as soon as the Antichrist shows up. See? Silver lining."

"I guess there's that," J-Dog said. Hit, swish and spit. "Man, I can't wait for the Tribulation."

* * *

ALL THOSE MILES IN THE BACK OF THE TRAILER GAVE TIME FOR THE boys to talk, bond, think, and explore subjects that they never really had before.

It was clear some of those discussions led Alfie down a road of deep introspection. "Alfie," Doc said, "you've been quiet over there for a while. What's on your mind?"

"Sorry, guys. I've been thinking. Thinking and questioning."

"Thinking and questioning what?"

"I don't know exactly. . . . Do I feel guilty about what we do? Or am I only starting to understand what we do?" He shook his head and shrugged. "I have much to unpack."

J-Dog closed his eyes in disappointment. "I knew this day would come. I warned you not to start thinking. You have to stay in your lane."

Alfie continued undeterred by J-Dog, "I just think we should be more careful."

Jonah leaned in. "Careful about what?"

Alfie exhaled. "Our videos. What we post on the internet. This might sound crazy, and probably nobody has ever thought about this before, but do you guys realize that once something is out on the internet, it's kind of there forever?"

BANG! The trailer hit a big pothole in the road and jarred everything and everyone in the trailer. The jarring caused them to sit in contemplative silence for a little bit as Alfie's revelation sank in.

Then, all eyes shifted toward Mac as he began to slowly unravel the gauze that wrapped both his burned hands that had been injured in the barn fire. The suspense built as layer after layer was removed until the final strands were peeled off, revealing the dead, burnt, dried out, crackly, flaky skin on the palms of his hands. He dropped the reams of gauze on the trailer floor and looked curiously as his palms. He bent his fingers into a fist, and the boys could hear the skin bend and crack.

Mac then broke the silence as he clasped his hands together in a way that all thought would hurt, but he treated it like an inconsequential afterthought. Next, he spoke with an unforeseen soft, deliberate, and even graceful tone. "I've long equated the all-encompassing, archival nature of the internet to be God's example for mankind in the natural of His omniscience in the supernatural."

BANG! The boys got jarred again by another pothole. Their eyes darted back and forth between each other as they maintained a concentrated, contemplative state.

"How in the world," Jonah said, as he sat fixated on Mac's chargrilled hands, "did Doc's thoughts come out of Mac's mouth?"

Alfie speculated, "I think we went through a worm hole, and this an alternate reality."

Mac reverted to his usual blunt choppiness. "Just because I don't talk much, doesn't mean I don't think much."

Doc nodded toward Mac's hands and asked him, "You good?"

He nodded back. "I'm good."

But then J-Dog stood up and threw his hat down in anger. He began pacing and flailing his arms as he talked. "Doesn't that beat all?

What I'm hearing is even in the Tribulation there is going to be an online record of my excrement eating exploits for all to see." J-Dog clutched his head. "The Tribulation isn't going to help me at all."

"Sadly, it appears that way, J-Dog," Doc replied, trying to hide a smile.

J-Dog turned to Mac. "Thanks, man. Thanks. I was this close—" he pinched his thumb and index finger together "—to a healing moment, but you couldn't even allow me that."

Mac grunted. "Don't hate the messenger."

"Don't you see what this means?" J-Dog pressed.

"Honestly," Doc replied, "I'm really interested to know what *you* think it means."

J-Dog adopted a slightly accusatory tone. "I expected you, Doc, of all people, to understand this."

"I apologize," Doc said, chuckling a bit. "Please enlighten me."

"If the internet will never forget that I ate horse poop, then God's not forgetting either."

"Uh, huh," Doc slowed rolled out his response, "and you think that's a strike against you?"

"Duh, yeah!" J-Dog replied. "God made a really big deal about not eating certain stuff. Tasty stuff, like bacon and chitlins. But God knew it went without saying: don't eat horse poop. He didn't even have to add a restriction in the Bible, because no one in their right mind would even think of doing it."

"So, you think," Doc replied, "out of all the things you've done, this is the one thing that puts you in a hole that's too big to climb out of?"

J-Dog shrugged like he was entertaining just that possibility.

"But you didn't mean to eat it," Jonah said.

"Yeah," Doc replied, "but ignorance of the law does not absolve one from the law."

"Thanks, Doc," J-Dog said, "really, that's the perfect response for this."

Alfie got excited. "Wait, wait, wait. I think we are all being taught a lesson from above. I think J-Dog's horse poop-filled mouth is a picture in the natural of J-Dog's sarcastic cracks in the supernatural! You see, you see?" Alfie's two index fingers pointed to each other. "He has a yucky mouth both ways!"

"Oooh, check it out," Jonah said. "Brother Alfie's prophesying."

"No, no, no," J-Dog protested. "You guys are supposed to be my friends. Friends don't point out life lessons in the midst of all the bad things happening. If we challenge that paradigm, then all is lost."

"Hold on, now," Doc waved his hands. "I think we need to flesh this out."

"What?" J-Dog said to his oldest friend.

"J-Dog, calm down," Doc said. "I think there are things here worth exploring."

J-Dog just shook his head. "Cue the dirge. I feel a monologue coming." Hit, swish, and spit. "Hey, Jonah," J-Dog said, "pass me some of your beef jerky."

"You don't need my beef jerky," Jonah fired back and laughed. "Fire Face just took a dump. Go get you some."

"Aw, come on!" J-Dog shook his head and looked away as the boys roared. "Let it go, man."

Doc stood up. "This road trip, brothers, is indeed an epic journey that will change our lives forever . . . collectively and individually. I believe this trip is challenging each of us in our own way, right where we each need to be challenged. I think we are all going to come closer to finding our true purpose and calling in life."

"Amen, brother," Jonah encouraged. "I'm living proof. I found the Black Blondini in me. He was always there; he just needed to come out. Now I'm ready to help all those skinny little sticks out there."

"Exactly," Doc said. "J-Dog, I believe you were supposed to have a dung-filled mouth so that you can learn that your gift of gab should serve a greater and higher purpose. You are selling yourself short."

"Yes," Alfie said. "Don't cheapen yourself. That's what's really making you feel dirty. It's not the horse poo."

J-Dog slumped up against the side of the trailer. "It's hard to stomach, I'll tell you that. I'm ruined by my own creation. It was my own internet giant that streamed my downfall. My greatness caused my own destruction." Hit, swish, and spit. He turned his head to cover up a teary eye.

"That's good, real good," Jonah said. "Just let it all out and have faith. Because when you hit bottom, where else is there to go but up?"

Alfie raised his hand. "Nah, he's got a closet full of shovels."

"Regardless," Doc said, "if you are so worried about everyone remembering you for being the boy who ate waste expelled from the rectum of a horse—"

"Really?" J-Dog responded, exasperated.

"Then do something good," Doc continued. "Something so good and on such a grand scale that it will surpass anything that you have ever done before by orders of magnitude."

Jonah slapped J-Dog on the back. "He's right. If you do that, no one will care that you're a horse dung connoisseur."

Doc nodded. "A fecal confectionary chef."

Mac smirked. "That you have your own dung delicatessen."

"I get it!" J-Dog shouted. "I get it. So, what do I do?"

Doc responded, "You have the platform of Wild Dog TV. You have millions of viewers. Use it for the greater good and rewrite your story. Rewrite your story right now, from this point forward. Fresh new life. Completely new. The old is gone; the new has come."

"Amen, amen," Jonah encouraged.

Hit, swish, and spit. "Okay, okay, but what about the Lord? I can't deny that I ate that which was unclean."

"True, J-Dog, that's true," Doc said, "but I think you're going to be okay with the Old Testament laws. I think He pulled some of those things back for you."

J-Dog's eyes got real wide and he shook his head as if he didn't believe Doc, and he nearly yelled, "Well, I'm still circumcised! If He was going to pull something back, one thinks He would have started with that!"

"Oh, no," Alfie said as he put his hand on his head and bared his teeth in remorse. "Sorry, J-Dog, now I'm certain I feel guilty. I've been streaming this whole time."

Mac quipped at J-Dog, "Rewrite your story, starting . . . now."

* * *

A FEW HOURS OF UNUSUAL QUIET TIME ELAPSED ON THE AMERICAN highways before J-Dog jumped up with a renewed vigor in his bones and tones. "I got it!" J-Dog shouted as he slid down from the gooseneck and landed in the middle of the other boys.

"You got what?" Doc asked.

"The event to erase all my previous events."

"Already?" Alfie asked. "I wouldn't rush it."

"Oh, no, it's big. This is it."

"Go," Mac said.

Hit, swish, spit. "I was thinking. I have millions of viewers, and if they are watching The Wild Dog, then that means they are in desperate need of better direction in their lives."

"Sound deduction," Doc agreed.

"I mean," J-Dog confessed, "I blather on endlessly, making fun of everything until Alfie and I come to blows. That's pretty much the scope and scale of what I do."

"Surprisingly self-aware," Doc replied.

Jonah bobbed his head a bit. "Maybe you have really changed."

Mac grinned. "It's an awakening."

J-Dog took a deep breath and exhaled as the rig bounced down the highway. "Therefore, knowing and understanding what I now know and understand, I want to use my platform for the moral good. Be a source of light and healing for people who have lost their way."

"Starting with you," Alfie said.

"Maybe." J-Dog nodded.

The boys were stunned by the out-of-character admission and revelation from J-Dog.

"Okay, then. We're in," Doc said. "What can we do to help?"

J-Dog explained his idea for the next episode, and his idea led to much debate, discussion, and then long, contemplative silences.

"So," J-Dog said after a while, "are we ready to change the world and get this show on the road?"

"We literally are on the road," Mac replied.

Doc cleared his throat. "J-Dog, let's just recap. Will what you propose make people forget about you being a horse dung eater? The answer is yes. Will it surprise people, jar people, offend people, infuriate, and even help some people? Yes. Are you morally justified in your message? Yes. Could you possibly start a civil war?"

Mac shook a fictitious object. "Magic eight ball says, 'All signs point to yes.'"

Doc raised a single eyebrow. "Well, friend, leave it to you to bring a grenade to a slap fight."

Mac showed unusual enthusiasm. "Let's pull the pin."

Doc nodded. "I'm in."

Jonah began waving a single finger in the air. "Hold on. Really hold on. I think we need to have a real conversation about this idea."

"We've just done that," Doc said.

"No. We haven't," Jonah replied. "Listen to me. I love your new direction, J-Dog. I'm down with what you are trying to do. It's real, it's needed, and it's kinda big. I get it. But shouldn't we see what Alfie thinks? I mean, I couldn't do what you're asking him to do. This falls into the category of 'only over my dead body' kind of stuff."

Alfie seemed to acknowledge Jonah's point. "Jonah, I understand what you are saying, and I understand what is being asked of me. But I'm willing to take one for the team."

Jonah shook his head. "Alfie, brother, this isn't taking one for the team. This is playing catch with a B-1 bomber."

Alfie argued back, "How can I tell J-Dog to do the right thing if I'm not willing to help?"

"Easy," Jonah replied. "Watch me. Hey, J-Dog, do the right thing! You don't need my help to do the right thing. Just do the right thing." He turned back to Alfie. "Like that."

"Jonah," Alfie quietly replied, "my parents sent me to this country in hopes of a better life. I must do my part to help my new home keep that better life."

With that, it was settled.

* * *

J-DOG SAT ON *THE DRAKON* AND LEANED HIS CHEST OVER THE HANdlebars. He was, without a doubt, a cool cat on camera, evidenced by the millions of fans that religiously clicked in to watch. And now he was about to embark on the most important episode of all time. One that promised to make everyone forget everything he had ever done in the past.

"J-Dog Dynamite is alive and well," he said as he kicked off another streaming event, and then he howled.

Doc entered the scene from the left as Mac manned the iPad.

"J-Dog," Doc said, "look over there. I think something is bothering our dear friend, Alfie."

"What?" J-Dog's demeanor changed to show a deep sense of concern. "Oh, Alfie, my dear friend, please tell me what doth trouble you?"

Alfie walked in with his head low, kicking at a piece of dirt on the trailer floor. "J-Dog," he said with a downtrodden voice, "can we talk?"

J-Dog took off his sunglasses. "I'm in the middle of a show, Alfie." He paused for a second, and then continued, "But for you, I'll do anything, because I like to put other people first. That's who I am. It's in my nature."

"Thank you," Alfie replied. He then continued with a distress that blanketed his face, "I've been wondering . . ." He stopped and stared shamefully at the trailer floor.

J-Dog walked to him and put his arm around him. "Hey, hey, it's me. You can tell me anything."

"Thanks, J-Dog. You see, recently," Alfie continued, "I've seen men wearing dresses, and blush and stuff."

"Go on," J-Dog warmly responded.

"So, I've been wondering," Alfie said with curiosity, "what gender am I?"

J-Dog thoughtfully raised his hand to his own chin. "I see. I see." He turned to the camera. "It appears we are witnessing the early stages of what we call Confusion Syndrome."

Alfie was shocked. "Confusion Syndrome? What's that?"

"Just as I feared. Asking such a question is another one of the symptoms."

"Oh no!" Alfie shouted.

"Simply put, Alfie, Confusion Syndrome is diagnosed when a person begins to believe something that goes against all common sense and stands against the entire collective bank of human knowledge."

Alfie reached out and clung to J-Dog's shirt. "What can I do? Oh, help me, J-Dog! I cannot lose my sense that should be so common."

"Fortunately for you, I have a brand-new, original t-shirt that has been meticulously designed, tested in our own laboratory, and proven to cure Confusion Syndrome in just one wearing."

J-Dog raised up a sleeveless white t-shirt to the camera.

Written on the front of the shirt, high across the chest, it stated: GENDER IDENTITY QUESTIONS?

Below that phrase was a giant red arrow pointing downward, and then underneath the arrow was a written instruction: JUST LOOK DOWN.

"Answer your question?" J-Dog asked Alfie.

Alfie followed the shirt's advice, and then he smiled and shouted, "I'm a boy!"

J-Dog slapped him on the back. "That-a-boy! This is J-Dog Dynamite, and you've been watching Wild Dog TV."

Alfie had walked off screen when he shouted with unscripted excitement, "J-Dog! J-Dog! I'm a boy! My hips don't lie!"

J-Dog pointed at him. "Nice."

* * *

THE NEXT STOP FOR THE GANG ON THEIR JOURNEY TO THE QUAD Continental was the Mare Motel breeding facility owned by Ben Fallow in southern California. That stop didn't mean a whole lot to most of the kids, but to Doc and Rachel, it signified the end of an era. The end of many hopes and dreams. With Dean still bedridden back in Bell Buckle, Rachel and Doc were going to finish the transaction of the rare stallion who was most famous for being the greatest racing horse who never ran a single race.

When Rachel pulled the truck and trailer into the horse stud, she couldn't help but think it looked more like a wine vineyard than a horse farm. Rolling hills of perfectly trimmed alfalfa spread everywhere.

Workers strolled the countryside collecting crops with barns so beautiful that it was obvious the horses lived better than the people tending to them.

Rachel slowed the rig down to a stop in a picturesque driving circle in front of one of the barns. There was a stable boy holding a big, beautiful, golden-brown stallion out on the lawn. A farrier was bent over, holding a hind leg, and filing down its hooves. The shimmering horse stood still like it was a bronze statue.

The boys peered out of the slats from the back of the trailer.

"Fire Face doesn't stand like that," Mac said.

Doc chuckled. "No, he doesn't."

The kids exited the trailer and made their way over to the farrier, while Rachel texted, called, and then went to go find Ben Fallow, Fire Face's new owner.

* * *

THE SKIN OF THE FARRIER'S HANDS MATCHED THE TOUGHNESS OF an old saddle. He had a huge handlebar mustache with unshaven scruff finishing off his face. He wore a beaten-up straw cowboy hat, stained with years of collected sweat.

He lifted his eyes to see the kids walking over, and he put the foot of the big horse down. "How ya doing?" he asked.

"Good," Doc replied, and then pointed at the stallion. "Who is this?"

The farrier took off his hat and wiped the sweat from his face. "This here is *the* Priceless Pete."

Doc couldn't hide his smile. "Priceless Pete?"

J-Dog turned to Jonah. "What the heck is a Priceless Pete?"

Doc overheard him and answered, "A world champion, that's what."

The farrier was impressed. "You know your horses."

"Yes, sir, my dad is Dean Copper. He's a trainer."

As soon as the farrier heard the name Dean Copper, he froze to attention. "Dean Copper? If you're Dean Copper's boy, and you're here with a trailer . . ." He spit some tobacco juice on the ground. "Then that means that's gotta be Fire Face in that there trailer."

"You have deduced correctly," Doc replied.

The farrier smiled. "I've heard of him. Or, at least, I heard the myth of him."

Fire Face could see, smell, and hear the other stallion so close outside. The presence of another stallion agitated him, and he snorted and began stomping in his aluminum cage.

The farrier tried to stare through the slats. "He looks like a biggin'." Fire Face's head banged into the ceiling. "And causes a ruckus, I see." The farrier looked a bit more. "Why do you have him in a livestock trailer and not a proper horse trailer."

"That's a long, drawn-out story you probably don't have time for," Doc replied.

"Fair enough," the farrier said. "I appreciate you not telling me then." He grinned. "Being in there is probably why he's so worked up though."

"No, not really," Doc replied and tried to explain. "He's always worked up. That's who he is, and there is a lot of bite to that bark, so you need to watch yourself with him."

The farrier offered a condescending grin. "Shoot. There isn't a type of horse I haven't seen or worked with." He turned his attention to Priceless Pete. "Take this horse for example. Priceless Pete wouldn't let anyone come within a country mile of his hooves. Now look at him. It took me an entire morning, but I got him calmed down."

J-Dog piped up, "Mr. Horse Whisperer, dude, what you have standing there," and he pointed at Priceless Pete, "isn't even the same species of what is in the back of that trailer. Fire Face would eat Petey here like chicken nuggets."

The farrier laughed off the remark. He found the kids entertaining. "Sure. Let's get that big old mean stallion unloaded and hope we live to tell the tale!" He laughed at the supposed naivete of the boys. "You know, how bad could this horse be if Dean let his wife and boy deliver him?"

* * *

RACHEL, PENELOPE, AND FLIP HAD MADE THEIR WAY UP TO THE BIG house on the ranch just in time to see Ben Fallow walk out of its front door.

"Hi, Ben," Rachel said with a smile. She noted that he looked a bit surprised. She wasn't sure why, but she didn't want to have any small talk. She needed this transaction to be done and over with. "I've got your horse," she said, "and I'd like to get this closed, if that's alright with you?"

Ben winced a bit. "There's this thing," he said as he shook her hand.

Rachel raised her eyebrows and responded with a bit of force, "What thing, Ben?"

He hemmed and hawed a bit. "The last few days have been kind of tough. I've made some financial moves that didn't quite go as planned."

It didn't take a crystal ball to understand what was happening. "Cut to the chase, Ben," Rachel demanded.

"Alright. I can't take on any more risk."

"No, no." Rachel shook her head. "You are not backing out of this deal. I just drove this horse across the country for you."

"Ma'am," Ben tried to apologize, "I'm truly sorry."

Every legal bone in Rachel's body wanted to drag Ben Fallow to court. She knew she would eat him alive in depositions. She looked around at the ranch, which was worth millions. "I know Fire Face is an expensive horse, but you clearly don't have to renege on our deal. What decisions did you make, for crying out loud?"

Ben's face flushed red. "I wired some money to buy some real estate from a guy who knew a guy who had a great deal. There was supposed to be oil, gas, and minerals on this property. I was going to make a fortune, and they had a website and everything. It was kind of a handshake deal, without really a handshake."

Rachel tried to contain herself, but she couldn't keep the disgust and anger out of her voice. "You're telling me that because you got suckered by an online scam, you can't buy my horse?"

Ben didn't even answer; he knew he'd been taken as the fool.

"What do you want me to do?" Rachel asked. "I know you talked to Dean. Our barn burned down and Dean's stuck in bed. We've got a race we're trying to get to down in Mexico. I can't take this horse with me a day longer. We are out of feed. He's been cooped up in that trailer because we weren't in a position to get him out. That's not good for that horse. He needs a pasture, and now."

Ben raised his hands. "Okay, okay. How about this? Leave the horse here until you drive back from your race, and then we'll talk. I'm not promising anything."

Rachel had to take what she could. "At least that's something."

* * *

THE FARRIER PRESSED HIS FACE BETWEEN THE SLATS OF THE ALUMINUM trailer. "I'll give you this, boy, he is big. Color me impressed."

Fire Face threw his head back and slammed the roof of the trailer. The farrier instinctively backed away.

"Wait till you see him run," Doc said.

"Is it true no one can ride him?" the farrier asked.

J-Dog spoke up, "Doc rode him."

The farrier looked disappointed. "I guess he's not quite the rogue they say he is."

"Yes, he is," Doc said. "I clung for my life and then fell off."

The farrier bit his bottom lip in a thought and looked at Priceless Pete, and then back at Doc.

"He does like to run?" the farrier asked Doc.

Doc smiled, "He'd rather run than breathe."

The farrier took off his cowboy hat and brushed it off as he thought out loud, "I really shouldn't do this with this horse, but I got a bad idea. You kids like bad ideas?"

Mac grinned. "Almost exclusively."

"What do you have in mind?" Doc asked.

* * *

THE PRISTINE FARM HAD LONG, BEAUTIFUL FENCED-IN RUNS ALL over the gorgeous acreage. Most were teeming with mares and foals, but there were two long thin runs, side by side, which funneled in and out of the vet barn where the collection of the stallions took place.

When the stallions were brought from their stalls and put into those runs, they were conditioned, via habit, to know that they were about to be collected. This caused their hormones to spike in their body, and that amped up their already aggressive natures that put the champion stallions on hair triggers.

The farrier and the other farm hands learned that when two stallions were put side-by-side in those two runs, usually as one was going in and the other coming out, that the breeding instinct for winning mares created a hyper aggressive competition between the two stallions. Their animalistic instincts demanded that they dominate the other for the right to breed.

They would prance, neigh, and dig up the ground with sharp hooves as they were separated and angered by the tall, reinforced fence between them.

One time, it happened quite by accident, that a pair of stallions, frustrated at the inability to fight each other, ended up in a violent sprint down the center fence. It was an incredible *mono et mono* match race between world class racing stallions but with the twist that no jockeys were involved.

The farrier figured it out that by pairing one of the horses who instinctively ran in that situation with another stallion that, consequently, the one taught the other horse to do the same. Over the years, through decisive pairings, the horses trained each other to race when they were put into those two long thin runs.

It was unbridled, instinctively driven match races. Champion versus champion. Legend against legend. Then it became the farm tradition, like all other horse races, to bet and to bet big.

The farrier was the ringleader, and he would take bets from the ranch hands. They'd toss their money on the ground into piles. The winners would take the piles and divvy up accordingly.

Priceless Pete was the reigning king of these special match races. He was naturally gifted to race. Everything about that horse showed man's best attempt to accomplish speed: his breeding, his trained temperament, his perfect diet that led to a slippery toned build. There was a reason he was a world champion. He was the very best of equine science and care. Only a few desperate gambling addicts at the stud would bet against him.

* * *

"As bad ideas go," the farrier explained, "this is really a good one."

The farrier went into great detail about the match race, the history of it, and then the idea of putting Fire Face into one.

"Sir," Doc asked, "are you suggesting that we pit Fire Face against Priceless Pete right now?"

"Only if you think your horse can handle it," the farrier egged Doc on.

J-Dog got hooked on the idea. "Dude, where's the all-in pile? Fire Face is going to curb stomp that pony."

Doc raised his hand in caution. "The question is, can your fences handle Fire Face? All hyperbole aside, sir, if that fence doesn't hold, Fire Face will kill that stallion if he rears up against him and anybody else that tries to get between."

The farrier shook his head at the perceived youthful ignorance. "I get it. You're from a small farm in Tennessee, and Fire Face is the biggest, baddest horse you've ever seen."

"Sir, I'm telling you—"

"You're about to find out what happens when your overgrown colt is next to a world champion stallion and not your 4-H hunter jumper, boy." The farrier laughed. "There ain't going to be no fight, and you're going to see your Fire Face is nothing but a fizzled firework. Trust me, if he were a real racer, he would have raced. The truth is, he's not as fast as people say, and your daddy didn't race him because he knew it."

Doc started to feel game rage run through his body, the same feeling he had when he was about to race *The Drakon*. His eyes sharpened a bit as he looked at the farrier. "Let's do it."

The farrier stuck his fingers in his mouth and blew out a piercing whistle. That was the signal for all farm hands to drop what they were doing and head on over to wherever that whistle came from.

He turned to Doc. "I need you to back up your trailer to this gate here." He pointed to the lot that was next to Priceless Pete's. "Can you do that?"

Dean had taught Doc to operate anything on the farm, and the truck and trailer was no different, even though he was only thirteen.

"Yep."

The ranch hands had begun to appear.

"Okay, gather around, boys," the farrier said. He took on a tone that was not unlike a boxing ring promoter. "Inside this trailer is none other than the fabled Fire Face."

"What?" some of the ranch hands asked aghast. "You're lying."

"No. It's true. The horse who has been on the cover of magazines and was touted as the next great champion is in this trailer, right here. Right now."

The ranch hands moved like a single amoeba and surrounded the trailer.

Fire Face let out a rumbling snort and spun in anger as he banged the metal sides.

One ranch hand spoke up, "He's the horse no one can ride? Okay. I get it."

Another hand looked at the run he was being put into and saw that the horse he was up against was Priceless Pete. The stable boy rebuffed the idea, "Are you joking? This isn't a race. Run him against one of the others first and see how he does. It's nothing to bet on if it's against Priceless Pete."

Doc didn't like that. "No, my dad says no horse is faster than Fire Face."

That remark got a chuckle out of the ranch hands. "No disrespect to your dad," one of them countered, "but he's dead wrong."

The farrier clapped his hands. "Let's do it, then. Get your money out." He used the heel of his boot to make two circles in the dirt. "This circle is for Priceless Pete. This one, Fire Face."

The ranch hands took out their wallets, and every single one of them threw down cash in the Priceless Pete circle. Not a dime was bet on Fire Face.

The farrier's face fell in disappointment. "Come on guys, we don't have a purse if no one bets for Fire Face."

One ranch hand spoke up, "I'm okay with losing a bet, but I'm not going to give money away by betting on this crazy horse. We already told you this isn't a race."

Another said, "What do you expect? You've got a world champion against a never been."

The farrier looked at Doc. "Do you want to back your horse?"

Doc had wished that he could. "Here's the deal," Doc said, "none of us have that kind of cash."

The group of ranch hands lost interest in the whole discussion. They picked up their money and started to disperse. "We got no race," one said.

Another added as they walked away laughing, "Besides, are we going to take the word of a trainer who can't even break his own horse?"

That ticked-off Doc, and he shouted at the guy who said it, "Would you bet your boots on that?"

The guy turned around. "What?"

Doc glanced down at his own boots and back at the guy. "I'll bet my boots against your boots."

The two groups were kind of intrigued at the prospect. "But," the ranch hand said, "I can't wear your boots. They're too small. What value are they to me?"

"Don't think of it like that," Doc said. "The boots are a trophy. Hang 'em off the back hitch off your truck and tell people how you won 'em. It will give you some moxie, which, from where I'm standing, I'm guessing you've had a hard time coming by in your life."

"Oooh," the other ranches laughed at the chutzpa of Doc, and they liked it.

The ranch hand was baited. "Alright, kid. You're on, boot for boot."

J-Dog piped up and looked at another one of the ranch hands, "My hat against your hat. Unless your head is so ugly it's just got to be covered. Why don't you just throw that toe ring in too, of which I am certain you have. I mean with a face like yours, you've gotta have a toe ring."

The farrier chuckled. "They got spunk. Let's match it, boys, hat for hat, boot for boot. Come on, this is Priceless Pete after all. This is going to be fun."

"Oooh, check it out!" Jonah squealed.

The farrier enjoyed the ribbing. "You boys are on, but I'm telling you, no one beats Priceless Pete."

"I want in. Ding! Ding!" Jonah said, "I've got my shirt, who'll go shirt for shirt with me."

One interested better piped up, "I'll take that bet."

That led off a fury of bets and trash talk. Boots, socks, belts, pants, shirts, hats, bandanas, and even two watches were on the line.

* * *

"ALL BETS ARE IN," THE FARRIER SAID. HE REACHED INTO HIS pocket and pulled out some sugar cubes. He walked over to the front corner of the long thin run, where Priceless Pete waited, and the farrier whistled.

Priceless Pete answered the call and came running. Everyone stared as this tall, lean golden-brown stallion glided over the ground with supreme ease and grace. His coat shimmered and gleamed from careful grooming. His tail was short and meticulously braided. His mane was cropped to his neck. Clearly, he was a show horse. He was a racing champion, and there was no question he was built to run.

The farrier climbed up on the bottom two rungs of the fence and reached his hand over. Priceless Pete carefully ate the sugar cubes.

"Man," Jonah laughed, "why don't people give me sugar cubes?"

"Because," J-Dog quipped, "they'd be too afraid to lose a finger."

The ranch hand who had a bet against J-Dog taunted, "You guys scared yet?"

"Not me, Glitter," J-Dog responded. "The fact that your cute horse licks sugar cubes from your hand tells me all I need to know."

J-Dog glanced over at Alfie. "We ready to go?"

"Already are," Alfie said as he pulled his remote control from behind his back and pointed to the sky. He had launched his drone, and this race was going live with aerial footage.

Jonah turned to Doc and whispered, "We got this, right?"

Doc never took his eyes off the champion horse. "We got it in spades, brother."

Doc backed the trailer right into the lot Fire Face needed to be in. All that had to happen was for the trailer door to be swung open, and Fire Face would exit into the lot next to Priceless Pete.

SHRIEK! A loud shrill battle cry came from the trailer as Fire Face recognized the nearness of Priceless Pete.

Fire Face reared up and smacked his head on the ceiling of the trailer with such force that it dented the aluminum.

Priceless Pete answered the call with a bowed-up challenge of his own. He reared up and kicked his front feet in the air. Fire Face took Priceless Pete's challenge as a basic affront to his very existence. He began slamming every side of the trailer with reckless abandonment.

"Everyone get out of the way," the farrier said. He pointed at Doc. "You got to get your horse out before he hurts himself."

The tension for the race was exhilarating. A world champion against a caged-up beast. The boys and the ranch hands climbed onto the fences of the outer run to watch the incredible moment when Fire Face came out of the trailer to meet Priceless Pete.

Doc grabbed the lever of the trailer gate, yanked it down, and freed the lock. He didn't even bother to swing open the gate. He dove out of the way to safety.

As soon as the door latch clicked free, Fire Face knew it. He launched at the gate, hitting it with his chest, and flung it open. It slammed into the gate of the run, bending it.

It happened immediately. There was no hesitation. There was not a moment to take it in. It happened without even one tick of the clock. Fire Face launched out of the trailer and charged Priceless Pete. The two horses reared up, and their chests collided through the tall fence between them. The collision sent a wave down the fence line. The huge mane and tail of Fire Face swished wildly in the air and got tangled in the fence.

Gasps filled the air.

"DUDE!" J-Dog shouted.

The farrier grabbed his head with both hands, crunching his hat, and shouted words that best remain unsaid.

Dread gripped the farrier. He had no idea this would happen. He hadn't believed Doc's warnings. He had chalked them up to a boy's exaggeration. He never would have done this if he knew just how aggressive Fire Face was.

The ranch hands got their first full, unencumbered look at the rogue stallion as he was reared up against the fence. His size was breathtaking. His head rose almost a foot higher than Priceless Pete's while they were standing on their haunches, and he was hundreds of pounds heavier.

The weight of the collision buckled Priceless Pete's hind quarters, and he stumbled off balance, falling backward, but he did not fall to the ground. Fire Face was still reared up and pressing against the fence, shrieking with a war cry.

Pure mayhem.

Then Priceless Pete did what Priceless Pete was bred and trained to do. He bolted like the bell had just rung and the gates had flipped open. He hugged the fence line like it was the interior fence of a racetrack and took off with rare, gliding speed.

A super relieved farrier exclaimed, "We got a race! Alright! We got a race! Son of a gun!" He was thrilled that Priceless Pete hadn't re-engaged Fire Face, but rather did what his training had him do, which was run and run fast.

Fire Face, not knowing what Priceless Pete would do, didn't immediately react to the stallion sprinting up the fence line. Briefly, he just stared at the bolting stallion, but then a flash went through that equine mind, releasing a bottled-up competitive racing spirit.

Fire Face pivoted on his hind legs and crouched low on his hind quarters, ripping out hair from his mane and tail that was caught in the fence. He called up unknown loads of torque and leaped forward like a big African cat coming out of a crouch. Wads of white hair were left hanging on the fence.

Fire Face gave chase. His neck and head completely flattened out, like a javelin piercing the wind, which could offer no resistance. The thin grace of Priceless Pete, being chased by the brute that was Fire Face, looked like a gazelle being hunted by the king of the jungle.

As fast as Priceless Pete was and as effortlessly as his strides responded to his will, he was losing ground with each powerful leap of the closing predator.

"Go!" Doc screamed at the very top of his lungs as he climbed the fence and hung over.

Fire Face found his next gear, one Dean and Doc knew he had in him.

"Would you look at that?" the farrier said with exasperation. "I'll be."

It didn't take long for Fire Face to pull neck and neck with the world champion. But when the two were running even for just a few strides, something snapped inside of Fire Face. A rage overtook him. He hated that another horse dared to run with him. He let out another screech.

Fire Face violently threw his head, and if a horse could peel out, he did. It was a gear that no one had seen before in a horse.

Soil and grass kicked up with the introduction of more horsepower, and the big stallion exploded forward with such anger that the sheer power of the move shocked everyone who was watching. He wanted the lead, and he wanted it now.

In a blink of an eye, Fire Face was a length ahead and accelerating still. His huge, untamed tail flung over the fence line and smacked Priceless Pete in the nose.

The world champion threw his head back. His strides became jerky and unsure. Priceless Pete was in a labored gait, clunky, like a rusted machine running without oil.

It was over.

Priceless Pete slowed to a lope and then to a choppy trot while veering off to his left. It was over as quickly as it had begun. The kids roared with the victory.

Fire Face kept running. And then, as if to celebrate his knockout of the world champ, he jumped and bucked, jumped and bucked. Flying hooves of fury. He let out neighs, snorts, and screeches along the way. His dominance over the challenger was complete. He knew it. Priceless Pete knew it. Everyone on Wild Dog TV knew it, and the legend of Fire Face went viral.

* * *

After Rachel and Ben's testy exchange about the state of their deal, Rachel, Penelope, Flip, and Ben walked awkwardly together toward the trailer. They were completely unaware of the events that had just transpired.

As they neared the trailer, they were treated with quite the scene. About a half dozen ranch hands, including the farrier, were hiding themselves behind the manure spreader wearing little but their underwear. Whereas Doc and his friends were sitting like triumphant champions in the bed of the truck, drinking longneck root beers and cream sodas while rummaging through their loot of clothes, boots, and hats. Rachel, the two girls, and Ben stopped in their tracks.

"Ben," Rachel said, "are your workers wearing any clothes?"

Ben struggled to find any answer that made sense. "I don't know what to say."

"Look away," Rachel said to the two girls, and then she focused in on her son. "Doc, is there something you need to tell me?"

"Nothing comes to mind," Doc replied with a grin.

"To the victor go the spoils," J-Dog toasted.

* * *

RACHEL EXPLAINED PRIVATELY TO DOC THAT THE SAGA WITH FIRE Face wasn't over. The stallion was able to stay at the Fallow ranch for the meantime, but they would have to deal with the situation on their way back. But for now, all eyes were on Calexico, the last fuel stop before entering Mexico and Baja California.

"It just got real, boys," Doc said as he felt his racing juices beginning to flow the moment they pulled into the last gas station on the US side of the border.

Many of the international race teams had been in California and had been testing their engines in Death Valley for weeks, and now the migration south to the legendary race was in full swing.

"Dude!" J-Dog said as he joined Alfie in pointing toward the rows of incredible semi-trucks pulling huge trailers.

"Those rigs easily cost hundreds of thousands of dollars," Mac said.

The rigs were painted and waxed to perfected shines and proudly bore the colors of their nations. The high gloss paint jobs perfectly blended from semi-truck to trailer and showed all the makings of teams with deep financial pockets.

"Where's our semi-truck?" J-Dog asked defiantly. "We're Team USA for crying out loud. I want a parade."

Doc's high-octane mind instantly went through a myriad of deductions, and the conclusion was like a punch to the gut. "I don't know. They never even offered one," Doc said. "It seems I've missed something."

They saw the Germans, Brazilians, Chinese, and even the North Koreans, which had a big painting of their leader riding a missile on the trailer.

Jonah looked worried as he elbowed Mac. "Are they in a different division than us? Like a super professional division or something?"

"No," Doc responded in a flat tone, "there are no other divisions, Jonah. This is our class." After a moment, Doc postulated an answer. "I don't know what happened, but I'll take a guess. I refused to use the USJRA crew, and I chose you guys as my pit instead."

Jonah asked, "You didn't get all this stuff because of us?"

"That's my only answer," Doc replied.

It sank in for the kids that the Copper truck and trailer was going to be a little bit out of place.

"Sorry, Doc," Alfie said.

"Don't be. I had my reasons. I didn't know I was giving up all of this—" He paused to let it percolate a bit. "But I made the right call. We got this."

Doc slowly walked up to Rachel right before she began pumping fuel. He stepped in. "I'll pump it, Mom." Then he asked her a question that she knew was coming, "Are you seeing this?"

Rachel sighed a little. "Eventually, we were going to have to have this talk."

"What talk?"

"Your dad and I made a decision, Doc." She looked at all the huge racing rigs. "And I think it might have been the wrong decision."

"Mom?" Doc asked.

"It was the wrong decision because we made it for you. Not that the decision itself was wrong necessarily, but we should have included you in it. I'm so sorry."

Doc's head swirled a bit. "Alright, I forgive you for not allowing me to be in the talks. Can you now tell me what they were all about? Because I wasn't quite prepared to see what I'm looking at."

"Long story short, the USJRA didn't want to back a team who had a thirteen-year-old rider with his bunch of friends as the pit crew."

"I figured." Doc nodded but saw there was something more to it. "And?"

"Then they were out and out irate when the barn burned down and the racer was destroyed. When I told them about it, the USJRA wanted to pull you out of the Quad Continental altogether. They wanted to simply forfeit your position."

Doc's anger began to boil. "I won the right to race. I'm Team USA, and the rules say I can ride my four-wheeler."

"I know, Doc, but the Quad Continental is big business, evidently, with big sponsors. They told us that they had already lost fifty percent of their sponsors with a thirteen-year-old racing for Team USA with nothing but his buddies for the crew. Then, when the actual vehicle was destroyed, all the sponsors disappeared. Those sponsors were the ones that would have paid for all this fancy stuff." She pointed to all the other racing outfits. "They knew that they couldn't legally stop you from racing, but they decided that they didn't have to help you either."

Doc shook his head. "I don't even have the support of my own country?"

"Sweetie, look around you. Look at Mac, Jonah, Alfie, Penelope, Flip, and even J-Dog." She cracked a smile. "Money can't buy that, son. Wouldn't you rather go through something this big with your best friends than with people you barely know just looking to make a buck?"

Doc agreed, even though he knew it put him at a disadvantage. He smiled at his mom. "None of this happens without you and Dad."

Rachel smiled and hugged her boy. She had no idea how this race would turn out, but she loved how her boy was turning out. "Let's not forget about the Lord either," Rachel said. "I think He may be more involved in this than we sometimes think."

Doc chuckled. "I think we are going to need Him involved in this."

* * *

RACHEL TURNED TO THE KIDS WHO WERE GATHERED IN THE PARKing lot. "Everyone, listen up. We are about to cross into Mexico, and I want everyone in the front with me."

The kids followed orders, and they packed into the truck cabin like sardines.

Rachel continued, "Get your passports out, and no one says anything unless I tell you to speak." She looked directly at J-Dog. "I will leave you in Mexico if you test me on this."

"What happens next?" Penelope asked.

"I'm not exactly sure, but when we get to the border, we'll be stopped, questioned, and probably searched a little. Then they will stamp our passports and let us on through. It shouldn't be a big deal."

She fired up the rig and headed toward the border.

As they kept driving south through the town of Calexico, the streets began to change. The crowds got bigger. The buildings, the signs, and the language also changed.

"Mom," Doc asked, "when do we actually cross the border?"

Rachel was a bit confused herself. "I'm not sure. Probably right up here. It's got to be close." She looked up. "Yep, this must be the border here."

A small, badly used 100cc motorcycle carrying a family of four passed right by Rachel's window, nearly clipping her rearview mirror.

"Woah," Rachel reacted, "that's not safe."

"This isn't America," Mac said as he looked out the window.

Rachel shook her head. "Yes, it is. We haven't crossed a border. We're still in . . ."

The traffic in the streets became very dense. Identifiable traffic patterns ceased. Lanes were not even suggested. Motorcycles were weaving in and out of traffic at dangerous clips, and some motorcycles even used sidewalks whenever they saw fit.

"*Uno momento, por favor*," J-Dog said and pointed at some road signs. "Unless those are English words I just don't know, this is Mexico."

"Where was the border?" Rachel asked. "Was that small, tiny fence the border?"

Jonah leaned forward from the back seat and pointed to some sort of Mexican military or police presence a few crowded blocks ahead. "What's up there?"

"So, let me get this right," Doc said. "We didn't even see the US border, and this is the Mexican border patrol a few blocks after we are already in Mexico? This makes no sense. Unless," Doc said, "no one cares about the border."

Rachel was about to reach a few of the Mexican military personnel ahead. "Sit back and let me do the talking."

As Rachel drove up, she rolled down her window and put on a friendly smile. She kept slowing and slowing, but no one indicated she should stop. She just rolled through whatever checkpoint it was.

"They're just letting us by," Jonah said with surprise.

"You have got to be kidding me," Rachel said under her breath.

The Copper truck and trailer was never stopped, at any point in time, by any governmental authority when going from the US to Mexico.

"That was non-eventful," J-Dog said.

"I guess we're on to Cabo San Lucas," Doc said.

"Guess so," Rachel replied, "I'll tell you what. I've been to eighteen countries, and this is the first time I've never been stopped crossing a border."

* * *

THE DRIVE IN BAJA CHANGED DOC'S DEMEANOR. THE BUTTERFLIES in his stomach began to flutter. Not in a fearful way, but they came with the promise of racing. His eyes tightened with intensity, and every passing thought was now only on the race at hand.

The gang followed suit. They took their cue from Doc, and they no longer acted like rowdy best friends on the road trip of their life. They were now vital cogs in a machine that was pursuing the Quad Continental world championship.

In a slight change, all the kids were riding in the trailer, even Penelope and Flip, and truth be told, the boys kind of liked the company.

"I know you saw the other teams and what they had," Doc said, relaying to the gang all that his mom had explained to him. "It stinks. It doesn't seem fair, but we're not promised fair in this life. So, simply put," he finished, "we're Team USA, but no one up there thought we were worth a dime, literally. We're the team that no one wanted. We're the team who was asked to quit, and we're up against the best racers in the world, racing the best machines, perfectly tuned for the desert. They have professional pit crews and the best racing tech money can buy. Because of that, we were told to quit as not to embarrass us, the USJRA, or the country."

Penelope put her hand over her heart. "I feel like writing a strongly worded letter."

"It won't even be opened," Flip whispered. "They don't think we can win."

Doc agreed, "You're right, Flip. So how shall we move forward? We can either prove that they were right, or we prove that they were wrong."

J-Dog took his hat off and scratched his head. "If you're saying what I think you're saying, Doc, then you're about to say that we're in it to win it."

"You got that straight," Doc replied.

J-Dog leaned forward. "Doc, I've seen you win every race you've ever been in, but this one is different, and you know it. *The Drakon* is simply outgunned. How can you possibly win this one?"

"I hear you, J-Dog," Doc said, "and oddly enough, you are pragmatically correct with your concerns. To say that the odds are stacked against us is an understatement. To say that we have one in a million chance to win probably gives us the benefit of the doubt. However, you know I've been working on a plan, one that takes into consideration *The Drakon's* shortcomings. I've calculated our average speed, their average speed, pit stops, driver fatigue, everything." He paused.

"And?" the gang asked.

"Winning isn't complicated," Doc said. "In fact, it's painfully simple. Emphasis on *painfully*."

"You're killing me," Mac said. "Spill it."

Doc replied, "For us to win this thing, we have to iron butt it."

The whole gang looked around at each other waiting for a punchline or something to make sense of what they had just heard.

After a few blank stares and seconds of silence, Jonah was the first to address it. "Did you say 'iron butt?' I feel like I should know what that means, but I really don't."

"Yeah, Doc," J-Dog replied, "I, too, find myself oddly unaware of this said iron butt."

"Iron anything is good," Mac smiled.

"Iron butt means we never stop. Never pit. It's one thousand miles, open throttle, the whole way. Our butts never get a rest."

Eyes darted back and forth between the kids to see if everyone else thought the idea was as crazy as they did.

Jonah whispered to J-Dog, "Did Doc take something?" He then looked at Doc. "You know that white powder stuff they were carrying over the border wasn't sugar."

"I'm with Jonah," Mac said. "Where's the punchline."

"No punchline," Doc said. "I had a local guy back in Bell Buckle modify a set of tires. They're not quite steel radials, but that's the idea. He did it on a quick turnaround. Hope they work, and if they do, we won't be swapping tires out. But they're heavy, and we'll burn more gas."

"No stops for oil changes?" J-Dog asked. "Filters and other stuff?"

"It's a Honda engine. As bulletproof as they come. In saying that, though, this race will be the swan song for *The Drakon*. We're sacrificing it on the altar of the quad. We'll burn the engine out and hope it makes it to the finish line."

"How long will it take to finish the race?" Penelope asked.

"Based on past winners, we need to get in under twenty-five hours."

Stunned silence hit the crew, and shock riddled Mac's face.

Jonah raised his finger. "Twenty-five hours, one thousand miles long, and you don't want to stop? Well, Doc, what about gas?" he asked. "Unless you have a magic infinity tank, you're going to need gas."

"That does need to be addressed," Doc acknowledged. "I've got a plan."

Mac fake-coughed. "Not to be the overly reasonable one of the team, but I've been wondering, where exactly am I supposed to be sitting for an entire day of racing? Because your four-wheeler is kind of built for one." Mac pulled out the owner's manual for *The Drakon* and waved it in the air. "See?" He pointed at it. "It says right here."

"That's where it gets interesting," Doc said as he looked out the windows. "Let's pick all that up tomorrow. We are pulling into San Felipe now."

The gang glued themselves to the windows as they watched in awe as San Felipe hopped with activity with the scores of international teams pulling in. San Felipe was the obvious layover before the final haul to Cabo San Lucas, the starting line of the Quad Continental.

* * *

AFTER A GOOD BREAKFAST THE NEXT MORNING, THE GANG LOADED themselves into the Copper rig for the last leg of the trip. That night, Lord willing, Rachel would roll them into the southern tip of Baja California, the starting line for the most aggressive, grueling, and demanding off-road desert race in the world.

Doc sat in the gooseneck of the trailer with his legs dangling off the edge and everyone else seated below. "Once we arrive tonight, we will have one day of rest and race prep."

"The racing part," Mac said. "Still waiting to hear about that."

"Yep," Doc replied. "This is how we do it."

"Finally," J-Dog remarked. "I've been waiting for the rabbit to be pulled out of the hat."

Doc turned to Mac. "This *should* take care of you." He reached behind him and pulled a collection of stuff down from the gooseneck.

"I took the passenger seat and the passenger footpegs from my dad's enduro motorcycle. I also harvested the handlebars off of my old bicycle and I had one of my dad's friends, who has a welding shop in town, create a skeletal structure for all of these components. So, now all we need to do is assemble it."

"It sounds like Bell Buckle chipped in to get this done in time," Jonah surmised.

"They did." Doc replied. "We may not have a country behind us, but we sure do have a town behind us."

Alfie's eyes widened. "It's going to look weird."

"It may look unorthodox, but it should do the trick," Doc replied.

"That's a lot of jerry-rigging, Doc," Jonah added skeptically.

Doubt washed over J-Dog's face. "We're attaching those handlebars and foot pegs off the back end of *The Drakon*? It's going to look like he's riding a pogo stick back there with a weird little seat."

Mac wasn't buying it. "It *should* work? That's your solution for me? For one thousand miles?"

"It will be attached to the frame of *The Drakon*. The seat is good, and I'm certain it will stay in place. That's not the problem. The problem is that you're kind of, sort of . . ."

"What?" Mac yelled.

"Seated right at the exhaust." Doc confessed.

Mac tilted his head and slowly asked, "Isn't that hot?"

"Scalding, I'm afraid."

Mac blinked a few times. "I know that I don't feel pain, but I'd rather not deep fry my skin, again." He waved his hands as if the kids needed a reminder of the barn fire.

Doc nodded, "I thought of that in advance, and I think I got a fix."

"Do tell," Mac replied.

"I've pounded out an aluminum piece of sheet metal that I'm using as a heatshield. I already fitted it under your seat. So that will block the heat from going through the seat and into you. Look."

Mac flipped the seat over. "Okay, that's a little something, but where's the heatshield for my legs?"

Doc gave an exaggerated nod. "I admit, that threw me a curve ball at first. I almost attempted to reroute the exhaust all together, but then Fire Face bailed us out."

None of the kids understood that one.

Jonah asked incredulously, "How did Fire Face bail us out?"

"When we looted the ranch hands at the Priceless Pete smackdown," Doc said as he turned around and grabbed the Farrier's leather chaps that they had won. He chucked them at Mac in a big, wadded ball.

THWAP! They hit Mac in the chest. "You wear these," Doc said.

Mac looked at them with disgust. "No. Noo. Noooo. You're out of your mind if you think I'm wearing these."

J-Dog doubled over, laughing uncontrollably.

Mac pointed at J-Dog and continued to protest, "J-Dog gets it! You got me riding on a pogo stick in a pair of leather chaps! I'm going to look like a circus act!"

Doc raised both his hands. "Mac, I know it's not ideal, but quite frankly, I'm glad we have 'em. I was out of ideas."

Jonah tried to console Mac. "There's just one simple question to consider. How much do you want skin grafts?"

Mac's face crinkled in a relented acceptance as he inspected the chaps. "This is just great."

Doc hopped down from the gooseneck. "Now, let's start building this thing."

* * *

It took a couple of hours, but the boys finished attaching the steel brackets and mounting the seating apparatus for Mac on the back of *The Drakon.*

"Sit on it," Jonah said to Mac, who reluctantly climbed onto what the boys had affectionately nicknamed the pogo stick. He tested it by bouncing, jumping, and throwing his weight around on it. "Funny enough, it's not half bad."

Alfie pointed at his feet. "Don't let your feet hit the tires."

Mac looked down. His toes were about three inches away from the back tires of *The Drakon*. "Thanks for the tip."

Doc was pleased. "We're getting there." He then pulled out a smartphone mount with a swing arm that he had modified to fit an iPad Pro. He attached it to the center of Mac's bicycle handlebars and fastened the iPad to it.

"This iPad is satellite enabled," Doc explained. "It won't hit dead spots like cellular."

"Sweet," Mac replied.

"I've loaded the most advanced GPS software available, including weather overlays, topographical data, you name it." He clicked it, and a little ATV emoji popped up. "See? That's us."

"What is it tracking, exactly?" Mac asked.

"The GPS tracker is in the flap of my right boot." Doc said. "As long as my foot stays attached, then it's accurate within nine feet of us."

Doc went to the tack box and opened it up, dumping out palm-sized boxes. About twenty of them. He opened one up and pulled out some sort of tech device.

"What's that?" Alfie asked.

"This is about you," Doc said.

Alfie sat up interested.

"These are signal boosters for your remote control on your drone. You can daisy chain them together to extend the range of your drone from where you are."

"That's awesome," Alfie said.

"Yes, but there is a cost, and a decision that has to be made."

"What is it?" Alfie said.

"Theoretically, with enough of these boosters, you could control your drone halfway around the world. However, you don't have the battery power in your drone to operate indefinitely."

"I see," Alfie said. "If the truck is too far away from my drone, it won't have the battery power to make it back to me."

"Correct. You'll lose your drone in this race."

"I understand."

"Okay, then," Doc said. "The decision is where to put the drone. Since it doesn't have the battery power to fly above us the whole race, we need to decide when and where we need it."

"How do we decide that?" Alfie asked.

"I think we need it toward the beginning. That's when there will be the most racers and probably when there will be the most danger. We'll need eyes in the sky during that time the most."

Doc walked to the cooler and got out root beers and cream sodas for everyone. They all popped the longneck bottles and drank.

"Now, this is how we win this race."

* * *

"THERE IS A RULE BOOK, BUT FOR THE MOST PART IT'S NOT ENFORCED all that much. There are only three major rules that they really care about. The first is that we cannot modify our vehicle to boost our horsepower to above the racing allowance. *The Drakon*, though, is so woefully underpowered in that regard, we couldn't break that rule even if we wanted to. We could pump the whole thing full of NOS, and still not have more horsepower than the bigger UTVs."

"Wow," Alfie said, "we're so lucky."

"Two," Doc said, "we must stay off the roads until we enter Tijuana and cross back into the United States for the finish line near San Diego."

"We can't just hit a highway, and open it up?" Mac said.

"Right, no streets of any kind before Tijuana," Doc confirmed. "And three: there are two major checkpoints all racers must pass through, but there is no pre-defined route to those points."

"What do you mean? There is no course?" Alfie asked.

"Correct. There is no course. It's a free-for-all. As long as we stay off roads, we can go where we want. The rules even allow us to ride through private property, but that is at our own risk, if you get my drift."

"Racing anarchy. I love it," J-Dog said.

"More than you know, J-Dog," Doc explained. "This is the most dangerous race in the world. It's not just the desert that can stop you; the other racers do."

"Explain that," Mac asked.

"The Quad Continental is notorious for collisions," Doc said. "Teams will try to crash us out. You may have heard that bumping is racing? In the Quad, running your competitor off a cliff is racing."

Mac looked at the pogo stick and his chaps. "This just keeps getting better."

"Don't worry, Mac. I can handle that. What we need to worry about is our fuel situation. Our entire race hinges on the fact that we have a two-point-seven gallon tank. The fact we'll be running heavy and with a wide-open throttle and no tune-ups along the way means our miles per gallon is downright awful. I'm counting on ten miles per gallon with the way we're going to be riding. That means, in our current situation, we are filling up every twenty-seven miles."

"Doc, I know you're a math genius," J-Dog said, "but that is like *a lot* of fuel stops. You said you wanted *zero* fuel stops. By my calculations, your math is off."

Doc walked over to a long, plastic cylinder jug that was sitting in a corner and picked it up. "This is called a dump can. Racers from every level use this at pit stops to fill up their stock cars, motorcycles, trophy trucks, whatever."

"How big is it?" Mac asked.

"Four gallons, but I filled it with exactly two point seven gallons of racing fuel. That huge tarp on top of this trailer is covering thirty-nine more. That should give us a few to spare."

"You were thinking ahead," Mac said.

J-Dog smiled and raised a root beer. "That's our Doc."

"Check it out! We got a plan!" Jonah squealed. "Now, as I see it, if we're placing these dump cans out in the desert every twenty-seven miles, then the pit crew needs a head start."

Alfie raised his head. "You probably want me to put the drone boosters at the dump cans."

"Exactly," Doc said.

"Where do you want the drone."

"Plant the drone near the starting line. You can launch it from there."

"Roger that," Alfie said.

"Now," Doc began before explaining the rest of the strategy.

* * *

Rachel and the gang would drop off Doc and Mac in Cabo San Lucas. They would then drive precisely twenty-seven miles and would place the dump cans at locations along with energy bars and drinking water.

"Wait," Jonah asked, "how do we know where to place 'em? You said there is no course."

"Right you are," Doc replied as he flipped open his laptop. "Jonah, I'm air dropping you a file now."

Jonah opened his laptop. "Got it. What is it?"

"I created our own GPS route for the race," Doc explained. "You guys follow that route, and then put a dump can exactly, and I mean exactly, on each of those pins. They are spaced out precisely at twenty-seven miles. Then, you message Mac and describe where you put it. Meaning, is it next to a big rock, a shrub, a cactus, is it in the middle of nothing, whatever."

"Check it out!" Jonah squealed.

"Now, guys, those dump cans have got to be placed in a location where Mac can reach down and grab them without us even slowing down. We're doing this on the fly."

* * *

It was now about two o'clock in the morning, and Rachel's exhaustion was real. She needed to cash it in and get some sleep. But as she looked around, she realized that this wasn't the time or place for that. "What is this?" she asked herself as she pulled the rig onto the dirt road located a dozen or so miles north of Cabo San Lucas.

The Quad Continental wasn't launching from the resort area of Cabo San Lucas with beaches, hotels, and BnBs. The starting line was north of the city in the harsh, untamed, and sandy terrain, and what she saw there was a tent city with thousands of people who had come from all around the world. "There's got to be at least fifty thousand people here, maybe more," Rachel said aghast. "This is unreal."

In this temporary city, there were makeshift booths, and generators rumbled as they powered LED lights that lit up the night. There seemed to be hundreds of floats, like those seen in a parade. But these floats celebrated the unearthly, mythical, and grotesque. There were giant art sculptures of every kind. Some took forms that could be recognized; others were so abstract as to not resemble anything at all.

People were walking around dressed in disturbing attire. Some like Vikings, some like vampires with capes and head dresses. Hair was any color but natural. Clothes were anything but modest.

"That guy is not wearing hardly anything," she said to herself and instinctively looked at the girls asleep in the seats next to her and behind her. "Oh, my gosh," she said as she saw a giant wooden statue of some humanoid-like form and people surrounding it partying hard into the desert night. "This is pure hedonism!" She shook her head as her motherly, protective instincts pushed forward, front and center. "This is supposed to be a junior race." She slowed even more and looked closer at this tent city. "What in the world is this?"

She slowed the dually to a roll, maybe five miles per hour, as she followed the makeshift dirt road which she believed was heading to the desert staging area for all the international race teams.

She tilted her head out the window and turned her gaze downward. Used needles, bottles, and drug paraphernalia covered the ground. Police were conspicuously absent. What she was witnessing was the human spirit, void of moral direction, completely untamed, unbound, and unrestrained.

Slowly, she made her way through the hordes of people. She rolled up her windows because they had started to move toward the truck. Their hands were now touching the hood, and their stoned faces were trying to look inside to find out who was coming.

"Just keep going," Rachel said. "Don't stop."

But then she had to stop. A young woman, wearing weird strips of rags as clothing, lay completely incapacitated in the middle of the road.

"Geez," Rachel gasped as she hit the brakes. Rachel's eyes popped out as she stared at the mess in front of her. She could easily have run the woman over.

It took a few moments, but bystanders saw the situation, and in a fit of laughter, they carried the woman off the road, waving at Rachel as if she was of a kindred kind.

Rachel whispered to herself, "This is not what we signed up for." She began moving forward again.

Rachel's heart continued to sink. She wasn't ready for this environment. Dean had told her of the mistake he once made by riding his motorcycle to Sturgis for the big biker rally. When he arrived, all he found was revelry, debauchery, and drunken depravity. That was the conversation that came to mind as she drove down this dirt road.

"Not good, not good, not good," she whispered.

Confusion and dread seized her. This was a junior race. How did the adults allow this? Is this what the Quad Continental always was? How was this not public information? How did she now know about any of this?

Rachel knew the plan was to let Doc and Mac camp in a tent for a night as she drove to drop the fuel off at the needed locations. This environment, though, changed everything, and the deeper she drove in, the sicker it became.

* * *

JONAH WOKE UP TO THE UNEXPECTED WORLD OUTSIDE. "WHERE are we?" he said to himself as he looked around at the mobs. "Hey, guys, you've got to see this."

It was easy for them to wake up. The sounds emanating from the parties outside were growing loud and more raucous at each turn. Doc and Mac crawled down from the gooseneck to see Jonah, Alfie, and J-Dog looking out the slats of the trailer and seeing things they should never see.

These people had less respect for themselves than for the trash they allowed to pile up in the desert. Suddenly, fireworks were shot up into night sky, and the light emitted gave glimpses of the breadth and depth of this modern Sodom and Gomorrah.

Most of the racers were also out that night, partaking in everything the bacchanal had to offer. Doc recognized many of the drivers, and none seemed to care that they had a thousand-mile race launching in under thirty-six hours.

The Slovakian team had a Ford Raptor truck brilliantly painted with their flag. It pulled up next to the Copper truck and trailer. The bed of that truck was packed with people. They were waving their flag and shouting. Teenage girls, wearing nothing but the tiniest bikinis, were already intoxicated and were starting to pass around drugs. All out in the open.

"This place must have the same mayor as San Francisco," J-Dog mused.

Doc was staring at the girls. "Swimsuit designers are the dumbest people in the world."

"Why is that?" Mac asked.

"Because they run out of ideas on what to cover so quickly," Doc replied.

Just then, the Ford Raptor peeled out without notice, nearly fishtailing into the Copper trailer. One of the drunk girls fell out of the back of the bed and smashed onto the desert floor. The boys gasped but didn't say anything. Some screams came from the people, but the partying just got harder.

Finally, Rachel made it to the pit area for the racing teams. She found the spot marked for Team USA and pulled in. It was less rambunctious here. The tent city didn't quite merge into this area, but its sights and sounds were still on display.

* * *

ONCE RACHEL PARKED THE TRUCK, SHE NUDGED FLIP AND Penelope. She was so grateful they had slept through that last portion of the ride. "Stay here," she said to them, and then she walked back to the trailer to wake the boys.

"Great," Rachel said sarcastically when she saw they were already awake. "Just great."

The boys filed out of the trailer and the gang congregated around the bed of the truck.

"Alright," Rachel said, "I'm guessing you saw all of that?"

The gang was quieter than usual, but they nodded while they processed what they witnessed.

Rachel gathered herself as best as she could. "I want you to know that I never would have brought you here if I knew this was the direction that the Quad Continental went."

"Never would have brought us," Doc repeated, understanding exactly where his mom was going.

"Correct, Doc. I was naïve," she responded. "I never thought a junior event would be so . . . adult." She paused to collect her thoughts. "What you are seeing is exactly what we've tried to shelter you from.

We are trying to raise you so that when you're older, you can see this for what it is: mankind's depravity."

Doc understood, and he already put two and two together, but he still needed to ask, "What happens next, Mom?"

"Right now, I want you all to get some sleep. Make sure the trailer is locked down. You all have headphones, wear them. Don't leave the trailer until I get you in the morning. The girls will sleep with me up in the truck. Tomorrow morning, we'll regroup and discuss next steps."

* * *

Somber and quiet, the boys climbed back into the trailer, but they didn't go to bed like Rachel said. They lined up next to the slats in the trailer and stared into the masses.

They slid open the windows, and they allowed the sounds of nauseous partying into their trailer and into their ears. The desert brought a cool, even chilly breeze, but it was nothing refreshing.

Their entire view was filled with dancing, shouting, drinking, stumbling, falling, and vomiting. The distinct aroma of drugs wafted into their trailer. The sights, sounds, and smells were a sensual assault on the boys.

J-Dog quipped as he looked at all those people. "Talk about the caboose end of the bell-shaped curve."

"Have you ever seen anything like this?" Doc asked.

"I have," Mac replied. "Where I used to live. Every weekend, you could see people stumbling on the streets. Drug dealers, hookers, drunks, drag queens. You name it."

"Really?" Alfie asked.

"Yep," Mac replied with a blank face, "things you can't unsee, man. My aunt used to come over and say she was sorry I had to grow up so fast."

"What did your dad do?" Jonah asked.

"He was out there with them."

J-Dog brushed it off. "They're freaks, man. They're weirdos and wackos. Without them, normal doesn't look normal. It's because of them we look so good."

Doc softly spoke, "What if we're the ones who are different? What if they're normal, and we're the outliers?"

"Say what?" Alfie asked.

"Just saying," Doc replied. "What if this is what we're walking into? What if the world we know isn't the world that is?"

"Hmm, hmm," Jonah's low gospel voice hummed. "Grandma used to say the gutters were getting wider than the streets."

"This is all gutter," Doc replied.

Jonah turned and tapped Doc on the chest. "But she would poke me, and say, 'In the darkness, the light shines the brightest.'"

* * *

THE NEXT MORNING CAME FAST. THE DAY BEFORE WAS LONG, AND the night was late. Doc stared at the ceiling of the trailer while lying in the gooseneck. It was seven-thirty, but it felt like five o'clock.

Mac, J-Dog, Jonah, and Alfie were still asleep.

Doc slid down from the gooseneck and moved to the side gate of the trailer. He opened it quietly, but it still clanked as he pushed it wide. He stepped out onto the side rail, and he felt the morning breeze, which felt good this time.

The rising sun was beautiful over the distant desert, and the sky was a piercing blue. But then he lowered his gaze and looked upon the tent city and the domain of man. The night of raucous partying had left a wake of stressed-out faces and used up bodies.

Instantly, Doc missed Tennessee. He missed the cleanness of the farm—the simple peace of the hayfield as the alfalfa swayed with the wind. He missed how each morning brought the excitement of a new day and not the hangover from the last.

He looked at the people passed out on the ground and wondered at what point in their life everything had gone wrong. Was it one tipping point? Or a gradual decline, inch by inch? He remembered his grandfather teaching him that evil was like a camel. If a camel's nose slips into a tent, it is only matter of time before the whole camel follows.

Doc heard a loud thump come from behind him. He turned around and saw that Jonah had finally pushed Mac off the blow-up mattress.

"Ugh," Mac groaned. The thump and grunt started to wake up the rest of the gang. Mac slowly climbed to his feet. "I guess I'm up." He looked and saw Doc on the rail outside and decided to join him.

"Look at the desert. They trashed it," Doc said to Mac as he leaned his head outside the gate.

Mac wiped his eyes. "They always do."

"It sounds like you know from experience," Doc said.

"Yep," Mac replied, and then he opened up in a way Doc didn't see coming. "My dad started calling me Mac long before I can even remember. He said it was short for my real name."

Doc listened and asked, "What's your real name?"

Mac kind of chuckled and was lighthearted about it all. "Michelob."

"Michelob?" Doc couldn't help but laugh. "Your name is Michelob Irons?"

"Yeah," Mac replied in his abrupt choppy way. "My dad had a problem."

Doc shook his head. "Shouldn't he have called you Mick then, instead of Mac?"

"Sure," Mac replied, "but I learned early on never to expect a drunk to make sense."

"How bad was he?" Doc asked.

Mac paused a bit. "You know, it was when he started beating me that I found out it didn't really hurt. At first, I thought it didn't hurt because he only hit me with his left hand."

"He really beat you?"

"Yep."

"With his left hand?"

"Yep."

"Was he lefthanded?"

"Nope."

Mac's demeanor was simply funny, even though the story was sad, and Doc kept chuckling. "Well, why did he beat you with his left hand?"

Mac nodded. "Because his right hand was his drinking hand."

Doc shook his head slowly. It was a sad story, but Mac had recalled it like it was just a normal part of this crazy thing called life. "Well," Doc said, "how's your dad doing now?"

"Dead."

Doc didn't say anything. He just waited.

Mac didn't laugh anymore. "He was drunk. He ran his truck into a telephone poll on the side of a country road."

That cut Doc to the core. He was instantly sorry for ever giving Mac a hard time about anything or thinking ill of him in any way. He reached out, put his hand on his shoulder, squeezed, and let go.

About five minutes went by as the boys stood there looking out at the sea of people who were still dazed by the depravity of the night before.

Mac finally broke the silence. "A man lives or dies by the choices he makes. That's what my dad taught me, whether he meant to or not."

Doc appreciated that pearl of wisdom, and then something in the distance caught Doc's eye. It was smoke. "Do you see that?"

Mac nodded, "Someone set a fire."

"I think they lit that big wooden structure. Remember that thing we passed last night?"

"I do," Mac said, "they were dancing around it like it was their temple."

Flames engulfed the dry wood human-like structure, and smoke billowed into the sky. About that time, crowds of people awoke from their slumber and began surrounding the burning structure.

"That's one of the most amazing things I've ever seen," Doc said.

That took Mac by surprise. "Really, why?"

"Look at everything. It's like something out of the Bible."

Mac had no idea where Doc was going with this. "How so?"

"Right there before us is a picture of mankind." Doc pointed at the scores of hungover, still drunk, and drugged up people. "If you live like this, then you'll end up like that." He pointed at the burning man.

"Dude, that's profound," Mac replied.

"It's right before their eyes. They lit the fire, yet don't even see it."

"Just like my dad," Mac replied. "He could never see anything before it was too late."

Doc then told Mac his grandfather's story of the camel and how, once it got his nose in the tent, it was just a matter of time before the whole camel was in the tent.

Doc paused and waited for Mac to say something. It took a few seconds but finally Mac replied, "I guess we know what we got to do."

"What's that?" Doc asked.

"Kill the camel."

* * *

Soon enough, Rachel, Penelope, and Flip were awake, and they climbed out of the cab of the truck and walked to where the boys waited at the tail end of the trailer, just staring at the tent city and the inexplicable burning man effigy.

"Hey, guys, how'd you sleep?" Rachel asked.

"Alright, all things considered," Doc replied.

"That is what we need to talk about. The all-things-considered part." Rachel let out a deep sigh.

J-Dog kicked the desert sand beneath his boots. "That's a bad sign. Whenever adults start using language like 'we need to talk,' it's bad for us."

Rachel continued, "I spoke with everyone's parents this morning and with your aunt, Mac. I explained to them what we drove into, and I apologized for putting you in that position."

Flip was sitting cross-legged on the ground with her head down. Her usual jovial self was gone. "It's not your fault, Mrs. Copper."

"But your well-being is my responsibility, and I'm just so sorry that you saw what you saw."

"Mom," Doc said with a somber tone, "what are you saying?"

Rachel responded, "I'm getting us out of here. We can't be a part of what the Quad Continental has become. Or maybe it has always been this, but we just didn't know."

Doc felt a gut punch. He dropped his eyes to the ground, put his hands on top of his head, and turned around. The kids were stunned, and Mac took it as hard as Doc.

Mac let out an angry growl. He was fighting on the inside, but was keeping it in.

"Mac, are you okay?" Rachel asked.

Mac shook his head and waved off the question.

Doc's eyes reddened. His whole life was being jerked from him. His work, his goals, his pursuits. He needed to race; it was breathing for him. His life didn't make sense without it.

He then thought about his dad, how he almost died in the barn fire, and all that they had lost. This race was a chance to do something, despite it all. His tears were being fought back, and a fighting spirit began to rise.

"Mom. No. Please don't do this."

Rachel's heart was breaking for her son. "Doc, I know this is the goal of your young life, but I am thinking of the rest of your life. This is no place for you."

"Mom. *No*!" he shouted. "Our barn is burnt. Dad almost died. We fought through that, and we made it here. We can fight through this, too."

Rachel understood so deeply this side of Doc, and her compassion was with him. "Doc, listen to me, Sweetie. There will be other races."

"This is the Quad Continental! This is *the race*!"

"I understand, but some things are more important."

Doc didn't respond. He knew the point his mom was making.

"You guys don't need to be a part of this," Rachel continued. "What you saw last night does nothing but hurt you. There are lines that need to be drawn in this life."

Rachel was heartbroken to see the sadness that engulfed the kids. She knew this would just be the beginning. The ride to Mexico had been brimming with the promise of something great, but the ride home would be the realization of much that was lost.

* * *

In utter silence, the gang loaded up the trailer. The girls sat up front with Rachel, but the boys wanted to ride in the trailer. The trailer had become their home, and it's where they belonged.

Rachel watched in the mirror as Doc climbed on the rail, but before he went in through the side gate, he turned. "Mom?"

"Yes, Sweetie?" Rachel replied from behind the wheel.

"The starting line," he said. "Do you think I can go see it? I just want to stand on it. That's all."

The starting line was at the end of the dirt road, positioned on the northern end of the pit crews.

"Of course," she agreed.

Rachel drove slowly down the desert path. The tent city was in her rear-view mirror, and the international racing teams now flanked her on both sides.

Doc hung on the outside of the trailer and didn't think his heart could break anymore, but it did as he passed the other teams that had come. The country flags lined the runway. Each nation had specially tailored uniforms and gear that proudly boasted their national colors. Their crews were out hustling and bustling all around for final preps before the race. This side looked familiar; this side looked appropriate.

Doc whispered to himself, "I wish we would have seen this first."

Each team had proper audio systems, and many of the teams turned them on now that the morning had come and the work had begun. Each was blaring news and music from their home countries, while the thunder of racing engines began to fill the air as the many technicians studied their diagnostics one last time.

Doc couldn't help but smile a bit when he saw the South American pit crews busy at work while rival soccer matches popped up between the nations' racers. The central American teams were quick to join them in the world's pastime.

The Europeans had the poshest of outfits, with hundreds of thousands of dollars evident in the rigs, equipment, and professional personnel. The European teams were the odds-on favorites to finish high in the event with the British team being the pre-race favorite. As the European pit crews worked furiously on last minute adjustments, the Euro drivers and navigators relaxed in front of flat screens with all the luxuries that vast resources could offer.

The Australians were stuck next to the Europeans, and they were getting away with insulting the rugby traditions of the British. Chants of "Aussie, Aussie, Aussie!" broke out periodically, which seemed to promise that someone would eventually get punched.

The Asian contingent were all work, no play. Diligent, stressed, and agitated to make things perfect for the honor of name, family, and country. Busy and fast, the techs scurried back and forth in the pit areas. Their pits were clean and organized. Doc thought they would need to be taken seriously in the race.

The African continent was represented by over two dozen nations. None of them had the funding of the Europeans, but nationalistic pride came with them. Those nations were newer to the high expense, high tech desert racing, but were catching up faster than some pundits thought they would.

The Canadian team had all the gear and tech of the Europeans but were lower keyed and seemed generally content. Not overly enthused, just an easy-going bunch. They were going to be fine whether they won or lost, just like in any other sporting event Canadians were in, save perhaps curling and ice hockey.

Doc saw the greatest racers and racing teams in the world, and he knew it. He was counted as one of them, and more than anything in his life, he wanted his chance to test himself against the best the world had to offer. He was driven by challenge, driven by the size of the obstacle in front of him, and now, he'd never know exactly how good he could have been.

Rachel began to slow as she reached the end of the dirt road. She stopped the truck and trailer ten feet from the starting line and the giant banner that read, "The Quad Continental."

On the other side of the starting line, all manner of civilization ended. It was a barren landscape for as far as the eye could see. A more foreboding race for juniors would be impossible to imagine.

She killed the diesel engine, and the kids slowly funneled out of the truck and trailer.

Doc walked to the starting line, bent down, and scooped up a palmful of the coarse sand, running it through his fingers.

"Was I good enough?" he whispered.

* * *

DOC SLOWLY WALKED BACK TO THE TRAILER AS HIS BUDDIES watched. Mac didn't even want to go up to the line. For him, missing this race meant missing the chance at a better future, and the more he saw, the more it hurt.

Alfie was leaning against the bed of the truck. "Maybe talking about it may help," he said as Doc walked back.

"What do you mean?" Doc asked.

Alfie lifted up his iPad. "Tell your story."

J-Dog piped up, "Wild Dog has been rooting for you. They're all behind you; we all are. If you don't tell them how this ends, it will be like kicking a puppy."

Jonah added, "Get it off your chest. Don't hold this in. You need to do it for you." Jonah put his arm around Doc. "And honestly, we all need this. We stand together as one."

J-Dog added, "Through the ups, and downs."

"Through thick and thin," Alfie added.

"On mountain peaks and through valley depths," Penelope added.

"The bood and the gad," Flip squinted her eyes. "I mean the good and the bad."

Doc motioned the gang toward him and then looked at Mac who was standing at the rear of the trailer by himself. "Get over here, brother. This is about you, too."

Mac slowly walked to them. "I'm here."

Doc nodded. "Let's do this."

"Mrs. Copper," Alfie said, "will you hold this, please? We all need to be in the shot."

Rachel smiled at the realization that she had just been roped into being an accomplice. "Sure, Alfie."

* * *

THE BELL BUCKLE GANG STOOD UNDER THE BANNER AT THE STARTing line of the Quad Continental. The journey had made them closer than friends; they were family, and it showed. Doc stood in the center, ready to speak.

J-Dog launched the stream. "This is J-Dog Dynamite. Welcome to the Wild Dog. We are live from Mexico at the Quad Continental. Now, before we start, I want to give a special shout out to Rachel Copper, our newest member of the crew."

Rachel winced incredulously, but then again, how could she be surprised? She bit her tongue.

J-Dog continued, "This is my best friend, the racer you know, the best in the land, Doc Copper." The kids stood there with all their arms over each other's shoulders.

"Good morning," an uncertain Doc responded. Rachel could see the fear in Doc, and she felt it, too. This uncertainty was new to him. He didn't know how to deal with the disappointment, let alone how to tell the world about it. It was a moment of murkiness and awkwardness.

"I feel like I'm about to let some people down," Doc continued. "I have to say some things I didn't think I would have to say."

The emotional toll on Doc was evident. All the kids felt it, but Penelope's nurturing sensitivities were too strong for her to suppress. She squeezed passed the other kids to get to him.

"It's okay, Doc," she said as she gave him a big hug, "none of this is your fault."

Doc genuinely appreciated the gesture as he stared into the camera to address Wild Dog TV.

He gathered himself, and he found that silver tongue he was always known for. "We started this journey," he said, "with the goal of bringing the Quad Continental championship back to Bell Buckle, Tennessee, but that is not going to happen. We will not be racing in the Quad Continental."

Doc let that sink in for a moment or two. To hear himself say it sounded like the tolling of a bell.

Doc continued, "This race meant the world to me. It was my pinnacle, my summit. I was ready to go to the ends of the earth and fight until the sun burnt out to make sure that we won this moment. But when we got here, we saw a reality that we were not expecting. We saw fallen humanity celebrating their own failure.

"There is no other way to say it, but for us to reach our goals, it would mean us throwing in our lot and giving a pass for the evil we saw, and more so, exposing ourselves to a type of evil whose only wish is to be exposed to us. That is something my parents wouldn't have me do." He paused and acknowledged their position. "I understand why. Because to become who we ought to be, we can't abandon the morals within. Not even for a moment. So, now I say this, in our farewell. I won't win this race, but that doesn't mean our day won't come."

Penelope was overtly moved, and she put her hand on her heart. "Doc, that was beautiful. And don't worry. I think you really did win this race today."

Doc smiled. "Thank you, Penelope. I understand what you are saying, but I didn't win the race." Doc's logic could never be circumvented by emotional sentiment. He explained, "We made different decisions, and that's fine, but someone else will win the race. Not us."

Rachel could almost see the ideas running through Penelope's mind. *Don't go there, Penelope*, Rachel thought to herself. *Just let it end.*

Penelope couldn't. "Perhaps in a material way," Penelope pressed back just a smidgen. "Honestly, I think in times like this, we are all winners. We all won this race because we did the right thing."

Doc straightened a bit. "Again, thank you, Penelope," he said with all courteousness. "That being said, we didn't win *this* race. None of us are winning *this* race. We made a decision based on other factors, and as important as they are, they led us, actually and factually, to the guaranteed outcome of not winning *this* race. Those are the facts." Doc smiled and tried to put it to rest.

Penelope turned her head a bit and shrugged. "Well, I think every body is a winner . . . as long as you try."

"Here we go," Rachel inadvertently whispered, and the internet heard it.

Doc twitched his head, and a sharpness came back to his eyes. "What did you say?"

Penelope was a little taken back. "I said everybody is a winner."

Penelope had just offered the sentiment that he was raised to reject. Perhaps at a different time and in a different place when a whole different subset of emotions were involved, Doc may have responded a little bit differently. But not today.

J-Dog saw it before it happened and whispered to Alfie, "Wait for it."

Doc delivered. "You're giving me the 'everyone is a winner' speech? You're telling me there are no losers?"

J-Dog whispered, "I swear, it's impossible for Wild Dog to have a bad show. I'm gifted."

Everything Doc was feeling came out. It was an eruption, not one of the irate kind, not like a volcano, but of a controlled, powerful, directional blast.

To his credit, he was able to compose himself and sift through all the emotional noise before looking square into the camera and giving a speech that could have won a presidency. "They say that children are the future, but that future can't be the sniffling, whining, bellyaching us. It must be the finest product of us. Refined through fire, honed by competition, toughened through failures so that, when we do overcome, it will actually mean something."

"Check it out!" Jonah said in his trademark way.

Doc rolled. "I'm disgusted at the world celebrating mediocrity, coddling failure, and taking a loss and calling it a win. I'm outraged at the concept of ribbons for seventh place, and don't even get me started on certifications of participation. Can we not discern for ourselves if we participated?"

"Ba-boom," Alfie said with a pistol pump.

"You want to know something? Sometimes you are going to try, try, and try again, and still lose. I'm not always going to win when I do participate. So, when I do get beat, don't pity me. Don't feel sorry for me. Give me the dignity of admitting it. When I fall, don't give me a handout; I'll do a push up. Don't you dare tell me that I'm a victim of some other force. Because blame is not the answer, for such frailty is not a virtue. Never tell me that the mere presence of a challenge is a reason to retreat from a challenge! You may think that we are down, but we're not out. A towel may have been thrown, and it may have been for reasons that I understand, but believe you me, the towel didn't come from my hand. I'll be back, we'll be back, and when we do return, even if the same forces of depravity and stupidity are here, we will drive a dagger through them and not lose ourselves when we do!"

The kids roared to an ovation.

Tears rolled down Rachel's face as she watched. She was so proud of her son. She watched him face the evils of the world, get something taken from him that meant everything to him, be thrown into the public eye at his most vulnerable moment, and then what happened next was one of the greatest moments a parent could have.

Doc responded, not as a young teen, but as a young man. Ready to take responsibility, ready to accept life, and ready to stand fast with who he was, what he was, and stare down, run down, and trample down the demons of this world.

In her eyes, this was a rite of passage. He faced an obstacle, and he not only responded to it, but he responded like a man. Like a moral, strong, and determined man. Rachel went from fearing the chance of losing him because he wasn't ready to deal with the evils of the world, to not wanting to hold him back from being a force in this world.

Her phone beeped. It was Dean. Of course, he was watching Wild Dog TV. She smiled and she shook her head.

Dean texted her. "He's ready. Let him race."

She smiled and nodded to herself through the tears. She whispered, "Yep, let him race."

Then her phone blew up. Texts from all the parents came in, because low and behold, they were watching the Wild Dog too, and with one collective voice, they had the same message: *Let 'em race.*

"Doc," Rachel said to her boy as tears stood in her eyes.

Doc looked up. He felt a bit of uneasiness, not knowing how his mom would react to what he had just done.

"Your dad and I and the rest of your parents have a message for you."

The kids waited in absolute silence.

Rachel said with a gentle voice, "Race." Rachel reaffirmed it. A bit stronger this time. "Race."

Doc thrust his hands in the air, and the kids erupted with an energy that shook the starting line.

Rachel then said one more thing, "And here is my personal message to you, Doc."

"Yes?" Doc waited.

"You're a Copper. You're in it to win it."

* * *

EVERYTHING HAD TO BE DONE AND DONE FAST. THE RACE WAS tomorrow morning, and the rest of the teams were already into their last-minute adjustments.

The gang moved like an army of ants toward a common goal. They marched in and out of the truck and trailer. They unloaded the gear that Doc and Mac needed in order to camp out in the desert that night, and then they begin the epic, blistering, one-thousand-mile race early the next morning.

The Copper rig sat in the dedicated Team USA slot between Team Canada and Team Mexico. Doc backed *The Drakon* out of the trailer, and it didn't take long before the entire Canadian and Mexican teams were looking at the incredibly under-gunned and oddly configured ATV that was Team USA. Chuckles began to trickle in from the international teams, and then it built into a full-grown laughing hysteria as teams passed and mocked the Americans.

"Oh, no they didn't," Jonah said from the trailer. "I'm about to go out there and bring a little Detroit with me."

Mac placed his hand on Jonah's chest. "Let it go. We'll settle this in the race."

J-Dog was busy on the campsite, pitching the tent and building a fire pit.

Jonah transformed the top of the trailer into a racing command center. First, he laid down a green artificial turf. He installed a special satellite antenna for better connection to Mac's iPad. He mounted a foldout camp chair that was embroidered with the words "Crew Chief." He secured two stainless steel coolers on either side of his chair that he packed with longneck ice-cold cream sodas and one thousand miles worth of his legendary homemade meat pies. He had stands for a laptop, an iPad, and he hung binoculars around his neck. "Check it out!" he squealed.

Flip and Penelope packed almost forty nutrition packs. They contained a variety of water and energy drinks, and every forth one contained protein bars. Each sack would be placed close to the dump cans for quick retrieval. Alfie was off flying his drone making sure its camera and operations were functioning perfectly.

Doc and Mac worked tirelessly on finetuning the seating apparatus that Mac would sit on for the race, tightening and adjusting it so that, at the very least, it was comfortable. They tested all the communication systems and worked on hand signals, taps on shoulders, and anything that could be used to communicate when they were in the chaos of racing.

Doc and Mac put on and tested the only thing that was not lost in the barn fire: the racing suits. The suits were designed specifically for desert racing with zipper vents in arms, chest, back and thighs for when the sun was scorching at midday, but then they could be closed to be wind-resistant in the cool of the night. The suits had state of the art armor at the chest, shoulders, elbows, knees, hips, and tail bone.

"It feels a little weird," Doc said as he zipped up his red, white, and blue racing jacket.

"What does?" Mac asked as he buckled his over-the-calf racing boots.

"I've always raced in my leather jacket," he explained. "This is the first time I've raced in something else." He pulled on his gloves that had armor reinforcements in the knuckles.

Mac replied, "We're Team USA. I suppose if you gotta change jackets, this is the time."

"You're right," Doc said as he buckled his enduro racing helmet that was gloriously painted in red, white, and blue. He turned on the comm headset in his helmet. "You got me?"

Mac heard Doc's voice come through his own headset inside the helmet. "Loud and clear, brother."

"Don't forget these," Doc said to Mac as he bent down and grabbed the farrier chaps up from the trailer floor.

"Agh," Mac replied.

It wasn't lost on Mac that J-Dog was right. He was going to look like an idiot wearing a racing suit with farrier chaps over the top while sitting on what looked like a pogo stick attached to the back of a four-wheeler.

It made matters worse when Penelope looked at him and said, "You look, um . . . nice."

* * *

IT TURNED OUT, AS SOMEBODY ONCE SAID, TO GET THE BEST OUT OF somebody, you give them too much to do and too little time to do it. That is exactly what happened.

Doc Copper and his gang from Bell Buckle worked at a feverish pace, and did they ever perform. The prep site looked great. The gang finished their tasks quick enough to take an early lunch, and with any luck, the truck and trailer would embark by noon on their trip to the finish line, placing fuel cans every twenty-seven miles.

"*Muy bien*," a voice said from over near *The Drakon*. Doc looked up and saw a Mexican teen walking around the ATV.

"I really like this racer," he said while giving a thumbs up.

This got the kids' attention, because *The Drakon* now looked like a Frankenstein creation that only a mother could love.

The Mexican teen was jovial. He had a big toothy grin, was thinner than a blade of grass, and his eyes seemed a little vacant.

"I'm sorry." Doc said. "Did you say you *like* my four-wheeler?"

"*Sí, amigo*. It's beautiful."

"Well, um, thank you."

"Do you know what you need are some reflectors," the teenager said.

Doc was polite. "Sure. I can see where that would be helpful."

The boy pulled out an old scratched up music CD. "Back in Tijuana, I hang these on my bicycle so the cars know that the thump they just heard was me."

"Okay," Doc replied, not knowing where this conversation was going.

Jonah elbowed J-Dog. "I don't think this kid is all there, man."

"A few beans short of a burrito," J-Dog replied.

"I'm sorry," Mac said. "Did you say you were run over by a car?"

"*Sí, amigo*. Cars. But don't worry; I bend very easy."

Doc wanted to be nice, and he never was far from his southern hospitality, so he walked over to the teen and shook his hand. "I'm Doc Copper. I'm the driver for Team USA, and this is my crew." He began introductions. "That's Mac, he's my navigator . . ."

The boy interrupted him. "I'm like you!" The boy said with a big grin.

Mac waved awkwardly.

"You're the navigator?" Doc couldn't believe it.

"*Sí, amigo*," the boy said and pointed to his shoes which had compasses built into the tongues.

"Why do you have two compasses?" Alfie asked.

"My driver said I needed two because if I lose a foot in the race, we would still have the other."

"Wow," Jonah said, "that's cut-throat."

"You don't know my driver. Her name is Magali. Since she began racing in Mexico, everyone else crashes. She wins."

"She?" Doc asked.

"Yes, *amigo*."

"She wrecks everybody?" Mac blurted.

"*Si*. Very scary."

"Thanks for the heads up," Doc replied. "I didn't catch your name?"

"Oh, I'm sorry," The boy said. "Do you know Billy Joel?"

"The Piano Man?" J-Dog said.

"No, the singer. We have the same name."

"Your name is Billy Joel?" Jonah asked.

"Kind of, but it's pronounced *Hoy-el.*"

"But you just said your name was like Billy Joel," Alfie jumped in.

"Because it's spelled like Joel. So, I tell everyone Billy Joel. My sister is Johanna. We tell everyone she is Johanna with an H."

"I think I speak for everyone when I say—" J-Dog raised his eyebrows as he was readying an insult.

Penelope cut him off in the nick of time. "—that we're all enriched by knowing such important details. Thank you."

"Joël!" a girl's voice shouted from around the corner of the fancy Mexican rig.

"I have to go," Joël said and quickly scampered toward the Mexican crew.

"I don't get it," Doc said. "How is he the navigator?"

A tall Mexican girl, wearing a race suit and a scarf, walked toward Doc while taking off her leather gloves, finger by finger. She had a striking appearance in more ways than one. Well-kept, manicured, proper, and walking with confidence, but there was certainly a hard edge in her eyes that told of a different side to her.

J-Dog gave a fake cough. "Not a friendly."

"I admit," the girl said with a curious grin, "I thought the American team would be, how should I say it, more formidable." Her mastery of English was superb. Clearly well-educated, and quick as a whip. Doc took her seriously.

"You must be Magali," Doc replied with a grin of his own. "Congratulations on making the Quad."

"I'm the first female ever to race in the Quad Continental," she said as she looked over *The Drakon*.

Penelope listened and smiled. "That's great," she whispered to Flip. "I like her."

Flip cracked her knuckles. "I don't." Game recognizes game, and she knew a cutthroat when she saw one.

"Is this what you are riding?" Magali asked with chuckle. "How do the mighty Americans send such an antiquated ATV to the most prestigious race in the world? Not to mention, how did they send *you*?"

J-Dog tipped his hat back. "Excellent fortune, I guess."

Magali raised her eyebrow at J-Dog. "Aw. The bravado of the American cowboy. What do they say these days? It's a dying breed, yes?"

"No, ma'am," J-Dog said with an ornery jest. "Alive and thriving. We're the type that would give you the shirt right off our back."

J-Dog took off his shirt and handed it to her, but she didn't take it. On the front was written *The Diplomat*. On the back was written, *Gulf of America*. "In the name of foreign relations, do I offer to thee," J-Dog said.

Magali looked at it and smirked. "I apologize if I don't take children seriously."

"Just wondering, Magali," Doc said, "racer to racer. How did you pick your navigator? Is he good in a race?"

"Oh, no. I picked him because he agreed to register as an organ donor."

The kids looked back and forth at each other. Jonah raised his finger and started pointing at nonexistent things. "Did she mean what I think she means?"

Magali walked back to her crew, "Joël!" she shouted. "*Firma*," she said as she waved a document that needed a signature in the air.

"Dude!" Jonah yelled out to Joël. "I'd be signing that thing 'Billy Joel!'"

* * *

Checklists were being ticked off. Final tie downs and last look arounds commenced.

"Gather around," Doc instructed as he stepped up on the back ledge of the trailer. Rachel made sure she stayed back; this moment was for them.

Doc gave a warm smile. "You mean more to me than you'll ever know. I love you all. You're my family." Doc then continued now with more of a command in his voice, "Jonah, you take your crew and head out. Get those fuel cans where we need 'em. Keep your comms on and open."

"You can count on me."

"I know I can. I trust you with my life, brother. J-Dog, thanks for the tent. Sorry that it's got to be sacrificed for the cause."

"It leaks anyways," J-Dog acknowledged.

Mac piped up. "I'm not much for speeches. So, I won't give one, but thanks for bringing me. I know that I wasn't really part of you guys before all of this."

"Mac, you were and are exactly what we need, and you're a part of us now," Doc replied.

"Amen," Jonah said.

"Let's go do this thing," J-Dog said.

"Honor, defend!" Alfie thumped his chest.

"Unrage the cage!" Flip shouted, giggled, and corrected. "Uncage the rage!"

"Just be careful," Penelope added as she cupped her face with her two hands. "The desert looks so daunting."

Rachel walked up and gave Doc a big hug. "Be who we raised you to be."

* * *

THE RIG WAS REORGANIZED AND REPURPOSED, AND JONAH CLIMBED up to racing HQ on top of the trailer. He used horse reins as a seat belt and strapped himself into his bolted down director's chair.

Alfie and J-Dog were in the front third of the trailer, in their newly worked up mobile studio for Wild Dog TV. Alfie prepped the drone.

Flip and Penelope continued to ride with Rachel in the cabin as she fired up the dually and slowly pulled out of the American racing slot, leaving behind her only son and his navigator for the most grueling and dangerous race they would ever be in.

Doc and Mac stood on the now vacated American pad. Everyone waved as the truck and trailer left them in the desert. They were miles north of Cabo San Lucas and one thousand miles away from the American border, with only their four-wheeler to get them back.

Doc sighed. "This is one of those real special moments in life."

"How so?" Mac replied as he also waved, knowing there was something different that Doc was thinking.

"Years from now, my mom is going to wonder how in the world she let us do this."

"Years? I give it three hours," Mac corrected.

Doc laughed. "Never waste a parental lapse in judgment."

"It's an international hall pass," Mac replied.

The two boys stopped waving at their friends as the Copper rig drove out of sight into the desert. They turned back around to be welcomed by the stunning reality of their new, and now quite isolated, situation.

A mass of riders and pit crews began gathering on the strip in front of the Team USA prep area.

* * *

THE SIGHT OF THE WORN-OUT TENT, *THE DRAKON* WITH THE JERRY-rigged seat added to it, and the two boys quickly became the laughingstock of the Quad Continental.

"Cross the Americans off," the Australian driver said. "That's the sorriest outfit I've ever seen."

The French added, "They won't even make it one hundred kilometers."

"This is joke," one of the South Africans said. "It's a ruse. This isn't Team USA."

Pointing, laughing, mocking, and scoffing ensued with relentless scorn.

The British navigator, Rupert, shouted out at the boys, "What happened? Did the American checkbook finally bounce?"

"By no means," Doc answered their mocking in stride and returned some fire of his own. "We just figured, why bring the fast one when we only need to beat the likes of you?"

That got some oohs and ahhs from the crowd.

Mac leaned over and muttered, "Way to win friends and influence people."

"This is racing; can't look weak," Doc whispered back.

The tall, lanky British racer, Ethan Oxidant, pushed his way through the crowd to the front. He was favorite to win the race and was considered the number one junior racer in the world. The hubris of that kid went beyond any normal brattish behavior. Everything about him oozed arrogance.

"Funny you seem so sure of yourself," Oxidant said in his haughty British accent. "The whole world knows America has already fallen, and it's the fallen that are the last to know, but I'll take it upon myself to instruct you on these matters."

"Feel free to let us know when you're ready to begin," Doc replied.

Ethan turned up his chin at Doc, and with a sneer, he turned to walk away. But he looked back. "What does that tell you, that *you* are the best America could send?"

"It tells me that we're the best that America could send. What does that tell you that you can't ask tougher questions?" Doc answered and got some chuckles from the crowd.

* * *

DOC STRUGGLED TO SLEEP THAT NIGHT. HE WAS FACING AN UNFORGIVING clock that read 3:00 a.m., and it was only five hours before the start of the race.

The sounds of the other pit crews doing last minute adjustments easily passed through the thin walls of the tent, but that's not what kept Doc up.

It was the imminency of the Quad. His mind was already zooming. He was visualizing the start and how he would maneuver in and out of those big side-by-side dune buggies. His mind wouldn't let him sleep.

He had always had those kind of pre-race mental activities, but never before a one thousand mile race the next day. If he didn't sleep that night, he wasn't going to sleep for a very long time.

Alright, Doc, he thought. *Breathe out, close your eyes, and just focus on breathing.*

But then some rustling outside the tent got his attention, and he snapped his head to the right. Doc stayed silent and listened intently.

There it was again.

Is it an animal? he thought.

There it was again.

He nudged Mac. "Wake up."

Mac opened his eyes. "Is it morning?" he said as he came out of a slumber.

"Shh. Listen." The seriousness of Doc's tone got Mac's attention, and he sat up. "You hear that?" Doc asked.

"What is it?"

"I don't know."

Then they heard it again. It was louder.

"Those are footsteps," Mac said.

"You're right." Doc clicked on a flashlight.

"I'm going outside." Mac grabbed the zipper, but it was too late.

A loud engine fired up and broke the night.

"Go! Go! Go!" Someone outside their tent shouted as tires peeled out, kicking sand onto the tent.

The boys locked eyes for a split second, and then everything happened at once. The old school triangular tent was pulled tight at one end, near the boys' heads. The tent lost its shape, and was wickedly yanked, ripping the tent stakes out of the desert floor.

Wretched violence ensued. The tent became a cruel sack being drug behind an accelerating desert racer.

"Aggghhh!" the boys yelled as their bodies were twisted up in the canvas, bouncing off each other and off the desert floor.

The vehicle banked hard right, slinging the tent like a water skier out wide. The tent tore a little, but not enough to break wide open. The boys tumbled over each other like shoes in a clothes dryer, pounding over desert rock. Mac's hand became a pin cushion as two-inch cacti needles thrust through the tent and embedded into his palm.

Doc's face slammed into the desert floor, bloodying his nose. In the chaos, Doc's hand fell through the tear in the tent and landed on a knot. He clamped on to it, hanging on for dear life. Doc tried to block out the chaos and reach into his cargo pockets.

Got it!

Doc pulled out a pocketknife as they were being drug across a flat desert terrain. For a brief moment, he realized the danger of opening a knife in their tumbling situation, but he had no choice.

He took the knife in his right hand and muscled it out up toward his left hand, which was clinging to the knot through the tent wall. Doc snapped back his thumb nail trying to open the knife, but he didn't care, he got the blade open.

As soon as the blade locked, he pushed the knife through the tent and felt the serrated edges lock onto the nylon rope.

"Agghh!" he yelled with force as he pushed and ripped that blade back and forth.

SNAP!

The Nylon rope broke. The boys skidded and then tumbled, hitting rocks and cacti along the way that eventually halted them in a bungled mess. Doc lost the grip on the knife in the tumbling ruckus.

The boys laid there, wrapped up in a tangled tent as they heard the desert racer speed away with sounds of laughter emanating through the night.

After a few hard breaths, Doc let out a belabored, "Mac, you okay?"

"Hard to say," came the reply.

Doc worked his way through folds of the tent and found the zipper. It was snagged, but he ripped it open. Worming his way free, he crawled out into the desert. It was still night, but the moon and stars gave off plenty of light. He began unwrapping Mac, but he felt something warm and wet on his hands as he pulled Mac out.

Mac grunted. "I got a thing going on," he said as he got to his feet and looked at his arm.

In the tumbling, Doc's pocketknife had skewered through the loose skin in the back of Mac's elbow. It was just dangling there, letting out a slow drip of blood onto the desert sand.

"Dude!" Doc yelled. "My knife's in your elbow!"

"Good work, detective," Mac said a bit comically, but seriously. "Can you get it out?"

Even though Doc knew Mac didn't feel pain, stark reminders like this were always shocking.

"Does it hurt?" Doc asked.

"It doesn't tickle. It's just there."

"Just pull it?"

"Be nice about it," Mac said as he reached out his arm.

Doc took a deep breath and pulled the knife out carefully.

"So, what happened to you?" Mac asked as the knife exited his elbow.

"My nose is bleeding, and I broke a nail." Doc held up his right thumb and tried to make a joke, but the pain began to rush in, and Doc didn't find the humor in his own joke.

"Does it hurt?" Mac asked as he saw Doc's thumb nail pulled nearly two-thirds of the way back, and up from the skin.

"You have no idea," Doc said as he was now free to concentrate on his own pain. "It's unbelievable how much it hurts."

Mac found the first-aid kit that was in the tent and pulled out the bottle of hydrogen peroxide and gauze. He poured the peroxide over his elbow, and it foamed like a polluted ocean cesspool. He looked back at Doc's thumb.

"What are you going to do?" Mac asked as he focused on pulling a cactus barb out of his own hand.

"I don't know. What can I do? Probably just tape it down tight, I guess."

"That's no good," Mac said.

With the sudden quickness of a cat strike, Mac grabbed Doc's nail and just ripped it off.

"Agghhh!" Doc screamed as his body contorted in pain and he dropped to his knees, clutching his thumb and pressing his forehead into the sand. His eyes instantly watered.

Mac looked at the nail. "I didn't know how deep the nail went under the skin. Do you want to see?"

Doc was screaming on the ground and didn't answer.

"Suit yourself," Mac said and tossed the nail.

After a minute of ludicrous pain, Doc opened his eyes as he laid flat on his back in the desert sand. "What's wrong with you?!" he yelled at Mac.

"Quit your whining, Doc. The nail needed to be removed. You know it, and I know it. It was best that I did it without you expecting it."

Doc stared up at the dark sky, letting out gasps and grunts. "I think my own judgment should have made that call. Aw, that hurts."

"Perhaps," Mac conceded, "but your knife did stab me. So, it's only fair. You know, blood for blood."

"Blood for blood?" Doc was incredulous over Mac's reasoning.

"Yeah, blood for blood. I owed you. It's my code," Mac said.

Doc was flabbergasted as he writhed in pain holding his now completely de-nailed thumb. "I was helping you with the knife. Can't your code take in the context of the situation?"

"Code's a code. You can't pick and choose when you apply it. That's what makes it a code. Anyway, I was helping you, too. See, it's all even now."

"You need to talk to somebody about that." Doc climbed to his feet and threw his head back. "Oh, why does this hurt so bad?"

"I wouldn't know about that." Mac looked around and saw nothing but desert. "So, we walk?"

"We walk. I think we're about a half mile out, and when we get in that race, you better believe what we're doing."

"Blood for blood," Mac said.

"Oh, yeah. Blood for blood," Doc said.

* * *

SIDE BY SIDE, IN A STONE-COLD SILENCE, DOC AND MAC WALKED back through the desert and to their pit. Doc dragged the tent behind him with the gear they needed for the race stored up in it like a bag, and in glorious defiance, they marched down the middle of the international strip.

It was past 4:00 a.m., and most the teams were already out working. Bright lights lit up the entire dirt road. Pit crews were changing filters, adding fuel, and firing up their engines.

As Doc and Mac passed each team, all eyes of the desert were on the two Americans. Everyone knew what had happened. Ethan Oxidant did what he did and let everyone know. But no one really cared. This was life in the Quad. If Ethan knocked the Americans out before the race even began, truth be told, everyone would have been pleased to have one less competitor.

The boys kept walking, and when they reached the Mexican team, Joël ran out to see them. "Are you okay?"

"We'll live," Doc replied.

"*Bien, amigo, y lo siento*. I'm sorry about your four-wheeler."

"What?" Doc asked and looked past the Mexican rig to see the abandoned plot. *The Drakon* was gone.

"Where is it?" Mac demanded.

"I found it," Joël said. "It's over there, about two hundred meters. You'll need these," he handed them big bolt cutters. "Don't tell them I helped you, please, *amigos*."

"Joël!" Magali yelled from inside the Mexican rig.

"I have to go," he said. "I'll see you in the race." He gave a thumbs up.

"*Adios, amigo*," Doc replied.

* * *

Doc and Mac hurried in the direction Joël had indicated, and they finally saw *The Drakon*. It was in a bit of a hole, but that wasn't the problem. It was also completely upside down, but that wasn't the problem either.

"Weren't they creative," Doc said.

The Drakon looked like it was in a metal cocoon. Chains and deadbolts weaved in and out and all around it, threaded through it, and banded together into a tight iron chainmail.

Mac growled, "I'm really starting to hate racers."

"If we get out of this mess," Doc said, "we're going to owe Joël a debt of gratitude."

"We should free him from Madame Caligula," Mac smirked.

"Let's get to work," Doc sighed. "First thing is to roll it over, because that engine is flooded. We still have a few hours before the race. We've got this."

Doc and Mac climbed down the slight decline and rolled *The Drakon* back upright. The chain-clad machine felt like a ton, but the boys managed.

Mac went to work on cutting the chains and deadbolts as Doc unwound it. They finished freeing *The Drakon* from the chains around 5:00 A.M.

"Any shut eye?" Mac asked as he wiped sweat from his brow.

"Two and a half hours' worth, if we can," Doc said.

The boys decided to simply lay down on the desert dirt. They closed their eyes and hoped for the best.

* * *

Doc sat up at 7:29 A.M., one minute before the alarm on his phone went off. He felt wide awake, but jittery, not refreshed. The pre-race energy rush of the biggest race in the world masked the violent, sleepless night they had just endured. It would have to do. The unforgiving desert monster called the Quad Continental had just awoken out of its four-year slumber, and it would suffer no delay. The racing world was at its feet.

The dry air in the desert buzzed with excitement. It was revving with a mechanical tension. The teams were scurrying, and the clinks of tools and shouts of orders were the soundwaves of the moment.

Doc tapped Mac on the shoulder. "It's time, brother."

Mac opened his eyes and sat up.

The boys used a military crawl to climb out of the hole they were in. They surveyed the starting line from afar.

"Wow, look at that," Doc marveled.

Huge crowds from the tent city had already made their way over to the eastern side of the starting line.

Mac chuckled, "Kind of surprised they made it."

"Me, too," Doc replied as they slid back down to *The Drakon* and supplies.

Doc opened the tent, which was nothing more than a giant knapsack at this point, and tossed Mac's gear his way as he pulled out his own. With deliberation and silent concentration, the boys beat the sand off their red, white, and blue racing suits.

The boys pulled on the heavy, weighted, armored pants. They snapped, strapped, and zipped them up. They slid on their tall endurance racing boots, tucked the pants into them, and snapped the five buckles tight.

They felt the weight of the protective armor as they put on the racing jackets. They zipped down the sleeves, cinched up the waist, zipped up the chest, and buttoned the flaps over top. They then connected the full three-hundred-and-sixty-degree waist zipper of the pants to the jacket, making it one continuous piece of protective gear.

Doc smiled and stopped to reflect on the past and the present. It had been filled with tumult and turmoil to get them to this point. Yet here they were. Still standing.

"You know," Doc said, "when we win this thing, it will all be worth it."

"Pure sweetness," Mac replied.

Doc pulled Mac's helmet out of a cloth bag and tossed the beautiful off-road racing lid to his navigator.

Mac slid it on. He turned on the Bluetooth headset and fiddled with the controls.

Doc picked up the iPad. "Let's get this connected."

The Bluetooth signals hooked up seamlessly.

"I'm live," Mac said. "It's beeping at me, and now it's talking."

"Hello," The GPS voice said, "you are connected."

Mac smiled. "She sounds cute."

Doc grinned. "I might have made a few modifications to the software." He then said, "Testing, testing."

"I hear you loud and clear, brother," Mac replied.

The GPS gave the instructions. "Turn right and proceed to the route."

Doc reached over and tilted the iPad his way for a moment. "Satellite's up, we should be able to have an open line with Jonah."

"For the whole race?"

"That's the idea."

"Let's try it."

"Come in, Team USA. Do you have your ears on? Jonah, are you there?" Doc asked.

The boys waited a few seconds. Nothing.

"Are we getting through?" Mac asked.

Doc shook his head. "Jonah, can you hear me?"

"Jonah, big fella, it's Mac. You there?"

Nothing but silence.

"I told them to be live by now," Doc said.

"Give it time."

Doc didn't like it, but he didn't let it bother him, either. "Here," he said as he picked up the old, dingy, leather farrier chaps and tossed 'em to Mac. "Don't forget these."

Mac grunted, "I was hoping we'd forget."

"That exhaust won't."

* * *

RACHEL HAD THE HAMMER DOWN. THE TRUCK AND TRAILER bounced through the desert kicking up a dust storm as she went.

"Woohoo!" Jonah laughed and screamed from the top of the trailer. He turned around in his embroidered "Crew Chief" director's chair and reached into the bag that was slung over the back. "That's what I'm talking about," he said as he found the racing goggles that Doc had left for him. He slipped them on over his big straightened blond afro. "Oooh, check it out!" he squealed. "In all my glory!"

"Hey, Jonah," J-Dog yelled from below and inside the trailer, "we're live on the Wild Dog. Put your headset on and say something."

Jonah slipped on the big Bose headset with the swing arm microphone. "Food's no foe! The Black Blondini! Check it out!"

"Are you snorting sand?" J-Dog yelled at him.

"What?"

"Talk about the race! Don't just shout random phrases. We're professionals! We're live!"

Jonah fiddled with his controls on his headset and pulled out his laptop. "So, Wild Dog, I'm the Black Blondini." He looked at the GoPro camera Alfie had installed on the roof of the trailer, and he took a swig from the bottle of cream soda. "I've got a bird's eye view from our mobile command center. I can see cacti. I can see boulders. I can see rocks. I can see sand. I can see—"

"Oh, sweet southern molasses," J-Dog chided. "The desert! Jonah. You see a desert! That's all you got to say? Now, tell 'em that you're the crew chief of Team USA, and then patch through to Doc so he can give us a real-time update. It's showmanship!"

Jonah opened the satellite connection, and then he piped the official broadcast from the Quad Continental right into the stream.

Jonah yelled out, "They're about to start!"

The world was watching now.

* * *

Eighty national teams revved their engines in the Baja desert. Pit crews buzzed with professionalism. The rowdiest and most ragamuffin fans packed the landscape around the starting line. They waved international flags and cheered and jeered as the greatest junior racers in the world readied themselves for the most grueling desert race ever conceived by man.

A Quad Continental broadcast booth sat ten feet above the ground looking down at the expansive starting line. It was an even, continuous line, wide enough for eighty racers. It wasn't stacked like Formula One, INDY, or NASCAR, because it didn't need to be. The width of the desert was the only constraint, not the width of a track. It made for the most intimidating starting line in all of motorsport.

Loud music pumped through the intercom system from the booth where none other than the Welsh racing legend Chester "Oil Slick" Hornback was ready with the call.

"Ladies and gentlemen, this is the Quad Continental!" Oil Slick roared into the mic with his thick Welsh accent, and the fans cheered with excitement.

The rapid-fire clicks of the hundreds of professional cameras rattled like the tail of a snake, and a dozen booths of translators chatted feverishly, taking the show to their corners of the world.

Oil Slick jumped into his intro, "This is the competition of our time. We are here to witness the writing of the next legend, to help build the foundations of many new glories. We are here to partake in the celebration of what the racing world can accomplish. We are here for the Quad Continental. The ultimate rave of racing, a mighty gala of game. I invite you all to imbibe the rising rush of glorious, unrestricted, devilish speed. Welcome to the altar of sports, and let us crown our next racing king!"

Raucous cheers thundered below from the sea of tens of thousands of fans.

"Racers, TO THE STARTING LINE!"

* * *

THE CHEERS FROM THE RABID FANS ONLY INTENSIFIED AS A LONG line of high-heeled flag bearers cat-walked through the windy desert. Each girl—dressed, painted, and polished to cover girl sheens—paraded their national identities with pomp and pageantry for the Olympiad of desert racing.

Side by side, the girls reached the starting line, and the international color guard stood at attention. Their hair blew, and the flags fluttered in the desert wind. The sound and sight that followed them was unmistakable as the engines rumbled in the desert.

"Here come the racers," Oil Slick decreed.

The competitors pulled to the line in their incredible desert racing UTVs. Then, with excited anticipation, Oil Slick announced each team, nation by nation. The constant cheering of the crowd ensued, but pockets of rousing applause broke out with each country announced.

"The bear of Russia!" Oil Slick bellowed. "From the land of dragons, China! From the sandy beaches of Rio, here's Brazil! Coming from one of the world's last untamed lands, Botswana!"

On and on Oil Slick trumpeted. The excitement increased with each national declaration.

"Here are the British! Led by the number one ranked junior racer in the world, Ethan Oxidant, and his navigator, Rupert Castle. They'll be a rowdy duo to contend with, believe you me."

Oil Slick glanced down at the pole positions to see the next national team.

"Hailing from the Red, White, and Blue, comes the youngest competitors ever to compete at the Quad Continental. Here are the . . ." He paused for a split second as he tried to find Team USA. He flipped through his papers to see if there was typo.

Oil Slick turned to the crew of production assistants and covered his microphone, "Where are the Americans?"

Everyone shrugged. Oil Slick continued.

"A big 'g'day, mate!' to the Australians . . ."

A starting spot was left vacant between the Brits and the Aussies.

* * *

THUMP, THUMP.

Jonah kept fiddling with the satellite uplink on the computer. It wasn't connecting to Mac's iPad. Something wasn't right, and he spilled his cream soda down his front as Rachel spared nothing driving through the desert over the uneven terrain. It sure made for a bumpy ride on top of the trailer, although he didn't mind, for there's little better for a young teenage boy than being strapped to the top of a trailer while blazing through a desert.

Flip stood in the bed of the truck with her hands on the roof enjoying the wind in her hair. "Hey, why didn't he say 'Americans?'" she asked as she held her phone in her hands, watching the stream.

"I was wondering that, too," Penelope said as she examined herself in a pocket mirror.

Rachel turned her head as she started to slow because they were reaching another fuel location. The girls didn't have headsets. All they knew was what was on the Wild Dog feed, and what they were being told by the boys. "What? Is something wrong? Are they not at the starting line? They should be there by now," Rachel asked.

Penelope shrugged.

"Jonah," J-Dog said as he climbed the side ladder of the trailer and popped his head over the top. "Have you talked to Doc?"

"No, it's not working," Jonah said as he continued to mess with the computer.

* * *

DOC AND MAC HEARD OIL SLICK RUNNING THROUGH THE TEAMS. They heard him stumble in their absence, and then continue on to the very last racer.

"Two minutes," Doc said. "We've got two minutes."

Doc cracked his knuckles and then tightened down his leather, carbon-reinforced armored gloves. He cinched his helmet tight.

Mac did the same and did one more double take at his ridiculous chaps, but then he put it out of his mind and climbed onto the dreaded pogo stick. He put his feet down on the pegs and made sure the iPad was secured on the center of his handlebars.

Doc did a walk around. One last inspection on *The Drakon*, and it finally hit him that this was it. This was the Quad Continental. He was the American champion, and this was the biggest racing moment of his life. He touched the front fender as he walked around, and he felt a small bit of emotion. He knew that this race would burn up his trusted ATV.

Doc swung his leg over *The Drakon* and took a deep breath. He looked at the starting line that was about a quarter of a mile away, and he triggered the ignition.

The Drakon roared to life.

Doc spoke to Mac through the headset, "It's time."

"Copy that."

Doc hit the gas.

* * *

PENELOPE HANDED HER PHONE TO RACHEL SO SHE COULD HEAR Oil Slick speaking through the stream.

"He's talking about Doc and Mac!" Penelope said.

Rachel kept driving despite every motherly instinct to turn around. But Dean had taught her the laws of racing. She had to let the unknown play out. She couldn't blow the whole Quad Continental by turning back now. At least, not yet.

Oil Slick nearly rested his lips right on the microphone as sand blew across the set. "The desert wind is flexing her might, isn't she? We knew the Baja wouldn't roll out the red carpet for us, and shame on her if she did! The Quad Continental is no place for the faint of heart, but that's not the news. The breaking story is, where are the Americans? We only have seconds till blast off. All the teams are ready, less one, and there wasn't even an American flag girl. For some of the people here, that's their favorite part. At the very least, they could have brought in a Southern Cal cheerleader. So, I repeat, I repeat, where are Doc Copper and Mac Irons?"

* * *

ETHAN OXIDANT REVVED HIS ENGINE. HE SPOKE INTO THE HELMET intercom, "It's a beautiful sight, isn't it, Rupert?"

"The desert?" Rupert responded.

"No, you fool. No Americans."

Rupert ignored the insult. He wasn't friends with Ethan. No one *really* was. He raced with him because of the perks of being on the British team.

"They could still make it, Ethan," Rupert said as he fiddled with his GPS software.

"Not a chance."

* * *

"Clock's tickin'," Mac said as the red countdown clock was getting low on time.

"I know; get ready for a jump," Doc said, and then in a synchronized move, the two boys stood on their pegs, bent their knees, and leaned back. The front tires hit a dip, sending *The Drakon* into the air.

WHEW! THUMP! They landed on the dirt path, and Doc hammered down.

"Got to move," Mac yelled.

"I know." Doc shifted as *The Drakon's* engine screamed in response. "Are you up for drive-thru?" Doc asked Mac. The Quad Continental had turned that barren desert into the worst parts of a carnival, and every type of vendor, selling every conceivable thing, lined the dirt path.

Doc veered over to the edge of the vendors. "Do you see it?"

"Old Glory?" Mac asked.

"Old Glory," Doc replied.

Mac leaned out wide and stretched out his right hand. Doc swerved perfectly.

"Got it!" Mac said as he snapped off the stars and stripes from the international flag vendor.

* * *

Panic set in with Rachel, and the kids felt it, too.

"Penelope, will you give me your walkie-talkie, please?" Rachel asked.

"Sure."

Rachel pressed the button. "Hi, Jonah, can you hear me? This is Rachel."

Jonah heard the static and the voice. He picked up the walkie-talkie from his mesh pocket slung over the side of his chair. "Hi, Mrs. Copper, how are you?" Jonah asked kind of awkwardly.

"I'm fine. Have you reached Doc or Mac? I'm starting to worry."

"No, not yet."

"What's to worry?" J-Dog chimed in on his walkie-talkie below. "We only left them one thousand miles away from the border with nothing but their four-wheeler among seventy-nine other teams who will do anything to win. I'm sure they're fine."

Alfie tried to console Rachel on his walkie-talkie, "I'm sure any mother would have done the same . . ."

* * *

OIL SLICK FINALLY SAW DOC AND MAC COMING. "WHAT DO MY Welsh eyes see?" Oil Slick rubbed his face. "Blessed Nessie, it's the Americans!"

Mac stood on his foot pegs and thrust the American Flag high into the sky as *The Drakon* kicked up a cloud of dust.

The crowd turned their collective heads in unison. A raucous cheer emerged from the tens of thousands of racing fans. Not because of any affection toward Doc and Mac, but the crowd had made the decision that loud, boisterous noise was the very height of their inebriated existence.

Jonah, Alfie, J-Dog, Penelope, Flip, and Rachel roared with the rush of relief as they watched and listened to the Quad Continental broadcast.

Oil Slick glanced at the countdown clock. "We may have a full cast after all!"

Doc sped toward the starting line and then slammed on his brakes. Skidding hard, *The Drakon* stirred up an opaque dust cloud that engulfed the boys.

Doc handled the brake to perfection, and *The Drakon* slid to a stop exactly at their poll position, equidistant between the Brits and the Aussies.

Simultaneously, Mac leaped with all he had, and with the help of momentum, he sailed over Doc and the handlebars and planted the American Flag in the desert sand as he landed.

"Present and accounted for!" Mac yelled.

"With time to spare," Doc said, looking at the clock.

"Holy Fourth of July!" Oil slick yelled. "And that is how you make an entrance." The crowd drank in the drama, and Doc and Mac became instant favorites.

Ethan griped, "I hate Americans."

As the dust settled, Oil Slick got a look at *The Drakon*, which now looked grossly overmatched next to the competition, and he sighed. "At least they added to the pageant."

* * *

A VIOLENT WIND THEN KICKED UP THE BAJA SAND, AND THOUSANDS of cheering spectators squinted in unison as the pebble-filled gust assaulted their eyes. But Doc was impervious to the desert elements. He embraced the wind, stinging sand, and the promise of unforgiving heat that waited for him. He longed for the agony of thirst, the threat of the unknown, and the danger of unmitigated speed. When he was in its throes, it meant he was doing the very thing he was born to do: racing.

But this time, it was more than just a race.

The American racing prodigy sat crouched on *The Drakon*, studying the desert. It was a living breathing natural force of waiting desolation, daring the racers to come on in, but Doc taunted back, because his racing persona had now hijacked his brain.

He was no longer just a southern kid from Bell Buckle, Tennessee. He was something altogether different. He gritted his teeth. Game rage had set in. He became an amalgamation of an adrenaline junkie and racing prodigy all wrapped up in the need for a reckoning.

He stared at the vast, barren Baja desert that stretched as far as the eye could see. Somewhere out there was the battle of his life and that chance for racing glory. His big, dark brown eyes popped with intensity and teetered on the tip of insanity, fueled by high octane adrenaline that flowed through his body. He felt the engine pulse beneath him as the pistons fired in perfect harmony. The heat from the engine began to steam up his leg, but it was the right kind of pain.

Doc pressed his chest against the bars. He pulled the clutch and shifted the high-strung racing machine into first gear while revving the engine within a millimeter of the redline. *The Drakon* roared, almost lurching forward, longing for the popping of the clutch.

Doc looked down at his trusted ATV, clearly outmatched by the brawnier UTVs surrounding them, and in a moment of sentimentality and knowing that this was *The Drakon's* swan song, his last ride on his trusted machine, he whispered, "I need all you got."

He tilted his head back and yelled out, "This is going to be legendary!"

Mac quickly responded in his customary blunt and choppy way, "Yep."

Mac's intense anticipation pushed beads of sweat down his brow and cheeks, and it began to soak into the padding of his helmet. He adjusted his goggles. "Gettin' antsy!"

Doc glanced to his right and to his left, seeing nothing but enemies flanking him, and he wondered how much violence was in him, because violence was coming, whether they liked it or not. "The entire planet's coming after us," he said.

Mac grunted back, "Yep."

"Let 'em come," Doc replied.

"Now you're speaking my language," Mac said as he slapped the plastic fender. "I owe 'em."

Ethan and Rupert stared at Doc and Mac, and if looks could kill, then they would be dead, and it wasn't like they hadn't already tried. Ethan yelled over the roar of engines, and as loud as the engines were, nothing could drown out Ethan's narcissistic scorn. "Hey, Doc! Nice ride. I'm a little surprised it still runs."

Doc knew exactly what Ethan meant, and his scoffing did nothing but add more fury to the raging fire. "Hold that thought," Doc yelled back, and then pointed to the desert. "We'll pick this up out there."

Mac spoke into the headset, "That punk would make a nun pull a switch blade."

The Australian team was on their right side, and the Aussie driver lifted his helmet and spit on Doc's front tire. "Let me guess," the Australian driver said. "You want to make this race great again?"

Mac stood up on his pegs and threatened with his fist. "How 'bout I make your face great again?"

Doc and Mac never wanted war so bad, and Mac yelled into the madness, "Doc, if you don't crush these guys, I'm going to let Fire Face kick you in the face."

Doc rifled back, "If I don't crush these guys, I'll let him kick me in the face!"

A young girl walked out into the sandy, cacti-riddled starting line. She began waving a flag in front of the greatest junior off-road racers the world had to offer.

"Mac," Doc yelled, "have you ever heard of American Exceptionalism?"

"Yep," Mac cracked his neck.

Doc grinned, "Here comes exhibit A."

"Roger that," Mac quipped back.

Another strong gust kicked up the desert silt. Doc pushed on his goggles, making sure the seal was tight.

The girl was waving that flag high above her head, and then Doc saw the slightest pause in her motion. "HANG ON!" Doc screamed.

The flag dropped.

Chaos.

* * *

THE FULL-THROTTLED GROWL FROM THE PISTONS STRIKING THEIR chambers brought a sonic flood that awed the crowd. Spinning rubber on the desert floor kicked up gluts of sand into the air, making a mirage of furious havoc.

A collective war cry from riders and navigators joined the dirt cloud, and exhaust notes created an audio-visual masterpiece of theatrical maelstrom that ripped the desert wide open.

Seventy-nine side-by-side racers and one undersized four-wheeler catapulted off the line. Violence and destruction didn't delay. The racers slammed into each other, bending, cracking, and splintering fenders, wheels, and bone.

The crowd oohed and awed as the left flank of the starting line, which was home to the Middle East contingent, became a meat grinder as teams rammed each other into oblivion.

"Oh!" Oil Slick yelled. "And that is precisely why you separate the Sunnis from the Shiites."

A gas tank ruptured when the Iranians rammed into the Saudis, and an explosion of gas and oil lit up the sky.

Oil Slick curled his bottom lip. "I suppose hugging it out may be a wee bit too much to ask."

More crunching collisions came seconds later as the North Korean racer saw its front tire fly off the axel. Its front axle wobbled with a spine-altering jar and then spun the vehicle into the Vietnam team. That, in turn, sent it into a horrific tumble, which was only arrested when it smashed into the South Koreans. They then rear-ended the Philippines, who skidded into Taiwan, who was trying to get away from China and had cut off the Mongolians in their escape. This caused the Mongols to plow into Estonia, who had been trying to steer clear of the Russians who had just gashed the tires of Ukraine in a clearly illegal move.

India and Pakistan broke free from the packs and began a senseless grudge match that resulted in the Indians being pushed into a boulder, utterly destroying their racing machine. Both the driver and navigator got tossed into air, while the Pakistanis tumbled down an embankment during the melee.

All in all, over twenty teams from the four corners of the world were crashed, rammed, injured, and eliminated from the race in the first thirty seconds. The shiny pre-race optimism now littered the desert in a mangled, oily, bloody mess.

Oil Slick exhaled. "Sheesh! This year's edition of The Quad Continental brought to you by the Whalers of Faroe."

* * *

DOC REACTED WITH GOD-GIVEN ELECTRICAL REFLEXES, AND IT showed. Smaller and lighter, *The Drakon* responded to the full twisted throttle and shot out in front of the heavier, larger displacement engines.

If Doc hadn't yelled a warning to hold on, he would have lost Mac right off the back. As it was, the physical jolt shoved Mac to the back of the seat and snapped his arms to absolute extension as he held on to his eBay special handlebars.

Doc cycled through the transmission with a redline assault.

REV, CLUTCH, SHIFT, REV, CLUTCH, SHIFT.

The Drakon responded, almost like it was alive, sensing the moment, feeling the urgency, loving the fight-or-flight octane firing in its block.

The quick start kept them free from all the chaos that happened behind them. It was the perfect first one hundred yards to a one-thousand-mile race.

Doc quickly discovered he had to overcompensate for Mac's added weight hanging off the back on the pogo stick. Doc leaned forward during hard throttles, putting his weight over those front tires, making sure he kept four on the floor.

He was able to open up a few lengths on the pack, but everyone knew that, once those bigger desert racers dug deep into their stables, those extra ponies would start to reel him in.

* * *

JONAH ADJUSTED HIS GOGGLES AS HE BOUNCED ALONG ON TOP OF the trailer. "Why can't we reach them? I've got everything on."

Rachel borrowed the walkie-talkie again. "Jonah, hi, any word on getting through?"

"No, ma'am," Jonah replied, "we're still trying to figure it out."

"If you can't reach them, how are we going to give them updates if we need to change where we place the fuel cans?"

J-Dog turned to Jonah. "Every once in a while, parents make a point."

"I can hear you, J-Dog," Rachel said through the speakers.

The boys grimaced.

Flip leaned forward from the back seat of the truck cabin. "I'll fix it." Within a second, she grabbed a red dodge ball and crawled through the back window of the dually, scurried up the gooseneck, and flung it at J-Dog.

BANG!

It twanged off the back of J-Dog's head, who was sitting in a chair on top with Jonah.

"Respect!" Flip yelled and giggled.

"Ow!" J-Dog yelled as the ball ricocheted off his head and into the desert. "Somebody's got to do something about her," he protested.

Alfie smiled. "She's my favorite human."

Jonah studied his communication software on his laptop, and coming up empty for answers, he shrugged. "It's got to be on their side. I think we're good."

* * *

DOC FELT THE SURGE COMING FROM HIS RIGHT, AND HIS INSTINCTS took over the moment. "Leg!" Doc yelled into the comm system.

Mac lifted his right leg just in time to see a front tire spin into the space where his heel should have been. "Whoa!" he yelled.

"Who is it?" Doc shouted back.

"The Aussies," Mac fired back, "and they caught us! They're running fast!"

Doc downshifted and loaded up on RPMs. He swung his body off the left side of *The Drakon*. Mac followed suit, and Doc twisted the throttle to the max. His back tires fished to the right, coming within inches of the Aussies' monstrous racer's front.

"Eat it!" Doc growled as *The Drakon's* back tires scooped up heaps of the Baja's grainy surface and slung it into the face of the Aussie drivers, pelting their exposed skin around their neck while obstructing their vision. The maneuver forced the Aussies to brake and swerve.

Mac turned his head back and raised a defiant fist. "BLOOD FOR BLOOD!"

"You may be saying that a lot," Doc cautioned.

Mac slowly lowered his fist as the victory proved to be just a skirmish in a much bigger war. A sea of racers were closing in . . . fast.

"Um, Doc," Mac said, "I hope you got something else up your sleeve, because they're catching us, and I don't think they're aiming to pass."

Doc glanced back just in time to see Ethan Oxidant veer into the New Zealand team. Ethan perfectly clipped their back tire. The driver panicked and tried to stabilize, but it was a useless gesture. The natural laws of gravity and motion pounded their gavel in judgment as the racer spun sideways and their momentum sent the Kiwis airborne.

BOOM!

The racer collided with the earth with unforgiving force. Landing on its side and in a merciless tumult, the New Zealand team barrel rolled as shrapnel and dirt filled the air. It was a raucous wreck that broke everything that had a part to break.

The Kiwis survived the crash only with their lives, and Ethan's victim count started to pile up.

* * *

Jonah, Alfie, and J-Dog were strapped down tight in director's chairs atop the trailer as they bounced across the desert. J-Dog took off his belt and wrapped it around his head to keep his cowboy hat mounted firmly on. He was proud that his buckle served as a chin strap.

Both Jonah and Alfie wore goggles, but J-Dog had his pilot sunglasses, and all three of them had faces caked in desert dirt.

J-Dog pointed at the sparse, arid landscape and shouted, "We must be living right, boys, living right!"

"Hey! I got something," Jonah said as he elevated his voice above the ambient sound.

"What is it?" Alfie replied.

"Doc and Mac! Check it out!" Jonah shouted and wiped the dust off his goggles. He clicked the trackpad on his laptop. "They're on! The world be watching now!"

The boys had worked hard in making *The Drakon* into one giant mobile action camera. One GoPro was mounted on the front fender that pointed dead ahead. Mac's helmet had a GoPro mounted on the side. Doc's helmet had a camera mounted on top. A camera was secured to the bottom of Mac's seat pointing backward, and cameras were mounted on the rear fenders pointing out to the sides.

Jonah raised a single eyebrow in disbelief as he saw the incredible racing action that surrounded Doc and Mac. "Are you seeing this? They're dancing with the devil in there!"

The three of them were glued to their iPads, soaking in all the views. "This is crazy!" Alfie yelled.

It was a cacophony of motorized chaos, and the world logged in to watch.

* * *

Doc glanced at the huge dust and exhaust cloud that emanated from behind them. It was a smoking cauldron. The horde had caught up. Doc's starting lead had evaporated a little quicker than he had anticipated.

"They increased their horses more than I thought," Doc said to Mac.

The larger horsepower of the dune buggies had a raw advantage over *The Drakon,* and the wide-open space of the desert fed that advantage.

"Tell me what you see, Mac."

Mac turned around to study the scene. "A lead pack is starting to form."

"How many in the lead pack?"

"Maybe twenty or so?"

"The Brits?"

"They're there, others are racing 'em hard though. Your move sent the Aussies back a bit. Good job. Hard to tell with the dust and smoke, but I think the rest of the field is falling back. They're not keeping up."

"Alright, we're seeing the contenders and pretenders then," Doc responded.

"Closing fast, Doc. Thirty feet back."

Doc lifted himself off his seat a couple more inches, letting his knees be his shocks.

"Woah!" Mac yelled. "Brits just did something!"

Doc turned his head just in time to see a handful of ball bearings flung into the air. They become demonic projectiles to everyone who was trailing the British.

Peru never saw it coming. They took a direct hit. An iron ball hit squarely in the center of the Peru driver's goggles, splintering the shield, and shocking him with the impact. His hands jerked and twisted his front tires.

The margin for error in that front pack was paper thin. The slight fishtail that ensued caused a chain reaction that claimed more victims with each millisecond.

Peru clipped the Norwegians, who curved into the team from Spain, causing a three-team pile up. They spun, flipped, and crashed into a blend of rubber, gas, and metallic carnage.

"Dude!" Mac gasped.

Doc turned forward again. "How many?" he asked. "How many are out?"

"At least three, maybe," Mac counted.

Other ball bearings tossed by the Brit bounced off the desert floor. Some were buried in sand, but others hit rock, bounced up, and drilled drivers and machines, bruising flesh and banging metal.

Doc saw how lethal this thing was, and he knew if he fell into the middle of the horde, those heavily caged up racers would make quick work of the small four-wheeler.

Doc felt the racers closing in. "Tight grip," he instructed Mac. "Bounce with your knees. Keep your torso loose."

Mac obliged.

Doc downshifted two gears, sending *The Drakon's* RPMs deep into the red. Then he broke hard to the right, kicking up as much desert sand and gravel as his knobby tires could grab. Doc let loose a tribal war cry as he buzzed inches in front of his competitors that were now directly behind him. His move was reckless and unexpected, and the other racers had to make a decision to either collide with them or be forced to brake.

Doc trusted that, if given no time to think, the reflexes of the best riders in the world would instinctively avoid the crash instead of T-boning them. He was right.

Doc's hard swerve caused the swath of racers to separate like a flock of birds. The whole pack slowed, and Doc found a momentary cushion of space. It was a perilous maneuver, but it kept him away from Ethan, and he knew this whole race was going to be predicated on more moves just like that.

* * *

"OH!" THE BOYS YELLED IN UNISON FROM THE TOP OF THE TRAILER. The GoPro cameras caught all the action and streamed it to the world.

"That's so dangerous," Alfie said as he cupped his face with his hands.

"There's no way they live through this," J-Dog remarked.

Rachel's nervous voice came through the headsets, "Hey, guys, is everything okay?"

"Oh," J-Dog said as he grimaced. The boys had forgotten the girls up front had smartphones too, and the boys' voices were coming through the livestream.

"Yeah, everything's great!" Jonah shrugged at the boys. "Thanks for asking. How are you?" Jonah clicked the trackpad. "I just muted us for a second."

"Good idea," Alfie replied.

Rachel answered, "It sounds a little scary. Are Doc and Mac okay?"

"Unmute it," J-Dog said.

"No," Jonah argued, "I'm not turning it on for you. I'll turn it on for me."

"No, I should talk to her," Alfie insisted. "I'm cool and collected."

"And I'm not?" Jonah furled his eyebrows. "I'm the Black Blondini."

J-Dog scolded him, "How does having hair like a pencil top troll make you the voice of soothing comfort?"

Alfie persisted, "Guys, guys. Mrs. Copper needs to hear a strong, reassuring, masculine voice. I think we all know that's me."

"Alfie, are you listening to yourself?" J-Dog asked. "I'm the one that millions watch to get advice on how to improve their miserable lives."

"But she knows you ate horse poop," Jonah said. "She can't respect that."

"Hey!" J-Dog shouted. "I thought we got past that."

Rachel hit a big rock in the desert, and the trailer popped up in the air, rattling the boys on top.

"Whoa!" Jonah yelled. "She's losing her grip! We gotta do something fast."

"Okay, okay. I know," Alfie said. "What if we say nothing? Maybe she'll forget she asked? You never know."

The boys went with that.

"Not to be the bearer of more bad news, but . . ." Jonah was looking at the GPS adjustments they had to make to get to the fuel route. "But if we can't talk to Doc and Mac soon, they may not make the right turn. We need to tell them to refresh their GPS file."

"Wait," J-Dog said, "how do we have the picture from the cameras, but we can't communicate with them?"

"I don't know!" Jonah popped with frustration.

* * *

"THEY'RE HERE!" MAC YELLED AS RACERS SWARMED ON EITHER SIDE of them and Mac dangled like chum off the backend of *The Drakon.*

"Watch your legs!" Doc yelled as the Uganda team sandwiched them up against Paraguay.

"Watch them do what?" Mac yelled back.

There was as much crash-up derby at this point as desert racing. *The Drakon's* frame could not survive the aggressive overtures of the larger iron-tubed UTVs that were designed for this kind of bumper battle.

"Good thing I've got chaps!" Mac's irony was unmistakable. "We need info, and I mean now!" He clicked through menu after menu, trying to find out why he wasn't hearing from Jonah as Doc fought to keep four wheels solidly on the ground while being banged back and forth between two heavy dune buggies.

"Stay steady," Mac told his fingers as he kept tapping all the wrong things on the iPad in the gyrating madness of the race. "Dang it! Stay still!" He held on extra tight with his left hand and tried to control his tapping finger on his right. "Forget it!" In a frustrated rage, he started pecking every single icon on the screen as fast as he could, and then something happened.

"Hey! I got it! I somehow got the update. I don't know which button it was, but it was one of them."

"Great!" Doc yelled back. "Are we good?'

"Nope," Mac yelled back, "right turn right now!"

At least seven racers formed a blockade between him and where Mac was telling him to go.

"Hang on!" Doc pulled the clutch and shifted down, engaging more RPMs to attempt a maneuver through the tightly spaced pack at crazy high speeds.

"Hang on?" Mac asked. "Kind of goes without sayiiinnnggg!" He yelped as his head and body were jerked, nearly forcing him right off the back. "Oh!" he shouted with thc thrill of the move, and he got his first true taste of why Doc Copper was a racing prodigy. *The Drakon* jolted forward and edged toward the front left tire of the Mercedes Benz-built racer that belonged to the powerful German team. Instinctively, the Germans also downshifted and tried to pull forward to block any move Doc was trying to make.

"*Vielen dank*," Doc said under his breath.

With the move, the German team opened a slight pocket of space between themselves and the Ducati-powered Italian team that was attempting to drag right behind the Germans.

"Perfect!" Doc pumped his front brakes, pushing Mac forward in his seat, banging himself against the handlebar post.

The move dropped them to the back-left corner of the German team, and they had a few milliseconds to take advantage of the newly created six-foot gap.

Doc cut into it. He forced the Italians and their high-strung Ducati to brake.

Mac gave the obligatory thank you wave as if he was a passenger in a car. The Italians did manage to wave back, but it wasn't as polite.

Game rage took hold of Doc again. "Mac," he said, "three racers back, is there a space?"

Mac turned and saw that there was room to get over behind the South African team, but things were moving so fast that there was no telling how long that space would be there.

"Maybe. Hard to tell."

"Good enough." Doc squeezed with his legs and throttled hard, jerking *The Drakon* over into the three-foot-wide alley between machines. Doc released the gas but didn't brake. Two racers on either side edged ahead, and then the South African team pulled up right next to them.

Doc tapped the brake, allowing the South Africans to jump forward, and then he deftly swerved in right behind them.

"Nice move!" Mac yelled, and then he saw something. "Hey, hey! The pack just broke up. The Brits broke away."

Doc looked back. "Ethan's going a different route?"

"Yep, and he's taking some with him."

"That helps us for now. The fewer the better."

"Speaking of routes," Mac warned, "our right turn is now or never!"

"I know!" Doc pulled hard to the right and gave *The Drakon* everything he had. The back wheels spun in the desert sand before they dug in. The screaming engine surged *The Drakon* forward, but it wasn't fast enough. The big Austrian super-machine was churning out upper echelon horsepower, and they were hot on Doc and Mac's tail.

A collision with Canadians had caused the Austrians to get off to a bad start, but after they crumpled the Canucks like a maple leaf, they began to chew up chunks of ground.

Mac looked back just in time. "Dude, uh, faster," he said with trepidation as he watched the big KTM built racer charging at them.

The Austrian engine was endowed with more horses than any other UTV in the race, and KTM had both years of desert experience and championships to back them up. This was serious, and Doc knew it.

"*Drakon*, I need you!" Doc opened up his small Honda engine and gave it all it had. They were scorching over the desert, but it wasn't enough. That supercharged KTM barreled toward them with bad intentions and the muscle to cash that check.

To Doc's left was Belgium, and to the right, rode the team from Singapore. Doc and Mac were pinned in.

"Mac! Keep them off!" commanded Doc.

"What?"

"If they slam your pogo stick," Doc explained, "I don't think I need to tell you what happens to you at eighty-five-miles per hour!"

"But my chaps should help!" Mac protested with anger.

"Let it go, dude," Doc replied while looking back at the big front end of the KTM and that tubular brush guard that was poised to do damage.

"This is going to get jacked up!" Mac yelled.

"Do something!" Doc yelled back.

Mac's eyes darted back and forth as he thought, and then he yelled a command at Doc, "Get down."

Doc dropped until his chin nearly touched the gas tank. Mac swung his left leg over Doc's head, and spun one hundred eighty degrees on *The Drakon*, remounting his seat backwards. He stretched out his legs toward the big menacing Austrian machine in a stunt sure to go wrong.

The Austrian driver flashed a devilish grin and hit the gas.

"Aggghhh!" Mac yelled as his feet connected with the giant bumper of the KTM. His legs instantly buckled. The Austrians downshifted and gave it more.

Doc felt the bump, and *The Drakon* moved forward slightly faster than it had the ability to go.

"He's trying to ram us!" Mac yelled as his legs continue to bend.

Doc was pinned in. Racers on every side, and *The Drakon* was maxed out.

The team from Greece suddenly shifted over directly in front of them. It was dire straits.

Doc and Mac were completely boxed in. Huge UTVs closed in on every side. It was a coordinated effort to wipe out the American team.

The crash would be deadly. The teams inched in tighter, and Mac couldn't keep the KTM off them any longer.

"Use your head! Do something!" Doc yelled.

Mac bobbed his head. "Use my head, use my head, use my head!"

Mac's pale blue eyes turned to daggers. The Austrians pushed Mac Irons one step too far, and something triggered inside of him. What came out next was the inner fight that was birthed on the streets of Memphis.

Mac snapped. He tasted metal in his mouth, and everything turned red. Mac pulled back his legs and planted them on his pegs. The Austrians surged forward.

"USE MY HEAD!" Mac yelled as he bent his knees, aimed his body at the Austrian driver, and thrust himself into the air. His body planked out as he torpedoed over the hood of the Austrian racer and delivered a flying atomic headbutt directly to the face shield of the Austrian driver, cracking it wide open.

The aggression rocked the Austrians' world, slamming the driver's head into the headrest. Doc glanced back as he felt the weight of *The Drakon* drastically change. He took a brief moment to take in the raging animal that his buddy had become. "He literally used his head," Doc quipped.

Mac was on top of the driver, headbutted him two more times, and then snarled at the gob-smacked navigator. Mac unbuckled the navigator's racing harness. "Some race, huh?"

Mac grabbed the collar of the stunned navigator and pulled him to his face. "In case of an emergency, look for your closest exit, and it may be beside you!" Mac planted his leg into the side of the Austrian, and kicked him out of the racer, sending him tumbling in the desert.

Mac looked back at the driver. "You wanted me. You got me."

The Austrian driver panicked, spastically jerking the wheel to the left and clipping the back tire of the Belgium racing team, sending the Belgians into a 360-degree spin, which led to a wicked tumbling roll that splintered their machine and sent shrapnel into the air.

Mac was hurled violently across the cabin, but he was able to slap the seat belt release of the driver as he went, undoing the boy's racing harness.

Mac collided with the front right roll bar cage that encased the KTM's cabin. He felt a rib pop with the impact, and then he got flung out onto the hood.

"Mac!" Doc yelled as he reached back with his hand. But Mac was out of reach.

The milliseconds ran in slow motion. Mac felt his gloves slipping down the painted hood, squeaking with each passing inch. Frantically, he tried to dig his hands into something to hold onto. He fought the fight of his life to keep himself from falling over the front bumper of the KTM and being bulldozed into the desert, first by it and then by every other racer following in the pack.

But Mac found nothing to grab onto with that glossy wax-finished hood. He felt the toe of his racing boots bang past the front bumper. His slide then accelerated into a sweeping fall until the inevitable happened. His feet touched down.

The force of the contact with the desert at that ludicrous speed grabbed his feet like demonic claws from below and thrust his legs under the UTV with mechanical-like rapidness, sucking him down much faster than gravity alone. His hands slapped at the hood, but to no avail.

"Mac!" Doc screamed with the passion of family.

Clawing and fighting, Mac felt his knees pass under the front of the bumper. He instinctively spread his legs to avoid the front tire, but now that left him straddling that spinning knobby devil.

Mac felt the thinnest fiber of his pant seat contact the ground, and the desert floor started eating into the seat of his racing grade Cordura fabric.

"Really?" he growled at the fact that his butt was the only place those ridiculous leather chaps didn't cover.

Mac crunched his abs as much as possible, trying to curl his body around the hood and bumper of the racer into some helpless grip.

BAM!

The front right tire of the Austrian UTV hit a rock.

The propulsion of the bump tossed Mac into the air like a rag doll, freewheeling and loose. The camera attached to his helmet disengaged with the spin and was sent hurdling through the air to smash into a rock in the desert, crushing it and killing its signal.

Thoughts of impending doom whisked through Mac's head. He braced himself for what was about to happen—crashing into the desert and being run over by the Austrian and then, for good measure, steam-rolled by every other member of the international horde.

A last thought dashed through Mac's head: "Dying probably won't hurt, either."

* * *

"AGGGHHH!" J-DOG, ALFIE, AND JONAH SCREAMED AS THEY TRIED to make sense of what they were seeing through Mac's helmet cam, and then it went to static.

"What was that?!" J-Dog yelled.

"I don't know!" Jonah yelled back, "But we lost both Mac's head cam and the camera under his pogo seat. It looked like it got smashed by a bigger bumper."

"If we lost Mac's head camera . . ." Alfie asked, "did we lose Mac's head?"

"Aggghhh!" they all yelled again.

* * *

"MAC!" DOC SCREAMED AS HE SAW HIS FRIEND LAUNCHED INTO the air and heading to a horrible demise.

Mac heard Doc's panicked cry through the headset, which only reinforced what he had come to gather about the peril of his own present circumstance. *Dicey,* Mac thought as he heard his own breath loud in his ears. Oddly, he felt a moment of serenity as he glanced up at the big beautiful blue sky and waited for the awful impact of the ground, and then the inevitable crushing blows of the stampede of racers.

"Here I come," Mac said to the Man upstairs as he caught a glimpse of his present foe coming right for him. The Austrian hit the gas with a vengeful hate. However, in the Austrian's rage to eliminate Mac, the Austrian threw out a lifeline, instead. He inadvertently accelerated under the falling boy.

THUMP!

Mac smashed onto the hood. Not the landing he expected. Never, in the history of mankind, has slamming onto the hood of a desert racer at full clip felt so good.

A surge of adrenaline pulsed through Mac's body and ignited his heart. The feeling of being jerked back from certain death gave an energy that no drug on earth could emulate.

"Mac's alive!" he screamed.

The momentum of the impact tumbled Mac into a backward roll down the hood again. But this, too, was calming. *Been here, done that,* he thought.

With the knowledge of the surroundings and the firm understanding of what was needed, he slammed his hands down with the adrenaline-induced strength of ten men.

PANG!

The palm of his hands slapped that front tubular metal bumper just as his legs got sucked under the front bumper . . . again. He smacked the bumper so hard that his bones rattled, sending hairline fractures throughout his metacarpals. It was well worth it though, because the break caught his body, and this time, he made sure to center himself on the hood and stay clear of the wheels.

"Not this time!" he screamed.

Mac did a chin up on the front bumper, but he allowed his feet to drag on the desert ground underneath the center of the racer. His eyes locked with the Austrian driver, but then he slipped.

Doc turned. "Mac!" he yelled as he saw his friend disappear under the KTM.

Doc looked up and saw the Austrian gunning next for him. He clearly had it in his mind to finish the American team.

Doc's eyes darted all around him. He was boxed in, and no one was letting him out, but he didn't care. He was looking for Mac on the desert floor, trying to see where he'd been thrown down.

The KTM accelerated, and Doc felt the front bumper hit the pogo stick in the back.

"Think, think!" Doc said, but nothing was coming to mind. He turned around and looked at his adversary when he heard a familiar voice in his headset.

"Yeah, you owe me. Big time."

"Mac?" Doc couldn't believe it, and then he saw him. Mac had used the frame and skid plates underneath the desert racer like a ladder, and grip by grip, he'd climbed underneath the KTM to the back, and he was now working his way up the back bumper.

Before the driver knew it, Mac hopped over the seat and landed in the navigator's chair. He grabbed the driver by the back of the neck, who now had a deer-in-the-headlights stare.

"Miss me?" Mac said to the Austrian.

The Austrian, shocked and shaken at the inexplicable arrival of the American, could only stare with saucer-wide eyes.

Mac pivoted his two feet toward the Austrian and tucked his knees to his chest. "Get out," he said.

Mac didn't even need to kick. The Austrian accepted his fate. He nodded and jumped out on his own, landing, bouncing, and tumbling in the desert abyss of fallen Quad Continental dreams.

Doc cheered, "Exhibit A!"

Mac's pale eyes squinted. They were reddened from the dry heat. He quickly situated himself into the driver's seat and gripped the steering wheel. He glanced at his feet and felt the pedals and the glorious feeling of adrenaline running through his body. Mac rolled his head and cracked his neck. "Uh oh, looky at what Mac's got."

"Sow some wild oats, brother!" Doc said.

"I'd never forgive myself if I didn't," Mac fired back.

Wide-eyed, Mac looked around at the pack of international racers, and they were all glued in on him, shocked at the spectacle of what the young American had done to the mighty Austrians, and for just a moment, Doc and Mac owned the pack. Every nerve and emotion was putty in their hands, but then something changed.

The voices of calm and cool heads soon prevailed in the headsets of the other racers. Seasoned crew chiefs, all watching from their own video feeds, quickly talked back their racers from the cliff of panic, and the teams slowed a bit, drifting back, giving both Doc and Mac some room to breathe.

"What's happening?" Mac asked.

"I don't know. Something though," Doc replied.

With the Austrian team ousted, a major favorite in the Quad Continental was no more. This was good news for every other racer still in the game.

Then, in typical Quad Continental flavor, the crews of the other race teams all had an eerily uniformed message to their drivers. *Eliminate the American navigator.*

The flag had dropped for the next stage of bedlam.

"Watch yourself," Doc said. "They're coming after you."

"Come and get it," Mac dared them.

* * *

"R U SEEING THIS???" THE TEXT CAME FROM DEAN AND BEEPED ON Rachel's phone, followed by a series of crazy, startled, and wacky emojis. Dean was following all the action of the race on Wild Dog TV.

Flip reached over from the back seat of the cabin and picked up the phone to read the text.

"Texting was obviously designed for me. Who needs wancy ferds," she giggled. "I mean fancy words."

"Let me see it," Penelope said, and Flip showed her the text. Penelope smacked her lips. "That is awful. I can't imagine a worse situation."

Rachel was concentrating on the desert, trying to miss rocks and holes as she had the pedal to the metal. "What's awful? What happened? What situation?" she asked as she swerved to miss a cactus.

Penelope sat up straight and spoke indignantly, "I'll tell you what has happened. Society is reverting to hieroglyphics with this unsophisticated emoji language. It's a real tragedy, if you ask me. Where is the joy of the perfectly, punctuated point? Or the grandiose delivery that stands on the sturdy foundation of the grammatically correct? Hmm? Next, we'll just be grunting to each other."

"Penelope!" Rachel said in exasperation. "Can you just tell me what the text says?"

Penelope answered, "It's Mr. Copper. He wants to know if you are watching what is happening in the race. If I lower myself to interpret the caveman lingo, there may be something that has caused him a fair amount of angst. Who knows for sure? I'm left to only interpret."

Flip nodded. "Definitely angst."

Rachel's irritation rose dramatically. "Well, what is the cause of the angst?" She glanced over at Penelope's phone, which was supposed to be streaming Wild Dog.

"Oh, I'm sorry." Penelope replied. "I wouldn't know. I switched over to the Hallmark channel."

"Hallmark?" Rachel was dumbstruck. "You're not watching the race?"

"No. It was barbaric. I found a lovely period film instead. It's placed in the early nineteen hundreds and it's about a young Hungarian girl working in her family's used clothing store. She dreams of playing the flute. It has subtitles."

Rachel rubbed her brow and glanced in the rear-view mirror. She spotted Flip watching her phone.

"Flip, you're watching, right?"

"Nope. I'm on eBay bidding for an autographed jersey of Cardale Jones. He signed it 12-gauge."

"But what about the race?" Rachel protested. "Can we not just focus on the race for a moment?"

"Don't worry, Mrs. Copper," Flip said as she bid again on the jersey, "if there was anything wrong, Jonah would say something."

Penelope agreed, "That's true. I feel Jonah is well-centered. It's not like we're counting on J-Dog. I fear he prefers calamity."

Just then the CB radio clicked and the static hissed. "Uh, Mrs. Copper, this is Jonah."

Flip clicked over to the stream on her phone and sat up straight and fast. "Not good," she blurted.

Rachel's maternal hopes confused what her senses told her. She saw glimpses on the smartphone but couldn't make heads or tails of it. It was too violent to believe.

* * *

THE GOPROS MOUNTED ON *THE DRAKON* AND DOC'S HELMET WERE allowing the Wild Dog to stream the most violent desert wheeled melee since Pharaoh tried to cross the Red Sea.

"You want a piece of me?" Mac screamed with revolutionary liberation. "Come and get it!" Mac made sure his wild-eyed tantrum met the faces of every racer surrounding him and then yelled, "ALL Y'ALL!"

Doc turned his head back. "Here they come!"

Like a school of piranhas, racers from every tribe and nation descended on Mac. A scorching haze of exhaust, mixed with sand and tribal screams, filled the air.

Tubular bumpers and guards smashed and rammed Mac. The big Austrian KTM absorbed the blows, but so many crashes from every side and angle would eventually topple the racer and cast it into a death roll.

Doc sped up just enough to clear *The Drakon* from the attack, and he turned and saw nothing but an opaque cloud of wheels, racers, helmets, and the sounds of bars crashing and bending. It was a whirlwind of action of which Mac was the tumultuous eye. It was war, and at these speeds, lives were at stake.

"I'm coming back," Doc spoke into his headset.

"No!" Mac replied from the center of action, his command accompanied with grunts and yells. "Get out of here! This is your chance; they can't hurt me. Might kill me, but can't hurt me."

The swooping attacks that had become a full crash-up derby in the middle of a desert had slowed the pack down to just under sixty miles per hour. Doc could have sped away safely from all the destruction, but that wasn't the way of Doc Copper.

He spoke with calm determination, "Never. Coming back on your right."

Doc pulled the clutch with a hard clank and downshifted *The Drakon*. He broke hard, swerving to the outer perimeters of the pack.

He stared into the circle of craziness.

* * *

The international pack acted in one mindful collective, all hoping to leave the KTM and Mac in one burning pile of destruction as they took turns blitzing in on Mac in a synchronized offensive. If this continued, they would eventually find their target. As tough as Mac was, he couldn't match their driving skill.

Doc glanced over and saw the Finnish team moving into position to ram the back of Mac. "Finns are closing in behind you."

But then the team from Yemen slammed directly into Mac's driver side, tilting the big KTM up on his outer two wheels. "Agh!" Mac fought with the steering wheel and managed to slam the big racer back down on all fours. Yemen wasn't done, though. Side by side, they bounced and slammed into each other in the desert, and then the navigator reached over and grabbed Mac's wheel, trying to jerk it into a sidespin. Mac fought for control as the pack had sped back up to over seventy-five miles an hour.

THUMP.

Mac felt a knock on his helmet from the fist of the Yemenite navigator. *He punched me.* Mac thought. *The punk actually punched me.*

The Yemenite had clinched Mac's steering wheel and wasn't letting go.

Mac glared at the Yemenite and yelled, "Let's see what you can feel!"

Mac built up as much power as his torso and neck could manage. He took aim at the hand of the Yemenite and then jackhammered his helmet into the clinched fist of his opponent, crunching the teenager's metacarpals.

* * *

Jonah, Alfie, and J-Dog were bouncing on top of the trailer, screaming at the top of their lungs at the computer and iPad screens.

"Get 'em, Mac. Get 'em!" Jonah yelled, as he shadow boxed, and then he inadvertently punched his iPad, knocked it off the mount, and it flew through the air. It landed on J-Dog's chest.

"Oh! That's lucky," J-Dog said as he grabbed it. "Can you imagine if that fell over the side?"

Jonah sighed, and he reached out his hand to get the iPad back from J-Dog.

J-Dog glanced at the iPad right before he handed it back and noticed something. "Jonah, you didn't turn the comms on."

"What? Yes, I did," Jonah argued back. "You see the little bars? We're connected."

"Yes," J-Dog said, "we have a satellite link, but you still have to click the 'share network' tab that allows Doc on with us."

"No way," Jonah said.

"Yes way," J-Dog replied. "Look." J-Dog clicked the tab, and it slid green. "See, now we're on. Speak through your headset."

"Um, Doc, you there?"

"Jonah!" Doc screamed back. "What took you so long? It's crazy out here!"

"Oh, it's so good to hear your voice. Funny story . . . I didn't click the link."

"Don't care," Doc shouted back. "We got a situation."

"Is it bumpy, Doc?" Alfie asked. "Because it's really bumpy where we are."

"It's bumpy!" Mac yelled back as he got rammed from behind.

"Hey, Mac!" the boys yelled.

"Hey," Mac grunted back.

"I'm glad you're okay, Mac." Jonah said. "It looked bad from the cameras. It looked like you got tossed around a bit. Was it not as bad as it looked?"

"It's bad, can't talk," Mac gasped as he took a broadside hit on his right side.

"What?" Jonah said. "Give us something."

"Shut up!" Mac yelled as he got bashed again.

"Woah, woah, what is *that*, Mac?" J-Dog scolded. "You're acting like you're the only one going through stuff. It's tough doing what we're doing, too. You're not the only one."

"That's right," Jonah said, "try not to focus just on yourself. The nerve, telling me to shut up. I'm the Black Blondini. No one tells the Black Blondini to shut up."

Mac growled, "Going dark!" He turned off his comms.

"Wait," Doc tried to intervene, "well, good job, boys, you really went and did it. He turned off his comms."

"That's not our fault," J-Dog said. "To be honest, he wasn't showing any gratitude."

* * *

MAC JERKED THE STEERING WHEEL AND SIDESWIPED THE YEMENITES. He pointed at the navigator. "Back off, or else!"

But they wouldn't back off. The two UTV racers were banging into each other as Mac was forced to defend. There wasn't more than an inch between the two vehicles. Mac reached into their cabin and grabbed the Yemenites broken hand and squeezed. The teenager doubled over in pain. He could feel the broken bones shift in the hand.

The navigator writhed in pain.

Mac let go, but then the Yemen driver veered hard into Mac, bouncing him to his right.

Then came another BOOM, but this one came from behind. It was the Finns. Mac's body flung forward, and his face mask crashed into the steering wheel. The Yemen driver, seeing the opportunity, pressed the advantage and sideswiped Mac again.

BAM!

The team from Angola quickly closed in on Mac's right and perfectly clipped his front right tire with their big tubular bumper. Mac's tire lost its seal and blew.

POP!

Rubber threads exploded. The scent of burnt rubber instantly filled the air.

Mac was out of time. "I can't hold it!" he yelled as his head gyrated on top of his neck like a bobble head doll.

The Yemenite increased their side ramming with bloodlust.

Mac had only moments. One more well-placed ramming could send him into a barrel roll.

* * *

DOC WAS ON THE OUTER PERIMETER, OFF THE BACK RIGHT SIDE OF the pack, and he knew that he had to do something fast. The incessant colliding actually slowed the pack down, which gave *The Drakon's* smaller footprint a tactical advantage in this tight, phonebooth type of battleground.

Thread the needle, Doc thought to himself as he saw the thinnest of gaps behind the Finnish team and in front of the racer from Belize, who was trying to draft behind. *Engaging now,* and he twisted the throttle, passing Belize and zipping into that gap.

Doc felt his front tire so lightly interface with the back tire of the Finns. It was the slightest of buzzes, but the loudest indicator that there was zero room for error.

Doc stood up on the foot pegs. He stretched forward and snatched the crowbar from the emergency repair kit attached to the back bumper of the Finnish racer. Then he shot through the other side and fishtailed as he straightened his line. Now he was back in the middle of a hornets' nest.

Wasting no time, Doc twisted the throttle, redlined *The Drakon*, and crossed behind the Yemen team. He zipped up right next to its driver, who never saw him coming. Doc tapped on the driver's shoulder with the crowbar. The racer turned with surprised eyes as Doc heaved the crowbar with all his might and harpooned it through the steering wheel, embedding it deep into the plastic dash—locking the steering in one final position.

The driver was dazed by the audacity of the maneuver, and then fear flooded his eyes and mind when he realized his steering wheel was locked.

Doc drifted back to his left and indicated that Mac should veer right.

Mac understood but muttered to himself, "But I don't have a front tire."

Doc glanced back to his left just in time for his peripheral vision to catch the Polish team charging him. They were on him, going for the kill.

Doc had to evade, and evade now. He crouched down, squeezed the seat with his knees, and hit all his brakes at once. Skidding in the desert. The Polish team flew right by him, but clipped *The Drakon's* front left tire as they passed, just enough to spin *The Drakon* into a clockwise donut spin at over seventy miles per hour. In the microseconds of the moment, in the midst of the tornadic spin, Doc felt his right tires begin to lift up. He was going to barrel roll if he didn't balance it out.

His left hand let go of the handlebars, and he completely swung his left foot over *The Drakon* and hung his whole body over the right side, sitting his butt down as far as it could go and throwing his head back.

"Hold it!" he screamed.

* * *

"Aw!" Rachel yelled as she saw a whirlwind on Penelope's screen, not knowing exactly what she saw, but knowing it wasn't good.

"Whoa!" Jonah followed suit, and he was joined by Alfie, J-Dog, and all of Wild Dog TV in one unified shout.

Doc spun three full circles in a matter of two ticks of the clock, but he was able to counter the gravity and get *The Drakon* to put four on the floor. Doc's body got flung back up into the saddle, and nothing but pure driver instincts kicked in as his right hand instantly twisted the throttle, allowing the back tires to dig in. Just like that, he was racing again. "Ahhh!" he nearly caterwauled.

The Polish team was stunned that Doc had somehow survived. Worse for them, though, they forgot to watch where they were going. The ebbs and flows of racing often depend on the cohesive understanding from all the racers of the turns, brakes, and accelerations. Thus, racing hordes often move like a flock of birds.

However, the Yemen team couldn't turn. Doc's crowbar attack locked them into a straight line, throwing an unforeseen wrench in the natural moves of a race. But the Poles didn't see it, and BAM! They slammed into Yemen.

A massive collision sent both racers into the air and busted parts ricocheted into the sky. As fast as the machines went up was as hard as they came down. Crashing into the hot desert sand, breaking tail pipes, ripping wires, and rupturing tanks as debris rained down on the desert, tumbling and flipping into oblivion. The Poles and the Yemenites were finished.

The suddenness of the action shook the rest of the aggregation, but not for long. There were now two fewer countries in the race. Everyone's odds just got better.

Unfortunately, Mac's situation hadn't improved all that much. He still had a crippled machine, and the rest of the racers still thought crashing him was a swell idea. The Finnish team pressed the advantage and began a relentless barrage of ramming.

Mac turned his comms back on. "Doc?"

"I'm coming," Doc quickly responded as he looked for an angle, a way, an entry point to engage, but the Algerians made a move and filled the alley, and the Sudanese pinched Doc from the other side, giving him his own problems.

* * *

Mac jammed his foot into the accelerator, trying to will his way through this chaos, but that busted tire wasn't going to have it. Then a flashing light on the center dash touch pad of the KTM got his attention. "That's new."

Mac didn't have any idea what it really was. "It looks like a button of sorts," he muttered. With Mac's comms back on, the gang could hear him speaking.

"What's new?" Jonah asked, but Mac completely ignored him.

Mac thought a little bit more about it. *What could it hurt?* He pushed it, and then a few beeps went off in his own comms. His headset was trying to connect with the KTM. Then it gave an elongated beep and a digitized voice confirmed, "You are connected."

Next, Mac could hear someone talking on the other side, but it wasn't anyone he knew.

"Hello, American. Come in," a deep, gruff, older foreign voice spoke.

"Uh," Mac muttered, "hi?"

Jonah, back on top trailer, replied to Mac. "Yeah, hi. You need something?" Jonah couldn't hear the voice coming from the KTM comms.

"Not you, Jonah. This dude."

"What dude?"

"Hello, American," the heavy Austrian accent repeated.

Mac tapped his helmet. "You can't hear that, Jonah?"

"Hear what?"

"The voice."

"You need water," Jonah opined. "You need water. You're dehydrated and hearing voices."

Mac tuned out Jonah, and answered whoever was speaking to him, "Hello?"

"Hello, American. I am Verggaandschlaat."

Mac shook his head as he absorbed another blow from the Finnish team and crinkled up his face in confusion.

"What? You're Vermin Snot?"

"Verggaandschlaat. I am *the* Verggaandschlaat."

Mac yanked the wheel and hit the Slovakian team who had decided to replace the Yemenites on the attack on him.

"I'm *the* Mac, and I'm kind of in *the* middle—" the Finns rammed him from the back "—of a situation. So, something on your mind?"

The deep gritty voice continued, "I am the chief engineer of the Austrian racing team."

"Oh." Mac grimaced at the knowledge that he was driving the Austrian machine. "This is awkward."

"Awkward is right, Mac." J-Dog tried to intervene. "Are you losing your marbles? It's okay if you are, because insanity is great for views. Are you seeing any images or visions, or just hearing voices?"

Mac was frustrated. "Shut up!"

Jonah shook his head. "There he goes with the shut ups again. He is really self-absorbed right now. I'm about ready to turn him off until he cools down."

"What?" Verggaandschlaat asked. "Shut up?"

"Not you, Vermin Snot," Mac replied.

"Verggaandschlaat!"

"Whatever, man!" Mac yelled as he got sideswiped by the Slovaks.

The heavy Austrian accent came through again. "I am the . . ."

"I get it. You want an apology or something?" Mac growled back. "Well, I'm sorry I had to let your driver go. We didn't see eye to eye."

SMASH. Mac was in a desert death duel with the Slovaks, and his busted tire put him on the losing end for sure. Mac yanked the wheel back into the Slovaks. CRUNCH.

SMASH! Now the Finns rammed him again from the back end, and Mac banged his head against the side tubular frame with the hit. "I can't promise you're going to get this thing back in one piece, Vermin Snot. So best prepare yourself for more disappointment."

BANG. The Slavs hit him.

Verggaandschlaat fired back, "I'm not worried about our driver. Truth be told, he wore on my nerves."

Mac didn't see that coming. "You're not mad?"

"No, I'm furious. The Finnish team stole my design."

Mac turned around and glanced at the big Finnish UTV. "Familiar hood," he quipped.

"I have a deal for you, American," the Austrian engineer said.

"I'm all ears."

"I will help you survive if you make sure the Finnish team does not finish the race."

Mac blurted in grim and gruff fashion, "Finnish don't finish, and I live. Sounds like a win-win."

* * *

DOC TURNED HIS HEAD JUST IN TIME TO SEE THE SUDANESE COMING after him, and they were holding something in their hands.

"I've got bad intentions coming my way," Doc said.

"Be careful," Alfie said on the headset.

"Good tip," Doc replied.

Doc twisted the throttle and gained just enough separation to glance back. Sure enough, the Sudanese team had a sharpened spike of some kind, one that had only one purpose: blowing tires.

Game rage intensified. "So, it's like that," Doc seethed in his helmet. He began twisting, darting, and fishtailing *The Drakon*, and its racing tires obeyed by spraying a cloud of dust into the cockpit of Sudan. However, Sudan wouldn't yield. Nor did they change course or intention. It was a cat and mouse game with Sudan closing in with one evil intention: crash Doc out. The Sudanese navigator raised his spear, but with each inch closer, their visibility diminished. Doc's dust storm was working.

"*Leuwih deukeut!*" The Sudanese navigator shouted at his driver, egging the driver to get closer. He was fully focused on getting as close to that back tire as he could.

Doc veered toward them in a sudden move, and the driver instinctively turned a bit away, but came back with foolish resolve.

Ten feet back. Seven feet. Five feet.

"Come and get it," Doc calmly replied.

Three feet back and the navigator raised his spear and took aim.

Doc muttered, "Consequences."

Now, Doc thought and broke to his right as a single needle from a giant desert cactus broke off on the front left tire of *The Drakon*. It was a razor thin margin that was executed at breakneck speeds, one that the Sudanese could never make.

The cactus had a trunk that was the size of a small oak, and the Sudanese never saw it until they plowed right into it.

Doc glanced back and saw the cactus rupture on impact like a grenade.

The Sudanese's back end launched straight up in the air as the racer floated in a vertical headstand for a moment, and then gravity had its way and the front end came back down. The desert won that battle with an ultimate lesson of absolute truth. The hood splintered on impact, sending fiberglass shards in every direction. Every item on the front end ruptured, and the racer exploded in a calamitous, fiery vortex.

Then, it got worse. Explosions built on explosions as other teams that were clustered in that mob barreled into the wreckage, causing half of the pack to fall prey to their own murderous desires. This was a continent killer. Half the African nations fell. A third of the Asian teams were rendered inoperable, and every South American team had crashed out.

As gruesome as the burning crash was, the Quad Continental gave no reprieve, but only magnified in intensity. The Quad knew no status quo. Each level of conflict seemed to only breed a higher threshold to reach.

In ice-cold Quad form, the crashes were met by cheers from the surviving international racers, because their odds just got better. In their greed, they gave leash and leeway to their most primal desires and submitted their soul to the anarchy, lust, and the promise of glory.

* * *

"Alfie, I don't think we can wait any longer," Doc said, both accelerating his machine and reassessing the situation. He saw a new fleet of UTVs coming his way. "I need a way to get to Mac, and I need all the help I can get."

Alfie picked up his drone controller. "We have daisy chained the boosters and connection is good. My drone is awaiting departure."

"Send it," Doc said.

Alfie removed his desert goggles and replaced them with a high-def, virtual-reality headset. On the screen, he could see everything that the GoPro camera on the drone could see, plus data on altitude, speed, battery power, air temperature, and precipitation. Absolutely everything a military grade drone could provide, Alfie's drone could also do. He and Doc had made sure of that.

He then wrapped a white silk scarf around his neck and announced, "Operation Save Doc and Mac from the Evildoers in the Desert now deployed."

J-Dog looked over at Alfie, "Operation Save Doc and Mac from the Evildoers in the Desert? That's what you came up with?"

"What? No good?" Alfie asked.

"It's too long," J-Dog said. "You need something, like Operation Razor Wire, or Shark Bite, or—"

"I got it," Alfie interrupted. "Operation Sky Talon!"

"Okay," J-Dog said, "that might be the coolest thing you've ever said."

"Oooh, check it out," Jonah added. "Operation Sky Talon deployed."

"Doc, I'm coming to get you," Alfie said as he pressed full throttle as the drone lifted itself off the desert floor.

* * *

Mac craned his neck. "Are you kidding me?" he yelled, his knuckles tightening up. "These guys don't quit!" He got smashed again from behind. "Vermin Snot, what do you have for me?"

The thick Austrian accent came back: "Under the steering wheel, you will find a yellow knob."

Mac reached underneath and found it. "Yep, it feels like a gear shift. What is it?"

"After they stole my design, I added something special, just for them."

"Okay, what do I do?"

"Pull it out, shift it to the right, and then up, and then push it in, but wait until the Finns are within three feet from your back bumper before you do it."

"Alright." Mac grabbed the knob and recited the instructions as he did it. "Pull. Shift right. Then up. Wait." Mac turned around and let off the gas just a smidge. The Finns took the opportunity to come in for a ram. "Waiting!" The Finns were no more than eighteen inches away. "Push!"

Mac heard clinking and rattling underneath the racer. The Finns were a micro-moment from collision. "Where's the magic, Vermin Snot?"

"Verggaandschlaat!" the angry Austrian replied.

POP! POP! POP!

Mac turned his head back and watched the whole thing unfold. The Finnish racer lost traction and went into a sideways slide in the desert. Doc was flying up the left side and had to quickly dodge the side sliding racer, which had started a 360-degree spin. All four Finnish wheels popped, went instantly flat, and the tire threads began systematic shredding until nothing was left.

Doc saw the cause and banked hard to his left to miss them. "Dude! You just dumped spikes out your back end!"

"Iron spikes?" Mac asked with hope and pride.

"Yep."

Jonah, J-Dog, and Alfie were listening intently to the audio and began jumping and cheering so hard that they almost knocked each other off the top of the trailer.

The old Austrian came through the headset. "American? Did we take care of our problem?"

"Dude. That was awesome!" Mac screamed. "Finns are finished."

"Good. You did your part. Now I do mine. Go to the flat screen."

Mac looked at the dash and began studying the touch screen embedded in the dash.

"Press the racer icon," Vermin Snot said.

"Pressing."

The display switched to a myriad of options and icons.

"Do you see the tire icon?"

"Yep."

"Press it."

Mac pressed it. "Got it. Go."

"American, you should see four tire icons. Press the front right tire icon."

"Okay. Done."

Vermin Snot continued, "Third bullet point down. Press."

Mac found the line item, but his finger was bouncing to the rhythm of the desert. "It had to be an eight-point font," Mac said incredulously.

BUMP. Mac missed the mark, and pressed bullet point two instead.

The flat screen went black and then flashed a skull and crossbones image. "Not good."

The heavy Austrian voice came through, "You pressed the wrong button."

CLUNK.

"Huh?" Mac looked up at where the sound came from.

WHEW.

The entire roof of the KTM flew up and off, sending it high and cartwheeling in the air. The team from Uzbekistan wasn't ready for that. The big roof landed directly on their hood, caving in the front with a big crash and blocking their vision. They drove right off a desert ravine. Another team bit the dust.

Evidently, the sequence of events from the mischievous bullet point two wasn't complete.

CLICK. BOING!

The navigator seat ejected. It tumbled in the air and landed right in front of the Philippines. The Filipinos deftly evaded the falling bucket seat with brilliant skill, only to crash into a giant cactus as the driver gave his navigator a high five. The impact flipped the racer, bending the axel, and taking another team out of contention.

Mac was unhinged. "Who are you people? Are you insane? You put in an ejection seat!"

"Sorry. That sequence is over," Vermin Snot said. "Was it too much? It might have been too much. Sorry, I get frustrated sometimes, and I fantasize about things." He paused and then continued, "It's my wife."

"Huh?" Mac asked. "Your wife is somehow connected to this ejection seat?" Mac shook his head and muttered, "What weird universe did I get sucked into?"

"Yes," Vermin Snot replied, "my wife. She talks and nags and talks and nags. She says I push her buttons. Well, I told her I'll give her a button to push."

"Yeah, that's a heck of a button," Mac replied.

"Don't push anymore wrong buttons."

Mac nodded quickly. "I'll make sure of that, but you're carrying emotional baggage, dude."

"That's what my therapist says."

"You got to deal with things as they happen. Can't let them fester. It's not healthy," Mac said.

"Is that what you do?"

"Yeah, I live by a code," Mac replied as he veered and sideswiped another team who had hit him.

"I want to hear more of this *code* you speak of?"

"Let's table that for now."

"Right, right," Vermin Snot said. "Pressing matters."

"Right, pressing matters."

"Okay, push the third bullet," Vermin Snot said.

"Yes, three." Mac found the screen again. *Still eight-point font,* he thought. "Careful, Mac," he whispered to himself as he slowly positioned his finger above the flat screen link. "And—"

"Wait!" Vermin Snot yelled.

"Wait?" Mac jerked his finger back. "What? Wait? Why?"

"Sorry. Bullet point one," Vermin Snot sheepishly suggested.

"What? Bullet one? You said three!" Mac screamed.

"Right. You are a very lucky American. It is most certainly bullet point one."

Mac shook his head in anger. "What's three? You know, the bullet point you told me to push?"

A slight pause, and then, "Uh, it's best if we don't go there. Muddies the water. I am certain it's one."

Mac was beside himself, but he steadied his finger. "Fine, one. Here goes nothing."

CLICK.

PSHHHH! The front right side of the racer popped up, and Mac felt the balance and handling of the big KTM come back full force.

"Vermin Snot," Mac yelled, "what happened?"

With no shortage of pride, Vermin Snot explained, "I repurposed airbag technology to created self-inflating spare tires."

"Dude, that's actually genius!"

"My thoughts exactly, my young friend. Now I have fulfilled my end of the deal. What you do now is up to you. But know this: the cage is made of high grade, reinforced Usibor 1500 aluminized steel."

Mac crumpled up his face. "Meaning what?"

"Your name is Irons," the Austrian engineer nonchalantly replied. "I thought you would have a proclivity for metallurgy."

"Low blow," Mac begrudgingly replied.

"Okay," Vermin Snot said, "your frame is super-duper, stupid strong."

"Understood. See? That's all you had to say." Mac looked around at the remaining racers that had been slamming into them and growled, "Blood for blood."

"Is that your code?" Vermin Snot asked with curiosity.

"That's my code."

* * *

Doc throttled hard, but the hole closed. "I can't get to you, Mac. I'm hemmed in on every side."

"Are they trying to kill you, too?" Mac said as he swerved at and away from every racer near him.

"It certainly appears that way," Doc replied. "Maybe if I can get loose and get up next to you, you can make a jump for it."

Mac gritted his teeth. "Sure, since crazy is the new normal."

Doc fishtailed to his left, avoiding a charging Croatian team. "You got any better ideas?"

"Evidently, I'm driving a tank with lots of bad buttons in it. I'm kind of thinking of just ramming everyone and pressing every button I got."

Jonah jumped in, "Hey, Mac, I got to tell you, we're a little worried about your frame of mind."

Mac gave a devious chuckle as he swerved toward a UTV, trying to ram it, but it got away. "My head is right where it needs to be."

"We're trying to put pieces together on this end," Jonah continued, because he still didn't understand that Vermin Snot was an Austrian engineer. "We all think you shouldn't press buttons you can't read. The instructions aren't in English, after all."

Mac's eyes were wide as owls as he aimed his front end toward another racer. "He was telling me to press the buttons."

"Who?" Jonah asked.

"Vermin Snot."

Jonah ran his fingers through his spiked blond fro. "He's hearing voices."

"Dude," J-Dog jumped in, "just embrace the voice, Mac. Do whatever the voice tells you to do."

Jonah gave J-Dog a dirty look. "Embrace the voice?"

J-Dog shrugged. "Do you see the views we're getting? I mean, we are moving the needle, brother. Plus, the voice seems to know what to do."

"Alfie," Doc jumped in, "you should be here by now."

"I see you now. I'm coming fast," Alfie said. "Watch your six; someone's coming."

Doc turned around just in time and saw the Japanese team with that big rising sun painted on the front hood. "Hey, Mac, they're coming after one of us."

Doc swerved to miss the first big collision. "Thanks, Alfie, I needed that."

J-Dog chimed in, "Show 'em you're riding a Honda. Shouldn't that get you some goodwill?"

Jonah almost responded to J-Dog, but he saw beads of sweat running down Alfie's face. "Alfie, you okay?"

Alfie didn't respond.

J-Dog tried to figure out what this newly found angst was that riddled Alfie's face. "Dude, you look like you're having a bad experience in a port-a-potty."

"Aggh!" Alfie yelled as he shifted his whole body right and thrust the joystick down and then back up again. "Climb, climb!" he yelled.

"What's going on?" Jonah asked.

"Enemy drones!" Alfie yelled as J-Dog grabbed a water bottle and sprayed a stream meant for Alfie's gaping, thirsty mouth, but missed, and soaked his head instead.

"Sorry, dude, that's what I get for being a good Samaritan." He shook his head and stared into a camera. "A man should know his limitations."

"It's okay," Alfie replied, completely consumed with the action inside his modified headset.

"Drones?" Jonah asked. "Who?"

"The Japanese!" Alfie yelled. "It's a dogfight!"

"Japanese? Dogfight?" J-Dog obliged with the rhetorical question: "Do we have a good camera feed?"

Jonah nodded. "We've got the GoPro on the drone!"

"Towel!" Alfie shouted like a surgeon, and Jonah wiped down the sweat from Alfie's brow.

"Dude," Jonah said to Alfie, "you look like a ticking time bomb."

Alfie pursed his lips. "Got that straight."

* * *

"WAAKAAA!" ALFIE SCREAMED AS HE PULLED HARD ON HIS JOYstick and his drone buzzed the needles off a desert cactus.

One Japanese drone aligned right above Alfie's and then plummeted in hopes to crash them both to the ground.

"No, you don't!" Alfie yelled and corkscrew-spiraled off to the side, evading the attack by a sliver. He dropped his drone to twelve inches from the desert ground at sweeping speeds, kicking up his own dust cloud. "Now watch this!"

Alfie throttled hard. The jet-designed drone dropped its backend, just touching the thinnest layer of sand, and brought its nose up to begin an aggressive climb. Alfie looked behind him, and the camera mounted on the top of the drone turned with him as the motion detector on the goggles controlled the direction of the camera.

Both Japanese drones matched the aggressive move and were closing fast.

"Hmm. So, you want to play hardball." Alfie banked hard right and yanked straight up, pulling the drone's path perpendicular to the ground. The Doc Copper–modified drone responded and climbed like a fighter jet all the way to twenty-five hundred feet. But the Japanese were up to the task. The enemy drones followed suit and climbed in a kamikaze pursuit.

Alfie zoomed in on them. "Those are the military issued, anti-ballistic J-5000 series super drones, and there are two of them. No one's been this close before!" Alfie huffed and puffed as he banked back and forth. "I'm dropping down to a couple hundred feet."

He entered a steep dive, quickly losing altitude, but then a warning icon flashed in Alfie's goggles.

"What? That's impossible," Alfie said as he clicked through his instrumental panel.

"What's impossible?" Jonah asked.

"I'm overheating. When I say heating, I mean really fast. My circuits will fry in thirty seconds if this keeps up. Doc, you will lose all aerial support. Are you hearing me?"

"Yes," Doc replied as he looked up in the sky.

"How is this happening?" Alfie asked.

Doc could now see the three drones locked in a dog fight above with massive swoops, turns, and dives. "Dude," he said, "I think you have two red dots on you. Almost like laser dots."

"What?!" Alfie turned his head and zoomed his camera in on the J-5000s. Sure enough, two blinding bright red lights were emitting a beam, and they were locked on him.

"Laser warfare," Alfie said. "They're heating me up!" Alfie shoved his joystick hard and to the side, going into a spiraling nosedive to the desert floor and temporarily losing the lasers that were on the drone.

"We need to put an end to this, Doc. Got a plan?" Alfie asked.

Doc looked ahead and saw what appeared to be an ancient dried out creek bed.

"Mac, do you see that wash up ahead?" Doc asked.

Mac was busy bashing guys around him, but he looked up. "Yeah, I got it."

"I got something if you're up for it," Doc said.

Mac smirked. "I got nothing else going on. What's on your mind?"

"How 'bout taking that tank of yours airborne?" Doc asked.

Mac grinned. "That's just my kind of crazy."

* * *

Jonah chimed in after Doc went through the plan. "I see what you're saying, but we could try this thing a thousand times and only hit it once."

Mac twitched his head. "Lucky for us, then, that we only need it once."

"Mac," Doc said, "throttle down hard right now and get into that creek bed."

"On it!" He shoved two other racers out of his way with his big tubular bumper.

"We got to hurry," Alfie said as the temperature reading on his drone reached critical mass. "They are hot on my tail. Increasing speed. Initiating cobra maneuverer now." Alfie put his drone in spiral nosedive to shake the drones, but they were able to follow. "I'm closing on the ground fast!"

"Pull up!" Doc yelled.

"I got it!" Alfie punched a button on his control panel and jerked the joystick back, barely leveling out before smashing into the ground. He zoomed forward and then curved around a giant cactus.

The first of the two enemy drones tried to follow him in the dive but couldn't pull up in time. CRASH! It smashed into the desert floor, obliterating everything about it.

"Splash one!" Alfie yelled. "That's what I'm talking about!"

However, the second J-5000 matched Alfie's high-speed maneuver, turn for turn, and it was now one on one.

Mac got free of his pack and jammed the accelerator with all he had and made a bee line for the dried-out creek bed.

The remaining J-5000 managed to regain the laser lock.

"I only have seconds left," Alfie said.

Doc replied, "Mac, once you're in the wash, find the best embankment that can be used as a ramp and hit it hard. Alfie, make sure you cross that front end as close as you can—and I mean inches—when Mac is in the air.

"Copy that," Alfie said.

"I'm getting to the creek," Mac said. "Here we go!" Mac's Austrian KTM flew off the edge and landed in the middle of the dried-out riverbed. He skidded, turned, and hit the gas. "I'm in."

"Okay," Doc said, "get your speed back up and find that natural ramp out. Alfie, get ready to cross his nose."

"Yeah, yeah, yeah," Mac said as he pointed his KTM toward his target. "I found my ramp, Alfie. Get ready!" Mac leaned back against his seat and stomped his foot on the gas.

"I'm coming!" Alfie yelled.

WHOOSH! Mac hit that embankment at a ludicrous speed, and like a missile launched from a naval ship, ripped into the air.

"Now!" Doc yelled.

"Ah!" Alfie screamed so loud that it startled Jonah and J-Dog on the trailer. He banked his drone and skimmed right in front of the KTM's nose, only inches to spare from a midair collision.

The timing of the trap was perfect. The J-5000 never saw it coming.

As the Japanese drone was a microsecond behind Alfie's drone and fully focused on its attack, it never envisioned meeting Mac in the air.

Mac's flying tank crunched the drone in mid-flight, pulverizing it. The resounding crunch sent a fuzzy signal back to the Japanese pit crew. Fragments of the drone showered the desert.

The boys screamed at the explosive collision.

"Splash two!" Alfie screamed.

Doc lifted a defiant fist in the air as Alfie's drone was now free and clear. Mac landed back on the desert with tumultuous force, bounced a few times, and found himself back in the race.

Vermin Snot's voice came through Mac's comms, "Yes! Yes! Blood for Blood! Ah, I like it. You are an engineer's dream. You get the most out of my machine. I wish you were my son."

"Too much," Mac replied. "That's way too much."

"Yes, sorry, I got carried away," Vermin Snot said. "My machine is good, no?"

"Yeah, it's a peach," Mac replied.

* * *

"The Japanese are coming at me, Mac," Doc said. "They want revenge."

"They want more, huh?" Mac asked the question, already knowing the answer.

"Copy that," Doc said as he veered to help Mac's line crisscross with the Japanese.

But the Japanese tossed Doc and Mac a softball without knowing it. The midair collision of their drone and the big KTM made the Japanese driver lose focus and he unwisely gave a prolonged stare at the falling debris. At that speed, those moments meant covering hundreds of feet on the ground. Not even the all-wheel drive Subaru-engineered machine could save that lack of focus.

The Japanese saw Mac's move to cut him off too late and only from the corner of his eye, which sent an involuntary reflex through his body, and he slammed on his brakes, jerking the wheel to his left. This error turned the Subaru forty-five degrees and sent his racer into an ominous side slide.

Mac hit the gas and evaded the skidding UTV, but not everyone escaped the sudden maneuver. The team from Greece trailed the Japanese by only a few meters, and the Greeks t-boned them at full speed. The two teams tumbled over each other in a locked somersault, spinning, flipping, and sputtering into a crumpled pile of twisted metal and broken dreams.

The Japanese were one of the favorites to win it all, and now they were out.

The Quad Continental, though, would not cease or desist. Violence begets violence, and Lithuania swooped up on Mac's left side, moving into the space vacated by Japan and Greece, and smashed into him.

The Lithuanian navigator was shouting all sorts of things at Mac and shaking a fist.

"I don't know what you said, but it didn't sound nice," Mac grunted. The rush of fight-or-flight adrenaline gave Mac another jolt. Mac chose fight.

Mac rebalanced himself and then jerked the wheel as hard as he could, slamming into the Lithuanian vehicle.

"Ah!" Vermin Snot yelled. "Blood for blood!"

The big KTM did its work and caved in the roll bar on the navigator's side. He stunned the Lithuanian into a moment of paralysis, and that was all that Mac needed.

With not an inch to spare between the two racing machines, they barreled through the desert, bumping into each other. Mac pressed his right knee against the steering wheel to steady it while he thrust both of his hands into the cabin of the Lithuanian racer. Mac was able to unclick the racing harness of the navigator.

"I could use a navigator," Mac seethed as his knees turned his steering wheel hard while he held on to the Lithuanian navigator with a python's grip. He yanked the shell-shocked teenager out of his racer and into the KTM.

* * *

ALFIE SHOUTED, "DOC, BREAK RIGHT, RIGHT, RIGHT!"

Doc didn't have time to look or think. He just reacted and banked hard right.

It was just in time to escape a charge from Madagascar. Fortunately, that team wasn't fast enough to follow the move. Their front left tire clipped a desert bolder and sent it into a spin that ended with them falling off the edge of a ravine.

"Thanks, Alfie," Doc exhaled, "you saved me that time."

"Just doing my job, sir," Alfie replied.

"Mac, I'm coming your way." Doc shifted up and adjusted his sights on trying to pull ahead of Mac.

"It's about time," Mac said. "Though give me a sec." Mac turned to his new passenger, and said, "You should be wearing a seatbelt."

Mac slammed his foot on the accelerator and jerked the wheel to the left, sending the KTM into a sinister G-force inducing spin at insane speeds.

His Lithuanian plus one flung out the side, but his right hand clung to the tubular roll bar as his body extended straight as a board as they spun in the desert, but the gravitational pull was too much, and, *whew*, the teenager was gone.

"Dude!" J-Dog's voiced came through. "We caught all of that from the drone footage. We're winning awards for this!"

Jonah jumped in, "I can't believe you did that, Mac. That was cold!"

"They started it!" Mac shot back.

Jonah turned to Alfie and J-Dog. "I think he left his conscience back in Tennessee."

Mac then went into full demolition mode, aided by turn-by-turn warnings and instructions from Alfie. He rammed every racer that had attacked him.

Tires popped, rims bent, and helmets were stress tested against dashboards. Mac was aided by the considerable advantage that he didn't need his machine to survive, at all.

The pit crews from every nation tried to get through to their drivers, but to no avail. Only the sounds of crashing, smashing, and collision came back through the headsets.

Iceland, South Sudan, Senegal, Romania, Nicaragua, and Jamaica were all crashed out, and by the time they were done, only a handful of teams were left from the entire pack that broke away from Ethan Oxidant's group and had followed Doc.

* * *

DOC HAD *THE DRAKON* RUNNING WIDE OPEN, AND HE HAD THE angle on Mac. "Coming up on your left, brother."

"Come and get me," Mac said. "I think I killed the KTM." Indeed, his hood was now spewing billows of smoke. "Kind of a shame really. It came in handy."

"I'm going to pull right up next to you. Just hop on the pogo stick."

"Funny how that sounds really easy at this point." Mac chuckled a bit and turned to check his surroundings. Only three other teams remained, but they were closing in: Georgia, Papua New Guinea, and Fiji. "Are you kidding me?" Mac said.

"It won't stop until the finish line," Doc said. "That's what this is."

Mac unbuckled his racing harness, pulled his left foot up, and crouched on the seat, still with his right foot down on the gas.

"Are you ready?" Doc asked impatiently from right next to Mac. "Those other guys are about to ram you."

"About that."

Mac tapped the icons on the flat screen in the familiar order and made it back to notorious bullet points. He then tapped the comm icon on the flat screen.

Mac's headset clicked, hissed, and a familiar voice came through. "Yes, Mac Irons," Vermin Snot replied.

Mac glanced backward, and he saw the team from Georgia waving threatening fists at him. "Tell me about bullet point three."

"I see you," Vermin Snot. "We're all watching you on the Wild Dog. ROOF! ROOF!" he barked.

"That's great," Mac said. "Three?"

"Press it, and then you have five seconds to get away. It goes, how do I say in English: Boom."

"It blows up?" Mac asked.

"Of course," Vermin Snot said. "In the case that my racer did not finish the race, I didn't want to leave behind my inventions for everyone to steal."

"You've got problems, dude. But, alright. Here goes nothing."

Mac clicked bullet point three, and the flat screen went red. He lunged out the side window gap and clutched those crazy pogo stick handlebars on the back of *The Drakon*. His body dropped with a thud on the desert, and he began dragging off the back end of *The Drakon*.

"Go! Go! Go!" Mac yelled and Doc didn't delay. He veered hard left, putting as much distance between the KTM and them as possible.

Mac turned to watch as the racers who were hot on the KTM's bumper stared in disbelief at what they had just seen.

BOOM!

The KTM exploded with such force that it knocked Papua New Guinea and Fiji up in the air and on to their sides. Georgia rammed the fire ball from behind. The fireproof race suits saved the lives of the drivers and navigators, but their UTVs were utterly burnt to a crisp.

"Dude!" Jonah, Alfie, and J-Dog gasped.

"What was that?" Doc asked as shocked as everyone else.

Mac pulled himself back onto that pogo stick and gave a huge exhale. "Button three."

Millions of dollars of research and development were reduced to nothing but a pile of burning metal and plastic in the desert. After the ash settled, Doc and Mac were the only ones left from the lead group that hadn't splintered off and followed the British.

"Clear sailing now," Doc said. "At least for a little while."

Mac looked up at Alfie's drone and gave a thumbs up.

* * *

THE QUAD CONTINENTAL TURNED THE PAGE ON ANOTHER CHAPter in its notorious existence, but this time, it was different. Thanks to streaming on dozens of international channels, not to mention Wild Dog TV, the Quad Continental's raw carnage was now exported to the world.

The guts, gruel, and its tantalizing carrot of glory, which was always met with the stick of cruel reality, was now on flat screens, computer screens, tablets, and phones all over the connected world.

Every social media platform in every nation had running threads rooting for and against their teams of choice. It was no longer millions who followed every last detail of the race. It was now billions. A viral event went super viral as the race consumed the hearts and minds of the masses.

The violence and the wreckage of the Quad Continental was not all that different from the carnage often carried out in the ancient coliseums of Rome, which is why the masses were drawn to it. But unlike the old coliseum, this new one wasn't made of concrete, but required a stage big enough for an axis to spin upon, and the internet provided such a place.

It was at this point, in this ripple in time, where the Bell Buckle Gang went from a flash in a pan to tipping their toes into the pools of legends, but legends of *what* exactly still remained to be seen.

* * *

DOC CROUCHED FORWARD AND WIPED THE SAND OFF HIS GOGGLES. He dug in nicely to his throttle as he and Mac skipped across the top of sand whoops and slalomed in and out of tree-sized cacti. They had been riding for hours now. Hundreds of miles were behind them, and the pack was gone. They were all alone on their own handpicked route, except for their friendly eyes in the sky.

The pandemonium of the starting line, the ruckus to survive the opening forays of the race, and the ludicrous maneuvers needed to wrench themselves free from the big mechanical menaces had passed. In Doc's mind, the waters had miraculously been calmed, and now the purity of the desert offered the euphoria of unspoiled nature as far as the eye could see.

"Awesome," Mac said. A kid from the inner city had never seen so much empty space. The best view he knew of was one that kept the back alley out of sight. He was mesmerized at the landscape of sand, rocks, and canyons.

The Drakon seemed to enjoy it, too. Racing engines were built to race. They were built to find mechanical balance at the upper echelons of their power output. The engine of *The Drakon* was no different. It was doing exactly what it was designed to do, and to Doc, it felt alive.

The independent shocks were sliding and absorbing every little bump in the desert and would have made its design engineers proud. The pistons were firing with precision, and the engine block perfectly captured the force of each miniature explosion, ushering power to the gears that provided the torque, turn, and punch along the entire RPM range.

Doc was one of the few riders who could push a machine to its highest performance. A grease monkey romantic might even wipe a tear, with an oil-stained shop rag, to see Doc push his engines into this mechanized nirvana now that the chaos of the crash-up derby had subsided.

Mac looked at his tablet mounted to the eBay special handlebars. "Jonah, you got me. Come in big fella."

Back at the control center, Jonah, J-Dog, and Alfie were also celebrating the new calm equilibrium that they found, and they quickly got back to their normal selves.

Jonah was lecturing the two others on his advantage, in a desert situation, to retain huge amounts of water. "Perfectly adjusted to my environment. You see?" He grabbed his belly and jostled it around. "I got reserves!" Jonah said as he heard the call from Mac and answered. "What's up? I got you loud and clear."

"Just double checking, dude," Mac said. "In about one mile, we are taking a pretty sharp turn. What are we looking at?"

"I've got you jumping into a dry riverbed for about fifteen miles," Jonah said.

Doc was listening and liked what he heard. "Perfect. We'll max it out."

"Yep, and you'll find a fuel can and supply bag at the end of that stretch."

"Great. I'm getting hungry," Mac replied.

"Now you should know, the other racers have broken off into two other packs. One pack is led by the British, and the Australians are close behind. The other pack is led by the Mexican team."

"Who's ahead?" Mac asked.

"It's close. Ethan seems the fastest. In saying that, though, that Magali's no joke. She keeps making up time. She knows the terrain perfectly."

"Makes sense. This is Mexico after all," Doc responded.

"Yep," Jonah replied, "one more thing. There aren't many teams left. They are dropping like flies. By the time we hit Tijuana, I bet there won't be more than a dozen racers still in it. We'll see."

"Wow," Mac said.

"It's a race of attrition. We just have to survive for now," Doc said.

"Yep," Jonah replied.

"So, we're currently winning, right?" Mac asked.

Jonah sighed and paused.

"Jonah?" Doc asked.

"Based on how far you have to go, you're kind of in last," Jonah confessed.

"What? We're flying," Doc said. "This is the fastest I've ever raced."

"It's not by *too* much, but it appears you'll be last to the check point. The British pack should be first, rolling in after midnight at about 12:35 with the Mexican-led pack closely behind about five minutes later. Then you and Mac right around 12:55 . . . if all stays the same, you know."

Doc felt a thud in his stomach. His tailbone was bruised and sore, hurting each time he allowed his legs to rest as he took a brief seat. His lips were chapped, cracked, and bleeding from the dry desert air. His eyes were bloodshot. The water and food in the supply bags would keep them going, but it wasn't enough to quench any thirst and fill their stomachs.

That far behind at racing speeds might as well have been an eternity, especially since they were already on the slowest vehicle.

"I don't get it," Mac said. "Doc has us full tilt."

"I know. You're preaching to the choir," Jonah replied. "And what stinks up the whole Mexican desert is that when the barn burnt down, it looks like it made it impossible for us to win the Quad Continental. No matter how great you guys are. Even with the speed modifications you made to *The Drakon*, it's still not fast enough. These big UTVs are just blistering fast, man. It ain't your fault."

The reminder of the barn fire lit a fire of its own in Doc's bones. He gripped the handlebars tight, which stung like fresh bee stings because of the broken blisters that had bubbled, popped, and seeped across his palm, even with the protection of the gloves. "Jonah," Doc almost growled, "where can we find those extra minutes?"

"I'd love to add a different perspective here," J-Dog said. "This narrative of the hero who lost everything and is far behind in the race of his life is playing great on Wild Dog." J-Dog smiled big. "It's actually . . . a tearjerker. I didn't know views could go so high. It's like we're inventing new numbers now."

"Glad we could help." Doc brushed off the comment. "Now, boys, we need to make up some time."

"Copy that," Jonah said with a fair bit of dejection.

* * *

THE NEXT TWO FUEL AND SUPPLY POINTS WENT OFF WITHOUT A hitch. Doc moved with the precision of a surgeon. Mac acted with the fearlessness of a boy who didn't feel pain as he snagged the fuel cans off rocks and arms of cacti at speeds high enough to bruise the body with every point of contact. Yet even with all of that, Doc knew their level of perfection was failing them.

"It's not good enough." Doc allowed doubt to find a place in his heart and mind. "I can't get more out of *The Drakon* than what we're getting."

"Got to," Mac said. "No choice."

Doc could feel a new vibration in the Drakon's handlebars. It buzzed a little more and the vibrations carried a touch more pop that began to numb his hands, which wasn't all bad—it helped dull the pain from the bleeding blisters across his palms.

Doc knew *The Drakon* was tapped out. Their decision to not stop, to not spend the time on oil changes and basic race maintenance, was starting to catch up, and *The Drakon* began to show the inevitable. It was dying. He knew it would give up the ghost for the race, but he never conceived in his eternally optimistic and idealistic mind that it would be sacrificed in a losing effort.

He never believed that the Quad Continental would cost them everything while they gained nothing. Nevertheless, he felt the unforgiving hand of time ticking away.

They were behind Ethan Oxidant, and unless Ethan made a critical mistake, it would be Ethan who would win the most important race of a lifetime.

* * *

"You feel that?" Doc asked Mac. They had been riding for more than twelve hours now, and night was coming.

"I do feel it," Mac replied. "It's getting cold. When you told me that we needed gear to keep us warm in the desert, I thought you were being a pansy."

Doc laughed a bit as night fell. The stars and moon illuminated the desert sky, and it was awe-inspiring beauty, an undisturbed arid masterpiece that told of the creative hand of eternal magnificence, but the wind still chilled with no sun at those speeds.

"Do we have any energy bars or drinks left over from the last supply bag?" Doc asked.

"Yep, here you go." Mac handed an energy bar over Doc's left shoulder. "I was just thinking; it would really be bad if we broke down out here. It's been a bit since we've seen any signs of life. Outside of an armadillo."

"Let's not bring that topic up again, especially since Alfie's drone can't last much longer."

"I heard that," Alfie said.

"But I'm right," Doc said. "I did some special work on it with the hybrid power source, but it's got to be close to dead."

"It is," Alfie said. "I was thinking, though, if I land it soon it would be possible for stand-by power to continue to send a signal to its location. After the race, I could come back and get it."

"Alfie," Doc replied, "that's probably not going to happen."

"But you never know," Alfie said.

"You're right. Crazier things have happened."

"Okay then," Alfie said with a little bit of encouragement. "I'll start looking for a place to stash it."

It had been a decent enough spell with little to no action that Mac was able to finally take a deep breath and appreciate the view. "I honestly didn't know places like this existed anymore," he said. "It's kind of cool. That is, as long as I don't have to live here."

"Nobody lives here," Doc said.

Mac peered as far as his eyes would take him. "What's that?" he asked as the moon gave just enough light to make out some shapes.

"That can't be a donkey, can it?" Doc asked. He soon answered his own question, "It is."

A scrawny donkey was tied to a post in the ground. As they got closer, some chickens scattered.

* * *

"THIS CAN'T BE WHAT IT LOOKS LIKE," DOC REMARKED, AND HE LET off the gas just a bit.

“Not a chance,” Mac responded with a bit of grief in his voice, as if he already knew he was wrong.

The structure was rectangular and about ten by fifteen feet in size. It was erected out of broken bricks.

The roof consisted of loosely laid metal sheets that were more rust than anything else. A makeshift awning of torn-up, fraying rags hung over the door, which was nothing more than another piece of metal laid against the outer walls.

Never had emotions changed so rapidly in Doc and Mac before. One moment, they were boys from Tennessee racing in a world-renowned desert race. Then, in a twinkle of an eye, a grim reality of life on earth pushed its way into their little, unsuspecting world.

Doc instinctively pulled the clutch and began to coast as he approached the inconsolable place. “Alfie, is your drone seeing this?”

“Yes,” Alfie replied, clearly as shocked as Doc and Mac.

“Is that a house?” Jonah asked as he leaned into his laptop screen.

“I think so,” Doc replied.

The noise of the chickens and the growl of the engine awoke the family inside. A Mexican boy ran out the front door clearly faster than he was supposed to. He was similar in age to Doc and Mac, and he was skinny. Too skinny.

A father who had the look of fear and distress on his face ran out, grabbing for the boy to jerk him back in. He was equally malnourished, and their clothes were dirty, raggedy messes. They were quickly followed by a young girl, maybe seven years old, and then a mom.

For the first time in his racing career, Doc coasted to a stop right in the middle of a race. Mac didn’t protest or even make a sound. Doc felt his heart pounding in his chest. He felt emotion. He felt pain, sorrow, and even embarrassment. He had never seen such abject poverty. He slowly reached back to Mac and handed him the energy bar. Mac took it without ever saying a word.

Mac slid off his helmet and climbed off his pogo stick of a seat. He gathered the supply bag full of energy bars and drinks. He slowly walked over to the father.

The man was apprehensive. Not sure of what was in the bag. Not sure of the intentions of the strange visitors. He pulled his son back behind him and took a protective stance in front of his impoverished, malnourished family. Mac noticed the action and stopped walking. He raised his hand in a kind gesture and placed the bag on the ground. It was all the food and drink the boys had.

Doc unbuckled and removed his helmet, dismounting *The Drakon.* He unzipped his pocket in his riding pants and pulled out five thousand pesos. It was something his mom had given him just in case he needed it. Doc waved the bills in the air and placed it in the bag of supplies on the ground.

The boys stood there and locked eyes with each member of the family. Suddenly, the little girl ran to the bag. Her mom tried to stop her, but she was too quick. Doc and Mac took a couple of steps back as the girl rifled through the stash of bars and drinks. It was in this moment that the boys saw something they would never forget. Real joy, real thankfulness, and real relief.

The boys backed up slowly, and Mac felt tears well up in his eyes because he saw the same thing in the father's eyes. He fought it back, choked it up, nodded, and put on his helmet.

The boys walked to *The Drakon.*

"Land it here," Doc said to Alfie. "Land the drone here. That way we know for sure how to find this place again."

"Copy that," Alfie said as he lowered the drone and landed it in front of the tin shack. The family looked at the drone like they'd just seen something from the future land in their dirt yard.

Doc and Mac slowly climbed on the four-wheeler that was meant to be their ride on their quest for victory.

Right before Doc shifted to first, Mac asked him, "Why are we racing again?"

"I don't know, Mac," Doc replied. "I'm not sure what I know right now."

To Doc and Mac, that was the most startling event that had ever happened to them. They had never witnessed the gaunt bodies, the eyes of despair, the absence of hope, and then the overriding joy of a promise that at least one night, that night, there wouldn't be hunger.

* * *

THE FLOOD GATES TO THE PHYSICAL PAIN OF THE RACE WERE OPENED as the adrenaline, excitement, and push to win at all costs subsided to the weight of seeing true poverty with their own eyes.

As they rode *The Drakon* away from the family, Doc's body began to ache in terrible ways. He felt the full weight of a body spent, his emotions jacked, and his spirit teetering on exasperation.

The Quad Continental toll bell was ringing, and the boys couldn't escape it, not this time. The desert had taken everything and left nothing but a sandy, gritty, affliction to their eyes, mouth, and now soul. Their tongues stuck to the roofs of their mouths. Eyelids hurt to blink, scraping with each pass over the pupil, and it was all magnified by the deeper hurt that comes from seeing true human suffering while they were racing for their own victory.

Doc's hands staged a full-on revolt against the crucible of gripping, twisting, and pulling. The muscles between his thumb and index finger maintained a steady pattern of succumbing to spasm attacks, releasing, and then repeating.

Mac looked at the GPS. Seventy more grueling miles were left until the big check point where all the riders would be resting for at least a few minutes to get a proper meal, proper hydration, a change of clothes, and even a cat nap for some.

However, there was a problem for Doc and Mac. Their strategy was to *not* rest while everyone else did. For any rest, any stop, any concession to the demands of their bodies, would irrevocably and irretrievably cost them the Quad Continental. Yet, every ounce of energy was syphoned out of them. Every thrill of the race had already been used to squeeze the adrenal glands dry. Every check was cashed, and the paper began to bounce. Pragmatism started to beat down the purity of idealism.

It was miraculous, some would say, that they even made it that far on the smaller ATV. Such sentiment, though, offered no condolences to the boys.

Another cruel pain was that the plan itself wasn't behind schedule. The stop at the dirt shack hadn't taken too much time away. They were going to enter the camp close to when they thought they would. The problem was that the other racers were faster than Doc had anticipated. Doc and Mac had done everything right; the others were simply faster.

For them to even think about a miracle finish that could get them across the finish line first, they would need a rapid fuel and supply stop at the mandatory check point, and then they would have to bust out while the others rested, giving themselves a precious gain to allow a fighting chance down the homestretch.

Yet, the need for sleep was overwhelming. The grit was gone, their hearts were drained, and through it all, they were still in last place.

Doc wanted to rest, and he knew he wouldn't get an argument from Mac.

* * *

THE MAJOR QUAD CONTINENTAL PITSTOP LIT UP THE BAJA DESERT like a small city. It was powered by portable halogen lights that flooded the sky with harsh white light, eclipsing the star power that had governed the desert since night had fallen. Every international team had their big rigs there and waiting, most in vain, as over three quarters of the field had been wiped out in the earlier mechanical melees.

The sanguine nature of the desert *au naturel* was drowned out by big diesel rigs rumbling and gasoline generators growling. It wasn't hard to see which international teams were in it, who were out of it, and those who still thought they could win it.

The British team hopped with activity. Ethan Oxidant had his team in first place and looked like the clear favorite at this point. His pit crew was operating like they were the front runners, and they did everything in their might to keep him there.

The Australians were doing well. They would come into the pit stop in second place. The Aussies were in typical high spirits, acting as if they didn't have a worry in the world, and would probably laugh about it if they did. They had a decent driver in Larry Gates, but everyone knew he had a way of shooting himself in the foot at some point. Time would tell if he could keep his ego in check long enough to make a serious run when it counted.

The Mexican team had taken full advantage of the home terrain. Magali Osario, the only girl in the field, had raced with keen awareness and wasn't afraid to get her hands dirty when necessary. Poor Ecuador had found out the hard way when she had distracted their driver with a flirty gesture and then slammed him into oblivion, tumbling him off a cliff. She had established herself as an absolute threat to win it, and word got around.

There were some other teams still in the race, but they were out of contention. For them, it was just a goal to finish.

Then, there were Doc and Mac. Dead last and falling further behind.

* * *

"COME IN, GUYS. COME IN," DOC SAID, TRYING TO GET THE ATTENtion of his crew.

"Gotcha loud and clear, brother," Jonah said as he slung long cords over the side of the trailer to Alfie, who was connecting external power supplies from the generators. "Where you at?" Jonah asked. "You should be at the pit already. Everyone else is."

"We're coming as fast as we can. Listen," Doc said, "we're exhausted. Is everything there waiting on us as planned?"

"You betchya," Jonah said. "This will be the fastest pit ever. We'll tune up *The Drakon*, and the other teams won't know what hit 'em."

"Wait a minute," Doc asked, "what'd you say? You'll tune up *The Drakon*? You guys aren't even supposed to be at the pit. You were supposed to drop stuff off and keep moving."

"About that . . . we ran into a hiccup," Jonah said, "but don't worry. We got a plan."

"You've got a plan?" Doc asked incredulously.

"I'd love to hear it," Mac said, "because all I know is that we need our fuel cans out there, and those are going to be tough to come by if you're not ahead of us."

"Chill, chill, chill. This is the Black Blondini. I've got everything under control, and I've got J-Dog buying us some time. I told him to go meddle."

"Okay. We'll talk about that when we get there," Doc said. He was too tired to care.

* * *

J-Dog flashed a big ornery grin as he and Alfie walked into the British pit area. "Excuse me, pardon me. Oh, I'm sorry! Am I in the way?"

CLINK. BANG. BONK. He knocked everything over he possibly could. Anything he thought could slow things down.

"What are you bloody doing?" one angry mechanic said as a quart of oil spilled to the ground.

"Oh, blimey," J-Dog replied. "Pardon the intrusion, good chap. I'm looking to interview Ethan Oxidant. We're a worldwide news organization with the largest online audience in the history of the universe. You've probably heard of me. I am J-Dog Dynamite, and this is Wild Dog TV."

"What?" the mechanic raised his eyebrows. "I have heard of you."

"Good, then, Ethan Oxidant please," J-Dog pressed.

"If you really want to, he is right over there," the mechanic said. "Be careful. He is a downright cranky creature." He pointed to the eighteen-year-old racer who was taking off his boots.

"Oh, for tea and crumpets sake," J-Dog said as he got an up close and personal look at Ethan. "Those argyle socks are a cry for help from a mile away."

* * *

Doc fixated on the big glow in the sky. The closer they got to it, the more he knew he needed it. He also knew that if they took any break for themselves, it would cost them the race. Plus, there was this giant conundrum of why his crew was still at the pit stop. That wasn't the plan, and Doc couldn't figure out how that didn't destroy any chance of even completing the race.

Normally, the prospects of a race being utterly lost would have sent Doc into a frenzied mess, but the despair he'd seen in the family at the dirt shack rendered any of that moot. His need to win above all else wasn't satisfying anymore.

There just wasn't enough game rage to overcome the weakness in his tired bones. No more thoughts of racing immortality could propel him forward. How could he race for a trophy when that family just wanted to eat?

Even more questions still assaulted his mind. What about the legendary status of being a Quad Continental world champion? The title no longer felt as thrilling, now that he knew the harsh realities of what the race was. The Quad Continental delivered brutal crashes, thrived on base animalistic instinct, and fed on the vulnerable with an insatiable appetite. What would it mean about himself if he did win? That he'd been the cruelest and basest of them all?

"Quarter of a mile out and closing," Mac said without expecting a response, and he didn't get one.

As the boys got closer to the first major checkpoint, they could see the countries' flags raised with spotlights, proudly illuminating their colors.

Doc pulled into the main drag. The racers were noticeably thinned out like a culling of the herd. He and Mac were the last ones to roll through. He saw all the teams working hard, restoring, refurbishing, and fueling up the racing machines that looked like they had gone to the depths of the abyss and back. Most of the surviving drivers were laid out flat on the ground in their pits, hoping to grab a ten-minute catnap while the work was getting done.

"How many do you count?" Doc asked.

"Less than twenty?" Mac replied. "And half of them look dead."

Jonah buzzed in, "Hey boys, let's go. We can still get you in and out. This is our chance."

Neither of the boys responded, and neither could figure out how that mattered if the dually wasn't out in front of them planting the fuel cans along the way.

"We're last," Mac said.

Doc didn't respond. Being last was nothing the racer from Bell Buckle had ever experienced before. Yet that disappointment beaded off of him like water on wax.

Jonah replied to Mac, "Maybe now, but we don't have to be. Let's go. We think we can get you out with the British. J-Dog's on it as we speak."

"What's he doing?" Mac asked.

"Buying time."

* * *

"This is the Wild Dog!" J-Dog beamed with an enthusiasm and energy that not many in the checkpoint had. "I am your host J-Dog Dynamite. You may see that I am in enemy territory," he said as Alfie panned the iPad to show the British team and flag. "We're here for Ethan Oxidant, the so-called number one ranked junior racer in the world. But I call rubbish. No number one in the world would be caught dead eating Duffy's Crumpets. That's just truth and reality."

Ethan watched with disdain as he picked up his leather racing gloves and slid them back on. "What do you know about truth?" he said to J-Dog as he grabbed his helmet and muttered to himself, "I create my own truth and reality."

J-Dog overheard the last remark and laughed. "Oh, thank you for being *that* kind of Brit. Honestly, I should have expected it. So, Mr. I Create My Own Reality, we often have on a Q and A session where people write in their questions, and we pick the most asked question to answer. What say you? Are you up for answering the most asked question we have ever received on Wild Dog TV?"

Ethan slowly turned his head in jest. "Sure, I'll enlighten your people."

"Excellent," J-Dog responded. "So here it is. Do you think it was the genetic bottleneck from all the centuries of royal inbreeding that led to the stupidest war strategy ever utilized by man, which was made famous in the Revolutionary War? The war, by the way, that we totally won and sent all you blokes back to the Land of Eng."

Ethan smirked. "That's the most asked question you have ever received?"

"We take the mathematical average," J-Dog replied. "There's the mean, the mode, and the median, but we utilize the fourth 'm,' the matter average."

"I've never heard of the matter average," Ethan replied.

"It's the thing that matters most," J-Dog replied.

"I'm only playing along out of morbid curiosity of how stupid you can be," Ethan scoffed. "What war strategy are you speaking of?"

"It's the one where you put your army in bright red coats, marched them out into an open field, and made them kneel down in a perfectly straight line, just so everyone could get a clear shot at them."

Silence from Ethan.

J-Dog smacked his own head. "I mean, who in the world does that?"

Alfie replied from behind the camera, "People who think they can create their own reality, that's who."

Ethan got up and stomped off to the loo.

"Tapping out so soon?" J-Dog shouted. "I'm just getting started."

J-Dog knelt on a make-believe battlefield and spoke in a horribly mocking old English accent. "But, sire, sire, they're only twenty feet in front of us, and their muzzles are pointing right at me. They'll snuff me out for sure." Then he stood up like an English commander of old. "Bloody stay still. Never mind them. Create your own reality."

Alfie radioed Jonah. "Diversion is working. J-Dog's talent to get under everyone's skin is a worldwide phenomenon."

* * *

DOC'S EYES COULDN'T BE HEAVIER. HE FELT HIS HEAD BOB WITH exhaustion. Six hundred and fifty miles of desert racing just tolled the bell and demanded the debt be serviced. His body tantalized him with the temptation of a deep sleep, and Doc wanted that low hanging fruit.

The adrenaline that had overridden any normal body fatigue had checked out. The impoverished family living in the dirt shack had shaken all that away. He was impacted; he was changed. Confusion overrode the confidence, and uncertainty replaced the resolve. What was once determination and a clear plan now gave way to uncertainty.

The Drakon growled with a new grind, and it didn't sound good. Not that it was unexpected, but it still was a sign that the Quad was killing it, and Doc felt the heaviness of having burnt *The Drakon* out for something he didn't even believe in anymore.

He lifted his eyes just in time to see that great Star-Spangled Banner lit up by a spotlight.

Doc and Mac saw their team lining both sides of a small dirt path heading into their pit stop. Jonah was smiling, Alfie was filming, J-Dog was hitting, swishing, and spitting, Flip was tossing a ball in the air, and Penelope jumped up and down like a cheerleader. Then, there was Mom, her expression a mixture of pride and concern.

Those people never looked so good to Doc and Mac, and as they pulled into the pit this family immediately jumped into action.

Penelope grabbed the clutch, relieving his cramping left hand. Jonah bearhugged Doc before he even knew what was happening and lifted him off *The Drakon* to put him in a soft reclining camp chair. Alfie killed the engine while Flip popped the fuel lid and filled up the tank.

Mac had purposely fallen off the back of his pogo stick, and landed mercifully on the desert sand, all sprawled out.

J-Dog and Flip came over, helped Mac up, and guided him to Doc. Oddly, though, Rachel didn't come. Doc could see her talking to a Mexican man. It looked like it was a rather significant conversation, but Doc was too exhausted to give it more thought.

Then the most unexpected thing happened. Another crew raced over to *The Drakon* with lots of equipment in haul. They immediately used hydraulic lifts and hoisted *The Drakon* to a height of five feet. Three men began working at a feverish pace to tune up that old ATV.

"What's going on?" Doc asked as he tried to stand up, but Jonah put a big hand on his chest and kept him seated.

"What's going on," Jonah said, "is we're going to win. They're on our side. Now, listen up."

The kids surrounded Doc and Mac, and so did Wild Dog TV, for that matter.

* * *

"First," Jonah explained, "we pulled into the pit stop right on schedule, just like you planned, Doc. We had every intention of leaving the fuel can and bag of supplies, and in fact, we did."

Alfie interrupted, "But we discovered that someone had stolen the supplies right before we left."

"That's right," Jonah confirmed, "someone figured out our plan of leaving fuel in the desert."

Hit, swish, and spit. J-Dog jumped in, "That means they would have stolen the next fuel can, too. You would have been stranded and most likely died."

Penelope gasped. "A little dark, J-Dog. Don't you think?"

"So, we thought you two dying was a problem," Jonah said. "We couldn't have a dead Doc and Mac. Then something great happened. Someone sabotaged the dually."

"Sabotaged the dually?" both Doc and Mac responded in unison.

"Cut the fuel line," J-Dog said.

"Removed the battery," Alfie added.

"Tashed the shlires," Flip tried.

Jonah summed it up: "Sliced every available wire they could see. So, the dually is dead."

Doc was beside himself. "How is that something great?"

Mac blurted in his normal choppy way, "Not ideal."

J-Dog wagged his finger. "Have faith, young ones."

"I'm trying," Doc pressed.

"So, your mom," Jonah continued, "found an old truck that this Mexican dude was willing to sell us for $500."

Doc and Mac glanced at each other, not sold on the transaction.

"A five-hundred-dollar truck to replace the dually?" Doc questioned.

"Can it pull the trailer?" Mac asked.

"Not a chance," J-Dog fired back. "It will be tomb-stoned in Mexico."

Mac shook his head. "Still failing to see the light."

"Wait for it," Alfie encouraged.

"As your mom was negotiating for the truck," Jonah continued, "some European dude named Vegas Slot or Vegan Brat or someone with way too many letters came by."

"Vermin Snot?" Mac couldn't believe it. "You talked to Vermin Snot."

Then a gruff man who was busy working on *The Drakon* raised his head and shouted, "Verggaandschlaat!"

"Hey Vermin Snot!" Mac gave a thumbs up.

"Hi, American. You are very lucky. I'm fixing your problem."

"How?" Mac asked.

"I'm increasing your fuel capacity," Verggaandschlaat said. "I'm taking motorcycle panniers, attaching them to your four-wheeler, and tubing them into the fuel tank. That will give you an additional one hundred twenty-four liters of fuel."

"Dude," Doc said as he did the calculation in his head. "The gas in our tank plus the extra in the panniers changes everything." That put a little pep in his step. "Alright, that's not nothing."

"Doc, we can do this." Mac got pumped.

Jonah did some quick calculations on the computer and cross checked it with the GPS system. "We are near a town called Preita right now. It is three hundred and forty-five miles to the last major pit stop just south of Tijuana. The other half of the Austrian Pit crew is already there. Once there, they will change your oil, give you street racing tires, change your filters, take off the panniers, and fill up your normal tank. Without the panniers, you'll be lighter and faster, perfect for in-city racing. Then, you head twenty miles north to cross the border. And guess what? Since that last fuel up is across the border, in California, we already Uber'd a fuel can to that location."

"Okay," Mac replied, "that's awesome. You guys are killing it."

Doc rubbed his chin. "You did come up with a plan. I mean, it works."

Jonah high-fived Mac. "Check it out!"

* * *

THE PLAN MADE SENSE. THEY HAD A FEW HUNDRED MILES TO GO, and they found solid footing on how to do it, but the weight of the race still hung heavy like a millstone around Doc's neck, and the physical exhaustion permeated every bit of his body.

"Listen, thank you," Doc said. "I'm hitting a wall, though, guys." Doc bared his soul. "There are racers back there in the desert that are going home a whole lot different than how they came. I knew this was a tough race, but I didn't know it was this. And I just don't get the what's and why's anymore—especially with that family in the dirt shack that we came across. We're busy racing to win something that I'm not sure is worth winning, and that poor family is just trying to eat."

Jonah replied, "You make sense."

"I mean really," Doc began to ask, "what's the point of a race when there is true poverty on one hand and wretched stupidity and greed on the other? Is there even a place to do what we are doing right now in this world?"

The conversation struck hard, and the kids felt it deep in their bones, but then a very unlikely voice spoke up. It was Penelope.

"You've been through a lot, Doc," she said. "From your dad being burned, the barn lost, the USJRA not backing you, you're losing your truck and trailer, and now you've seen a different side of life that you weren't ready to see. I get it. Everything seems to be going wrong, and you didn't even get to sell your horse."

"She's right," Jonah said. "It's a lot."

Penelope continued, "You may feel like everything is piling on. You may even feel like you've lost a little bit of yourself and be wondering why some things happen. But I have learned that everything happens for a purpose."

"How do you mean?" Mac asked.

"At first, I didn't know what purpose I had in coming because you didn't really need me for anything, and I was different. But you accepted me, and guess what? I was here for a purpose. I needed to, first, learn from you. I needed to see how you see, and I'm better because of it. And now it's my turn to give back."

"Ooh," Jonah whispered, "something's happening."

Penelope continued, "Your dad is healing. Your mom loves you and is making a way. We are your friends. No, scratch that, we are your family. You are not alone, and just because other people are messing up this world, doesn't mean you can't use the strength and stability of your family, your friends, and your faith to have joy in the midst of the mourning. You have the chance to live right when so many others have lived so wrong. So, don't give doubt a seat at the table where faith belongs. Be who you were meant to be. Go fight the good fight, Doc Copper, and that fight is whatever shows up at our doorstep each day. Today, it's this race."

In that moment, in that time, no more profound words could have been spoken. The petite, soft, eloquently spoken Penelope Parsippany, the poet of epiphany, dropped an anvil of truth that night.

Doc smiled at the warm, sweet and, more importantly, wise words. They brought a spring of renewed strength, and another reservoir of vigor and vitality began to build.

Alfie then spoke up in a way that he often didn't, and it was clear something was moving him. "Doc, I think you need a different perspective on the dirt shack. Suffering is something I understand. In Malaysia, there is much poverty, too. But there is a different side to it, my friend. That family in the dirt shack is forever grateful because you and Mac were an answer to prayer for them when you gave them food. Without you in this race, they would have even less than they do now. God brought you to them for such a time as this."

Between Penelope and Alfie, the message of grit, endurance, faith, and perseverance hit home.

Doc breathed in strength and looked Mac square in the eyes. "Then, it's settled. We race."

"To the end, brother," Mac replied.

* * *

The international pit crews steamed with activity. Torque wrenches spun and the smell of rubber, fuel, and grease filled the desert as the last remaining racers geared up for the final third of the grueling race.

The British were the first to release from the pit stop, followed closely by the Australians, and then the Mexicans. They shot out of the pit like canons. A second crop went out about a minute after the leaders.

"Vermin Snot," Mac yelled, "we got to go!"

The Austrian engineer cracked the whip on his team and motioned to Doc and Mac. "Come. Now!"

He didn't have to tell them twice. The boys got on as the last tube from the panniers was inserted into the gas tank, and the holes were sealed off with a quick and dirty rubber cement smudge.

Vermin Snot also installed two LED super lights on the front, and when he switched them on, it didn't even look like night anymore.

The moment before Doc pressed the ignition, the Austrian reached over and covered it with his hand. "Americans," he said, "you know that this four-wheeler cannot beat the bigger side-by-side racers."

"What's your point?" Doc asked.

"I've made a slight modification to your engine. I gave you more power. Still not as much as the other racers, but I got you closer. The problem is, is that it comes with a price."

"What'd you do?" Doc asked, not all that excited about someone touching his beloved *Drakon*.

Mac shook his head. "It's not a button, is it?"

"I've been experimenting with a next generation NOS application. It works on a constant micro drip, and I've added my own proprietary chemical, which is an additional heat accelerant to it."

Doc was skeptical. "If it is so good, why didn't you use it in your KTM?"

"It runs too hot, and it cracks the engine block. I could never get it to last the needed thousand miles for this race."

"Can it last three hundred and fifty?" Doc asked.

"I don't know, but this is what I do know. It will make you faster, and it *will* crack your engine block. I just don't know when it will happen. Will it happen in twenty miles, one hundred, or three hundred? I don't know. You might make it to the finish line, but you might not. It's fifty-fifty. I'm hoping the Honda engine can handle it longer. If any engine can, it's this one."

"I'll take those odds," Doc said.

"Good," Vermin Snot replied as he reached below the seat and flicked a switch. "It's on."

Doc looked down and saw four cannisters of the special formula NOS. He took a deep breath and fired up *The Drakon*. Instantly, it roared with a new energy and a deep guttural note sounded from the exhaust. Doc felt *The Drakon* buzz under him with a new lethal vigor.

J-Dog shouted, "*The Drakon* lives!" He laughed like a villain.

"You on?" Doc asked Mac.

"Hit it," Mac replied.

Doc gave it full throttle, and the launch of the four-wheeler thrust both boys back as *The Drakon* surged, leaving a thirty-foot dust cloud in their wake.

Vermin Snot smiled at the wicked torque that the four-wheeler had just unleashed. He turned to the gang as they watched Doc and Mac rocket ahead. "What do you Americans say? Houston, we have lift off?"

* * *

"This is why we have insurance," Rachel texted Dean.

BEEP.

"THAT'S MY TRUCK!" Dean rifled back.

The texts had been going on for a good time now, and Rachel had given up on consoling the inconsolable.

"I know it's bad," she texted, "but we've got to roll. I'll keep you in the loop."

Rachel wasn't trying to be short with Dean, but the truth was, she didn't have a choice. She was in battle conditions and, quite frankly, didn't have time for sorrows. It appeared someone had cut every single line that could be reached in the dually, and even snipped the brake lines in the trailer as well, and she wanted to get out of there.

"Honestly, Dean, I feel really good that we found this five-hundred-dollar truck. It showed up at the right time."

Dean finally relented. He knew Rachel was in the heat of battle, and if she was happy with a five-hundred-dollar truck, then that means she really needed that truck.

"Alright, you're right," he texted. "Sorry. I didn't get the situation. Please be safe. Get across that border."

Rachel texted back, "We will. Talk soon. Love you."

She turned to the kids, "Everyone load up, we've got to get out of here."

The kids, in a distinct change of behavior, all followed instructions to a "T," even J-Dog. The bed of this new "junk" truck just became the command center for Team USA at the Quad Continental.

Once in the bed of the truck, Alfie slid back on his virtual reality headsets. "I'm back in the game," he said.

J-Dog tilted back his flask. "I thought you left the drone back at the shack."

"I did," Alfie grinned ear to ear. "I got a new one."

Jonah looked over at him as he got situated in the back of the junk trunk. "How'd you do that?"

"I bartered with the Thailand team at the checkpoint. They had one they never used. Malaysia shares a border with them."

"Thailand?" Jonah replied. "I didn't know they had a team in this race."

"They did for twenty-seven seconds," Alfie said.

"That's all they lasted?" Jonah replied.

"That makes sense," J-Dog thought out loud. "They probably entered a rickshaw. What did you barter with?"

Alfie pulled the joystick back, and the drone rose up into the sky. "I told them they would have exclusive rights to manufacture all of our Wild Dog TV shirts."

J-Dog took a hit from his flask, swished, and spat. "You did what?"

"You heard me," Alfie said as he started swooping the drone around in the sky. "Didn't you ever realize that you were selling shirts that we weren't making?"

"I chalked that up to crossing that bridge when we got there."

"We're on the bridge," Alfie said.

J-Dog's face turned to consternation, and Jonah thought it was time to intervene.

"Now, J-Dog," Jonah said, "take it easy. I'm sure Alfie only had good intentions. Plus, you do kind of need to deliver these shirts."

"Alfie, Thailand?" J-Dog took off his hat, rubbed his hair, and then looked up. "I don't know what to say, so I'll cut to the quick of it. This is awesome! I've always wanted my own sweatshop."

Jonah grabbed a meat pie out of his cooler. "I didn't see that coming, but I should have."

J-Dog inquired, "Seven-year-olds? Four-year-olds? What are we talking about?"

Alfie shrugged. "Pregnant women, too, probably."

"Dude, so our labor pool will literally hit the ground running. Can we put a big oil painting of my face up in the factory?"

"With some good luck and fortune," Alfie replied tongue-in-cheek as he was swooping his new toy in the sky. He changed subjects, "I put a GoPro on it. Boys, we've got our eyes in the sky."

"Alfie," J-Dog put his arm around him, "when I took you in off the streets . . ."

"I flew first class," Alfie interrupted.

"Semantics," J-Dog replied. "I knew one day my investment in you would pay off."

"Nuff talking," Alfie said. "Doc and Mac are off; I gotta fly."

* * *

THE ROUTE THAT DOC AND MAC HAD, WHICH KEPT THEM ISOLATED from the other pack, was now over. Their best route was also the best route of everyone else.

"Mac, this is about to get real," Doc said as he pointed ahead. *The Drakon* hummed at extraordinary speeds aided by Vermin Snot's next gen NOS kit, and they were catching up to the main pack. The Brits and the Aussies were now dead ahead.

"Woah," Doc said, "did you feel that?"

"Sure did," Mac replied as *The Drakon* seemed to be pushed sideways like a sail.

"Check the radar," Doc said.

"On it," Mac replied and tapped a few icons. He grunted. "Not good."

"How not good?"

"I'm afraid you're about to see for yourself. Look!" Mac pointed west as they were heading due north.

Doc turned, and what he saw he wasn't ready for. "And the hits just keep on rolling."

"About thirty seconds?"

"Yeah, if that."

"Here it comes!" Mac said as he tightened the goggles around his face.

"Jonah," Doc said, "what do you got for us?"

"Alfie's new drone is trailing you, but he's worried he won't make it through what's coming your way."

"It's that bad?" Doc asked.

"It's that bad," Jonah confirmed.

A flash windstorm hurled billions of silty particles into the atmosphere. It was a dust storm of biblical proportions. In a matter of seconds, the visibility was down to twenty feet max, and at their speed, they were easily outpacing their field of vision.

The Dutch released the throttle due to the impaired visibility, and Serbia never saw it in time. They crashed right into the back of them, sending both into a horrific tumble. Serbia flipped down a jagged outcropping of rocks that busted their fuel tank. A wicked fiery blast burst into the air.

Doc's exposed neck felt the heat of the explosion hit and spread up to his helmet, leaving his neck blackened with soot.

Mac felt the powerful pulse of the heat, but was mostly shielded from it by Doc.

Next came the pile up. One after one, teams slammed into the racer in front of them. The crash cut the remaining field in half as Switzerland, Indonesia, Nepal, and The Ivory Coast all got caught up in the grisly wreck.

Doc's instincts kicked in as the pile of burning twisted metal built a mine field right in front of him. He immediately deployed evasive maneuvers.

"This is going to be close. Lean left!" Doc pulled his body completely off the seat and hung off the left side of *The Drakon*. Mac followed suit. Their weight lifted *The Drakon*'s right two wheels off the sandy ground just in time to miss the metal carnage.

The four-wheeler, up on the left two wheels, snaked through the smallest of windows. The two boys rocked their bodies back, and *The Drakon* came down, just missing the wave of wreckage.

Mac turned his head back to see the carnage behind them. "It looks like we're racing again."

"Right! Right!" Jonah was yelling on the comms.

Doc heard the urgency in Jonah's voice. His visibility was down to only feet now. He knew he didn't have time to question, nor did he know what he was evading, nor what he was driving into.

In a leap of faith, Doc banked hard to the right, and then he felt the ground disappear from underneath the wheels.

"Woah!" Mac yelled as they unexpectedly soared through the air. Mac's left hand flung up and clasped onto the left handlebar as he grunted and caught his balance as the four-wheeler landed back on all fours in a whiplash sequence that only lasted a second.

BOOM. BOUNCE. And steadied.

"Check it out!" Jonah squealed.

"What the heck was that all about?" Doc yelled.

"I just saved your butts! That's what that's about," Jonah replied.

"How?"

"Because if you didn't turn right, that five-foot drop would have turned into twenty. Look behind you."

Through the sandstorm, the boys could barely make out a pile of rubble.

"I think that's Fiji," Jonah said as he studied his laptop. "Now, continue north to a canyon that should be deep enough to get you out of the dust storm and, hopefully, give you a little cushion between you and the rest of the pack. Which, if you haven't guessed, is pretty thinned out right now."

"How thin?" Mac asked.

"I only count four left," Jonah said. "Brits, Aussies, the Mexicans, and you."

"Four?" Doc asked with shock.

J-Dog took a hit. "That's cuatro, *amigo*."

"We can win this thing," Doc said. "All we need is for our engine to last. How did you see that ridge, Jonah? I thought the drone's vision was impaired. We couldn't see it."

"It wasn't the drone. I made an estimated guess based on your GPS location and the topography map you overlayed on it. I guess it was a good one."

"Dude," Mac said, "you just saved our lives."

"Check it out!" Jonah replied. "The Black Blondini needs a cape!"

J-Dog's voice, in an ill-appropriate calm, came through their headsets. "Guys, awesome stuff. Viewership off the charts. But next time, Jonah, let them get closer to destruction before the daring save. Also, I'm thinking of selling ad space to Band-Aid. Any thoughts?"

* * *

Jonah was right. The canyon provided the perfect cover from the dust storm. More importantly, though, they were the only team to take that route, and it allowed *The Drakon* to hum with its new mechanical NOS injected force, skimming across the desert sands.

For Doc and Mac, it was the highlight of the race. Nothing but flat canyons and dry riverbeds was in front of them for three hundred miles. Plus, with the huge fuel capacity, courtesy of Vermin Snot, there was absolutely no delays for fuel stops or anything else for that matter. Only pure unmitigated speed, piloted by a driver gifted for precisely that.

About a quarter of a mile away, and a few hundred feet higher in altitude, the British, Mexicans, and Australians were fighting the desert, winds, sands, and each other.

Ethan Oxidant had a magnificent machine with the best engineering that Land Rover and Jaguar could put into a desert racer. It was deadly fast. It had the speed of a Jaguar, but the legendary off-road performance of a Land Rover.

Ethan, also, for all his issues, was still one of the best racers in the world, and he pressed that machine to its limits. He gradually began to create some distance between him, the Mexicans, and the Australians.

Magali milked every bit of power possible out of the Mexican racer, and she was lethal in her approach. She was not afraid to take out anyone, at any time, and with no regard for their safety.

Her knowledge of the terrain gave her a distinct advantage. She and Joël knew every inch of Baja California, and it showed. They were skilled in finding shortcuts that no one else knew existed, and it allowed them to overtake the Australians and hold down the number two spot in the race.

The Australians were in third, and even though Gates had the flare of a winner, his brain didn't quite fire to make good on it.

According to times and distance, Doc and Mac were in fourth, but not a distant fourth, and they were gaining. Doc and Mac were cruising at a blistering pace that would have them rolling into the pit stop in Tijuana right with the others. Things may have finally turned the corner for the Bell Buckle Gang.

"Hey, Mac," Doc said.

"Shoot."

"I'm feeling smooth sailing for a while," Doc said. "You got anything?"

Mac clicked through pages of data on his iPad. "Copy that. Keep the throttle wide open, brother. I say next stop Tijuana."

* * *

RACHEL HAD THE JUNK TRUCK SPEEDING AT ABOUT FORTY-FIVE miles an hour. For a vehicle like that, though, that was a feverish tempo, and so it was a blessing that the fuel situation with Doc and Mac was all sorted out. She could now just focus on getting these kids back across the border safe and sound.

In the bed of the truck, J-Dog sat on the side wheel well. "Alfie, we need to cut into the action and do an official update on where we're at."

"I can't," Alfie said. "I'm flying my drone."

Hit, swish, and spit. "I've got to do everything? Fine."

As the gang bounced around in the bed of the junk truck, J-Dog fired up his iPhone for a special stream. "Welcome to the Wild Dog, junk truck edition. I am your super host, the one and only, incomparable, irreplaceable, the one you all love to love, J-Dog Dynamite." He added a deep throated howl. "You might notice that the girls are riding in the back with us. But don't worry; they are under my chivalrous protection."

Flip beaned J-Dog on the forehead with a wiffleball that she had held onto religiously since Cabo San Lucas. "Who's protecting who?" The ball bounced off his head and back to her.

Hit, swish, and spit. "Dang it, Flip! You're going to make my head explode."

Flip giggled as she drilled him again. BAM! "Is that really possible?"

J-Dog held up two hands in surrendered. "Time out. Truce. Let's just think this through."

"Ahem," a doubtful Penelope entered the fray. "Think this through? That would be a first for you, J-Dog."

Hit, swish, and spit. "Are you kidding me, Miss Bo Peep?" J-Dog protested, "I'm Mr. Thought Process. My thoughts have thoughts, and they give birth to even greater thoughts. Heck, I've got fifty trillion brain cells in my head, and I told them all to think for themselves."

Penelope pulled out a pump bottle from her purse and sprayed a cooling mist on her face. "Have you ever seen a therapist? Because I think you may have narcissistic disorder."

"No!" J-Dog brushed off the idea. "Why would I need a therapist? If I need expert advice, I just talk to myself, and trust me, those are riveting conversations. I would invite you in on those conversations, but the mere invitation would make the former cease to exist, and so I'm plagued by the fact that I alone am aware of my greatest moments."

"I think you just made my point," Penelope replied.

"That's right; I made your point. That's what thinking men do, we make points. Now, if we're done with the pleasantries, I've got a show to do."

But, Penelope didn't stop, and began to pontificate a bit. "I must admit, I never thought sitting in the bed of a truck would be so rewarding."

J-Dog was annoyed that Penelope was talking during his stream.

She continued, "I do believe the dry desert air is good for my pores," she said as she examined her face with the selfie camera on her phone, "but, there is something deeper happening as well. This desert, it stirs my spirit. The very grit of the sand seems to be born from the grit of its people. I'm inspired to write."

J-Dog sat blank-faced. "You know, you just spilled that girly, gobbledygook all over my show. I've got a standard to uphold."

Penelope was going to respond, but before she could, the junk truck did what every junk truck always does. It began coughing, spitting, sputtering, and then finally stalling.

* * *

"NO, NO, NO," RACHEL SAID AS SHE FELT ANXIETY TIE HER STOMach into knots. As the truck died and coasted to a stop, they were still quite a bit away from the border and not at a place where anyone wanted to be stranded.

By the time she opened her door, the kids had already climbed out the back. She could see a village in the distance. "Not ideal," she said, "but let's all stay together and start walking. We should find some help up here, I would think."

As the gang walked, and as they got closer, they realized that the village was barely a village at all. The local grocery wasn't much bigger than a closest, and all the structures were made of the same brown concrete with flattened roofs.

"*Hola, amigos*," a kind looking older man walked out into the dirt street to greet the newcomers. He wiped oil off his hands with an old, faded shop rag.

Rachel tried to speak, but J-Dog beat her to it. "*Hola*, my good friend. We've hit a snag."

The man could see the junk truck behind them in the distance. "Broke truck?"

"Yes, I'm afraid." Rachel replied.

"Okay, okay," the man said. "My name is Jorge el Ocho."

"The eighth?" Jonah replied.

"*Sí, amigo*. I'm from a long line of proud Jorges."

Rachel noticed the oil-stained rag, and she asked with hope and expectancy, "So, are you a mechanic? Can you look at our truck?"

"Sorry, *señorita*, I don't work on trucks. I work on airplanes, or mine at least. Do you want to see?" He motioned with his thumb back to a large shack.

Rachel shook her head, but once again, before she could talk, she was cut off by J-Dog. "Totally," J-Dog said, and Jonah and Alfie agreed. "Let's see your plane."

"Good, come. Come," Jorge said as he now led the worried mom and intrigued gang to a makeshift garage and a plane covered by old tarps.

"Look at the beauty," he said as he pulled the first tarp off the front, and a well-aged, wooden propeller peaked through. "It's an old freight aircraft. But I modified it to be a crop duster."

Jonah stopped, looked behind him, and did a double take on the landscape. "Um, you have a crop duster?" he asked, his voice too high. "Do you know you're in the desert? Not a lot of crops."

"*Sí!*" Jorge exclaimed and tapped on his temple. "I'm very smart. There are no crops because there hasn't been a crop duster. So, now I'll have a monopoly, but I think maybe, I can help you, no? You have somewhere to go? Maybe we work out a little business?"

"Oh, no," Rachel said, "that's not what we are looking for. We need a mechanic for our truck. I would love to be able to pay you for your time to help us find a mechanic if you know one."

"*Sí, señorita*, our town has a mechanic, but I don't know when he'll be back."

"Oh, good. That's okay. We can wait. When did he leave?"

"You can wait," Jorge said. "He left about three months ago. Don't know when he'll be back."

"Oh, that's not really . . ." Rachel rubbed her head. "Okay, is there a hotel nearby? Somewhere we can stay for a night as we sort this out?"

"*Sí, señorita*, there is a hotel about seventy-five kilometers from here. But you'll need to drive to get there."

Rachel's frustration started to mount. "Right, but we wouldn't need a hotel if our truck could drive seventy-five kilometers to it, now would we?"

Jorge nodded. "*Sí*, you have a broke truck."

"Right, broke truck." Rachel's patience was running thin. "So, is there anyone who can give us a ride to the hotel?" As soon as Rachel said it, she knew shouldn't have.

"*Sí, señorita*, why stop at the hotel? You are American, no? Let Jorge help. There are trucks and vans all the time carrying people all the way to America that pass through here. I know conditions are tight, not much air or room in the vans. Sometimes you lay under floors or on top of each other."

"Yes!" J-Dog shouted and pointed. "That's exactly it! We want that!"

"Wait," Penelope asked, "that seems seedy."

"Absolutely," J-Dog replied, "do you know what that would do for Wild Dog TV if we stream a coyote crossing in real time!" J-Dog slapped his hands together. "We're shaping culture."

"Check it out," Jonah squealed, "we'll be on the History Channel."

"I'll make the call," Jorge said as he pulled on his phone.

"The plane!" Rachel shouted. "We'll fly in your plane. Everybody gets a plane ride."

"*Sí, señorita*," Jorge said, "you are a very smart woman."

* * *

BUZZ. THAT PROPELLER SPUN, AND THE OLD BIRD FOUND LIFE AS it started to pull itself down the old dirt road that now had become the last fading hope for the Bell Buckle Gang to finally get out of Mexico.

It made noises that no engine of sound integrity should make, and the soft tires didn't help as it clanked and clunked its way down the road.

"Here we go," Jorge yelled as he throttled up and pulled back on the stick. "Hang on tight."

The nose lifted itself up as the old airplane wobbled, hopped, and bopped like flying was merely a suggestion, but it did gain altitude.

"Welcome to the Wild Dog, air danger edition!" J-Dog had convinced the others to let him sit in the co-pilot's chair. "In our pursuit of internet excellence, I have chartered a plane to provide the best access to the world-renowned Quad Continental. Let's give three hoorays for Jorge, our very own Wild Dog pilot."

Jorge gave a shaky thumbs up that didn't look too confident as the wind blasted through the cabin because of its missing windows.

J-Dog took a hit, swished, and spat out the window, but his spit went out the window and then into the open windows in the back, showering everyone with used yellow Listerine.

"AGGGH!" they groaned in disgust.

"My bad," J-Dog said with half a chuckle as he continued with the stream. "We don't know if we can catch Doc and Mac before they hit Tijuana, but we're going to try."

"Uh . . ." A grunt came from Jorge, and then another one that was deeper and sadder.

J-Dog looked at him. "Dude, you okay? You kind of look green."

"I think, uh . . ." Jorge was struggling to speak and had begun sweating profusely. "I think we have a problem." He was staring out his window down at the ground, which was now hundreds of feet below him.

"Problem?" Jonah leaned up from his cramped seat. "This is not the time for a problem."

"I'm sorry, *amigos*, but . . ." Jorge paused to catch his breath. "I think I'm afraid of heights."

At that, the cabin erupted with rapid fire questions and comments from everyone.

"How can you be afraid of heights?"

"Aren't you a pilot?"

"Airplanes operate in high spaces! Didn't you think of that?"

"But wait, how are you just now figuring this out?"

"Have you ever flown before?"

Jorge was overwhelmed. "I'm sorry, *amigos*. I really am. I got my pilot license online, and this is my maiden voyage. You know, as they say, there's a first time for everything. Well, this is mine."

Jonah was squealing, "What are we supposed to do?"

"I think someone else should fly," Jorge said nervously as he unsnapped his seat belt. "*Sí. Sí.* That's it. Someone else can fly, and I can sit over there with my head down between my knees. I think I'm going to get sick."

Jonah ran his fingers through his blond fro and commanded Jorge, "Sit back down, son."

"Where did you get your license?" Alfie asked.

"Online at Pilots-Are-Us," Jorge replied.

J-Dog adjusted his pilot glasses. "Let me get this straight. You've never flown, but you bought a plane, got your license from an online hack-a-shack, and you talked us into going up with you on your maiden flight?"

Jorge nodded nervously.

"I gotta give it to you, ace. That's a boss move. Respect." J-Dog thumped his chest.

"Hey, guys." Alfie looked up from his iPad just as the plane started to bounce with turbulence.

"What?" everyone answered.

"I just got my Mexican pilot's license," Alfie said proudly. "I'm a pilot!"

"How?" Jonah asked.

"At the online pilot store. They asked me two questions. One, do I have flying experience, and I said yes, because of flying my drone. Two, which way should the nose point?"

"Which way should the nose point?" Jonah asked.

"I guessed up."

"And?"

"I was right."

"Huh," Jorge said, "I answered down." He quickly got up out of the pilot's chair. "We have another pilot on board." Jorge then plopped down on the floor and put his head between his knees. The plane instantly began to lose altitude.

Penelope peeked at the website on Alfie's iPad, "Boys, Pilots-Are-Us isn't really real. This is a toy website. You get a free plastic plane with your license!"

Rachel leaned forward, "Alfie, can you do this?"

"Well, we don't know that I can't," Alfie quipped and handed his drone's control panel to Jonah as he hopped into the pilot's chair and strapped himself in. He surveyed the switches and gauges. "Okay. I see. That's that, this is this. Alright. Guys, this is simple enough. It's not a jet. I think we're good."

"Oh no," Jonah said.

"What?" Alfie fired back, "What's wrong?"

"Man, this isn't my fault. You handed me the joystick," Jonah replied. "You did this. Don't blame Jonah. Jonah good. Jonah not bad."

J-Dog started chuckling. "Uh oh. It's never good when he speaks about himself in the third person."

"What'd you do?" Alfie asked.

Jonah didn't answer, but J-Dog did, "I bet a full ten pesos that he didn't keep the nose up."

The radio comms beeped. It was Mac. "What the heck! You guys trying to kill us?"

Alfie leaned over and grabbed the iPad, but when doing so, he jerked the stick, and the whole plane banked hard to the right.

"Ahhh!" everyone yelled.

Alfie panicked and swerved back to the left.

"Ahhh!"

Alfie finally composed himself, leveled out the plane, and hit Mac back, "Why? What happened? Is my drone okay?"

"Is it okay? You just torpedoed it into the ground, and you almost took my head off."

"No," Alfie moaned. "Jonah, how could you?"

Jonah shook his head. "It's not Jonah's fault. You just handed it to Jonah!"

"Jonah? Why was Jonah flying the drone?" Mac asked.

J-Dog answered, "Because Alfie's flying the airplane!"

"What airplane?" Doc shouted.

J-Dog cackled uncontrollably. "The desert crop duster that belongs to the pilot who's afraid of heights. We've gone *loco*, man, and the best part is that it's parent approved!"

"Excuse me. Excuse me," Jorge interrupted. "I'm sorry to interfere, but I inadvertently saw a beeping spot on that screen. Is that your friends' location?"

"Yeah, why?" Jonah asked.

Jonah moved forward and showed Jorge his iPad with the GPS map that was tracking Doc and Mac.

Jorge grimaced. "Do you want the good news or the bad news?"

"The good news," Jonah replied.

"There is no good news," Jorge said, "and that's part of the bad news, because that's drug cartel territory, and that's a river."

* * *

Jonah was on the call with Doc and Mac. Doc shook his head, "You want us to cut nearly ninety degrees due west, back track fifteen miles, find that natural bridge, cross the river there, and only then head toward Tijuana?"

"That's impossible," Mac blurted, "too slow."

"Jorge says there is no straight way through that territory," Jonah argued. "You want to stay clear of the cartels."

"Who's Jorge?" Doc asked. "And why should we listen to him?"

J-Dog thought about the question. "Honestly, we have no history to suggest we should ever listen to Jorge."

Jonah smacked J-Dog in the back of the head. "What good does that do?"

"You know how Doc thinks," J-Dog said. "Logically speaking, does Jorge have a good track record?"

Jonah thought it through. "Alright, Doc. Jorge is unreliable in every way, and we think you should listen to him." He waved his hands. "It is what it is."

Rachel couldn't stay silent, and she inched forward in the cramped plane and spoke into the iPad microphone, "Doc, just do it. As your mom, I would really feel better if you didn't run into the cartels."

Doc conceded to his mom's desire. "Fair enough. I'll think of something."

THWAP. A dusty piece of paper that seemed like trash smacked Doc right in the face. The wind stuck it to his goggles. Doc grabbed it and was about to discard it, but something in him made him think twice. "Mac, look at this." He handed it back over his left shoulder.

"It's in Spanish. I don't know what it says," Mac protested.

Jonah overheard it. "Hold it up to one of the cameras. We'll have Jorge read it."

Jorge read the crumpled sheet, and his eyes popped. "*No es bueno,*" he said. "It is a public service announcement from the cartel."

“A PSA from a cartel?” J-Dog replied. “That seems oddly out of place.”

“You want good news or bad news?” Jorge asked.

“Bad news,” Jonah said, still upset with the previous outcome of such a question.

“Good,” Jorge replied, “because there is only bad news. The flyer says there is a drug war going on in Tijuana between two rival cartels and the police.”

“Wait,” Mac asked, “two cartels *and* the police are all fighting each other in Tijuana, and this paper is a flyer from one of the cartels warning to stay out of the way?”

Jorge explained, “Yes. Cartels are a way of life in Mexico, *amigo*. The cartels depend on all the small villages in Mexico for hideouts, and they pay the poor people to keep quiet. The drug war is against the police and against other cartels for territory, not usually against normal people. People learn the safest thing to do is stay out of the way.”

“Well, geopolitics aside,” Doc said, “if I read you right, we should avoid the drug war in Tijuana.”

“Right,” Jorge replied.

“But we have to go directly through Tijuana,” Doc said.

“It’s a pickle,” Jorge replied.

“So be it,” Doc said to Rachel’s deepest angsts. “Alfie, can you be our eyes in the sky from the plane?”

“Still trying to catch you, but you can count on me. Operation Sky Talon 2.0.” Alfie pulled back on the stick to gain altitude and throttled up.

“We got you on our GPS, Doc.” Jonah studied his laptop. “And we’re coming.”

“Good! We’re rolling the dice. See you in Tijuana.” Doc hit the throttle hard.

* * *

THE TERRAIN BEGAN TO CHANGE FOR DOC AND MAC AS THE SAND, rocks, and small mountains gave way to pavement, Pemex, and clustered concrete buildings.

"There," Mac said.

"I got it," Doc replied as the boys saw the last mandatory check point for the Quad Continental in the distance.

"The pit takes up the whole city block," Doc said.

Mac tapped Doc's shoulder as he saw the other teams cross their field of vision. "Look! See 'em?"

Doc clinched his jaw. "Yep."

The British, Mexicans, and the Australians were almost in a dead heat as they came racing toward the pit. They were about a half mile ahead of Doc and Mac.

"I bet they came from Ensenada," Mac said.

"Yep," Doc agreed, "then went directly north. I'm sure they cheated and hopped on some roads."

"We got to make up that time somehow," Mac said.

"We're close enough to catch 'em in Tijuana."

"Catch 'em? Vermin Snot's modifications are that good?"

"Yes, and there's more to it than that. After the pit, the race fundamentally changes. It becomes a street race all the way to the Naval Air Station at North Island in San Diego, the finish line."

"A street race is good?" Mac didn't quite understand.

"Really good. We're smaller and lighter. We'll actually have the mechanical advantage for once."

"Dude, if we have the advantage," Mac said with excitement, "we're going to kill 'em."

"You got that straight." Doc grinned. "Lock and load, brother. It's about to be our turn."

* * *

"Alfie's in the house," Alfie whispered under his breath as he realized all those hours working on his aviation skills as a drone pilot were actually, weirdly, paying off.

Jonah tapped Alfie on the shoulder. "Let me have a turn. Let me fly."

"Not a chance, Pillsbury. You crashed my drone," Alfie snapped with an out of character slam on Jonah.

"Hey!" Jonah and J-Dog glanced at each other. Neither knew how Jonah would or should react. "I'll let that one pass, cause we're in a situation. So, you get grace."

"Seventy times seven type of grace?" J-Dog smirked. "Can I get in on this window?"

Jonah shook his head. "I'm not that sanctified yet."

Penelope and Flip squeezed themselves foreword into the flight cabin.

"Ahem," Penelope began, "if you boys would pay attention to what is important, maybe you'll see what we have been watching forever back here."

"What?" a perturbed Jonah responded.

Flip pointed and shouted, "Moc and Dac!"

Alfie glanced down. "I see them!"

The old plane made up time when Doc and Mac had to reconfigure the route to cross through the hills, canyons, and the river.

"Breaker, breaker," Alfie spoke into the headset, "Doc, Mac, come in."

"Hey guys," Mac hit back, "you still in the air?" he asked with some jest.

"Yes, and we are on your six."

Both boys turned around and saw the old propeller coming in behind them.

"Yeah!" they yelled.

Alfie throttled up. "What's our next move, boss?"

"We're almost to the check point," Doc replied, "and Vermin Snot will take our extra fuel tanks off, juice-up our NOS, put on street tires, fuel up, and then it's the last stretch for the border."

"What do you need from us?" Alfie asked.

Doc nodded. "When we pit, that will give you two minutes to get out in front of us. Your job is to identify the cartel hot spots and keep us away from them."

"Copy that," Alfie responded, and then yelled, "Thy honor defend!" Then he banked hard for absolutely no reason at all.

Jonah shoved his eyebrows high, and he glanced over at J-Dog. "This is getting to his head."

"I was afraid of this," J-Dog replied. "Alfie's drunk on power."

* * *

Doc saw the Brits, Mexicans, and the Australians racing into the pit at wicked speeds, and their professional pit crews moved with rapid fire efficiency to swap tires, fill tanks, replace the sand-filled filters, and get them back out there racing again.

"Mac, can you get Vermin Snot on the comms? We need to be fast when we come in."

"On it." Mac switched over a frequency in his helmet and began making the call. "Vermin Snot, do you copy? Come in, Vermin Snot."

"Ugh. My name is Verggaandschlaat," the deep graveling accent came back. "You are really trying my patience, American."

"Sorry, Vermin Snot, we're going to have to agree to disagree," Mac said. "Listen, we're coming in hot. We need all hands on deck."

Doc and Mac weren't that far behind, as the eye sees, but in terms of racing, they were still a distant fourth.

Mac patched through Doc. "So, we are taking off the extra fuel tanks, and giving me street treads, right?"

"That is correct. There is one more thing, though," Vermin Snot said.

"Hold that thought, we're coming in now." Doc looked up and saw the Brits get in and out of their pit. They took an odd turn to the right. That was off the route that Doc was certain they would take. Then the Mexicans did the same, and oddly enough Australia followed suit. "Do you see that, Mac?" Doc said.

"Yep, don't know what to make of it. They shouldn't be going that way."

Doc came into the pit hard and slammed the brakes. The Austrian pit crew was there and moved with Formula One precision. A jack came out and lifted the four-wheeler, with the boys on it, three feet in the air with perfect balance.

The Austrians moved like a single organism, all in one movement, each with perfect execution of what they needed to accomplish, and before Doc and Mac knew it, that crew was done.

"Awesome!" Doc yelled.

The hydraulic lift dropped *The Drakon*, and the entire pit took less than fifteen seconds, but Vermin Snot came through the comms before Doc had a chance to shift into first: "Americans."

"Yes?" Doc answered.

"We have a problem," Vermin Snot said. "Southern California has been swept up in hundreds of acres of wildfires."

"Are you kidding me?" Mac replied. "Why does California always catch on fire?"

Vermin Snot continued. "The Tijuana River National Estuary is engulfed in flames. It's impossible to cross there. The finish line at the naval base has been completely blocked off."

Mac nearly threw the GPS off the side of *The Drakon*, "Where are we supposed to go now?"

"The finish line has been moved to a location called Rohr Park, California."

Mac clicked through the maps app and found it. "Okay, I got it. It's not too much of a difference, but we have to go east, and I mean now. Where is everyone crossing the border then?"

Vermin Snot answered, "An emergency border crossing is being set up near American route 805. It will be top speed tarmac racing from there on in. You'll need every ounce of NOS you got, and I hope your engine can make it."

"You're telling us we have to go straight through the guts of Tijuana and out the other side?" Doc asked.

"Yes," Vermin Snot replied, "and if I were you, I would follow the others."

Just then, that old plane buzzed above. Alfie stuck his hand out the window and waved. Alfie's voice came through the comms. "That is a big, fat negatory," he said.

Jonah filled in the blanks, "It's a jungle down there, boys. Drug war directly to the east. We can actually see the gun fights! But we got your back. Head north up the coast and then make a hard right. That is your best chance to avoid the fighting. It's a touch longer, but it's stupid down there."

Doc agreed. "We'll the ride the coast until you tell us to turn, and I'll burn rubber to make up the time."

"Copy that," Jonah said.

* * *

ETHAN OXIDANT TURNED HARD AND DOWNSHIFTED. HIS MACHINE answered the call as its new street tires bit the pavement and slung itself around the corner. He made all the pedestrians dive out of the way as the Quad Continental took over the city streets. He clipped the tires of a street vendor's burrito cart and beans, tortillas, and sauces exploded all over the sidewalk.

The Mexicans were right on their tail and Magali ducked, but Joël took a full facial of guacamole.

Larry, the Aussie, had fallen back a little bit, about fifty yards. He was struggling to keep up with the torrent pace of Ethan and Magali as they slalomed through the urban course.

BAM! Larry slammed right into the bowling pins of a street juggler who dove out of the way, just in time. The pins bounced off his helmet and UTV. Fortunately, the juggler avoided being a casualty in the deadly Quad Continental.

Ethan tried to accelerate more in the tight streets, but he was having a hard time putting distance between him and Magali. She grew up in Tijuana, and from the time she was five, she was riding her bikes in these very streets. She kept taking shortcuts and back alleys, even though every street looked like a back alley to Ethan.

However, Magali then heard something. The sound broke through the hum of the engines, and it was all too familiar to the border towns.

Gunshots . . . lots of them.

People began running into their homes and buildings.

* * *

TWO RIVAL CARTELS BATTLED OPENLY AND BRAZENLY IN THE STREETS. The melee consumed a whole city block, and it kept moving from one street to another. The police were barricaded behind their SUVs and shot when they could, but the officers were fine to let the cartels thin each other out as they played wait and see.

Ethan turned a corner, and he found himself in the hotspot of the street fight. A full city block engulfed in machine gun rounds filling the air.

"Bloody, Mexico!" he shouted as his navigator fell to the floorboards to take cover. In the only move Ethan could make, he downshifted twice and forced that racing engine to give everything it had. The engine block growled itself deep into the redline and Ethan began to swerve and bend between assailants as bullets whizzed by his head.

BANG!

A bullet deflected off the frame of the racer and hit the side of a building, sending fragments into the air.

It seemed like an eternity, but Ethan made it through the city block in merely seconds. The only thing left between Ethan and freedom was a blockade of round barrels and heavily armed cartel fighters crouched down on the other side of them.

Ethan snarled under his helmet, and that Jaguar engine tipped its hat to the Land Rover brush guard as Ethan accelerated and collided with the barricade. The muscular racer overcame anything in its way as barrels and fighters went flying in the air to the sound of banging metal, spraying bullets, and crunching bone.

Ethan was free, alive, and still racing toward the border.

Magali's shrewd racing kept her and Joël away from the gunfire. Instead of following Ethan into the gun zone, she braked hard and pulled to the left through an alley. It put her a little bit behind, but she was going to live, and she knew she could make up the time on Ethan as more streets of Tijuana were still ahead.

Larry was not so lucky. About fifty yards behind Magali, he came to the epicenter of the fighting, and instead of trying to find a way around, he went straight through.

"Aussie, aussie, aussie!" he yelled, maxing out his lexicon.

He went right through the motherload of gun fire, and his custom made, lightweight, fiberglass hood of his UTV was penetrated like butter, and his engine block was riddled with bullets. His tires exploded as hollow points chewed them up, and then he let go of the wheel and dropped to the floor with a wild cry as his machine went into a spin.

His engine exploded, and he spun up onto a sidewalk and collided with concrete wall.

CRUNCH!

His frame met the building, and a spectacular obliteration followed as pieces of everything erupted and the frame was tossed back into the city street, barrel-rolling to a stop.

He and his navigator, mostly protected in the cabin, sat there silently as the fighting continued, waiting for the worst. Fortunately for them, the cartels turned their attention back to each other, and the fighting moved onto the next block, leaving behind the broken, burning wreckage of the Australian racer and the two scared-out-of-their-wits Aussies, who radioed their team to come and get them.

The race was down to three.

* * *

To say that all sensibilities had been tested would be an understatement, and Rachel had to eschew all parental norms to even endure what was happening in front of her. The assault on her senses of having her own child race in something as barbaric as the Quad Continental inevitably changed her, and nothing but a survival instinct for her child and his friends controlled her decision-making processes.

So close to the border and finding herself on an airplane piloted by Alfie, she knew that now was the time to make a move and get everyone across the border.

"Okay, guys, we are so close to the border, and we need to figure out how to land this plane. Now, do you see what I see?" she asked as she looked out over the densely populated areas of Tijuana.

"What's that big green space?" Flip asked.

"Exactly," Rachel said. "That's what I'm looking at."

In the midst of all the impoverished neighborhoods stood a pocket of exorbitant wealth. It was a golf course community complete with 10,000 square foot homes, pools, and tennis courts. It was a giant walled complex with its own border patrol.

"Wait, wait," J-Dog said with a renewed excitement about the prospects of a landing. "Mrs. Copper, are you saying what I think you are saying?"

"Yes, I am."

"What? What are we saying?" Alfie asked.

"Dude," J-Dog was beside himself with excitement, "you get to live the dream, brother. You're going to land a plane on a golf course!" He then looked around. "Can we find the eighteenth fairway?"

* * *

J-Dog began an epic monologue on Wild Dog TV, giving a play by play of every single event as tens of millions were glued to their screens.

He howled, "This is why you tune into the Wild Dog! Because I am the founder of entertainment, the creator of content, the host with the most, and the one who put the bang into dynamite."

Rachel grabbed Jorge by the shirt and pushed him up to the cabin. "You are going to help him."

"Okay, I just can't look." Jorge buried his chin into his chest. "It's a small plane. Can't we just glide it down by pulling back the power?" Jorge asked.

"I don't see why not," Alfie replied. "Slow down and go down." Then he pointed to one lever. "What's that?"

Jorge replied, "That's the pesticides for the crop dusting. I made that lever myself. Don't pull it; it's full."

Alfie circled one more time to line up with the longest, straightest par five the golf course had, and to J-Dog's delight, it looked like it was, in fact, the eighteenth fairway.

"Everyone grab onto something," Alfie instructed.

"Keep the nose up," Jonah yelled with angst as he prepared for a hard crash landing, of which he didn't think any of them would survive. He turned to Jorge. "I hope you know Jesus, because you're about to meet Him."

The wings toggled back and forth as the plane got lower.

Alfie passed over a water hazard and came in way too fast. J-Dog stuck his head out the window and yelled, "FORE!" as loud as he could.

Golfers and caddies scattered as they looked up. Then . . . BOUNCE.

The plane's tires hit the fairway hard, and it kicked the plane back up. The wings tilted to the right, nearly clipping a ridge on a sand trap, but Alfie pulled it back level, and the plane came down again, chewing up the soft fairway and carving divots that were always going to remain.

Alfie kept the plane on the ground this time for good.

The plane had landed, sped down the middle of the fairway, slowly skidded sideways, rotated completely backwards, and finally scooted and slid to a stop right on the eighteenth green.

Jonah touched his body all over. "I'm alive. Praise Jesus, I'm alive."

J-Dog reached over and shook Alfie's head back and forth. "You hit a hole in one!"

A caddy who had been on the green and had dove away, slowly walked back up to the green and marked a ball.

* * *

RACHEL NEVER FELT MORE RELIEVED THAN SHE DID AT THAT moment. "Come on, guys. Get out of the airplane."

"Should we bring our stuff?" Alfie asked.

"Yes," Rachel chuckled, "we're never getting back into this thing," But then she heard it. It came from the front entrance of the golf development.

POP, POP, POP. Rachel's face flooded with worry again.

The drug war somehow found itself at the front gates. Two cartels were warring, and the security personnel, armed only with small police batons, were overwhelmed by the machine guns.

The cartels busted through. The fighting was now taking place inside of the golf course community, and the kids could see it.

Rachel ran toward the action to see if there was a way out. She covered about fifty yards like a trained sprinter. The view she saw was bad. Real bad. One small band of cartel hitmen were heading their way in a pickup truck with their cohorts shooting wildly from the bed.

Rachel saw it, felt it, and knew it. There was no way out of this but one. She turned and yelled back at the kids, "GET ON THE PLANE!"

"Say what?" Jonah squealed, "on the plane? Oh, this is bad. Mrs. Copper telling us to get back on the crazy plane and fly way."

"Alfie, get your wings!" J-Dog yelled as he spun his iPad around, filming the moment.

Alfie scrambled to the cockpit as all the other kids piled in.

"Jorge," Alfie yelled, "Jorge!" But Jorge was nowhere to be found; he had fled the moment he heard the gun fire.

"This is up to me," Alfie said to himself. "Alfie, the Malaysian real-life hero." He fired the engine, and the propellers began to spin. He throttled up and turned the plane back down the 18th fairway.

Jonah pointed at Rachel. "We got to pick her up."

"I'm on it. Hang on!" Alfie said as everyone crouched down inside the plane and hung on to each other.

POP, POP, POP.

The gun fire was now everywhere, and even the hum of the airplane didn't drown it out.

"Faster, dude," J-Dog said as he saw the pickup truck filled with outlaws heading their way. "Faster!"

Alfie pushed hard down the fairway, trying to pick up speed. He was going toward Rachel, but she began waving frantically to not slow down at all for her, and she sprinted off into a heavily treed area of the course.

"Where is she going?" Alfie asked.

J-Dog couldn't believe it but understood it. "Dude, she's saying to leave her. We got to take off."

Jonah spotted the truck right at their wings. "Faster!" he yelled.

Alfie throttled up hard, and the front end begin to lift, "Up, up and away, into the wild blue yonder!" His yell turned into a song.

The truck was too close, though, and it pulled beside them as the plane's front wheels came off the ground, and its back began to lift. A man, from the bed of the truck, dove at the plane door and slammed against the outside, clinging to the handle. It popped, and the door swung open with the man dangling on it. But the plane was airborne and not coming down now.

Alfie throttled more and climbed quick, barely clearing a row of trees. The Mexican outlaw pulled himself into the plane, closed the door behind him, and plopped down on the floor, huffing and puffing.

The kids stared at the man for a few stunned seconds, and he stared back. Then J-Dog nudged Jonah and showed him his iPad. "Dude," he whispered, "do you know who that is?"

Jonah looked at the picture that J-Dog had just web searched. Jonah swallowed hard.

"That's Kiké Enrique, the most wanted drug kingpin in the world," J-Dog said.

"Oh, boy," Alfie gasped.

Kiké caught his breath. He anxiously grabbed for his bag and looked relieved when he saw that he still had it.

J-Dog whispered to Jonah, "Dude, we're streaming."

"So?" Jonah whispered back.

"Say something to him," J-Dog said.

"What do you want me to say?"

"I don't know; be the Black Blondini, intrepid reporter. No one has ever gotten this close to him before. This could be your big media break."

"Um . . ." Jonah looked around, and then at Kiké. "So, how's the drug business?"

Penelope gasped, "What are you doing? Don't ask him that."

Jonah answered in an exasperated fashion, "I don't know. I've never spoken to a drug kingpin before."

J-Dog zoomed in on the interview.

Kiké hemmed and hawed as he looked through his bag, "Ups and downs. Today was down. It's hard finding good people you can trust."

"Uh huh," Jonah replied as he tried to think of what else to say. "Have you ever tried to not be a drug kingpin?"

Penelope gave an encouraging nod.

"*Sí*, of course," Kiké replied. "I dabbled in kidnapping for a little while."

"Oh," Jonah replied as he rubbed his forehead, "how'd that go?"

"I liked it at first," Kiké replied, "because you're always meeting new people."

"Sure, sure," Jonah replied as Penelope looked aghast.

Kiké continued, "But those relationships never seemed to end well."

"I can see that," Jonah replied.

"So I went back to my roots, which, by the way," Kiké rummaged through his bag and pulled out two packaged bricks of some sort of illicit narcotic. "I'll give you these two kilos if you can get me across the border, *amigos*."

J-Dog adjusted his glasses. "While the generosity of your offer warms my heart," J-Dog replied, "that's not really a currency we trade in."

"No, no, *amigo*," Kiké said, "this is really good stuff."

"We'll have to take your word for it," Jonah said.

* * *

RACHEL WAS FACE DOWN ON HER BELLY IN THE OUT OF BOUNDS OF the eighteenth fairway. She peeked through the long grasses to see the remaining cartel members from the truck get completely gunned down by the rival cartel. She shivered at the scene.

Her Spanish was certainly not very good, a product of high school Spanish class, but she did seem to pick up that the other cartel was leaving, and she thought they were going to try to follow the airplane. She wasn't sure, and she hoped she was wrong.

She quickly pulled out her phone and messaged the boys' iPad. "Cartels left, they may try to follow you. Do whatever you have to do to get across the border. Don't worry about me. I'll be fine. I'm safe. GO!"

* * *

"LEAN!" DOC SHOUTED AS THEY CORNERED SO HARD TO THE RIGHT that *The Drakon* was forced up on two tires. The two boys threw all their weight against the turn, urging the machine to bring four back to the floor.

"Ah!" Mac yelled amid the maneuver, but finally weight won the day as the tires slammed back down. Doc accelerated hard out of the turn.

"Alfie, come in," Doc said. "We need your eyes."

Alfie fired back and explained all that had transpired.

"Where's my mom?" Doc slowly eased off the accelerator, fully prepared to turn back for a rescue.

"She's fine," Jonah said, "The cartel left, and she texted us and said she was good."

"Dude," J-Dog said, "It's actually a sweet golf club. She may want to stay and take in a round."

"Okay, okay. That's good, I guess." The news calmed those fears for Doc, "Where are you now?"

"Right behind you," Alfie replied.

Mac turned and lifted his gaze upward and spotted the plane buzzing their way. "The gang is back together. Now let's do this. What's our next turn?"

Alfie accelerated over the dense population, looking for routes. "We need to get you to the eastern side of Tijuana, and you're halfway there now," he said.

Jonah jumped in, "Hey, boys, you're about to have company."

"Of what kind?" Doc asked.

"The racing kind," Jonah replied.

"Can confirm," Alfie added. "I see them, too. In about ten blocks you are going to intersect with the other racers."

"Who's left?" Doc asked.

"The Brits and the Mexicans," Jonah replied.

"The Australians are out?" Mac asked.

"Bit the dust," J-Dog replied.

"I can't say I'm shedding a tear," Mac replied.

"Seven blocks." Alfie gave a play by play.

"Do we avoid?" Doc asked.

"Hate to say it, but no," Jonah replied. "Ethan is leading, and it looks like he's got a bead on the best route, and we're only ten miles from the border. After that it's a wide open sprint to the finish line."

"Okay. So, we'll fall in with them and race to the border." Doc gave a quick turn of the head to Mac. "This is it, brother."

"Copy that."

"Three blocks," Alfie counted down. "Two blocks."

"Here we go," Doc said.

"One block," Alfie continued. "Contact!"

* * *

The Drakon's back wheels squealed with racing glory as the boys slid into the intersection that met Ethan and Magali head on, Doc turning left and Ethan turning right. Ethan had the edge and narrowly beat Doc for the lead as Doc plugged the tight space between Ethan and Magali. Both the British and the Mexicans were flabbergasted to see the Americans come out of nowhere. Doc waved at Magali as he squeezed in front of her.

Magali wasn't one to take a third-row seat, and she crushed the accelerator in her dual clutch, automatic transmission, bringing that Yamaha-made racer into the redline as it screamed with a high-pitched shrill. She hopped the curb as she busted through a food stand, sending tortillas high in the air. Spectators were forced to jump out of the way as they shrieked, but then cheers ensued. Such a reckless, dangerous spectacle is what the people wanted.

All the windows in the two-story buildings that layered the streets were open, and Mexican flags were out as they cheered the greatest chance their country had ever had at winning the legendary Quad Continental. Magali fed on the enthusiasm and the license to barrel through anything that stood in her way.

Ethan shot through the city streets with the skill of a seasoned pro. He was trained by the best and raised to subdue any competition by any means necessary. Ethan was a lethal combination of brains, ruthlessness, and skill and had the mechanical menace to back up the whole concoction.

He banked hard and accelerated through a corner, skillfully blocking the slightest of paths that Doc could have shot through to overtake him. Ethan knew that this guerilla type, city-racing favored Doc, and he did all he could do to block him.

"Are we passing?" Mac shouted.

"Can't," Doc said as he swerved to the other side, only to be blocked off again by Ethan. "If we get beside him, without getting by, he'll ram us right into the side of a building. We have to be patient."

But patience wasn't on their side as Magali closed in.

"Um, Doc," Mac said, "we're going to have to do something."

Doc glanced back, and sure enough, they were about to be in the middle of a metal sandwich. Ethan looked in his rear-view camera and saw the opportunity. He decelerated without braking.

Doc saw it and knew what was happening. The Brits and the Mexicans were taking this chance to make it a two-team race.

Doc's head swiveled left and then right. "Street's too thin," he said.

If he swerved to either the left or the right, they would have met the brick façade of a two-hundred-year-old building, and Doc knew that the building would be the one that survived.

"Gotta do something," Mac blurted. "I've been here before, and it's not fun!"

Doc had to slow to keep from ramming Ethan, but Magali was right behind them.

"Watch out!" Alfie's voice screamed in their helmets, and then he buzzed them in a low flying pass.

The flyby caused both Ethan and Magali to look up and lose a moment of concentration on Doc.

"The cartels!" Jonah screamed.

Two pickup trucks zoomed in at the next intersection with machine guns blazing. The racers zipped right through the middle, but two more trucks pulled in at the next intersection and made a blockade.

The racers were trapped, one cartel behind them and the other cartel in front of them, and they found themselves in the kill zone. Bullets flew by them as the war ignited the two blocks. The racers had nowhere to go, and the cartels didn't care.

The three best junior racers in the world went into emergency maneuvers as they spun, broke, and accelerated, trying to find a crack in the wall of bullets wide enough to make a run for it through the blockade. But it was impossible. The gunfire was as thick as smoke, and the Quad Continental was about to end in the most inglorious way imaginable.

POP.

Doc felt it, the front left tire ruptured as a bullet passed through.

BANG.

A bullet ricocheted off *The Drakon's* steel handlebars. This was the end. No one could survive this.

Back in the airplane, the kids saw the battle playing out and saw that their best friends were about to be another casualty of the senseless violence.

"We got to do something!" Jonah yelled.

"I'm doing another pass," Alfie said.

"We need more than a pass," J-Dog exclaimed.

"Wait," Alfie said as a light went on in his brain, "Jorge made this into a crop duster."

Jonah was exasperated, "you want to de-bug the bad guys?"

"Alfie, you're a genius," Doc said as he overheard him in his comms. "You guys have to release it, and light that stuff."

J-Dog turned to Kiké. "Please tell me you have a lighter."

"Of course," the drug lord said as he seemed completely unmoved at the raging gunfight below. "You smoke?"

"I do now," J-Dog replied.

Kiké handed the Zippo lighter to J-Dog who took off his custom-made shirt that said *I believe in gun control . . . use both hands.*

He made the shirt into a wad and took out his flask and soaked the shirt with the ethanol-based Listerine. "Oral hygiene is so important," he said as he looked over at Alfie. "Say when."

"What's going on?" Jonah yelled. "Why are you soaking your shirt with mouthwash?"

Doc replied through the comms, "Listerine has a flash point. Be careful, very dangerous."

"I believe," Penelope said, "we may be lighting the plane on fire."

Jonah squealed, "Oh man, we going to blow up!"

"Perhaps," Alfie said, and turned around to them. "But let's hope for the best."

J-Dog sparked the lighter, and the flame glowed, and he held the shirt up, "Make the call, Alfie."

"Roger that," Alfie said, and he banked hard, pulling the crop duster above the city street, lowered to an altitude of under fifty feet, and then accelerated into an attack speed. "Doc, Mac!" he yelled. "It's about to get hot!"

Alfie reached the two pickup trucks from Kiké's cartel first.

"Hey, those are my guys," Kiké protested. Then he relented, "Never liked them."

Doc slid *The Drakon* to a stop. "Dive now!" he yelled, and he and Mac dove off and belly flopped on the old, cracked pavement as Alfie passed over.

Alfie made the call, "Echo! Bravo! FOXTROT!"

J-Dog lit his shirt, and it went up like a torch. He flung it out the window as Alfie jerked down the lever releasing the pesticide spray on the city streets below.

WHOOSH!

The burning shirt ignited the pesticides, and the crop duster metamorphized into a flying blow torch with a trail of fire that was grander than anyone could have imagined. The city block glowed from the blue burning flames, and the gunfire stopped as the assailants stared in horror as their judgment descended upon them.

Wild eyed and sweaty browed, Alfie buzzed the first two trucks, which immediately set off explosions from the cheap cans of gasoline in their beds. That set off a chorus of piercing screams and yells from the kids, mostly in fear, except for J-Dog, who found the highest moment of euphoria he had ever know.

Two gunmen in the trucks got tossed in the air from the inertia of the explosions, singeing their clothes, eyebrows, eyelashes, and heads, in addition to receiving a concussion shock from the explosions.

The heat from the flames was ridiculous, but Doc and Mac's race suits were designed to resist heat and burning, and so with the helmets on, the boys came out relatively unscathed.

Both the British team and the Mexican team also survived due to the high-tech race suits and helmets, but the drug cartels got waylaid into next week.

Mac rolled over just in time to see Alfie fly away, and he turned to Doc, "Talk about being burned into your memory."

Alfie pulled the lever back on the pesticides, and the flames receded as cheers erupted in the headsets that the stunt worked.

"Time to go," Doc said as he and Mac climbed back onto *The Drakon*. He peeled out but instantly felt the flat front tire thumping with each rotation. "Not good."

"We'll deal with that later," Mac said and pointed.

Doc looked up to see what Mac was talking about. Two of the gunmen struggled to get to their feet.

"We got to get by them," Mac said.

Doc accelerated as the explosions of the trucks caused a separation big enough to drive through the burning blockade. But the flat tire slowed them just enough that two gunmen dove at the boys and nearly tackled Mac off the back.

"Ah!" Mac yelled as he gripped down on his handlebars. Mac swung a wild right elbow and clocked one of the assailants. That guy slid down and clung to his right leg. That marginally worked, and so Mac swung his left elbow and drilled the other in the face, and he fell down from Mac's torso to his left leg.

The two drug hitmen clung to Mac like pythons. The three struggled as Doc drove, and it was clear that one of them was reaching for some kind of weapon.

"Doc! Doc!" Mac yelled as he kicked and squirmed but couldn't jar this pair of paid muscle.

Sure enough, the guy pulled a knife from a sleeve in his boot.

"Hey, anyone!" Mac yelled. "We've got a problem."

Alfie doubled back, the airplane buzzing toward them and what appeared to be Flip hanging out the door with Jonah holding her by her midsection. She held Kiké's two kilos of powder, one in each hand.

"Ahem," a dainty voice came through the headsets. "Do you take sugar?" Penelope asked the two boys.

"What?" Mac replied.

Penelope smiled. "One lump or two?"

Doc thrust two fingers in the air.

Like missiles coming from an F-35, Flip threw the powdered rounds and drilled the two gunmen right in their heads. The illicit powder exploded into a white cloud, and the impact blasted the drug runners off Mac. They toppled, turned, and somersaulted into a road rash mess.

Flip screamed in glee. "Best bodge dall game ever!"

J-Dog, always streaming, zoomed in on the faces of the two beaten hired thugs. White powder covered their burnt and blackened faces.

J-Dog turned the camera toward himself. "This is your brain," he smiled, and then panned back to the thugs, "and this is your brain on drugs. Any questions?"

That threat was gone, but the race continued, and Doc could feel the blown tire. "This isn't going to work." He glanced back and saw his competition.

Ethan took advantage of Alfie blowing up the blockade, and he too was back to racing and coming fast. With *The Drakon's* weakened state, it would only be a few seconds before they were caught. But they couldn't see Magali.

"Where're the Mexicans?" Mac asked the eyes in the sky.

Alfie did a quick survey of the grounds. "I think they are out. I think our fire attack melted their wires."

"They're out, really?" Doc said.

"Yes," Alfie confirmed, "their UTV is melted. It's down to two!" Alfie replied.

"Congratulations, Alfie," J-Dog said. "You just destroyed the hopes and dreams of the Mexican people."

"Thank you!" Alfie replied.

* * *

DOC TRIED TO GUN IT, BUT IT WAS NO USE. *THE DRAKON'S* FRONT left tire was only running on a rim. It emitted a fountain of sparks as the cracked pavers of the road fought against the metallic rotation of the wheels. The whole side was about to burn up.

Doc didn't care about the damage it was doing to *The Drakon*, he cared about his speed, and at this rate, he didn't have a chance in the world of keeping ahead of Ethan.

Mac looked over his shoulder. "Here he comes."

Doc glanced back. "I see 'em."

Ethan came up hard on his flank, downshifted, and nearly rammed them. But Doc conceded the right of way. He knew he didn't have a chance of dueling with him with his busted wheel, so he let him pass.

"Guys," Doc radioed up to the gang, "I need answers. As of now, all the hard work we've done is about to be for nothing. I don't think *The Drakon* can make it to the border crossing, and I know as sure as the sky is blue that we can't catch Ethan. Any ideas, because I'm running on empty."

"Come on guys!" Mac yelled, sensing that things were slipping away fast.

"What about a tire change?" Jonah asked. "Can't we just change tires?"

"Not on the Mexican side," Doc said. "We don't have time to stop, find a tire, and get it swapped. It's not like we have Vermin Snot setting up a pit."

"If we can get you across the border, can we do it there?" Alfie asked.

Doc and Mac could see the United States, for they were only a quarter of a mile from the border as the crow flies, but they couldn't cross at that location.

"That would make it easier, but we're still a bit away from the crossing, and I honestly don't think *The Drakon* can make it," Doc said as he could feel the heat rising up to his handlebars, and that wasn't a good sign, no matter what the situation.

"Uh, excuse me," the thick Latino accent was overheard in the headset.

"Yes?" Doc replied.

"I may have an answer to your problem, if you do something for me," Kiké, the drug lord said.

Doc replied, "I'm willing to listen, but I certainly can't promise anything."

"If your friends fly me over the border, then I can help you quickly get across, but we have to act fast. Your window of making it is about to close."

Jonah interrupted, "Why do you want to cross the border?"

Kiké pointed downward and showed that they were being tracked by the rival cartel from the ground. "As you can see, if we land in Mexico, I am a dead man. I'd rather take my chances with the Americans."

Jonah saw the other cartel. "Uh, Doc," Jonah said, "I'm not real interested in landing on this side either, all things considered. Maybe we should just fly across the border."

"Okay, Kiké," Doc said, "I'm listening."

Kiké continued with his plan, "Do you see Los Pollos?"

"That fast food joint?" Doc asked.

"*Sí*, turn in."

Doc almost missed it, but he squealed out a hard left turn.

"Now, go around the back," Kiké instructed.

Doc listened.

"Do you see the two big freezer doors?"

"Yes," Doc said.

"Open them and drive in."

"*Drive* in?" Doc asked.

"Si, and welcome to La Ciudad de Fiesta."

* * *

MAC JUMPED OFF HIS POGO STICK, RAN TO THE FREEZER DOORS, and flung them open. What he saw next, no one would have expected. It was a giant new world.

La Ciudad de Fiesta wasn't just an illegal tunnel crossing from Mexico to the United States, it was an underground corridor that looked like a midway at a state fair welcoming thousands of people each day as they traveled freely in the tunnel system between California and Mexico.

Though there were many tributary types of tunnels, there was one long, straight, and wide tunnel that was the obvious main superhighway between the two countries, and it was packed with pedestrians, cyclists, and small engine motorcycles.

Doc and Mac didn't say a word as no words could serve as a summation for the experience they were having. So, Doc did what Doc does, and he accelerated as much as he could as he dodged women, children, and babies as the boys sped through the tunnel on three wheels and a sparking rim. Funny enough, they kind of blended in.

Ciudad de Fiesta was nothing if not efficient. The boys cut through the couple hundred yards in no time flat, and they felt the tunnel start to ascend.

"What's on the other side?" Mac asked.

"I'm hoping America," Doc said as the NOS infused engine began screaming as the back wheels dug in deep.

"Look," Mac pointed, "there's literally a light at the end of the tunnel, and a sign."

The sign read: GODSPEED.

"Hitting full throttle." Doc gave *The Drakon* all it could handle, and *The Drakon* gave it back as Doc wrestled with the handlebars to keep the hobbled four-wheeler in a straight line.

The tunnel ascended sharply upward as the boys hunkered down for whatever came next.

"Here we go!" Doc yelled as the boys went up the ramp, leaving Mexico behind.

* * *

BACK IN THE AIR, ALFIE HAD QUESTIONS. "WAIT A SECOND," HE began to ask, "are we allowed to just cross the border in a plane? Don't we need permission?"

J-Dog replied, "No, we're fine. I'm a card-carrying NRA member."

Alfie checked his gauges. "Okay, due north."

"Praise God!" Jonah said. "We're going home."

"How do we know when we've passed into America?" Alfie asked.

"I didn't see a sign," J-Dog said, "but we're not over Tijuana anymore. Maybe we're already here?"

Just then the airplane radio comms kicked on, and a voice came through, "This is the flight tower at Naval Air Station North Island. You have entered American air space. Identify yourself."

J-Dog shrugged. "I guess we're here."

Alfie turned around and whispered, "What do I do?"

"Talk to him," Jonah replied. "These are the good guys."

"Okay," Alfie said, and then leaned toward the radio. "Hi. I'm Alfie."

A stern voice came back, "You are hereby ordered to reverse your heading and re-enter Mexican airspace."

J-Dog whispered to Alfie, "I got this." He leaned up. "I have authorization. Please stand by as I read off my NRA membership number."

The voice was completely unamused, "We have scrambled jets, and you will be intercepted in thirty seconds. You are ordered to reverse your heading and fly back to Mexico. We have been cleared to shoot you down if you persist on your current heading."

"What?" Jonah went hysterical. "They went all war on us! They going to blow us out of the sky! They think we're terrorists! Alfie, turn around!"

J-Dog bowed up. "How much pesticide do we have left?"

"What are you boys thinking?" Penelope counseled. "Just talk to them."

"What do you want me to say?" Alfie replied.

"For lying out crowd," Flip scolded, "tell them we have Kiké Enrique, and game over. We win."

"Oh yeah," Jonah said and scratched his head.

"Hey guys, I got an idea," J-Dog pepped up. "We got a bargaining chip with the drug guy. We need to use that."

Flip rolled her eyes. "Did you think of that all by yourself?"

Jonah's ebullience couldn't be restrained. "Yes, tell 'em we've got a known fugitive on board."

But the drug lord wasn't going along with the plan, and without any warning, he rushed to take control of the plane. But, in a twinkling of eye, Jonah pivoted and cold-cocked Kiké in the jaw, dropping him like a sack of powder.

The kids stared at the unconscious drug lord who was sprawled out on the cabin floor.

Alfie shouted, "Your daddy can whip any man in the county!"

Jonah smiled big. "And I can whip my daddy!"

"Now I understand!" Alfie said.

"Do you know what we are?" J-Dog asked with electric enthusiasm. "We're bounty hunters! We are globetrotting bounty hunters! I'm going to make leather wristbands. Oh my gosh! To call ourselves The Bell Buckle Gang sounds so cool now!"

J-Dog leaned into the comms of the plane. "Yes, Pacific fleet commander, we are the Bell Buckle Gang bounty hunters and we have captured our target, the notorious Kiké Enrique. He is in tow with us. We are looking for safe passage to deliver our bounty and to receive our public props for being great American heroes."

Alfie saw two Hornet fighter jets coming their way fast. He pointed ahead. "Here they come."

The naval base came back, "You are claiming to have captured Kiké Enrique. He is on board with you, and you wish to turn him in? Confirm."

"That is affirmative," J-Dog replied, "and we would like to meet the President of the United States of America."

A few seconds went by. "You will be escorted to a landing site where you will be forced to land. Any deviation from that plan, and we *will* shoot you down."

Penelope shook her head. “Is that really necessary? That’s such a strong tone.”

J-Dog replied, “We’ll land, and you’ll want me to sign your hat.”

* * *

The Drakon ACCELERATED UP A RAMP THAT CLEARLY WASN’T designed to be accelerated into, and it soared twenty feet into the air as it left La Ciudad de Fiesta behind.

“Ahh!” Doc and Mac screamed as they overshot the landing and headed directly into a side tributary of the dirty, pollutant-filled water of the Tijuana River.

SPLASH!

The Drakon cannoned into the water, sending both boys over the handlebars as *The Drakon* flipped in a speedboat-like catastrophe. Then, all too quickly, the ATV found itself completely submerged, sinking into the gunk of the riverbed.

Doc and Mac skipped like stones before tumbling to a watery stop. The weight of their gear dragged them down. The somewhat shallow river still had a twelve-foot depth at this spot, deep enough to drown and not think twice about it.

The boys feverishly fought to take off as much weight as they could and shed the helmets and gloves quickly. Next, they fought to rid themselves of jackets, but those big, buckled boots weren’t coming off.

Doc was able to free himself enough, and he kicked hard, and sucked in that American air as soon as he breeched the surface. Once up, he frantically looked around, but he saw nothing.

“Mac! Mac!” He yelled, but there was no reply, and no swirling water to suggest Mac was coming up. A sudden fear ripped through Doc. “MAC!”

Doc dove hard and fast, but he couldn't see a thing. The polluted water gave no sight. It was opaque as smoke. He erratically swung his arms in every direction hoping to make contact, but he felt nothing.

Then his own lungs began to give way. He had expended too much energy, and he ran out of breath much too quickly. He needed air.

Doc thrust himself back up, and as he broke the surface, he quickly scanned the area, and had a sinking feeling in his gut. "One shot left," Doc said, and saw the slightest turbulation in the water ten feet away to his left. He raced to it.

DEEP BREATH.

Doc torpedoed down, and in what felt like a last ditch effort to save his friend's life, he thrust his arm down, and a long two seconds went by.

Then Mac clutched back!

The two boys gripped hard, and Doc contorted his body back toward the surface, and then he swam with all his might pulling Mac up behind him. Doc broke the surface first, but then Mac's face appeared, and his lungs sucked in so hard that it made an awful wheezing sound as oxygen rushed into his body.

"Go," Mac blurted, and as soon as he could muster the word, he added, "chaps!" Those dang chaps were like an anchor wrapped around Mac's waist.

Doc never let go of Mac's arm as the boys began to swim. They were splashing against a death grip in some of the nastiest, smelliest water on planet earth, and they had to survive about forty yards of it.

But finally, and fully exhausted, the two boys reached the bank. They sloshed, stumbled, and struggled, but they made it to their feet. Mac's arm was draped over Doc's shoulder as Doc nearly carried him out of the river, and then they collapsed onto the dry shore.

Both boys laid there, spread eagled, and stared at the sky. Their minds and bodies were mush, and they stunk like a septic tank.

"Thanks," Mac sighed, "I wasn't going to make it."

"Don't mention it," Doc replied.

Doc raised his head for a moment, and looked at the sludge-filled grave of *The Drakon*. They were never getting that thing out.

The race was over. Doc knew it. Mac knew it.

Knowing it was over, the boys just lay on the ground and breathed.

* * *

"YES, SIR, WE CAN HEAR YOU," ALFIE SAID INTO THE COMMS.

A serious voice responded, "My name is Lt. Commander Higgins, and I have been tasked with landing you safely on American soil."

"Okay," Alfie said.

"How much experience do you have flying an aircraft?" Higgins asked.

"Today is my first time flying a plane, but I have already landed on a golf course. So, I'm good."

"Today? A golf course?" Higgins said back.

"Yes."

Higgins was all business and didn't let the shock of the situation impact him at all. "The first thing to do is keep your nose up, even as you are descending."

Alfie turned around to the kids and tapped the middle of his forehead. "I told you. Alfie very smart."

"Do not be alarmed," Higgins said, "but we are bringing up the two fighter jets on your wings. You will lower as they lower. As they slow, you slow, and you are to stay parallel with them. They are your guide."

The two jets whooshed in and bracketed the small plane on either side.

J-Dog turned and pressed his face against the window. "Oh, this is legendary." The pilot of the jet acknowledged him and gave him a thumbs up. J-Dog motioned to the pilot to blow its horn.

Jonah smacked him in the back of the head. "He ain't a semi-truck. He's got no horn."

"Oh, yeah," J-Dog replied, "I lost my head for a moment."

Alfie covered up his mic. "You lost your head many years ago," he said before continuing the conversation with Higgins, "Do we have a landing site?"

"Affirmative," Higgins replied. "We have a grass landing target at Rohr Park. It is two miles due north. Get ready."

"Rohr Park? That's the new finish of the Quad Continental. That's perfect!" Alfie cheered.

Higgins explained, "From satellite images, there seems to be a cleared path long enough for a landing. That's why we chose it."

Jonah jumped in, "That's because they made a stretch for the finish line. Are you allowed to use it?" Jonah asked Higgins.

"With all due respect," Higgins explained, "I have clearance to do absolutely anything I want."

Jonah whispered to the gang, "Let's stay on his good side."

Higgins continued, "You are now going to begin to slow. Pull back on your throttle and allow the plane to gently lose altitude."

* * *

THE PARK AT THE NEW FINISH LINE BUZZED WITH THE CREWS OF the international teams and bustled with media who had shown up to broadcast the finish of the legendary race, but the sound of the fighter jets turned all heads upwards, and the sight of an old plane being escorted by the two jets was a dead giveaway that something different was going down.

Instinctively, the media went into breaking news mode as cameras aimed upward and started filming the dramatic sight. One reporter, from a local affiliate, was the first to turn the aerial scene into a news story.

The tall, thin, sunshine-blond reporter flipped her hair back and peered into the camera. "This is Billie Riggs reporting live from the finish line of the Quad Continental. We have breaking news. We have, what appears to be . . ." She tapped her ear as if getting information. ". . . a military escort of a small propeller plane. It seems the finish line of the Quad Continental will be used for a runway for this small aircraft. We do not know who is on this plane, but it does have a military escort. We will report back as we learn more. To be sure, though, this is a very unusual occurrence."

The red light of the camera went off, and she lowered her microphone and told her cameraman, "We need to find out who is on that plane."

The cameraman pointed to three black SUVs pulling into Rohr Park. "They might know." Half a dozen FBI agents got out, and they had weapons drawn.

* * *

"Continue to slow," Higgins instructed Alfie. "Stay between the jets."

"Roger that, continuing to slow. Preparing for landing," Alfie replied.

The people on the ground scattered from the finish line, hoping to evade the makeshift landing strip and the plane coming down on it. Then, as is the modern way, the everyday person became a part of the media as hundreds of mobile phones began recording and posting on social media the extraordinary aerial spectacle.

Alfie pulled gently back on his throttle, and though the plane seemed to teeter a bit on its axis, it sailed down more gently than one would expect. Its tires hit the ground with a bit of a skid and bounced a couple of times as Alfie pulled back all the way on the throttle to achieve a much smoother contact than what he had at the golf course.

"Practice makes perfect," he uttered to himself, and he let the plane coast to a stop. He killed the engine, and nothing could remove the smile on his face. "Alfie's got skills," he beamed.

J-Dog put his hand on Alfie's shoulder. "Yeah, I'll give you that. You had yourself a day."

Once the plane had stopped, the two fighter jets shoved their throttles and shot back up into the sky as quickly as they arrived. The thrust of their turbines left a tornadic dirt cloud wowing the spectators.

* * *

THE NEWS REPORTER FLIPPED HER HAIR. "BILLIE RIGGS REPORTING live from Rohr Park. We are here because this is the new finish line of the Quad Continental. What has just happened, though, no one could have foreseen. After talking to the FBI, I am reporting that Kiké Enrique, the infamous drug lord, and the number one person on the FBI's most wanted list, is aboard this small plane. It is being reported from an internet channel that goes by the name of Wild Dog TV that this drug lord has been captured by a group of fearless bounty hunters who call themselves the Bell Buckle Gang. As you can see, the plane is now surrounded by FBI agents, and they have weapons drawn."

A gaggle of reporters and their cameramen chased the armed agents to the plane, and they were followed by the crowds of the Quad Continental. It was a mass of humanity encircling this little plane who were all fighting for the first glance of whomever was going to step off.

Alfie unbuckled, and the kids moved to the door.

J-Dog tried to prep the gang, "Okay. We are heroes. Do you understand me? People of the year award kind of heroes. So, let's act like it. Get your tough faces on."

Jonah lifted the dazed and confused kingpin off the floor, and he and J-Dog dragged him off the plane, while flashing the most intimidating faces they could muster. The image of them coming out of the plane was memorialized on every major news outlet in the world with the heading: *Kiké Enrique CAPTURED! By the Bell Buckle Gang!*

* * *

BACK IN MEXICO, MACHINE GUNS STILL RIDDLED THE ALREADY war-torn streets of Tijuana as the black-masked *policía* unloaded their guns at the cartels. Block after block of the deadly gun fighting left all sides broken and bleeding with men who would never get back up.

For Ethan Oxidant and the British team, this race wasn't over, but as good as Ethan's equipment was, it wasn't bulletproof, and this time, he got caught up in the fight of fights. A back tire was blown out by a bullet, and he and his navigator had no choice but to hunker down and wait. He slammed on the breaks, and the two teenagers jumped out of the British racer and belly crawled underneath it.

"Get over here *now*!" Ethan screamed into his headsets at his pit crew. "I need out of here!"

A worried British voice came back, "Nothing we can do, Ethan. The police have us blockaded out. We cannot get to you."

"I've got a flat!" he screamed.

An exasperated crew chief yelled back, "Bullets are flying, Ethan. There is nothing we can do but wait!"

"Waiting isn't racing!"

"If you want to live, it is," the crew chief said.

* * *

DOC AND MAC WERE STILL FLAT ON THEIR BACKS STARING INTO THE sky. Not resting, not thinking, not anything.

"Agh," Mac finally let out a slow, sorry sound, "I don't know what this is. But I don't like it."

Doc slowly turned his head to look at him. "What's wrong?"

"It's this thing," he put his hand on his side. "I feel my ribs when I breathe. I don't like it."

"We hit really hard. You may have bruised ribs or something," Doc postulated.

"Bruised ribs? But that doesn't explain—"

"Pain," Doc said with some astonishment. "Dude, are you feeling pain?"

"Pain? Is that what this is?" Mac asked.

"What does it feel like?" Doc asked.

"Every time I breathe in, it's really uncomfortable."

"You're feeling pain, Mac."

Mac's face distorted to an intense throb in his side. "I think I want to say something I've never said before . . . ouch."

Doc propped himself up with his arms. "It's a miracle. You're healed."

Mac grimaced. "Sorry if I don't share your enthusiasm," he said as he gripped his side, "but I thought miracles took the pain away, not the other way around."

"That's the thing with miracles," Doc said, "we don't decide how they go."

BUZZ.

Doc patted one of his zippered pockets. "That's my phone," he said, surprised as he pulled it out.

"How does your phone work after all of that?" Mac asked.

"Who knows, right? I'm just glad my mom sprung for the waterproof model."

"Did someone text?"

"No." Doc looked at the locked screen. "It's nothing. It's just reconnecting to the American network, but at least we can let people know we're alive but out of the race."

Dejection hit the boys again.

"We were so close," Doc said.

"I know; we had it," Mac replied.

"Let's FaceTime the guys. Let 'em know the news," Doc said, "and I'm kind of curious to see how Alfie's plane landing went."

Mac tilted his head. "I hope they're not dead."

* * *

THE FBI AGENTS SWARMED THE DRUG KINGPIN, AND IN A MATTER of seconds, Kiké was face down on the ground, with an FBI agent's knee pressing into the small of his back.

J-Dog grinned. "Seeing that guy being sent to perdition is a true joy."

Penelope frowned. "That sentiment feels misguided to me."

J-Dog waved her off.

"Hey," Jonah said as his iPad pinged, "it's Doc and Mac!" Jonah answered the FaceTime request, "Hey, guys!"

"Hey! Real quick," Doc said. "How's my mom doing?"

"Don't worry," Jonah replied. "She's good. She texted again. Evidently, she found a ride in a big truck with like fifty other people wanting to cross the border, too. So, I say ship shape."

Doc replied slowly, "I guess that's good." And with that, everyone filled everyone in on everything.

After hearing Doc and Mac's account, Jonah blew out and flapped his lips. "Man, that hurts to hear that *The Drakon* is out of commission; we just knew you were going to win. Especially, since, you know . . ."

Doc realized that there was something more in Jonah's voice than just the hope of winning. "No, I don't know. What do you mean?"

Jonah replied, "You know, because Ethan is stuck in Mexico. He's being blocked by a fight between the cartel and the Mexican police."

"He hasn't crossed the finish line yet?" Mac was astounded. "We thought it would be over by now, or at least real close."

"No. He's still miles from the border, and he's at a dead stop."

Doc's mind went into full gear, and he felt the subtle pulses of hope starting to build up in his body, but there was still a problem. *The Drakon* was down and out, and there was no salvaging it. Even if they could drag it out of the muck, which they couldn't, it would never start.

"Think, Doc. Think!" he said to himself. "I got it! Jonah, get a rule book."

"No, no, no." Jonah knew where this was going. "You want to see if you can get a new ride? They'll never let you do that."

"Just get the book," Doc commanded. "I have an idea."

"Okay. I'm on it," Jonah replied with skepticism. "Geesh." He looked at the gang. "They do get demanding, don't they?"

Doc turned to Mac. "How do you feel? Can you race?"

Mac looked at him with confusion. "Did I miss something? Do you see where we are? *What* are we possibly going to race?"

"I think we're still in this. I just got to double check my memory."

It didn't take long for Jonah to get back to Doc. "Hey, Doc, I found Oil Slick, and he gave me the rulebook, and since I knew what you were thinking, I had him show me the clause that says you cannot swap vehicles. I read it myself. I'm sorry, Doc. It can't be done."

"Do you have the rule book?" Doc said with frustration.

"Yes, it's right here."

"Just read it, word for word," Doc said, "the part that says you can't swap vehicles."

Jonah shook his head. "Okay, here it is: *No team or driver shall attempt to substitute or replace any race vehicle with another motorized vehicle for the purpose of continuing competition in the race once the race has commenced."*

Doc listened intently. "That's it!"

Jonah replied, "Yeah, that's it. That's pretty final."

Doc turned to Mac. "I've got an idea. But it is not without its challenges."

"I'd expect nothing less," Mac said.

Doc put his hands up to beg permission for something crazy. "The rule said no *motorized* vehicle could be used as a substitute."

"Sure." Mac shook his head. "Not seeing where you're going."

* * *

A rather nervous Ben Fallow shook his head while Doc explained his unique predicament to him on the phone. "Doc," Ben said, "first off, you know if I do this, your dad is going to kill me. Hold on, Doc," Fallow said. He shouted to one of his farm hands, "No, we've got to move these horses ASAP. The wildfire is coming our way. Get on it."

There was a slight pause as Fallow listened to a response from his farm hand, and then he gave an exasperated yell, "Then hire more truckers!" Another pause. "I'm back, Doc. I'm sure you overheard that. That's another reason we can't do this."

Ben Fallow's stud was in the midst of a full farm evacuation due to the California wildfires. Every trailer he had and a whole bunch of hired trucks were at the farm loading up dozens of million-dollar stallions. They were in a hurried and haphazard effort to protect the animals in the face of these raging wildfires.

"Then there is this," Fallow continued, "I can't even get your horse on a trailer. All my farm hands are scared of him, and let me tell you, it's for just cause. He's the most aggressive horse I've ever seen. Heck, even I'm scared of him."

"I can help you with that," Doc said. "Just load a mare up on the trailer, and Fire Face will follow the mare. Then have your farm hand slip out the front gate with the mare, and you got him. That's what my dad learned to do with him."

"Fine, I get it. But guess what? I kind of don't even want to."

"Why is that?" Doc protested.

"Because you and your crazy little friends have been a real pain in my back side."

"How so?" Doc asked.

"That stupid internet show, or whatever it is, has caused more problems than you can possibly imagine."

"Wild Dog?" Doc said as he wringed water out of his shirt from his plunge into the river. "What does that have to do with you?"

"I'll tell you. Because that Dog fella was talking about Fire Face. Then, of all things, these wacko animal right activists got to listening, and they thought that protesting *my* racehorses was a good idea."

"Oh." Doc frowned. "Sorry about that, but don't penalize me because of those idiots."

Fallow nodded. "Right, Doc, but as I am trying to protect my horses from the fires, I've got one hundred or so freaks blocking the road that I'm using to get my horses out of here."

"Sir," Doc said with the utmost respect, "it is obvious that they are proper fools because they are hurting your chances to care for your horses."

"Exactly," Fallow replied.

Doc continued in his legal like rationalization. "When people of sound mind capitulate to the irrational just because the irrational scream louder than everyone else, then we, in fact, become enablers to them. Just ignore them, and let's do what we do. They are little people with little minds. Move on."

"My goodness, boy," Fallow replied with a chuckle, "when you run for President, I'll vote for you."

"Before I enter that race, sir, help me win this one."

Fallow smiled on the other end. "Gosh, you can argue good. You just make sure you tell your dad how convincing you were."

"You got it."

"Text me your location," Fallow said.

* * *

The farm hand who literally drew the short straw was tasked in giving Fire Face one last go of it. He did exactly what Doc recommended, and a mare proved to be too much for Fire Face to resist as the big, brooding stallion stomped his way into the trailer.

"Of course, these lunatics would protest now," Fallow said in disgust as his mirrors were filled with the place he had to leave, and his front view was packed by a crowd of animal rights activists that had swollen to at least one hundred and fifty people.

Fallow lowered his window as he rolled to a stop in front of the crowd, hoping to have a civil, rational conversation. However, as his window lowered, his cabin was filled with the chant, "Horses are human, too! Horses are human, too!"

The leader of the protestors strolled up to Fallow's window and began yelling gibberish at Fallow. Fire Face then let out a violent shriek at the chaos outside and part of his nose stuck out of the aluminum slats.

Someone in the crowd recognized the markings of the face and shouted, "It's Fire Face!"

One protestor rummaged through his pockets, pulled out some sugar cubes, and began walking toward the big stallion.

"Son," Fallow shouted out, "if you're thinking to feed that horse those sugar cubes, I am warning you, do not do that. I'm not kidding."

"Why not?" the angry protestor snapped back.

"He bites. He's a dangerous horse. You need to let him be and let me pass."

"He only bites because he's abused," the man lectured. "If you treat them like animals, then animals are all they're ever going to be!" The crowd gave a raucous roar of approval, and he continued to walk toward the horse with his outstretched hand.

"I'm telling you, don't do it," Fallow warned again. "I'm not responsible."

Fire Face tilted his head and slammed it through the tight space in the trailer, and extended his neck toward the hand holding the sugar cubes.

"Here you go, friend," the man said.

CHOMP! Fire Face got the cubes and one finger.

The man screamed in pain as he clutched his crushed index finger. The agony of the man screeching left the crowd in confusion and disarray. Fallow saw the opening, shifted into first, and hit the gas.

Fallow called Doc. "Hey, you there?"

"Yes, sir. You're coming with my horse?"

"Yes, but . . ." Ben looked in the rearview mirror and saw Fire Face tossing his head about. "I really hope you would reconsider. This horse ain't safe, son."

* * *

DING. DOC'S PHONE RECEIVED A TEXT.

"Who is it?" Mac asked as he wrung out his chaps.

"It's Jonah," Doc replied. He answered the FaceTime call. "Go."

"Bad news, Doc. Ethan's coming," Jonah said.

"He got through the fighting?" Doc asked.

"Yep, and he's got a fresh set of tires. He's only minutes from the crossing."

"Thanks for the heads up. We're working on a plan."

"What plan?" Jonah asked.

"I'll tell you when it works," Doc replied.

Fallow then texted Doc: *I have an emergency; we have more trailers than we do trucks. So, I have to unhook the trailer and leave it. Come and get 'em.* Fallow then sent Doc the final location of where that trailer would be.

Doc texted back: *Absolutely, that's only a mile and half from us. We'll get there. Thanks so much.*

Fallow replied one more time: *By the way, your leather jacket was left at the farm. It's in in the trailer, too.*

Thanks, Doc texted back. He turned to Mac. "We got to run. Fire Face is one and half miles from here."

"Go," Mac replied as he hadn't put his pants back on from wringing them out. "I'll catch up."

Doc sprinted with all his might.

* * *

DOC GASSED HIMSELF WITH THE FASTEST MILE AND HALF HE WOULD ever run. He was sucking in air by the time he saw the trailer ahead, and he still wasn't there yet.

The anxiety from the fires and the protestors had the stallion on a knife's edge, even more than usual, and he was rocking the trailer back and forth with incessant spinning.

Doc pulled out his phone and FaceTimed Jonah. "Hey," Doc yelled into his phone, "Jonah."

"Yeah, what are you doing?" Jonah asked.

"I'm running," Doc replied.

"Why?"

"It's a part of my plan."

Jonah crinkled his face and scratched his head. "Your plan is to run to the finish line? Doc, I'm not sure that's one of your better plans."

Doc ignored the comment and then texted Jonah his location. He asked, "What's the route like from my location to the finish line?"

Jonah got the text and did some checking. "You'd be fine if you could do a straight line as the crow flies, but it's mostly suburbs. You'll be turning corners the whole way. It's a horrible route."

"Where's Ethan?"

"Still in Mexico, but he's cooking now, looks like he's through the tough parts."

"Okay," Doc replied, "send me a GPS route based on the straightest line possible. Don't worry about the streets, houses, or anything. I just want a straight route."

"You're talking crazy, but I'll do it." Jonah hung up and went to work on customized waypoints.

Doc slid the phone in his pocket and glanced back. Mac was coming, but he was holding his ribs as he ran.

Doc couldn't help but smile . . . Mac had put the chaps back on.

* * *

"Easy, boy," Doc said as he reached the trailer and tried to catch his breath. The big stallion looked more violent than ever. He kept spinning and banging into the metal sides. Doc spoke to himself, "If there was ever a time to reconsider, it would be now."

As Doc was having second thoughts, he decided to FaceTime Jonah again.

"Yeah," Jonah answered.

"I found my vehicle," Doc said casually.

"But you're not allowed another vehicle?"

Doc corrected, "The rules say I'm not allowed another motorized vehicle. It doesn't say anything about an unmotorized vehicle."

Doc turned the iPhone toward the trailer, and Jonah saw the big stallion's chest that was now pressed up against the aluminum slats.

Jonah's eyes bugged out. "Oh, I get it. You decided to make a deal with the devil."

"Do you have my route?" Doc pressed.

"Sending it now," Jonah replied, "but are you expecting him to follow a route?"

J-Dog's face appeared in the camera view behind Jonah. "Hold your horses, are you thinking what I think you're thinking?"

"You got a better idea?" Doc asked.

"There is no better idea than that!" J-Dog clapped his hands and said to himself, "Best day ever."

"Do you see?" Jonah asked. "J-Dog's on board with your plan. What does that tell you?"

J-Dog pushed his face in front of Jonah's. "Doc, I want you to know that I fully support your decision to go crazy. You're going to get the first annual Wild Dog Dog of the Year award. So, congratulations."

"See?" Jonah said.

"Duly noted," Doc replied, "but we don't have a choice."

Mac reached the trailer, and he clutched his bruised ribs. "Oh," he gasped, "breathing hurts so bad."

Jonah overheard the comment. "Mac hurts?"

"Yep," Mac explained, "evidently, I'm the blessed recipient of a miracle." Mac looked up at the massive stallion that only promised more injury. "Why couldn't God have just waited a few more hours?"

"Are we ready to do this?" Doc asked Mac.

"Wait," Mac said. "Listen, you know me, and I'm with you till the end. Which we may be looking at right now. Honestly, what makes you think we can ride him?"

Doc looked at Mac. "Do you trust me?"

"You know I do, brother," Mac replied.

"Something happened at the farm before. When I rode him, he didn't buck me off. I just fell off when he jumped that gate. He let me ride him."

"You said no one could ever ride him," Mac said. "That's why he was never able to be raced."

Fire Face stomped hard in the trailer.

"You're right, no jockey was ever able to ride him, but I think I figured it out," Doc said. "It's about control. I rode him bareback and unbridled. He was in control. So, he didn't really care if I was there or not. I think it's possible to ride him if we don't bridle him."

"Well, that's good and dandy, Doc." Mac sarcastically answered. "How do we know he'll go in the right direction?"

Doc nodded a little sheepishly. "Valid question. I'm not going to lie. I'm hoping we caught a break with the direction of the trailer."

"How so?"

Doc pulled up the GPS route that Jonah had just sent him. "See, the back of the trailer is facing the finish line. I'm hoping he runs straight out of the gate."

"Hope?" Mac asked.

Doc relented. "I know it's not great, Mac, but it's all we have left. We either try this right now or we give Ethan Oxidant the Quad Continental, the punk who dragged us through the desert."

That sunk into Mac. "I can't believe we're actually going to do this, but I owe him. There is one more thing, though."

"What's that?"

"I've never ridden a horse," Mac said with his arms wide open.

"Never?"

"No, not many stables in the inner city, Doc."

"Okay, that's more complicated, but really, you just have to hang on to me with both arms." Doc tilted his head.

"You mean like a hug?"

Doc grimaced. "I guess a lot like a hug."

"I'm supposed to be on a horse, sitting behind you, and hugging you?"

"Listen, it's not ideal. I'm not excited about it either, but it is what it is."

"This is worse than the chaps! You know we'll be streamed online. Can you imagine the memes?"

"Okay," Doc replied, "I get it, so when you get to the finish line, just kiss the first girl you see. That sorts out everything."

"I'm going to have to," Mac replied. "I got to save face."

"I'll apologize to the unsuspecting girl for you," Doc replied.

"Are you kidding?" Mac grinned. "It'll be the highlight of her life."

* * *

Now that they got that sorted, Doc took a deep breath. "Here's how we do it. I got to get in there and get on him. As soon as I do, you unlock the gate. He'll blow the thing open, and you grab my arm as we pass."

"We are out of our minds," Mac said.

"Something like that," Doc agreed as he slowly moved toward the front of the trailer. He started talking to Fire Face. "Shh, it's okay, boy. It's okay."

The giant of a horse snorted a warning, but Doc pressed on.

There were two compartments in this trailer, and they were divided by a swinging gate. Doc entered the front compartment from the side of the trailer, and as his foot stepped in, he felt the aluminum trailer tremor beneath him from the big stallion's movements. Doc's heart pounded in anticipation, a bit of fear, and the fact that everything he knew about horses was telling him that this was a bad idea.

Doc glanced by happenstance into the gooseneck part of the trailer, spotting his leather racing jacket. It was like an old friend, and oddly enough, it felt like reassurance to him. He grabbed it and put it on. He zipped up the front of the jacket and zipped down the sleeves. He then slowly flipped up the collar.

"Shh. Easy boy, easy. I don't have a bridle, see?" he spoke softly and calmly. "I don't have a saddle or anything. Just me." Doc moved to the latch, and slowly lifted it, and it clanked as it unlatched that center barrier.

Fire Face stomped and shook his head. His ears pinned back for a second, and Doc froze, but then the ears eased back forward, so Doc slowly swung the gate toward himself and stepped on the other side of the barrier, now with nothing separating him from the stallion.

Doc's heart raced, but he breathed in deeply, knowing the horse could sense his fear.

Fire Face spun, and Doc's life flashed before his eyes as the huge hind quarters of the horse passed in front of him. For the briefest of moments, Doc thought he was going to get kicked into oblivion, but Fire Face continued the spin until he faced Doc. The horse tried to rear up, smashing his head against the top of the trailer, making an awful banging sound.

Doc spoke in slow, soft, soothing tones, just like he had seen his dad do thousands of times. "Easy, easy. We've done this before, remember? Back in the barn? I rode you, and you didn't kick me off. You and I both know it. I understand you. You don't want to be controlled. Shhh. I don't want to control you."

The horse gave a loud shriek and a snort.

"I won't try to hold you back. This is your moment, too," Doc said, "to show everyone what you can do. Because the whole world is going to watch you run. I guarantee it, and I need you to run. I need all you got, and I need it now."

Doc held out his hand. Fire Face tossed his head back, and then took a stomping step toward Doc. Doc didn't retreat, but slowly took a step toward the stallion and extended his hand as far as he could reach.

The horse's lips quivered with a small snort, but that was all. Doc reached forward more. The two touched. Doc's fingers graced the front, soft part of Fire Face's nose. Fire Face jerked his head back, and Doc took another small, slow step forward.

Then Fire Face pushed his head into Doc's hand. Doc pressed his palm against the big broad nose and rubbed up between the horse's eyes. Doc couldn't believe it. It was the first time anyone had had a moment like this with the stallion. "We gotta go," Doc said, and didn't take his eyes away from the eyes of the horse as he addressed Mac. "Hey, Mac, as soon as I am on him, you need to open that gate. It's going to happen fast."

Doc moved toward the neck of the horse, rubbing him along the way. "Are you ready?" Doc asked both Mac and Fire Face.

Doc's left hand grabbed a wad of the horse's thick mane, and he twisted it around his fist like a bull rider tightening up the rope. "Mac, pull the pin out from the gate, quietly, and stand off to the right of it, and get ready. We have one shot."

Mac lifted the pin, and it made the faintest clink as it went up. Fire Face heard it and knew exactly what it meant. Like a Texas tornado, he spun with twister-like force. Doc nearly had his arm pulled out of its socket as he clinched down to the mane and held on as he twirled around with the horse.

Doc planted his left foot and used the momentum to jump with all his might and swing himself up onto the stallion. "NOW!" Doc yelled, and Mac flung open the gate.

The horse launched toward the gate as it was opening, and Fire Face moved faster than the gate smashing it open with breaking force. Fire Face leaped with extraordinary strength out of the trailer.

Doc gripped the mane with his left hand and blindly swung down his right arm. They had one chance to make it. The speed and force of the gate opening nearly took Mac's arm off, but his reflexes saved his life as he sidestepped the gate and reached up his arm on a plan and a prayer.

SLAP.

The two boys' hands smacked and clinched down on each other as Mac found himself instantly airborne. Doc was nearly pulled off, but his legs gripped as tight as they could around the rock-hard midsection of the stallion, and he managed to stay on. Mac's body bounced to the rhythm of his heels banging onto the ground. It took about one second for Mac's senses to catch up to his dire situation. He thrust his other hand up to Doc's arm and grabbed it.

Doc bent his body over to the left side of the horse as Mac began climbing Doc's arm like a rope. Mac raised both knees up to his chest and kangaroo kicked his legs down to the ground, contacting the surface and jumping as hard as he could.

The momentum and Doc's pull brought Mac high into the air, and he kicked his left leg as wide as possible. Gravity then shoved him down on the broad back of the mad fast horse who was tasting total freedom and sensed that Doc didn't have the will or the way to slow him down.

* * *

Fire Face's strides were nothing short of joyous aggression fueled by equine excellence. He ripped through trees, leaving snapped branches in his wake, crossed a road, leaped a ditch, and blasted through another treed area on the right of way.

Mac hugged Doc tight and yelled, "Shouldn't we run on the road?"

Doc buried his head into the huge thick mane of the horse. "Decisions up here aren't being made by committee!"

There was a row of wild shrubs coming up, and Fire Face showed no intent of slowing down.

Doc gave a preparatory warning to Mac, "Best hang on like your life depends on it."

"I'm already grabbing you," Mac replied.

"Squeeze with your legs!" Doc shouted.

"My legs?"

"Yes! The harder you squeeze the better you'll stay on."

"But the harder I squeeze, the faster he'll run!"

Doc looked back at Mac. "And the faster he runs, the harder you better squeeze just to stay on!"

"Now we're getting crazy!" Mac yelled.

Fire Face launched himself into the air and cleared the six-foot high bushes. The boys clung to everything they could and soared with the stallion. As powerful as the take-off was, the smooth landing took the boys by surprise. Fire Face never broke stride, never stumbled, never seemed to feel his own weight contacting the ground again. It was an effortless act of grace and balance that the mechanized ATVs that Doc raced could never achieve.

"You making it?" Doc shouted back.

"I think you'll know it when I'm not." Mac winced in pain from his aching ribs, but he was finding his seat on the horse. "It's actually easier to balance on him than I thought it would be."

"I know, right?" Doc replied. "He's smooth."

* * *

Doc's phone buzzed in his jacket, and he balanced himself and pulled it out. He handed it back to Mac.

"Go," Mac said as the thundering hoofs brought an ambient sound that was unmissable.

"We got problems," Jonah said. "Ethan is coming. He's passed the border and absolutely flying."

"We got another set of problems," Mac replied. He panned the phone so Jonah could see just how nuts things had gotten.

"Oooh, check it out!" Jonah squealed. Jonah turned to the thousands of people who were waiting at the finish line. "THEY'RE RIDING FIRE FACE!"

That call of the wild went far and wide, and the rest of the gang ran to the phone in extraordinary anticipation of seeing the one thing they thought could never be seen. Then other spectators, race officials, and interested bystanders also found themselves running over to the American crew out of morbid curiosity.

J-Dog grabbed the iPad out of Jonah's hand and quickly reconfigured it to do a direct stream to the Wild Dog. Instantly, that signal from the palm of Mac's hand went around the world.

"Mac, J-Dog here. We got to keep this stream going."

"I knew it," Mac relented. He snapped off three leather cords from his chaps and tied the phone, tourniquet style, to his right leg.

"Look," J-Dog chimed, "a *mounted* camera."

Jonah fist bumped J-Dog. "I see what you did there."

* * *

CHESTER "OIL SLICK" HORNBACK SAT AT HIS BROADCAST BOOTH AT the heavily crowded finish line. He, along with millions of other people around the world, logged onto the Wild Dog. He tapped the mic to make sure it was on and began the play-by-play finale.

He slapped his cap on the table and put it back on in haste. "Welcome to the Wild West, Quad Continental style. This a Quad first. The Americans are attempting to finish this race on a horse! I suppose it is how the west was won, so let's see if it can win the Quad as well. To all of our TV partners out there, our producers are now delivering live drone aerial footage for you, and you are definitely not going to want to miss this."

A fleet of official Quad Continental drones had launched into the air, and the first one reached Doc, Mac, and Fire Face.

"My gosh, look at that horse! Is it even a horse?" Oil Slick said, marveling at the sheer size, sight, and majesty of the stallion. "Or is it some creature from the antediluvian world?"

Oil Slick grabbed his rulebook. "For you fans out there wondering if it is even legal for a racer to ride a horse, I've got weird and wacky news for you. It appears the Americans have found a clever legal loophole. According to the officials at the Quad, nothing prohibits them from riding a horse, because an animal is not a motorized vehicle. The rules state a racer cannot replace their vehicle with another motorized vehicle. Well, bless constitutional law, that horse isn't motorized, now is it? Obviously, no one ever thought anyone would try to ride a horse in the Quad Continental. It's insane. It's ludicrous. It's wildly absurd. Yet here we are, watching it unfold. Now, there is another rule we found as we fact-checked the legality of riding a horse, and this rule is so apropos to our situation, because it states that you must be able to cite your vehicle's horsepower upon request. Well, holy engine block, they have *one* horsepower! So, my friends, hang on to your knickers, for we've got ourselves a spectacular finish shaping up here."

* * *

"Hey guys, get over here," Jonah said to J-Dog and Alfie.

The three of them congregated near the finish line. "What is it?" Alfie asked.

Jonah pulled up the aerial footage that the Quad Continental drones were broadcasting. "Look at this." Jonah pointed to Ethan. "Look where he's going."

"That doesn't make sense," Alfie said.

"Not at all," J-Dog replied. "That's not his best route to the finish line."

"I know," Jonah said. "What are they doing? They're not dumb. They got something up their sleeve."

"Hold on," J-Dog said as he waved over Flip and Penelope.

"What is it?" Flip asked.

"We got a situation," J-Dog said. "The Brits are up to something, and we don't know what. We need you to find out."

Penelope pursed her lips a bit. "Why do you think we can find out?"

"You want me to beat it out of 'em?" Flip asked.

"No," Jonah said, "walk over, smile, and listen to what they are saying."

"Smile and listen?" Penelope asked. "What makes you think they'll just talk about their plans with us around?"

All three boys answered at once, "You're girls."

Penelope objected, "I find that totally demeaning."

"Good," J-Dog said, "so help us foil the plans of those who will be doing the demeaning."

"This isn't going to work," Penelope said, "but we'll try."

"I think it will be fun," Flip said. "Undercover spy."

"That's the spirit, kid," J-Dog replied. "Go get your Bond on."

* * *

PENELOPE AND FLIP MEANDERED IN THE MOST INCONSPICUOUS WAY they could until they were within earshot of the British crew. When some of the British team noticed the two girls standing there, Flip whispered to Penelope, "Act confused. It makes boys think they're smart."

Penelope smiled wide-eyed and stupefied and pointed at one of the big British support vehicles. "Oooh, what's in that big truck?"

The ruse worked. The Brits ignored them, and Flip and Penelope overheard everything.

J-Dog, Jonah, and Alfie watched Penelope and Flip listen in. Jonah then jerked his head back. "What's going on?" he asked as he saw Flip clinch her fist and cock her arm like she was going to punch someone. Penelope held her back though and convinced her otherwise.

"Dude, Flip's about to flip," J-Dog said.

"Yeah, something bad's going down," Alfie said.

Jonah waved his big hands in the air to get the girls' attention. Flip saw it and did a dead sprint to him. Penelope ran too, but she couldn't keep up.

Flip slid to a stop and tried to get out what they had heard, but she was so flustered she couldn't get it our right. "They're going to fit Dire Face like a fear! I mean dit Fire Dace like an ear. Agghh!" she screamed. She took a deep breath. "They told Ethan to hit Fire Face like a deer."

* * *

MAC YELLED AT DOC AS FIRE FACE ONLY INCREASED HIS STRIDE AS he approached Highway 5 in southern California. "Those are cars, man!"

The busy highway ran perpendicular to the horse's chosen route and Fire Face seemed wholly unconcerned.

Mac turned his head and saw a big Chevy Suburban coming their way. "That's going to hurt!"

"You got to jump off!" Doc screamed.

"Too late!" Mac shouted.

The boys were shocked into silence as they grabbed everything they could, trusting that the big stallion didn't want to get hit either.

Fire Face notched it up a gear. His head extended out, and his ears pinned back. He shot over the ditch and into the four-lane highway without flinching. The Suburban slammed his breaks, car horn screeching as Fire Face crossed right in front of it.

Fire Face met an empty space on the second south bound lane, jumped the median straight into north bound traffic, and barely crossed in front of a semi-truck, whose safety camera caught the whole event. The truck driver slowed and veered ever so slightly as Fire Face's tail swished the front grill of the truck as he passed by.

But there was no way to miss the touring motorcycle in the next and final lane of traffic.

Doc's eyes met with the glazed eyes of the motorcyclist who saw his own life pass right by. The gang back at the finish line screamed in horror as the camera strapped on Mac's leg streamed everything along with the Quad's drones in the sky.

That is when it happened. With a shortened skip, Fire Face packed his energy into his haunches and threw his head back and up toward the sky, smashing his muscular neck into Doc's face and rocking the boy back into Mac.

Fire Face jumped with the spring of a large jungle cat going straight up a tree. The boys soared in the air with both their backsides losing contact with the horse. Doc hung onto the only thing he could, which was the thick mane, and Mac held onto Doc.

The motorcyclist closed his eyes for an impact that never came, as he passed directly underneath the stallion.

The front hooves came down in the grass, and the rear hooves extended with incredible elasticity even farther forward. The stallion pushed off again, never thinking twice about his incredible leap.

The boys came down exactly where they left off, on top of that giant of a horse.

Doc gasped. "I can't believe—"

Mac finished the thought, "THAT just happened!"

* * *

After the crossing at the San Ysidro Border, Ethan Oxidant hopped on the 805 Highway. He juiced that Jaguar turbo as he eclipsed one hundred and thirty miles per hour, screaming past the traffic in the slower, normal commuter lanes. It was a sight to behold, but Oil Slick couldn't peel his attention away from the other view on his split screen.

"Holy Frogger!" Oil Slick yelled. His eyes bugged out as his drones delivered the video of Fire Face navigating the highway. "Never in all my years have I seen such a thing." He then glanced at Ethan's aerial shot. "And I've got an inkling that even more mayhem is on the horizon."

It didn't take a genius to see that the British had monarchal-sized violence on their minds.

Oil Slick wiped sweat from his brow. "Ethan Oxidant has left Route 805. He has gotten on 905. I repeat, he has gotten on 905, and is heading back west. Let me explain to you what that means because it is completely whacked. He had a straight shot to the finish line on route 805! His best chance of winning was simply hunkering down, opening up that Jaguar turbo, and lettin' it eat. So, I think he's off to intercept the American team, something that I don't think he needs to do to win this race. He's got bad intentions, my friends."

* * *

FIRE FACE FELT THE EXHILARATION OF DOING WHAT HE WAS BRED TO do: running. His equine mind knew no fear, knew no caution, and knew not an ounce of panic. He was the alpha male, and he wouldn't hold back.

After passing Highway 5, Fire Face scorched through city streets. Running stop lights, passing kids with backpacks, not stopping for stopped buses, but then . . .

"Dude," Mac said as he saw a sign on the road, "this is a dead end!"

Doc replied, "That's a concept lost on a horse, Mac."

Sure enough, Fire Face reached the dead-end of the urban development and found the obligatory dumpster and fence which was followed by a brushy, unkept field. There was room to go around the dumpster, but that was another idea absent for a horse bred for steeplechase.

Fire Face increased his speed, surprising the boys who didn't think there was more speed to be had, and he thrust his body in the air with nearly hydraulic ease. The stallion soared over the dumpster with the shell-shocked boys as cargo.

WHEW!

The air was soothing to the boys as the clappity-clap sound of the hooves was briefly suspended. He then landed with the usual grace that the boys had become accustomed to, and he continued his galloping ways through the now knee-high grass.

Then Doc heard a high-pitched crack that Flip could identify a mile away. It was the sound of a baseball hitting an aluminum bat.

"This will be something," Mac said, as he looked at the barrier of trees ahead of them, and having a good idea of what was on the other side.

The ball diamond had two teams locked in an extra innings battle, and thirty or so parents crowded onto wobbly aluminum stands behind the backstop.

Fire Face crushed through the treed barrier, branches snapping off on all three of their bodies, and CRACK! A high bouncing grounder was hit toward the second baseman as the giant stallion jumped over the inground dugout, passed the first base coach, and was heading toward second. Gasps reverberated from the stands, followed by a stunned silence from the crowd and teams.

The cheap infield was more recycled gravel than suitable dirt for a baseball field, and the grounder struck a jagged rock and popped up, nearly hitting Mac in the face, but his reflexes saved him as he snatched the ball with his hand.

"What do I do with it?" Mac asked with the ball in his hand.

Doc gave him the first thing that popped in this mind, "Throw him out!"

Mac turned, and side-armed the ball to first, which the first baseman caught in a state of complete bewilderment.

"Out!" the umpire shouted, not knowing what else to say.

The crowd was silent for a few moments, and then everyone erupted in cheers as Fire Face jumped over the left field fence, gone as quickly as he appeared. But he left behind a few short seconds of action that became a lifelong memory for everyone at the ballfield.

* * *

MAC GLANCED DOWN AT HIS LEG TO CHECK THE GPS, AND HE wasn't happy. "We've got 905 coming up. It's a big road, Doc."

Doc crouched down like a jockey with both hands choked up high on Fire Face's mane. He looked over his shoulder. "We got to trust Fire Face. We really don't have a choice."

Mac's FaceTime video rang; it was Jonah. "Dude, you got to WATCH OUT!" Jonah screamed into the phone.

"905," Mac replied. "We know. Big road."

"Not that!" Jonah yelled. "Ethan's coming for you!"

"What?" Mac said, trying to process the information.

"He's right there!" Jonah said. "He' going to try to hit you guys like you're a deer."

"I really hate that guy," Mac grunted.

"Hang on, brother," Doc blurted as the embankment to the 905-state highway came into view. "We got to live in the moment."

"Live is right!" Mac gasped as Fire Face hit the embankment and ramped up. A small compact car was coming eastbound, and a collision was imminent. "This doesn't get any easier!" Mac yelled, his eyes as wide as saucers.

Doc shouted back, "Just pretend you're at the farm, riding in a field."

"Okay." Mac closed his eyes. "I'm at the farm." He opened one eye. "During California rush hour! And that guy's texting!"

"Here we go!" Doc readied.

Mac growled, "Holy emoji!"

The boys leaned forward, squeezed with their legs, and they felt those hind quarters shift underneath them. Fire Face launched with a full stride into the air the moment he hit the paved berm. His muscular body streamlined itself as he soared, his feet tucked up tight beneath him. He cleared the diminutive car like it was nothing more than a hedge of bushes in a race. He did so with ease, without angst, and as if he simply did the reasonable and natural thing to do.

A big SUV was in the next lane, and that driver slammed the breaks at the action. Fire Face seemingly took note and simply powered through the lane, running down into the large grassy median.

Mac, not sure if he was breathing or not, glanced right, and that's when he saw it. Ethan Oxidant's desert racer was ripping down the highway, in and out of cars, right toward them. Ethan had timed it perfectly. He was going to meet Fire Face exactly when the big stallion crossed the westbound lanes of traffic.

"Doc," Mac said.

"What?"

Mac pointed. "The British are coming! The British are coming!"

The warning was no use. Fire Face crossed the median, and his big hooves clunked down on the pavement.

Ethan pulled to the right berm, off the highway, and down the embankment. When he hit the bottom of the ditch, he yanked back hard and downshifted, giving that wicked engine all the fuel it had.

Fire Face crossed the first lane of traffic without needing to jump. Cars slammed on their breaks, giving Fire Face a clean route to pass through. Fire Face's right ear flickered from a pinned back position to a quick upward tilt in the direction of Ethan. Fire Face had seen him.

Ethan's tires spun in the grass as he climbed the ditch and took aim with deadly intent.

Fire Face's last stride was on the paved berm, and then he jumped, like he always did, to clear the charging Ethan.

The embankment, though, acted like a ramp, and just like Ethan had planned, his vehicle came up that embankment and soared into the air, too. Fire Face was in midair, unable to turn, stop, or accelerate.

He was at the mercy of momentum, and his flight had already been established.

The top bar of the bruising metal cage of the racer connected, mid-air, into the upper curled front legs of Fire Face, clipping them and missing the boy's legs by inches.

The horrific collision flipped the stallion in the air, catapulting Doc and Mac off his back. The forward momentum kept all three away from the highway, but nothing could arrest their tumultuous airborne twists and then tumbles.

Fire Face landed first, and the downward slope of the embankment gave him and the boys a saving grace. The stallion crashed and then smashed the side of his head so hard that he was knocked unconscious. He rolled and flopped down the embankment, before hitting bottom. The big, glorious stallion, for the first time in his existence, stayed completely still as his body was unnaturally sprawled out in the wet ditch.

Both boys were flung far and came down hard on the embankment. Their appendages whipped around like rag dolls. When their bodies did finally stop, they laid motionless, unconscious, showing no signs of life.

Ethan took one glance at his work, and evil contentment soothed his malice. He drove off the highway and arranged a final pit stop with his crew to ready his vehicle for his imminent victory. There was no need to rush, for he was the only racer left.

The highway seized up as onlookers couldn't help but stop, and gawk at the scene. At first, no one knew what to do. The culprit of the crash was gone, and no one had ever seen anything like it.

The police dispatch was flooded with nine-one-one calls, but the roads were so backed up that no emergency vehicles could get through.

* * *

JONAH, J-DOG, ALFIE, FLIP, AND PENELOPE SCREAMED WITH AS much force as their vocal cords could allow. The streaming iPhone strapped to Mac's leg had caught the entire midair collision, and then it was crunched at impact, killing the phone and killing the stream.

Tears hit the girls first, but the tears came to the boys quickly as well. There was no response from them but fear, no comments . . . just silence. They didn't know what do to, what to think, and panic froze them.

Their friends were down. The invincibility of Fire Face was destroyed. Nothing was uttered. Their young minds had never thought this end was even possible.

Jonah tried to FaceTime, but there was no answer. He rang again. Nothing.

Dead silence and complete motionlessness ruled for some moments. The kids lost a little contact with time, not knowing how long the shock took over, but eventually, Jonah spoke up, his voice cracking, "Check it out." He wiped away some tears. "We're down. We're down, but . . . but this is what we do. When we're down, then we've got to look up."

"What do you mean?" Penelope asked.

"Pray," he replied.

The kids huddled up with arms over shoulders, and then the big gospel voice of Jonah prayed. He prayed with panic, prayed with angst, but prayed with faith, and all Wild Dog prayed with him.

* * *

THE BOYS STILL WEREN'T MOVING, AND NEITHER WAS FIRE FACE. Onlookers got out of their cars, and a few of them kept people away from the horse, knowing that such a large animal, when injured, was just too dangerous to approach. A group of about a dozen good Samaritans ran up to the boys.

One well-dressed, sharp looking man got out of a car and quickly got to Mac. "Give me room, please. I'm a doctor," he announced.

The doctor examined Mac first and immediately noticed a bad shape to the shoulder. He checked the boy's vitals. "He's still alive," he said and then pressed in on the shoulder. Mac winced, and he came to as the pain acted like smelling salts. "He's got a broken collar bone," the doctor said. He looked at a young woman who was standing nearby. "Miss, would you kneel and hold his hand, and try to keep him calm as he wakes? I need to check the other one."

The doctor then shuffled over to Doc and knelt beside him. "He's alive, too," he said loudly after checking his vitals. He then inspected the boy closer. Everything looked miraculously intact. He whispered, "Someone's looking out for you." He turned back toward Mac. "How's he doing?"

The woman replied, "He's waking up."

The doctor exhaled. "Try to keep him calm."

The doctor continued to examine in triage fashion. Doc's racing pants and his leather jacket kept away the scrapes to the skin, and amazingly, the bones were intact. "Any news on an ambulance?" the doctor asked those around him.

"Nothing," a bystander said, "the whole highway is locked up. It's backed up for miles."

The doctor took over the moment. He pointed at a bigger guy. "Then you need to get up there and direct traffic. You've seen police officers do it. Just take charge and get cars moving."

The man listened.

The doctor continued and pointed to another woman. "And you, get us a couple of bottles of water from somewhere."

"From where?" she asked.

"Just ask people in their cars what they have. Tell them we have boys who are hurt."

"Okay," she said.

Then there came a sound of stirring and rustling coming from the horse, and all the attention shifted.

"Careful," the doctor said as people started to get too close to Fire Face. "Please stay away from that horse."

A big, burly fellow said, "I don't want to, but I've got a sidearm. I can put that horse down. You know he's hurt."

A petite woman quickly cried, "No!"

The man explained, "We don't know what a horse that size will do. If it wakes and panics, he could do a lot of damage."

"Not yet," the doctor said. "Once you shoot him, we can't bring him back. So, let's make sure."

Fire Face flung his head, and his mane swished in the ditch water. The horse blinked, his eyes turning in circles for a moment. A big snort came from the stallion as he struggled for a moment on the ground, but then he surged to his feet.

Gasps filled the crowd at the size of the creature. They stared at the huge wet, matted mane, the flame-like face, and the blood running down his shoulder and dripping from his nose.

The people kneeling around the boys stood up, and so did a groggy, slightly confused Mac, whose senses were so scrambled that he didn't quite know where he was, or who all the people were standing around him. The woman entrusted to care for Mac helped him stand straight, but wasn't sure if the boy should be standing at all. Then there was the horse.

The burly man drew his sidearm.

"Please don't, please," the meek-spirited woman begged.

The man replied, "I don't want to ma'am, but we have to be humane to the horse and also protect all of us."

"Just wait," the doctor asked.

Fire Face reared up and let out a huge shriek, shocking the crowd.

The man aimed the pistol for the center of the big muscular chest but still didn't cover the trigger with his finger.

The doctor raised his hands. "Wait, wait."

Fire Face's hooves came back to the ground and stomped, and then he saw Doc lying on the ground, still unconscious.

Mac was slouched over to one side, clearly favoring a shoulder. "Fire Face," Mac softly said. Then a bit louder, he said, "Fire Face, easy boy."

The horse recognized the voice and seemed to stomp in response.

"It's alright," Mac said, and then he winced from the incredible pain in his shoulder and neck. He realized he couldn't move his arm.

Fire Face took note of the crowd standing around the boy on the ground. It was Doc, and the stallion knew it. In an amazing act of instinctual protection, Fire Face stomped and began moving forward slowly, but not in a threatening manner. The man moved his finger to the trigger, but the doctor saw something and grabbed the man's arm.

"No, no, no. Everyone back away from the boy, now."

"What?" The burly man was livid, thinking they were going to sacrifice the boy to an angry, wild horse.

"Doc?" Mac said as he finally recognized that his best friend was lying there and not moving. "Doc!" Mac shook himself free from the people trying to hold him. Not caring about his pain, he rushed to his friend and knelt beside him. "Doc, wake up, buddy. Wake up," he pleaded with his friend. "Come on, you're tougher than this. Don't you dare go all pansy on me now. Let's go. Get up, man. Come on, Doc."

"Watch out!" someone yelled from the crowd as Fire Face quickened his steps toward Doc and Mac. Snorting, stomping, and swishing his tail, the horse neared, but his ears weren't pinned back now. Rather, they were forward and alert.

Mac didn't care. Mac wasn't afraid as the stallion moved toward them. Fire Face didn't stop until his head was directly over the two boys.

"Come on, brother," Mac said.

Then the amazing happened. Fire Face lowered his head past Mac's, and the big horse pushed Doc's face with his bloody nose, smearing blood onto the boy's face and hair.

Doc didn't move.

Fire Face nudged the boy again, this time a little harder, making the people in the crowd more uncomfortable. Fire Face pulled his head up for a brief moment, sucked in air through his big nostrils, and put his nose right on Doc.

SHRIEK! He neighed with all his might, right in and on Doc's face.

The shrill, siren-like sound blasted Doc. The volume and intensity broke through Doc's consciousness, and the boy's eyes popped open.

Fire Face raised his head, neighed, snorted, and stomped.

Doc looked straight up at the stallion and cautiously said, "Hey there." Doc's eyes darted around, taking in the surroundings as Mac leaned over him.

"There you are, brother." Mac smiled and then grabbed his own shoulder, grimacing.

"Are you okay?" Doc asked.

"Sure, just living the miracle life." Mac winced in pain.

"You hurt?"

"If by hurt you mean it feels like my arm is about to fall off, then yes."

Doc's mind started to recalibrate a bit. "Sorry, dude. Are we still racing? Is it over?"

Mac rolled back to a seated position and then decided to lay down flat on the ground next to Doc. Mac stared at the sky and touched his shoulder. "My arm doesn't work, Doc. If we are racing, I can't do it. I wouldn't be able to hang on."

Doc glanced at the horse. Blood dripped from the stallion's nose and abrasions covered his body. His majestic mane was caked in drying mud. What used to be the endless flames of his beautiful coat were now extinguished by blood mixed with water and dirt. It felt like a giant rock dropped on Doc's chest. All the emotions hit him at once as his mind unforgivingly ran the gamut of all he had endured for the Quad Continental.

From the beginning of this race, he felt the anticipation of the unknown and the anxiety of impending calamity, but as sure as the sun would rise the next morning, there was always a new hope, just tantalizing enough for them to press on toward the prize.

But so much had been lost now. He didn't even know how he could point Fire Face in the right direction . . . if he even could get on him, and Mac was clearly out of commission. It seemed the Quad Continental had finally taken its claim. He breathed out and let the exhaustion sink in.

* * *

A FEW PEOPLE IN THE CROWD STARTED TO WHISPER, AND THEN THAT turned into chatter.

"Hey," the man with the sidearm, which was now holstered, asked, "are you those kids from the internet?"

Doc and Mac turned to the man, but the petite lady answered for them, "It is you, isn't it? You're the Bell Buckle Gang." She got excited. "My daughter loves you."

Mac leaned over to Doc. "At least we got that going for us."

The woman grew embarrassed. "I mean . . . the whole Bell Buckle Gang. She loves all of you."

The man saw that he was right. "I knew it. Wait, this is that race? The Quad Continental?" The man paused, and a deep relief came over him. "Ah, I'm so glad I didn't shoot your horse."

Doc and Mac didn't even know that had been an option. "Me too," Doc said as he looked at Fire Face.

The man was juiced up now as more thoughts came to his mind. He turned to the crowd. "This is Doc Copper!"

Doc smiled. "In the flesh."

"You're Mac Irons," someone else said.

"Guilty as charged," Mac quipped as he grabbed his shoulder, which made the doctor begin working on a makeshift harness for him.

Another bystander was watching something on his phone. "Guys, we're all on TV."

That got the crowd's attention, and they rushed to his phone to watch the aerial footage from the two drones circling the area.

"Wait," the burly man said, "if you're Doc, and you're Mac, and you're in the race right now, then that jerk that hit you was the British kid."

"Yep." Doc finally stood to his feet, and he cracked his neck. It hurt.

The man couldn't understand why Doc was still standing there.

"Doc, you gotta go. The race isn't over," the man said.

Some of the group started to get on board with that idea, but others just saw two boys who were lucky to be alive, and an argument ensued between the adults on the issue.

Doc moved his arm and mentally checked his body for damage. "Sir, it's too late," Doc answered. "Ethan would be to the finish line by now. There's no way."

The man shook his head. "No, he's not. He took a pit," The man said as he watched the race coverage on his phone. He tossed the phone to Doc who watched the feed.

"Can I make a call?" Doc asked the man.

"Yeah, absolutely."

Doc dialed up Jonah on FaceTime.

Jonah didn't recognize the number calling him, but he swiped to answer as he wiped down his saddened face.

"Hey, Jonah," Doc said.

"Oooh, check it out!" Jonah said. "You're alive! We just saw the drones above you and Mac and Fire Face, but we didn't see you moving." Jonah turned to the gang and shouted to everyone, "They're okay! Doc and Mac are okay!"

Hit, swish, and spit. J-Dog pushed his face in front of the phone. "Dude, I talked to God for you and cashed in some chips. You can thank me later."

"Jonah," Doc asked, "where's Ethan at?"

Doc heard excited whispers from the adults behind him. "He's talking to the Black Blondini," one said.

Jonah pulled over his laptop and brought up the GPS window. "He's one mile northwest of you doing a pit, and he's taking his sweet old time. I think they are actually polishing up his vehicle. They want a stupid parade."

Doc was flabbergasted. "He should have won by now."

Jonah replied, "But he's the only racer left, Doc. He's going to drink in all the fame."

Doc felt the slightest inkling of hope building up in him, but it was measured. "What's his route?"

"It's downright awful," Jonah replied. "When he came after you, he left his good route. Now, he's got nothing but dense California suburbia all the way between him and the finish line. But they don't think it matters because it's nothing more than a leisurely Sunday drive for him. Again, he's the only one left. Outside of you and him, no one else even made it out of Mexico."

Doc thought about it a bit. "He'll never get that fast turning through all those city blocks," Doc said. "Real quick, Jonah, if we go straight as the crow flies, how many miles is it?"

Jonah did some quick calculations. "You mean if I ignore the houses and stuff and just go straight?"

"Yes."

"I'm seeing about six miles."

Alfie added, "Give or take."

"What does Ethan have?"

"Sticking to the neighborhood roads?" Jonah replied.

"Yep."

"Eleven point two."

Doc quickly calculated his approximate speed on Fire Face and Ethan's speed. He turned to Mac. "He'll never see it coming. I'm not doing this without you, though. I'm not leaving you here."

Mac looked at Doc. "Brother if you think you can go, then go. I can't ride."

"We're in this together. I'm not leaving you behind."

Mac used his good hand and grabbed Doc. "You're not leaving me behind." Mac gritted his teeth. "If you're really telling me you can beat this punk and actually win this thing, I'm not going to let you check out now because of me."

Penelope's face popped up on the FaceTime. "Doc, listen to me. If anyone would say that you shouldn't do this, it would be me. If anyone would be afraid for you to do this, it would be me. But I've seen what Ethan is capable of, and sometimes there is only one way to stop people like that, and sentiment isn't going to do it. So, man up, find your reason to win, and let speed and fury chase it down."

"Oooh! Check it out!" Jonah squealed.

J-Dog raised his flask. "I'll drink to that."

"Unrage the cage, baby!" Flip shouted. "I mean, uncage the rage!"

The crowd began cheering, clapping, and urging Doc on.

Doc flipped up his collar on his beaten-up leather racing jacket and looked at Mac. "Are you sure?"

Mac was dead serious. "We owe him. Blood for blood."

Doc looked at Fire Face and then back at Mac. "He's going to have to listen to me."

"What do you mean?"

"I can't just straight line him. I've got to direct him."

"Does he know how to do that?"

"My dad says he knows what leg pressures mean, and I can pull his head with his mane, but . . ." Doc paused.

Mac finished the thought: "He'll freak out if you try to control him."

"He always has. You and I just let him run straight. It just happened to be in the right direction. That's not this. He has to follow my lead if I'm going to have a chance of reaching the finish line."

Doc turned to the big stallion, who remarkably stayed close by. Doc began walking slowly to Fire Face. He reached out his hand and softly began to speak, "Easy, boy, easy. Are you okay?"

For the first time in Fire Face's life, a type of kinship was formed. Doc had proven himself worthy to the big stallion. They'd gone through a fight together, and Doc was still there, and Doc hadn't tried to "break" the horse. Rather, they just came to an agreement.

Then, in that moment, something happened, something special. Fire Face trusted somebody. The big horse found a comfort, a connection, a partnership.

With building tension, the stallion began prancing toward the boy's outstretched hand, and Doc touched the horse's nose and gently rubbed the long face. Fire Face snorted.

"Easy, boy," Doc said. Then, a realization struck Doc, and he tilted his chin to the side in a bit of awe. "My dad was wrong about you. You're not a racehorse at all. You're a warhorse."

Although the horse couldn't understand the words, he sensed the rising emotion in the boy's chest. He could feel the boy's game rage grow and the intensity mount.

Fire Face flung his head back and let out a loud snort. Doc grabbed a fist full of mane, jumped, and swung his leg over the muscular stallion. Doc turned the horse's head by pulling on the thick mane, and the stallion allowed it. Doc glanced back at Mac for just a second. "This is for all of us." He then turned and squeezed his legs. "Go."

Fire Face's body ignited as his muscles rippled. The crowd gasped at the explosion. Fire Face hit full speed in five strides, and he and Doc were gone. The final reckoning with Ethan Oxidant had begun.

* * *

ETHAN HAD LEFT THE PIT, AND HE BEGAN RIDING THROUGH THE maze of city blocks and endless stop signs, lights, and turns that was California suburbia. But he did it with a calm, calculated measure. His arrogance overflowed as he began rehearsing his victory speech in his head and then out loud.

"Give it a rest, Ethan, and speed up already," Rupert said. "I'm getting nervous."

Ethan could only scoff. "What could you possibly be nervous about? I've won. There's nobody left but me. Just be grateful you're along for the ride."

The navigator didn't want to spend one more moment than he had to with Ethan. One thousand miles sitting next to the narcissist was too much, even for him.

The flat screen in the cockpit lit up with an incoming video call. Rupert answered it.

Their pit chief began speaking frantically, "Bloody well better go faster, and I mean now!"

Ethan shouted back, "You too? We're the only ones left."

"Not anymore!"

The two teenagers looked at each other, and the navigator flipped the touchscreen view to show the Quad Continental official broadcast. Ethan and his navigator looked on in mortification at the aerial shot of Doc Copper riding Fire Face through the suburbs.

"Turn it up," Ethan demanded as he wanted to hear Oil Slick give the call.

The thick Welsh accent poured out of the speakers, "The Quad Continental has raised its mighty voice again and has said this story's not done yet. The Americans are back!"

Ethan sat there dumbfounded.

Oil Slick continued, "Doc Copper was out of it. Literally dragged out, knocked out, and left for dead. But, as if laughing in the face of the sickle itself, he has rebounded, and is on that magnificent steed once again. I'm just going to shut my big mouth now and let everyone take this in. It is the best racing has to offer, my friends, and our fleet of drones has it covered. Watch and behold!"

The aerial view captured what only the imagination could have envisioned. Fire Face raced and roared through the suburbs, paying no heed to streets, curbs, signs, and lights, and doing what the Coppers knew he was able to do. This was the steeplechase of steeplechases.

Fences, bushes, pools, cars, and yards were run through, jumped over, and splashed about in the most epic display of equine athleticism the world had ever seen. Women in pools shrieked as the horse soared over them as they sunbathed. Gardeners had hearts ripped out as giant hooves cratered yards of growing vegetables and flowerbeds. Privacy fences were rendered obsolete.

It didn't take long until everyone followed the racing duo on Wild Dog, and people began to fill the streets as communities emptied their homes and waited on porches, streets, and driveways for the horse and the boy to pass by.

Gangs of kids were on bicycles, hoping for the chance to ride next to the legendary horse and rider for just a few breathtaking moments, and Fire Face didn't disappoint as he galloped through it all to cheers of new lifelong fans.

Doc felt more alive than ever before as he acknowledged the fans of what had quickly become a great procession. "This is racing," he said as he felt the muscular back underneath him move with grace and might. His hands pulsed to and fro in perfect rhythm with the powerful surging neck and bouncing mane.

The age-old sensation stirred inside of him, multiplied to infinity, of what made horse racing as old as domestication itself. It was the thrill of riding something that we have no natural right to ride, yet the horse submits to it out of their own nature and will. It's a bond, an agreement, and it won't ever be understood until the horses tell us why.

* * *

HOWEVER, ETHAN WAS TOO COCKY TO FEEL THREATENED BY THE new development, and he was driven to destroy. "Where are they?" he screamed.

"I don't know how to say it," the navigator replied.

"What road are they on?"

"This is bonkers, but they're not really on roads. They're cutting through neighborhoods. This is bad, Ethan."

"What do you mean?"

"What I mean is they could actually win!" Rupert yelled at him.

"How? They're on a horse!"

"LOOK!" the navigator screamed and forced Ethan to look at the flat screen. "The shortest distance between two points is a straight line. The horse is squeezing between the houses and running through yards, and you, you bloody imbecile, took us away from the highway. We're stuck on these stupid city streets!"

"Shut up!" Ethan yelled. "I know what I'm doing."

"I hope so, or you'll go down in history as the moron who lost the Quad Continental to a rider on a horse!"

Ethan was incensed and screamed untellable things. He pushed his vehicle hard but had to slow yet again to make another ninety-degree turn on the city street.

* * *

Hit, swish, and spit. "Live, and in living color, I am J-Dog Dynamite, and this is the Wild Dog. As I speak, our boy Doc Copper and the beast, Fire Face, have the place lit!"

The finish line was hopping to loud music, and a raucous party erupted as the crowd anticipated thee most exciting and improbable finish in the history of the Quad Continental. In astonishing chutzpah, the chairman of the United States Junior Racing Association showed up at the finish line. He wanted a chance to speak on Wild Dog TV about the great support the USJRA has had for Doc Copper.

"Oh," J-Dog responded to the request from the suited man in the eight-hundred-dollar shoes. "Let me submit your request to the committee."

He and Alfie conferred in whisper tones for a moment and J-Dog returned.

"The committee has determined that it is quite ironic, that you, being a racing organization, were so slow on the uptake. Request denied with prejudice."

* * *

The intercom blasted in the local hospital all the way back in Bell Buckle, Tennessee. A firm voice commanded, "All available hospital staff immediately report to room 108 and . . . bring a sedative."

Dean was jumping on the bed in the hospital room like a five-year-old at Christmas. IVs ripped out of his body, rendering his hospital-issued garments useless in providing dignity. Both hands were thrust in the air as he watched the aerial footage.

Dean was yelling uncontrollably, "I knew he could do it! I knew he could do it!"

A big orderly, who got to the room first, started watching the TV more than watching Dean. "Knew who could do it? The horse or the boy?"

"Both!" Dean said, beside himself to finally see Fire Face race under a rider, and he couldn't calculate the internal jubilation of seeing his own boy as the one who did it.

More staff flooded the room. "Mr. Copper. Mr. Copper, we need you to calm down," an older female nurse scolded as she prepped a big needle. "Your lungs cannot handle this kind of exertion."

Dean began to wheeze a little bit and winced in pain, but that wasn't stopping him one iota. He grabbed his phone and texted Rachel: *Are you seeing this???*

His phone rang, and it was Rachel FaceTiming him. He answered. He was a bit taken aback when he saw her. Her hair looked like it hadn't been combed for days, and it was clear she hadn't slept in that long either. She said to him, "Just tell me he is going to live. That's all I want to know."

"He's going to do better than live. He's going to win! Copper racing, baby! Copper racing! We're in it to win it!"

Rachel was simply relieved her son was alive. "And yes, *I'm fine*, Dean. Thanks for asking," she said with deflated sarcasm. "I just swapped my ride with a coyote, hopped on the back of a motorcycle—with a family of three mind you—to the border, and now I'm in an Uber heading to Rohr Park."

Dean completely checked out on what Rachel was saying.

Two big orderlies grabbed him by each arm and forced him down while a nurse, with the touch of a gorilla, injected him in the rear with enough tranquilizer to subdue a herd.

"Hit him again," Rachel's voice could be heard.

* * *

Fire Face found himself on a paved straightaway, and he took full advantage of the obstacle-free runway, moving with unearthly power. So fast, yet so smooth. Fire Face could sense the freedom of unfettered speed, and he moved with an uncaged spirit, never even thinking that one day he would stop.

Doc's bond with Fire Face had grown as close as a boy and horse could have it. He crouched on the horse with the skill of a natural born jockey, leaning forward and matching the rhythm of the mane with his hands. He found that view dead ahead, seeing between the bobbing ears in front of him.

The clap of the hooves on the pavement was loud. "Be careful," Doc whispered to Fire Face, knowing that pavement was slick for a horse, but Fire Face wasn't going heed that warning as he only moved to maximize his strides.

Doc pulled out the man's phone he'd apprehended at the highway to check the GPS. They were on course, but he needed to veer to his right soon, just a touch. An unpaved gravel parking lot was straight ahead. He would need to start curving Fire Face to the right after that.

"Careful," Doc said as Fire Face was full tilt. "Keep your feet," Doc warned and took a deep breath as Fire Face's first hoof hit the loose gravel of the parking lot.

Doc never wished he was wrong more than now, but he wasn't.

It happened in slow motion in Doc's mind. He felt Fire Face's front right foot lose a sure hold when that hard hoof hit the gravel. He saw and felt the front shoulder dip on the stallion and his body sling forward.

Fire Face was going down.

Doc's mind went into hyper speed as he thought through what was happening. *Hit and roll,* he thought to himself. He knew the danger was not the ground, but the giant horse rolling on top of him if he couldn't get out of the way. That would crush him.

Doc had nothing to push off from. No stirrups to launch from, but only a lurch from his body.

From there, it happened fast. Doc threw his body as far to the right as possible, and he tried to time his roll as best as he could when he hit the ground. As his body thudded into the gravel, he instinctively began a dizzying roll, and he heard and felt two cracks in his right leg.

The blunt force of all the impacts were numbed by shock, and as he flipped and turned with each rotation, his eyes caught the tumultuous horse rolling toward him, like clothes in a spin cycle.

Three, then four turbulent rolls, and then he planted his left foot and sprang up to his feet, jumping farther away. As he landed, he felt his right leg give way with a numbing tingle that shot all the way up to his hip. He knew what happened. He'd broken his right leg.

He turned his head to find that Fire Face had bounced up from the fall as well and was shuffling around flustered, tossing his head with a neigh and a snort.

Doc looked down at his right leg and touched it right below the knee and above where the racing boot ended. The leg throbbed like it was going to bust out of the skin. He hobbled over to Fire Face, quickly scanning the horse to see if the stallion had broken a leg or if there were other external injuries. "You okay, boy? You okay?" he asked as the horse pranced toward him. Doc looked him over, and the stallion seemed fine at a cursory glance. "Shh, shh," he soothed the horse, trying to calm him down, but the horse seemed more worried about him.

Fire Face came right up to him and allowed Doc to lean against his strong shoulder. Doc tilted his forehead into the mane and kept weight off his right leg as he leaned against the horse for stability.

He reached down and unbuckled his right boot, and he opened the tightly, overlapping flaps. When he did, pain assaulted his leg, and he threw his head up to the sky and gasped in anguish. He didn't notice that the GPS chip, which was adhered to the inside of the flap, had fallen out of the boot when he had unbuckled it, and it became lost in the gravel.

Doc fought to clear the cobwebs from his brain and took stock of his surroundings. He knew that unbuckling the boot was probably a mistake and that he needed to keep the break in his leg compressed. So, he screamed in agony as he re-buckled the boot tight, like a cast.

His thoughts didn't venture much. He knew he was in the race, and it looked like Fire Face could still run. He breathed heavy and looked at the map on the phone. "Okay," he said to himself. "There it is." He saw the finish line on the map. He did a few quick calculations in his head, and he figured he was still ahead of Ethan, but he was losing time. "It will be close, and it's easy enough to get there."

He went to instinctively mount the horse and pushed off the wrong leg. He fell to the ground in agony. "Aggh!"

The shock had worn off, and now the pain was there in full force. He stayed on the ground, catching his breath from the throbbing. A real moment of doubt came through his mind as unchained suffering coursed through his body. "I can't do it. I'm sorry, boy. I can't do it," he said to Fire Face who had turned his head to look at the boy kneeling on the ground.

Doc put weight on his left leg and used the mane of the horse to help pull himself up. Fire Face pushed Doc's head with his own, almost willing the boy to keep going. Doc shook his head. He couldn't find any more strength to pull on. Every ounce was gone. He was wrung out like a twisted rag and left mangled and hurt.

The horse nudged him again, and Doc leaned against the side of the horse, flopped his arms over the big strong back, and dropped his head upon him. The horse stood steady, strong as a statue, and was pleased to be the boy's rest.

Then Doc's mind began turning, like it always did, without request or permission. It just turned and churned. Memories flooded his mind of everything that had happened to bring him to that very moment, to be standing there with this horse at this time and place.

One memory, one thought, one idea persisted and would not retreat. It was the revelation of all that his family and friends had done for him to be exactly where he was, right now.

His mom and his dad. Mac, Jonah, Flip, J-Dog, Alfie, and Penelope. He knew the sacrifices they had all made, the pain they all had endured, and that this championship meant as much to them as it did to him. This was not his championship anymore. This was not him etching his name in the hallowed halls of racing, for he knew those pursuits were empty. This race was now for all of them. He patted Fire Face and knew the race was also for him.

Doc needed to leave no question unanswered and no bell un-rung, but he was exhausted. He was hungry and thirsty, bruised, bloodied, and now broken-boned. His whole body hurt. He didn't even know how he could stay on that stallion with his leg the way that it was, but he needed to try.

So, Doc reached down to find more within him, more fight to finish this race, and he discovered that his body had no more adrenaline to give. His muscles had nothing in reserve. His bones were indeed broken, and there wasn't any more emotional game rage that could be mustered for this final stretch. Those springs had been run dry. Everything was spent and the search for that type of energy returned void.

However, it's not as if he didn't find anything within him. He did, and what he did find, was the strongest thing of all.

He found love. Love for his family, love for his friends. And these were not merely friends anymore—Mac, Jonah, Alfie, and J-Dog were knit to him as tight as brothers, and Flip and Penelope were grafted in as strong as sisters. It was love that would push him. It would be love that would rise and be his strength, and it would be love that would conquer all.

He opened his eyes. He used his good leg and hopped around to the other side of Fire Face. He balanced himself and then jumped, flinging his broken leg over. It hurt as gravity let it drop on the other side and bang against the barrel-bodied stallion. He dropped his face in pain into the horse's neck. But he gathered himself, took a breath as he cinched his hands deep into the mane, and leaned forward, preparing for the coming surge.

"Fire Face," he said, "lets finish this," and he simply tapped with his good leg.

The big fiery stallion responded as if he had never fallen at all. He put a foot in the ground and launched with the suddenness of a sprinter, the power of a titan, and with the endurance of a marathon runner, but this time, he was running for Doc.

* * *

Alfie squatted on the ground and covered his eyes. He simply couldn't watch any more. His head was straight down. "Is he coming?" Alfie asked.

"I already told you, Alfie. I don't know," Jonah replied. "We don't have the footage. The drones left him once he hit the trees, and they came back here." Jonah pointed to the sky as the drones circled above the finish line. "They didn't want to miss the end, and his GPS signal just stayed put. Maybe it malfunctioned or fell off. I don't know, but it's not moving. So, I don't know what's up with that."

J-Dog took his hat off and ran his hands through his hair. "I can't believe we've lost all contact this close to the finish line."

"Before you ask," Jonah said, "he ain't answering his phone. I tried."

"I just hope both of them are alright," Penelope said. "That was a nasty fall."

Just then, a car pulled into Rohr Park. It started beeping its horn at the crowds in front of it. It was trying to get through.

"Who's that?" J-Dog turned and asked.

A hand waved out the window.

Penelope squinted and grinned ear to ear. "If my eyes don't deceive me, that, ladies and gentlemen, is none other than Mac Irons."

The good doctor had loaded Mac up in his car from the crash site on the highway and drove him to the park. The kids ran toward the car, but the crowd was thick enough to cause a blockade. Mac swung open his door, yelled for his friends, and began pushing his way through the hordes of spectators.

Billie Riggs, the bombshell blond reporter, noticed that it was the Bell Buckle Gang who was trying to reach this other boy, and then she put two and two together. She signaled to her cameraman to begin rolling. She fixed her hair to ready herself to go live and then pushed her way through the crowd to reach Mac.

"This is Billie Riggs, reporting live from the finish line of the Quad Continental. It appears that the navigator of Team USA, who I believe is Mac Irons, has just arrived, but he is not with Doc Copper." The crowd parted for her and her camara crew, and she reached Mac first. "Mac Irons," Billie Riggs said, "can you tell us what happened?"

He looked at the blond reporter and saw the rolling cameras, and before anyone could say another word, he went right up to her and laid a big old kiss right on her lips.

"Check it out!" Jonah yelled.

Once Mac was satisfied that his masculinity was well-documented, he pulled back and quipped, "Had to be done." He winked at her and walked away.

He left Billie Riggs just standing there, wide-eyed and speechless.

Flip finally got to Mac and slammed into him with a giant hug, which was less like a hug, and more like a linebacker filling the gap. She gave no attention to the fact that Mac had a sling around his shoulder and arm. Neither did the rest of the gang. Mac grunted as the wind got knocked out of him, which impaired his ability to gasp at the incredible pain she had just induced on his broken collarbone.

Then, in a second swarm, he was engulfed by the mass of humanity called Jonah, who picked him up and shook him around like a rag doll, which still made it impossible for Mac to properly explain the excruciating pain he was in.

J-Dog reached over and shook Mac's head hard and wild and Alfie jumped up on his back.

The good doctor, who had driven Mac to the finish line, pushed his way through the mini-mob, yelling, "Stop, stop! Let go, let go, let go!"

"What?" Jonah said. "Who are you?"

"He has a broken collarbone! Let go of him!" the doctor urged.

"Oh," Jonah set Mac down, and by extension, Alfie who was clinging to Mac's back, who then slid off.

"My bad," J-Dog said. "Good thing you're Mac Irons, right?"

Mac grunted and moaned. "It's okay. I love you guys, too." He caught his breath as he tried to reconcile the extraordinary pain he was feeling. "But I'm not quite the man I used to be."

Jonah grinned. "Try telling that to Billie Riggs."

Mac laughed. "Enough about me. Where's Doc?"

* * *

THE GANG MADE THEIR WAY BACK TO THE FINISH LINE AS JONAH pulled out his iPad. "We lost him after the crash. We don't know where he is, and there's no way to find out."

"He fell? Again?" Mac's eyes popped.

"Yeah," J-Dog said, "it was bad. Fire Face wiped out and went down."

"Are they okay?"

Jonah exhaled. "I'm not going to lie, we don't know. We lost them. Tracker stopped moving, and the drones bugged out. We're in the dark, brother."

"Well, if Doc is alive, he's going to be here. I know that," Mac said.

Then the sound of an all too familiar rumble came from the distance. It was the distinct growl of a throaty engine and piercing RPMs that signaled the driver was giving every bit of fuel to an engine that was purposely built for speed.

"Oh no. Oh, no, no, no!" Mac growled. "Ethan."

The British crew came to life with a raucous cheer and came running to the finish line from their support vehicles. Plenty of them jeered at the gang as they prepared to become champions.

"Doc, where are you?" Mac said. "Come on."

"Nothing, man." Jonah shook his head and tapped on his iPad, but he knew there was no information there to be had.

"Do we see the British yet?" Alfie asked.

"I don't see him yet, but by the sound, he's getting closer," J-Dog said.

Jonah pulled out his binoculars and started scanning the area from where the sound was coming from, "Oh man," he said with dejection, "I see him."

Ethan had that machine full throttle as he bounced across curbs, yards, and medians.

"Where?" Flip asked.

"Give it about five seconds," Jonah said, "and you'll see him kind of come out in the clear."

"No sign of Doc." J-Dog took off his hat and threw it on the ground. "Come on, brother. Anybody but Ethan. Where's Billy Joel when you need him?"

"I see Ethan," Mac said. "I see 'em."

"Where?" Alfie asked.

"He's still a little bit away," Mac said. "Do you see the white house?"

"Okay, I got it," Alfie said.

"Now just looked to the left a bit. See him?"

"Oh, I see him," Alfie said. "Maybe he gets a flat."

J-Dog added, "Maybe he gets struck by a meteor."

The gang stood in silence as they watched Ethan Oxidant racing toward them with nothing in front of him but a clear shot to the finish line.

"This thing's going to be done in under a minute," Mac said.

"Shoot." Jonah bent over at his waist, and then in fit of anger, he slammed the iPad down on the ground. Smashing it.

"Let's just hope Doc makes it here safe," Penelope said, trying to shift the conversation to the next best outcome. "It was a grueling race. That's what's important at this point," she said.

Jonah stood back up and put his hands on his waist as he watched Ethan getting closer and heard the engine noise growing louder. The British team started chanting something. It sounded more a like drunken pub gathering than anything else, but it had the sounds of victory in it.

J-Dog turned his back to the race and just shook his head. "I'm so glad we don't have their king. Or their climate. You know, they don't have sun," he kept muttering, eventually trailing off.

But then Flip saw something from the corner of her eye. She saw trees rustling, branches moving. She couldn't tell what it was—it was coming from the right side, about a quarter of a mile away perhaps. She looked back at Ethan. He had a straight shot and was probably still more than a half mile out.

She looked back to her right, and there was definitely something there. Something in the trees. It was moving and moving fast. She glanced back at Ethan and then back at the trees. Back to Ethan and then back to the trees.

Then she saw it. It was a bolt, moving like a violent shock of electricity.

Flip ran and jumped up onto the back of Jonah and punched her fist high in the air as she screamed with every bit of power in her lungs, "DOC!"

Her voice pierced every other sound in the vicinity and people looked in the direction of her gaze, and they saw it too. Fire Face and Doc Copper burst into full view, coming in from the right side, running on a tankful of force and fury.

The crowds erupted in cheers as Fire Face banked like a fighter jet with his hair flowing ablaze. Doc's left knee was bent into a tight angle as if he was riding a motorcycle around a tight corner, almost waiting for his knee to skid the ground below. He leaned into the bank, completely trusting the horse to keep his footing and make that turn, and Fire Face did not disappoint.

Fire Face dug deep into the turf, leaving divots, as he carved out the corner and pulled upright as he straightened to make the final stretch of the epic race. Doc glanced back at Ethan Oxidant who was still a bit back but moving fast. Doc pointed at him, daring him to come and get 'em, and then he swung that hand forward and pointed toward the finish line.

Doc's breath quickened, and he found himself saying, "Go, go, go," and his broken leg throbbed up to his throat, but with the rush of the final drive, he didn't care. Those words grew to great shouts of, "GO! GO! GO!"

Fire Face found another gear deep within him, and he delivered the maximum amount of speed he could muster, and his body straightened like a plank as he sensed this was the reason they were running. His adrenaline surged and super-fed his strides. He found the very reason he was bred, and perhaps even why horses were ever created to begin with. To merge unspeakable power, grace, beauty, and speed, and allow man to come along for the ride. And what a ride it was.

Doc crouched up right behind his shoulder blades. His hands were stretched forward and buried deep in the long, thick, fuming mane as it bounced like a raging inferno. His hands flowed in perfect rhythm with the surging neck and head. His breathing matched the loud huff and puffs of the horse, and his ears enjoyed the distinct punctuated sound of thundering hooves hitting the ground in a perfect rhythm and covering ground faster than any horse that had ever come before him.

Some of the British crew dropped to their knees like they were sucker punched. All their pride and pomp were getting stomped out of them as they saw this incredible beast charging toward them.

The Bell Buckle Gang was enraptured with cheers. They were captured by jubilation and exultation at a level where their voices would pay the price for it later as screams and yells tested their vocals cords to the breaking point.

The crowd followed suit with the fanatical frenzy of enthralled spectators. Media broadcasted live. Oil Slick gave a running, nearly incoherent commentary, juiced with roars and exclamations. The internet servers around the world were breaking as the traffic brought them to their knees.

Banners were up, and crowds now lined the path to Doc's right and to his left, but his eyes were fixed on his best friends who were locked arm-in-arm, waiting for him to finish what they had begun long ago back in Bell Buckle, Tennessee.

Doc glanced back to see where Ethan was, and what he saw was fitting. Ethan wasn't gaining. Ethan wasn't coming. Ethan had quit.

Once Ethan Oxidant saw Doc take the lead, he had thought that that lead was insurmountable. It seemed that Fire Face was too far ahead, and there wasn't enough ground to catch him. He could have made it close, yes, but he wasn't going to catch him in time. So, instead of finishing the race set before him and finishing second in the Quad Continental, Ethan chose dishonor over dignity, and quitting over achievement.

Doc shook his head at the sight. "You are who you are," he said as he watched Ethan sitting at a dead stop with his hands on his helmet. Rupert, the navigator, had already gotten out of that super-charged, super-powered, desert racer and was screaming things unknown.

Doc then turned his gaze back toward the finish line and saw his friends, and the rush of victory they were experiencing brought him a joy he had never had before in racing. They were going to win that day, and that made him choke up just a bit as a deep satisfaction overtook his heart and soul.

Doc closed his eyes and slowly released his grip on the mane, even though Fire Face was still moving like a rocket. His nerves tingled for a moment, but his seat was sound, and he slowly raised his hands to the sky. He tilted his head back and allowed the sound of hooves, the wind in his hair, the sensation of raw power underneath him, and most importantly, the love of family, friends, and his horse to encapsulate his senses.

The move looked a bit daring for the onlookers, but it wasn't. Doc believed in his horse, believed in the reasons that they raced, and believed that this was their time, and nothing was going to stop them now.

He blasted across the finish line as confetti and fireworks shot up into the air. He pointed to the sky, opened his eyes up to heaven, and whispered, "Thank you."

Oil Slick's voice flooded the airwaves, "Your Quad Continental Champion, Doc Copper! And boy, did he ever do it with style!"

As Fire Face blasted past the finish line, he didn't slow. He continued to rush past the swath of spectators, and Doc knew this horse wasn't inclined to stop, but he needed him to.

Doc leaned forward, and spoke with a calm, almost soft voice. "Whoa. You did it, buddy. You did it. Whoa." Fire Face's ears twitched backward.

Doc sat back up straight. "It's done." And Fire Face felt the intensity of the boy subside. He felt the completion in the tone, and the true friendship in the spirit.

The stallion obliged and pulled back his gait. Fire Face slowed to a canter, to a trot, and then a soft walk, and finally he stood completely still. Doc could hear and feel the strong rush of breath going in and out of those mighty lungs as the powerful body simply absorbed the rest, and for the first time in the stallion's life, Fire Face was perfectly at peace.

But then the raucous crowd started coming their way with reckless shouts. The stallion tossed his head, giving a loud shriek which halted the masses in their tracks. Doc laughed a bit, "It's alright, buddy," he patted him. "Let's just be."

Doc scanned the people, trying to locate his friends again, and then he saw them. They were running towards him with their arms stretched high. There was jumping, waves, cheers, and hugs. Their joy seemed endless, as did the smiles on their faces.

Their passion for the victory permeated the entire atmosphere, and their joy brought a deep satisfaction to Doc, greater than any other victory he had ever had before.

And with that, Doc lost all of his physical strength. All of his energy was depleted. His body gave out and he collapsed forward and wrapped his arms around the big neck of the stallion, burying his head into the wild mane. "We did it," Doc whispered as he almost lost consciousness.

A few seconds past when Doc felt a hand on his shoulder. "Doc."

It was J-Dog.

"Hey, wake up, Doc. Would you mind jumping off the back of the horse with a flip or something? It's for Wild Dog."

Doc slowly opened his eyes and saw J-Dog, with all the gang behind him. Doc's face was awash with dismay at J-Dog's request. His look said it all.

"Alright," J-Dog replied. "You're tired. I get it. We'll do a big thing later."

And with that, the rest of the gang surrounded Doc and Fire Face. In their exuberance, they pressed in, and even leaned into the big stallion, and yet the horse didn't move. He allowed the hugs, the cheers, and the rush of exhilaration, all around without giving a flinch.

"You know," Penelope said, "they are going to want to talk to you."

"Who?" Doc asked.

"Everyone," Jonah replied.

Then Doc saw Mac, all bandaged, and with an arm in a sling as he gingerly slid his way through the others.

"Copper," Mac grinned.

"Irons," Doc smiled.

Doc slid off of Fire Face and landed on his one good leg, making sure his broken leg didn't touch the ground.

"What?" Mac asked. "You broken, too?"

"I'll live. You?"

"I'll live."

The two boys laughed, and then embraced in a big bear hug.

"Ow, okay," Mac grimaced at the aches that coursed through his body. "Still dealing with the miracle of pain."

"Right," Doc laughed. "Sorry you're normal now."

"Not sure I like it," Mac replied.

The crowd continued to press in, and then an outstretched microphone shoved its way through the kids nearly into Doc's face. It was TV reporter Billie Riggs, and she was already in mid-sentence reporting live.

J-Dog jumped up and down, and gave a big thumbs up to Doc. He was also streaming live.

Doc agreed. He looked the reporter in the eyes and gave her an affirming gesture.

Billie showed no hesitation. "This is Doc Copper, the winner of the legendary Quad Continental. As it now stands, you will probably go down as the single greatest champion in the history of this race."

"No, ma'am," Doc stopped her there, and his smooth southern accent came through. "I didn't race alone, and I sure didn't win this alone. Look around you. These are your champions." He pointed to the gang, and his horse. "I just played my role, just like them. I couldn't be here in this moment without them supporting me the entire way. We all won."

Billie Riggs nodded. "I appreciate your humility, but it is your name on the trophy. You alone are the champion, and I think your friends would be okay if you took your bow. Don't you deserve this moment?" She pushed the microphone even closer to this face.

"My dad used to say to me that if someone sings their own praises, then it's going to get real quiet, real quick, because they'd be the last one singing. And maybe I didn't understand all that he really meant, until now. But now I know. This race has a way of teaching you things, whether you like it or not."

Billie Riggs leaned in, "What did you learn?"

"It's what I learned, and it's how I changed," Doc explained as the crowd hushed to listen in.

"The boy I was when I left Bell Buckle could not have won this race. I had to change from the inside out, ma'am. This race was a crucible. It never relented, it never paused, it threatened and attacked at every corner. In some ways it didn't feel like a race at all—it was life itself. And, if it was just my strength alone that I raced on, then you'd be picking up the wreckage of my body and machine a few hundred miles from here in that Mexican desert."

"Then how did you do it?"

"It's what my dad was trying to teach me. You don't want to go it alone in life—a single strand is just too easy to snap. But a cord of many, when braided together, becomes something altogether different. It gives you a steel in your spine that is not easily bent, and then you can stand with the strength of many, and not falter with the frailty of a few."

"You had your team. I get that," Billie Riggs replied. "But so did every other racer. Everyone had a team. What made yours different?"

"We raced for something greater than ourselves, ma'am. We raced for the love of one another. A lot of those other teams raced on greed, ego, and hate. They raced to crush enemies, but we raced for the love of our friends. And I'll tell you what, hate burns hot, but hate burns quick, and it leaves you thirsty, broken, and spent. Everyone that ran on hate ended up with a tank as dry as the desert sand we just raced through. They stalled out, burned out, and crashed out. Look at every mile behind me and you'll see hate only left a pile of wreckage, debris, and empty dreams."

"Why is that?" Riggs asked.

"Because everyone who trusts that type of anger reaches a point where the costs are just too high. But love never finds that limit.

"Love was the fuel that burned strong. It was there when times were dire, it was there when all seemed lost, it was the strength that never ran dry. It was love of God, family, and friends that gave me the strength to finish the race. The trials and tribulations of this race prove yet again what the Good Book has taught us all along—love never fails."

THE END